Cold Cases and Sweet Redemption

J.M. Dabney

Hostile
WHISPERS PRESS

COLD CASES AND SWEET REDEMPTION

J.M. DABNEY

HOSTILE WHISPERS PRESS, LLC

For my readers who make telling my stories worth it.

COLD CASES AND SWEET REDEMPTION

COLD CASE UNIT #5

When two broken men find redemption together, will one survive to accept it?

Chance

Everyone assumed I was a magnet for trouble, or maybe I searched it out on my own. By the age of forty, I almost destroyed my life. The tragic event that changed my entire perception of myself is haunting me. When a friend is in danger, I volunteer to keep them safe and momentarily distract myself from my problems. Yet my demons keep hunting me down.

Bart

For twenty years since my divorce, I'd completely cut myself off from all physical connection with another person. PTSD has taken everything from me, and a time bomb lives in my head—ready to go off at any moment. For the most part, I've learned to control it. When Chance needs help learning a healthier coping mechanism, I offer my assistance, but when he's healed, will I be able to let him go like I'd promised?

Nothing had prepared two traumatized men for each other. Can they heal and find redemption, or will the danger around them take one from the other before they realize they have more than their demons?

(TW: Mentions of childhood sexual, physical, and mental abuses. Passive Suicidal Ideation, self-harm, eating disorders, and mental illness. These are mainly off-page, but there are detailed flashbacks and conversations of said acts. Yet if these are triggering for you, please feel free not to read the story. Your self-care and mental health are more important. Thank you.)

CHANCE

The air refused to enter my lungs as I gasped like a suffocating fish on the sidewalk outside the home of a murder suspect. I tore at the front of my shirt, trying to get to my vest underneath it. I'd made a rookie mistake and didn't pay attention to my blind spots. For my fuck up, I got a shotgun blast, almost full-contact to the chest.

A strong hand jerked down my mask as an oxygen one replaced it. My blurry vision cleared to find a paramedic above me and my team off to the side. The pain was threatening to make me pass out, but I refused to show weakness. I'd learned that was the easiest way for enemies to find out where to hit you.

"What's the damage," my commander, Dolan Sharp, asked.

"A few superficial wounds, but as close as you said, best case scenario, he's probably got some bruised ribs. We're gonna transport him. Someone riding along?" one of the paramedics asked.

"I-I'm fine. Go back to HQ. I'll just call for a ride." It took everything in me to get the words out without whimpering in pain.

I didn't want any of them coming with me. Dolan, especially.

My ex-husband didn't need to know about my medical stuff unless it affected my job. In the past year, nothing about me was a secret anymore, and I needed to be able to keep some things to myself. Dolan had gotten bossier with age, and while we were friends outside work, I didn't need him to run my life.

"I'll be up as soon as I finish the paperwork. Call if you're done before. Don't fuck with me, Bowers. I'll sic Deacon on you."

I snorted and groaned as pain bloomed outward from the center of my chest. "Don't threaten me. I'm wounded."

"Then behave, or my husband will have you on the couch so he can watch over you. Call me." It was an order, pure and simple.

I nodded as they loaded me into the squad, and I instantly collapsed as I clutched my chest. The pain choked me, and I couldn't get my breath again. An oxygen mask covered my mouth and nose, but soon it was too much. The world slowly transitioned from the bright overhead lights to nothing but black as they called my name.

IT SEEMED like only seconds had passed before my eyes opened again, and I was in an exam room with monitors all around. My nose was dry and itchy from the oxygen from the cannula. I moved my head around and frowned when I found Deacon, aka Boss, Dolan's husband watching me.

"Hey."

"Hey." My voice was barely a croak.

"You have something to tell me, Chance?" I knew that disappointed voice, which was why I hated when Boss became upset with me. He wasn't a yeller or anything. He could chastise you with nothing but a softly spoken question that made you question every life choice you'd ever made, and to be honest, I regretted them all.

"I tried to stop."

"Is that why you wouldn't let Dolan come with you?" I

nodded. "There were a lot of them. More than you had when I found out."

"Did you see?"

"Yes, I was here when you came in. One of my kids got picked up. He's off his meds. When they stripped your shirt and vest away, the nurses froze. Honey, we talked about this. You can't punish yourself for it. Cutting to hurt yourself every time you get a hard-on is not the way to deal with your sex addiction and rape."

"I don't like who makes it happen."

"Chance, I love you, but you have to talk to someone…other than me. You need to find some way to work through the sexual trauma. Wanting someone isn't wrong, honey. You've seen that enough in the support groups every week."

He didn't know. The Outreach's kitchen was the only place I'd felt safe in the last year. Bart, the kitchen manager, was a big husky man who looked like a teddy bear. He complained about me in his kitchen dozens of times per night when I volunteered. The man would huff. I'd noticed I'd started messing up on purpose to get his attention. He was a nice, caring man, but he had an ex-wife and kids. I'd even asked if he was gay, and he'd said no, but it was a regular misconception. Not something that offended him when people asked him.

"Chance," Deacon called my name until I realized I'd faded out thinking about Bart.

"Could I talk to Remy?" I asked. Remy was a detective in the Cold Case Unit, friends by association. He was a psychologist specializing in trauma, but he wasn't licensed—I just trusted him.

"Of course. Remy keeps offering. You need to talk to Dolan."

I shook my head. "I don't want…want anyone to know, especially Dolan."

"I can't tell him, but I'd like you to reconsider talking with him. He's your friend. And as much as you fought it, we're family, and you can't escape."

3

"That sounds like a threat. What's the damage?" I asked to change the subject away from Dolan and any talks Boss wanted me to have with him.

"You have a bruise the size of a dinner plate in the center of your chest. Nothing appears broken, and they cleaned a few grazes. You're going to be sore for a while. Ice will be your best friend for at least a few days."

"I didn't check my blind spot before clearing the room. I made a rookie mistake."

"You've been under extreme stress for a year. You need to take some personal time. I hear you're benched until a doctor clears you."

I groaned. I hated sitting at home with too much time to think. And if I couldn't work, that meant going to the Outreach was out. If I couldn't help, I had no excuse to study the tall, fluffy Black man. It was the best part of my evenings, seven days a week. The husky man wasn't my type. I always went for muscled men, physically perfect ones. He had a belly that, for some reason, I'd become fascinated with. *Straight man*, I screamed in my head. My self-destructive tendencies and impulse control issues were at least familiar.

"They're going to keep you in the ER overnight just to make sure there's no complications. That blast was almost close enough to shred your vest."

"Can't I just go home?" I asked.

"No. You have a lot of impact trauma, and right now, you're medicated for the pain so you can breathe. You want me to stay all night?"

"You got the kids." He and Dolan had two adopted children, a girl and a boy. I'd never seen Dolan as happy as he was with his husband, Gabby, and Todd. Seeing him so relaxed made me feel guiltier for what I'd put him through, especially for what I'd denied him.

"That's not what I asked. Gabby and Todd will be fine for one night. Bart will even drop them off for dinner if I call to ask. You know he's weak when it comes to the kids. He's more overprotective than I am."

"I'll be fine. I'll probably just sleep. That's been in short supply recently."

"Chance," he called my name as he stood and came to sit on the edge of the bed. "I'm not telling you that you have to heal today or even another year from now, but you have to try." He leaned down and brushed a kiss to my forehead. "Call us when they start your discharge paperwork. Dolan or me will be here to pick you up."

I nodded, and I almost wanted to call him back as he disappeared around the curtain, and out the door. I relaxed on the bed and attempted to take the pressure off my chest. Which was almost pointless. Other than that, abdominal injuries were meant to take you out of the game. Yet I should be used to pain. There wasn't much I'd gotten right in my life. When I'd escaped the rundown trailer in my tiny Texas border town when I was eighteen and enlisted, I'd thought my life would be different.

No more stepfather taking me out on the weekend to *cure* me when he caught me looking at a boy. Sex should've repulsed me because of my childhood, but I'd quickly learned that if I used my body right, I could get what I wanted. I'd felt needed, and that need had turned into something that haunted me every day.

When I'd met Dolan Sharp, he was gorgeous and interested, and I'd had his focus and love until I'd fucked all of it up. I'd lied to keep him until one day, he'd grown tired of my cheating and lies. He'd moved across the country to get away from me. Those four years apart, I'd searched for that same focus, countless men, one on one and in groups—I'd bend over for a brutal train because I could pretend those men wanted more than to get off.

The night would end, and the next day, I'd be back to drowning in my self-hate and addiction to being used—something I'd confused with actual desire. I looked a lot younger than my age. I knew I was an attractive man, but that's all I'd ever been. Perfection I'd fostered with disordered eating and extreme workout. Chance Bowers had become nothing more than a walking list of disorders, and I didn't know how to change that.

I'd thought I could heal from my sexual assault. It hadn't been the first time I'd had sex when I hadn't wanted to. I could've treated it all the same. But just as I had my entire life, I'd lied to myself. The cutting was about the release, but it was also to make the outside as ugly as the inside. My breath hitched with the pain as I shifted my arms to run my fingertips over the thin gown that covered my chest and stomach. The scars and scabbed razor wounds were in neat, orderly rows from my chest down and were a testament to every nightmare. To all the men who'd viewed me as nothing more than a body to use. They also sadly represented the one pleasurable thing I had.

After my first support group, Deacon had asked me if I wanted a distraction, and I'd instantly agreed, only to regret it minutes later when I was introduced to Bart Hastings, the Kitchen and Pantry Manager at the Outreach. His presence overwhelmed me, and I didn't understand why. Then after a week of volunteering, I'd entered my own personal hell.

Dolan and Deacon's daughter, Gabby, had said something, and Bart had let out the most unrestrained belly laugh I'd ever heard. It was warm and happy, and I'd never once felt that way. Of course, I faked it well. Yet I'd never been free. Even during my marriage, where I assumed I was where I wanted to be, I was dying inside. Bart's grumbling bass was comforting and gentle when it needed to be. He was firm about his rules for the kitchen but never cruel.

Even at six-two, he towered over me and probably outweighed me by a good hundred pounds. He had beautiful dark brown skin, a neatly trimmed beard on his broad jaw, and short twists that he kept covered with a bandanna in the kitchen. He was thickly muscled yet soft, and he made me think of things that I'd never considered until my new group of friends I'd met in the past year.

Being in the closet was like a prison. A constant battle to make sure your masculinity was above reproach. Yet being around my friends, they had their husbands or boyfriends sitting on their laps, cuddled up close to each other without fear. I stared in frightful wonder at the closeness and intimacy, and it became a lure to know what that experience felt like. But it wasn't mine to have.

Damaged goods. Lightyears away from attaining any form of redemption. That didn't mean I didn't wish for a small sliver of what my friends found. I couldn't give in, though. Forty years of conditioning, and no matter how much everyone told me I'd be okay, the broken thing I was would always remain. I couldn't have a cuddly kitchen manager. There were some secrets best left hidden.

2

BART

COLD CASE
UNIT

The frigid air of the walk-in freezer felt almost painful on my face. All I could do was wait for the panic to subside. One of the volunteers had dropped a metal pan that echoed like a ricochet through the cavernous space of the Outreach kitchen. Some days were better than others, but for some reason, I was on edge and couldn't figure out why. The flashbacks of the explosion which had sent me home still as clear as it was twenty-five years ago. I'd gotten stateside, healed, and became a drill sergeant until I'd retired from the military.

Being a soldier had been a point of pride for me. I'd served and gotten a college degree, then I'd been respected and exemplary at my job. I'd gotten my twenty and retired, but the horror hadn't remained in the past. I focused on my breathing, a slow inhale and exhale, repeating the motions until my heart returned to its normal rhythm.

My marriage had only lasted a year after retirement, and the shit living in my head told me that my wife and daughters would be better without me. I'd packed up a duffel bag, and hours later, I was walking the streets looking for a place to bed down for the night. I'd spent four years in an underground homeless community. That's where I'd met Boss my first week on the streets. He'd offered me a job, and twenty years later, there I was. At fifty-nine, I hadn't expected to be a kitchen manager at a massive community program only known as the Outreach.

But between the homeless settlement and Outreach, I'd found a family—a community of people who knew what pain and loss were. Boss had given me a second chance at life. Thankfully my wife and daughters understood. While homeless, I kept in contact even if I could see the helplessness in their eyes. They wanted to help, but there was nothing they could do. My demons were my own to slay, and for the most part, I had, except on days I was on edge and unprepared.

I exited the freezer once I felt calm enough to return to my job. We were cleaning up for the night after another busy dinner service for low-income and homeless people. Everyone was welcome. I was proud of what I'd accomplished. Boss had given me the kitchen. He called it my territory. I'd been thankful for something to focus on except for my PTSD.

As I looked around, I found the kitchen spotless and everyone had cleared out. I did my walkthrough inspection to make sure that everything was sterile and ready for the next day. My people never fell below my expectations. I quickly turned off the lights and went to my office at the back of the kitchen.

I removed my apron and bandanna and ran my hand over the short twists of my hair. I'd sworn there was more silver that morning as I'd studied myself and trimmed my neat beard. I'd had dinner with a few of the regulars I knew from the settlement and caught up with them. Every night was busy at the Outreach, but life just seemed to be overwhelming me more as I aged.

My feet dragged as I made my way through the maze of halls, into the common room, and out the front door, locking it behind me. I was always the last one to leave unless there was an emergency. As I headed across the parking lot to where I parked, a familiar figure sitting on the hood of a truck made me change directions.

S.W.A.T. Lieutenant Chance Bowers stared off into space. He almost seemed unaware that he was no longer alone. He was forty and almost pretty. His hair—which used to be platinum— grew out over the months until the color was rich as honey. His crystal blue eyes were always filled with pain, no matter how broadly and expertly he smiled to fool everyone else.

"Hey, honey," I said from a safe distance. He shook himself before he brought his attention to me. "Abandon me, leaving me short-staffed to stare up at the stars." I smirked at him. I knew he'd gotten hurt a week and a half earlier. He was horrible in the kitchen, probably worse with an injury. But I liked that he always kept coming back, no matter how bad he was.

"I don't think not having me was much of a loss."

I agreed, but I didn't respond. "Not an answer. You okay?"

"This place fills my evenings, and, well, my apartment was a bit too quiet...too much thinking."

"Thinking isn't always a bad thing." As impatient as I was to get home to my place, I approached and turned. I leaned back next to his legs, but not close enough that he'd feel crowded. I'd seen the rooms he came out of on support group nights.

"Sometimes it's the worst thing." He sounded broken, and it was odd because even with the sadness haunting his eyes, he always looked and sounded like a man with no problems in the world. But again, his eyes made him an open book.

"Sometimes. I spent a good twenty minutes in the freezer because someone dropped a pan."

"Sorry."

"No need to be. It's just a side effect of the life I chose. Boss told me you were hurt and completely forbidden from working until a doctor cleared you. What happened?"

Boss was a man who didn't share someone's secrets. If you told him something, he held onto it. You never had to worry about him flaying you alive for the world to see when the confidence was broken.

"We were called in to help with a capital murder suspect. Armed and dangerous, barricaded in his house with possible hostages. We made entry, started clearing the structure room by room." He shook his head and pushed out a heavy breath. "I didn't check my blind spots, and he got the jump on me. Almost got a contact wound from a shotgun center mast."

"Ouch, I bet that's a nice bruise."

"Yeah, the bruise radiates out from the center of my chest. It wasn't as bad as it could've been, I guess. But I have impact trauma and severe muscle bruising. There were a few hairline fractures to my ribs, but nothing having them wrapped with a bandage won't take care of. I've missed working in the kitchen."

"Glutton for punishment."

"You do berate me for my knife skills."

"You should've learned to slice by now." I grinned as he gave me a small smile.

"Knives are for self-defense, not vegetables."

"You just come in for the free meal."

"I do."

"Brat," I growled. I felt better when I heard a chuckle with a little less edge. "What are you doing out here?"

"This is the first place I've ever felt safe. Do you have a place like that?"

That answer was easy. "Here. When I returned home after an injury, all I did was bring stress to my wife and daughters. I spent four years working here during the day, spending my nights in an underground homeless settlement several blocks from here. The Outreach is where I got my life back. This place definitely gives out more than it gets, but we keep pushing forward." I wanted to ask what his demons were. How hard they hunted him every night, but it wasn't my place. I'd admit I was overprotective of the people who came to the Outreach, and by extension, I'd kept a close eye on Chance. When I told Boss I'd take care of Chance, I'd taken that seriously.

"Why did you leave?"

"I woke up from a nightmare, and I had my hands around my wife's throat. She left claw marks trying to free herself. It was safer if I left. If I did that to her, what would happen if one of my daughters were around? I couldn't put them in danger. They were hurt, and I had to make amends when I was better, but I only did what I thought was right."

"How many daughters?"

"Four."

"Four?"

"Yes, and two of my daughters are married, and each of them gave me a granddaughter."

"That's a lot of girls."

"It is, but I loved being a girl-dad. Tea parties. Letting them paint my nails or do my hair. I loved it all. They were everything good in my world."

"Did they forgive you?"

"My youngest Cora took a while. She didn't understand and had to work through her feelings of abandonment, but when she was older, we sat down and came to an understanding. The others were older and could sense something was wrong with their dad."

"Did you ever think about reconciling with your wife after you got better?"

"No. We divorced, and she met a really great guy a few years later. She's happy. I even approve of her husband. We're not *have beers best friends*, but we get along well. You have any family?" I asked and saw him tense up. "You don't have to talk about it. We can just sit here and stare up at the sky."

"That's a very Boss-like thing to say."

"I learned from the best."

"My mom died when I was fourteen. I don't even know who

my biological father is. My stepdad had adopted me, and until I left, it was just him and me. He was a bastard. He believed he'd beaten the gay out of me and trained me well with all the sex workers he paid to *cure* me. He told me he'd show me what a real man was."

I jerked my head around and saw the tears that shimmered on his thick lower lashes. "There's nothing wrong with being gay. Some of the best people I know are. I'm ashamed to admit how bigoted I was to the community when I came here. Boss broke down my misconceptions. We all have the ability to change but being gay isn't something to cure."

"I was deeply embedded in the closet until recently. I didn't even acknowledge my husband for the decade we were together. Dolan definitely got a winner the second time around."

"Sharp and Boss are completely obsessed with each other. It's good to see Boss happy." I crossed my arms over my chest. "It's normal to deal with internalized homophobia after childhood trauma like that."

"Everyone wants me to talk. Spill all my secrets to make it all better. What if it doesn't make it any better? What if this is as good as I'm going to get?"

"Is that what you believe? That you're just broken and not worthy of healing?" I knew the answer as soon as I looked at his face under the parking lot lights. "Have you eaten today?" He shook his head. "Come on, honey, let's go get something to eat. You up to walking a few blocks?" Again, all I earned was a nod as he gingerly slipped from his perch on the hood.

We walked in silence to the main drag and then turned left as I headed to Mama Sue's diner a few blocks away. He needed some comfort food. I'd found that I fed people to let them know I cared. Sharing a meal with someone was an intimate experience —it contained physical closeness and conversation. Years had passed since I had a one-on-one dinner with someone.

I opened the door as we stepped up to the old subway car

turned diner. They'd extended the back out for a good-sized kitchen, but there was a total of six booths and a counter to sit at. I motioned him inside, and he hesitated a minute, staring up at me from under thick lashes. "I can go in first if you need me to." He shook his head, ascended the three steps, and then entered.

"Bart, what are you doing here so late?" Mama Sue asked as she moved around from behind the counter.

She was an ageless woman. She'd been around here longer than all of us, but it was almost as if she hadn't changed from the day I met her. "Give me some love." She opened her arms, and I fell into them to find the comfort she offered everyone who stepped through the door. I barely let anyone into my personal space, but even as used to being alone as I was, an occasional comforting embrace was nice to experience. Especially from a woman who became the mother of the strip and loved every one of us.

"Don't hug him," I whispered in her ear and felt her nod. Over the time he'd worked in the kitchen with me, he always put a physical distance between him and everyone else. The way he'd cringed the first time someone brushed against him told me physical touch was too much for him. It was probably more so with the injury. "Mama Sue, have you met Chance, yet? He's one of my volunteers."

"Nice to meet you, Chance. Find a table. What do y'all want to drink?"

We both ordered sodas and made our way to a booth at the end. I took the seat that put my back to the wall, and he slid into the bench across from me. He seemed uncomfortable.

"Do you have to take any medicine?"

"I took it earlier. I'll be good until I get home. It makes me tired. I've passed this place on the way to the Outreach but never stopped to come in."

"This place is a staple. Her son was a cop. He patrolled here, and she bought this to be able to see him. He was killed on the job, so she kinda adopts everyone who comes in. She's particularly fond of the Cold Case Unit. Remy and Vega have been around here for decades. The strip becomes a bit like an addiction. Once you're here, you experience the culture of it, and you don't want to leave. Down here, you're accepted without condition."

"I noticed that. It's almost like visiting a different world."

"We believe if we can't find it on the strip, we don't need it. What about you? That southern accent is pretty thick."

"Texas, born in a border town, it barely had a name, enlisted at eighteen to escape, and after I did my two tours per my contract, I applied to the Houston S.W.A.T. Team. Lived there until I ended up here in Winston Harbor. I came here to get Dolan back."

"That didn't work out for you. Do you like it here?"

"I do. It's a city but not as crazy as Houston was." He stopped speaking as Mama Sue came back with drinks and menus.

"Do you trust me?" I asked him, and he looked confused.

"Yes."

"Mama Sue, my usual times two."

"Keep an eye out while I cook."

"Got it." I smiled at her as she turned to head to the kitchen. She ran the place alone. She was the cook, server, and hostess. If you wanted a rushed meal, this wasn't the place for you. You came in, and you knew it was a family dinner. Regulars would jump behind the counter to ring up someone who was done. Someone was always ready to refill a drink or two if she was busy.

"She doesn't have a cook?"

"No, this is a one-woman operation unless she lets some of the teenagers earn a bit. She's only open from six PM to six AM. There's a homeless guy who comes by in the evenings to wash dishes for a meal. We take care of our own around here."

"I can see that."

Under the bright lights, I noticed the dark bags under his eyes. "You're not sleeping much, are you?"

"No, maybe a few hours at a time. I'm always on guard, and the floor I live on has a lot of people in and out all night. I can't relax."

"You know if you want to talk…" The sharp shake of his head cut me off. "The offer is there if you use it tonight or a month from now."

"Everyone keeps telling me to talk about it. What's that going to help?"

"It shares the burden with someone who can help you carry it for a few. So it doesn't feel so heavy."

"No one wants that burden, Bart."

"I do, especially if it helps. You know where I am seven days a week. And I expect my kitchen help back to fighting strength soon. I have no one to yell at." I winked at him and finally got a real smile, but even when he dropped his head forward to hide it, I still counted it as a victory.

Something about him made me want to help heal him, I was just as broken as him, but I wanted to mend the hurt in some way. No one should look as alone as the man seated across from me.

3

CHANCE

Three drops of blood made a tickling journey down the once-ripped plane of my stomach. I hissed through my clenched teeth as I pushed a bit harder with the razor. An odd tingling traveled over my bare skin as I sat there on the side of my tub, preparing for another day of existence. I'd sworn I'd stop, but I couldn't. It's just a thing I did, a normal morning routine before I cleaned up and dressed. When I left the house, I could pretend that all was normal.

All of it was a fallacy. My new and old routines were unbearable, and I was ill-equipped to make the change everyone said I needed. What change? Self-destruction was the only thing familiar. I added a second cut for good measure before I cleaned and bandaged myself.

The Outreach *Kick-Off to Summer Block Party* was starting in a few hours, but I'd volunteered to help with the food. I still had another week at most before a doctor would clear me for duty, but I couldn't stay in my apartment anymore. I dressed in jeans—a few sizes larger than last year—and a baggy t-shirt that would hide the bandage covering the cuts.

If nothing else, I needed a distraction, and the chaos that the

Outreach induced would be a great way to allow me to forget for a bit. The tape holding the wound cover in place pulled as I leaned over to lace up my boots, along with the pain of my bruise managed by some over-the-counter meds. That's why I kept trying to talk the doctors into freeing me, but, also, unless Dolan felt I was ready, he'd put me on a desk. I couldn't handle that.

I left my apartment, went to the parking garage for my truck, and on the drive over to the Outreach, mentally prepared myself to be normal or at least my brand of normal. I pulled off into an alley and went the back way to the parking lot behind the Outreach where the training center was. They'd set up volunteer parking there.

I opened my door and jumped down from the driver's seat, then I used my keycard to open the cafeteria entrance and walked inside. The first thing I heard was Bart's booming voice directing the volunteers. I followed the sound of it and froze to find him in the middle of the kitchen barking orders with a beautiful toddler with tiny puffs of dark hair on either side of her head.

A snort slipped free as I caught her mimicking his arm movements as he pointed here and there.

"Honey, you're late." He spoke without turning around, and I just stood there because I hadn't made a sound yet. "Chance, are you here to help or look pretty? I don't pay you to look pretty."

"You don't pay me at all," I grumbled as I crossed the room to wash my hands and grab a pair of gloves.

"I pay you in food, which I've seen you cook. My granddaughter could do better. A wonder I keep you around." He pointed to a large aluminum pan and ordered me to take it outside to the grills that Dolan and Marcel were manning that day.

"I didn't sign up for this abuse." I glared at him as I passed him.

"You know what to do if you can't take it, right?" His thick brows arched and waited me out. When I just walked off, his booming laugh followed me all the way down the hall and out into the community room.

I squinted as the bright early afternoon sun hit my eyes, and then I looked around until I spotted Boss and the Cold Case Unit around two massive grills. I weaved through the crowd.

"I think you need to fire Bart. He has a terrible attitude," I grumped at Boss, and all he did was shake his head.

"If you can straighten him out, you're more than welcome to try. I gave that up fifteen years ago. Once I gave him the kitchen, he was drunk with power."

"We were wondering if you'd show up," Dolan said from where he stood sideways behind Boss with his arm looped around his husband's chest.

"I said I'd be here. I'm actually a half hour early." I set the pan down. I looked over to a sitting area under a large tent with collapsible chairs and loungers with the rest of my friends and their significant others. Simon, Marcel's husband, was slathering all the kids down with sunscreen and then sending them off to play.

I almost asked was a grownup going with them, but I realized they were all wearing the trackers that Vega outfitted all the adults with, too. The teenagers herded the little ones away to go find games and the street food carts set up. The community took care of its own, so they'd be safe, but I still worried.

"Honey, you're not done yet. Play on your time," Bart yelled from the door.

I shot a glance over my shoulder and was about to flip him off before one thick brow lifted as he shifted the toddler on his hip. And then he disappeared back inside.

"Can I escape and go home?" I asked as I turned back to an amused Dolan and Boss.

"I think he'd hunt you down. Get to work," Dolan said, and Boss shooed me away with a motion of his hands.

The afternoon was non-stop work as Bart's errand boy, going

back and forth to the kitchen. I'd introduced myself to Sierra, and she started helping me carry small things, a bag of buns or more napkins, something to keep her busy. Even with the block party, Bart was still hard at work preparing lunches for people to pick up for their kids or themselves the next day.

With Summer break in full swing, the need for help with food was at an all-time high as they worked to feed the kids three meals a day and snacks. No one went without on the strip as long as the Outreach was going, and no one ever had to worry about food or medicine. I'd never realized that truly selfless people existed in the world. And they did everything for so little payback. It was grants, fundraisers, and calls for donations.

They did it all. They fought every day for enough funding, and sometimes it was reaching into their own pockets to cover things. I felt so unworthy to be around them. I'd spent most of my life as a selfish man. My looks earned me all the attention I needed. My body paid my bills when a man enjoyed it enough to turn me into a kept man for brief periods.

I shouldn't even be there. I wasn't one of them—I didn't deserve to be included.

THE PARTY WAS WINDING DOWN, and dusk was starting to turn the sky darker as the Outreach and Cold Case Unit relaxed around the tent. I was sore, but Bart had slipped me a one-dose pack of pain relievers, and I hoped they'd kick in soon. Bart's granddaughter, Sierra, was roaming around. I kept an eye on her as Bart went to get her some juice in the kitchen. He'd said his daughter's band was playing at the end of the strip, and that's why she was with him. The toddler didn't like the loud noises of the drums so close.

Vega was off to the side talking with her wife, Cash, who was away on a band gig and wouldn't be back until the next day. I scanned the otherwise deserted parking lot as everyone prepared to go off and have fun since they'd finished with the food and cleanup.

I frowned as I saw a small flash across the street on one of the rooftops. Shaking my head, I started to turn away when the first shot rang out. It hit the ground inches away from Vega's feet. Vega and Sierra were in the line of fire, only five feet apart, and I was already on the move. Sierra cried out as I jerked her up and spun to put my body between her and the sniper. Next, I ran up behind Vega and grabbed her around the waist.

I cursed as fire ripped across my shoulder, but I kept moving as I saw the Cold Case Unit and Dolan running across the street as I tucked my two small bundles behind an SUV.

"What the hell, Chance," Vega cursed as she shook where I had her pressed to my chest.

Instead of answering, I muttered soothing words to Sierra as she clung to my injured shoulder and buried her face right over the fading bruise on my chest.

"We have a sniper on the building across the street. Stay down and stay quiet," I warned Vega as I released her, and luckily, she didn't fight me and stayed where she was.

"Sierra!" Bart's panicked voice came from the doorway.

"Stay there."

"Chance, where's—"

"She's right here, but we don't know if the sniper is still active. So stay." She fought a bit as she heard her grandfather's voice, but I held her close no matter how agonizing it was. I touched my shoulder, relieved to find nothing but a groove in the skin where my shirt had a ragged tear.

"All clear," Dolan yelled, and I peeked around the side of the SUV to see him standing on the roof.

Vega was shaking, and I think the adrenaline was wearing off, letting reality set in. I struggled to my feet and took her hand, pulling her up as I led her to the front door of the main warehouse. Bart walked out, and I saw him stumble, and then I realized Sierra and I were smeared in blood.

"It's mine. Sierra's fine. Just a flesh wound." I wasn't going to tell him Sierra was on that side when I got hit. He already looked as if he was going to lose his shit.

Vega was talking loudly into her phone, and I realized Cash had heard everything, and she went into Mommy Domme mode to reassure her babygirl. She was rushing around Bart to get inside.

"Come on, honey, let's get you two cleaned up." He took my hand, and when he went to take Sierra, I turned away. He frowned but didn't try again, and he led me inside and sat me down on the couch. He was gone a few minutes and then was back with a first aid kit. "Honey, take off your shirt."

Then it was my turn to panic. "I can't."

"Put her down, and I'll help you."

"No, Bart, I can't take it off, please." I stared into his light hazel eyes and silently begged him not to make me.

"Okay, Chance, it's fine, but just let her sit beside you so I can see your shoulder better."

She fought me a bit. I guess I was her comfort for the moment, but finally, I got her on the cushion next to me. She buried her adorable face against my ribs. Bart's features were strained as he cleaned my shoulder up. He placed a clean rag over it and held it to stop the blood so he could see better.

"Thank you," he muttered.

"For what?" I played dumb.

"You know what. Sierra was out in the open, right?" I opened my mouth to lie, but I earned another arched brow. "Thank you."

"I was just closer."

Cora came running inside screaming her daughter's name, and then Sierra abandoned me for her mother's comfort. I watched them cling to each other, and she was jerking at Sierra's clothes.

"It's mine. She's fine," I explained. I'd only met her for a few minutes before she'd had to go off to find her band.

"You might need stitches."

"Dolan's going to fire me."

"Why's that?" Bart asked as he lifted the rag to check the bleeding.

"First a shotgun blast to the chest, and now this." I motioned to my shoulder with my right hand.

"Maybe you just suck at your job as much as you do in the kitchen."

"Don't be mean to the wounded man."

"Pouting ain't getting you out of seeing a paramedic, at least."

I groaned, and he chuckled at me, but it seemed sort of tight and forced.

"What's the damage," Dolan demanded.

"Graze to the shoulder right above his upper arm. Definitely needs to see a medic. He might need stitches," Bart answered for me.

"I'm fine. A bandage after it quits bleeding, and I'm good to go."

"I don't think I asked your opinion, honey." Bart's stern tone caused me to nod.

"What the hell happened?" Boss asked.

"I was just scanning the parking lot. I saw a flash like the sun hitting a scope, and then the shot hit a few inches from Vega's feet. I think whoever it was tried to cause chaos so he could take the final shot. I'd already grabbed up Sierra and Vega before he could get the next round chambered. When he did, I already had them hidden behind me, and he hit me. What did you find?"

"Nothing. He used a rope to do a controlled descent from the roof, and he policed his brass. He was already gone. The crowd freaked out and went in all directions. We had to fight our way through. We have a forensic team on the way to collect the rope and carabiners to check for prints and DNA." Dolan sounded frustrated and instantly reached for his husband to cuddle the man to his side.

"Who's doing crowd control?" I asked.

"Remy, Doc, Simon, and Stevenson are trying to calm the situation and check for witnesses who may have heard or seen something," Boss answered as he rubbed Dolan's chest and as per habit. I tried to sense any jealousy over the two, but it wasn't there.

"Vega was the target. It was too open out there for it to be anyone else," I whispered as I heard Vega's voice, softer and calmer from the side where the support group rooms were.

"Shit, that's going to be a long fucking list of people she pissed off." Bart shook his head.

"We need a closer look at that shoulder," Dolan said as he moved forward and started to lift my shirt.

"No, I don't..." I turned my gaze to Bart's, and shame filled me when the first tear fell.

"Dolan, he's mine. I can take care of this." His tone was sharp as he held my shirt down, but thankfully Dolan backed off. His big hand fisted in the fabric at my waist to keep it in place until Dolan cursed and stormed away.

I briefly caught Boss's gaze and couldn't miss his disappointment. He wanted me to confess to Dolan, but I couldn't. I'd fucked up so much in my life that my ex-husband may not say *I told you so*, but he was going to be thinking it. Boss went to talk to Dolan.

"Thanks."

"What you're hiding is your business...no one's unless you want to tell them. Yet whatever you bandaged it with...the blood seeped through."

I glanced down to find a small bloody spot but not over where the gauze was. The rescue must have torn the scabs that had formed on the ones from the day before.

"Chance, right?" Cora asked as she stood beside Bart and me.

"Yeah. She okay? I jerked her up kinda hard...if she's bruised, I'm sorry."

"We can live with a few bruises. Thanks."

"Just doing my job."

"Doesn't change the fact I want to thank you, so say you're welcome." Cora sounded exactly like her dad.

"You're welcome."

"Are you okay?" she asked. "I'm a doctor. I can check it out for you."

"Yeah, no, flesh wound, no permanent damage."

Dolan shouting Vega's name had me off the couch as I saw Vega sprawled on the floor. I grabbed the first aid kit and ran across the room. I fell to my knees. She was breathing heavily.

"Vega, where are you hurt?" I demanded as I lifted her baggy shirt and, without thought, I ripped my shirt over my head to slam the cotton over the wound through her side. "Medic," I yelled as I checked her pulse. It was strong but a little too fast, but pain and terror were probably the cause.

Suddenly Cora was there. She'd handed Sierra off to someone, and she peeked under the cotton as she reached for the first aid kit.

Tears seeped from the corners of Vega's eyes. "I did *not* consent to being shot."

I weakly laughed at her bad joke. "I didn't either, but here we are."

"Cash—" She tipped her head back and stretched out her arm as if looking for her phone.

"Vega, Boss has it. He's talking to Cash now. Just relax. Paramedics are on their way. They had a squad parked about a block over, and they're having an issue getting through the crowd," Dolan told her, and she relaxed a bit. "Luckily, it looks like we had a doctor in the house."

"Did you know that density of fat can make you bulletproof, they lied."

"Don't believe everything you read." I squeezed the fabric tighter to the wound and just felt it turning wetter. I glanced at Cora, and I couldn't read the young woman, but she didn't seem panicked, although that could simply be because of her training.

"I'm not going to die, right?"

I briefly looked at Cora, and she shook her head, giving me a wink that I assumed was comforting and good news. "Vega, you're not, it's through and through, and you're bleeding, but it ain't bad. They're going to need to stitch the wound, though." She nodded, but it was in a weird spot, so it could've hit anything on the right side. Thankfully, it was too low to have pierced her lung, and her breathing was fine, but I didn't know the exact angle the bullet had entered her body.

Finally, the paramedics arrived and took over. Cora filled them in as she stayed to assist. I struggled to my feet, and then I had a button-down shirt wrapping around me. My eyes widened as I glanced at Bart and saw the way he focused on my chest and stomach. Next, I looked at Dolan, who looked pissed, but I wasn't ready for that argument. Yet in my panic to help Vega, I'd exposed the secret I hoped to always remain between Boss and myself.

Bart jerked the two sides together to hide me, and I looked up at him, his face was devoid of all emotion, and I couldn't read him. He simply helped me put my arms into the sleeves and then buttoned me up. Was he going to be mad at me, too?

BART

Cops weren't my favorite people outside the Cold Case Unit, and being forced to give statements made me crankier than normal. It wasn't helping that a friend was in the hospital getting fixed up, and Chance was on the other side of the room swimming in my shirt. I could see he was losing steam and drawing into himself with every second that passed.

I don't know what came over me. I'd been in the kitchen when I heard the shot ring out, then three more, and I'd run to the front door. I'd kept the heavy steel door between me and possible danger as I frantically searched out Sierra and Chance. My heart dropped to the pit of my stomach when I couldn't see them.

I hadn't relaxed until I'd seen Chance coming toward me with my granddaughter on his hip. Then I'd stumbled at the horror of both bloody. He'd assured me they were fine, but I knew I wouldn't be satisfied until I checked them over. The fear in his gaze when I told him to take his shirt off said he was hiding something. When I'd claimed him as mine so Dolan wouldn't touch him shocked me. I just wanted to protect Chance and his secrets.

My imagination hadn't conjured the full picture until he'd

ripped his shirt off to tend to Vega, and my throat closed up at the number of scars and fresh cuts. They covered him from his mid-chest to the waistband of his jeans, and the sickly yellowing bruise center mast made the scene almost grotesque. The uniformed cop ended his questioning, and I stayed, leaning against the wall, but never took my attention from Chance.

"You okay?" Boss's voice came from my right, and I turned to lower my gaze to him.

"Yeah, my heart got a workout, that's for sure."

"I'm sure."

"Heard anything about Vega?"

"She said it went through her muffin top, and she needed the wound cleaned, and they stitched it up. Remy and Robert are there with her."

"Who has the kids?"

"Simon and Marcel took them all to their place. They're a little scared because we told them Vega got hurt, but our kids are strong and know we'll never lie to them. Dolan is about to read Chance the riot act."

"Why?" I absently asked as I kept staring at Chance and studying the blond man.

"I found out about the self-harm several months ago. He was spending the night, and I walked into the bathroom to find him cutting. It wasn't my story to tell, but I tried to talk him into letting Dolan know what was going on. Chance rips his shirt off, and there it was, in glaring clarity. The fresh bandage didn't help."

"I know why you didn't tell Dolan, but are you in trouble, too?"

He shook his head. "No. Dolan and I have an understanding about what's told to me in confidence stays that way. He's irritated but understands. I think Dolan's looking back over the last year and trying to figure out if his ex-husband-turned-friend is a danger to himself on the job."

"Chance is worried he's going to get fired."

"No. Dolan will make his life hell but won't fire him. What happened to—" Boss cut himself off with a sigh.

"I've seen which groups he comes out of, so I'm pretty confident what happened. But I'd rather him tell me...to trust me."

"You like him." He sounded amused.

"He sucks in the kitchen, but he doesn't give up, and he amuses me. He's surprisingly good with everyone. He told me he was in the closet until recently."

"Yes, and after what happened, it spread pretty quickly who he went to a motel room with. I'm sure no one has said anything to him at work. Dolan's too scary for someone to pop off with some bigoted bullshit."

"He does like bragging about you." I finally smiled as I caught the slight blush on Boss's cheeks. The level of happiness my friend had attained in the last few years was good to see. We all kept telling him he needed more than the Outreach, and he'd finally found it with Dolan. I wasn't sure about the two of them together, but Dolan was obsessed with his husband. The number of locked-door lunches in his office with a K-9 guard was an ongoing joke around the place.

"He does. Mama Sue said you were in there on a date with a pretty blond the other night."

I barked out a laugh. "I was feeding him, that's it. Despite what everyone believes, I'm straight. Maybe I should cut down on the endearments."

"You have, but you still call *him* honey."

"I'm fifty-nine, Boss. If I was going to get curious, wouldn't it have happened in the past twenty years?" He shrugged, and I rolled my eyes. "Dolan's turned you into a bigger brat."

"That I won't deny. Go on. I know you want to check on him. Simon paid for a private charter to get Cash home. I gotta get to the airport to pick her up."

I nodded as he pivoted on his toes and crossed the room back to Dolan, who was still giving Chance a death glare. As soon as the cop talking with Chance walked away, I headed straight for him. He caught sight of me, and his gaze locked with mine. There was fear and embarrassment in those pretty blues, and because I was the man I was, I wanted to take care of wiping those emotions away.

"Hey, honey." I stopped a few steps away from him to keep from crowding him. "You okay?"

"Yeah. They said I'd have a nice scar, but I'm okay. Thanks for..." He plucked at the front of the shirt.

"Look like a little kid wearing it. Sorta cute."

"Thanks, what every man wants to hear." He rolled his eyes, and I smirked at him.

"You're welcome."

"Dolan's waiting to pounce. I can see it." He glanced to his left.

"Might just want to pull that band-aid off and let it happen."

"Are you mad at me?" he asked, and I was surprised by the question.

"Why the hell would I be mad? I'm concerned about the number of scars, but you're not the first one to cut to deal with shit. Would I prefer you didn't? Yes, but that's a decision you have to make. Not my place to tell you to stop."

"I wanna stop, but...I don't know how."

"Come with me." I didn't wait for him to agree. I simply took his hand and led him through the hallways, into the kitchen, and then into my office. I sat him down on the small loveseat. I released his hand to grab my desk chair, pulling it over until I could take a seat in front of him.

He looked scared, but I wrapped my hand around the back of his neck. I pulled him in until our foreheads touched. His eyes locked on mine. "Don't look away."

"What are you doing?"

"Sharing pose. I did this with my girls all the time when we had to have serious discussions. It made them focus. So just go with it." He gave me a small nod. "What are you scared of?"

"Love." His voice broke.

Nothing much shocked me anymore, but his answer made me lose my train of thought for a minute. "Why is love so scary for you?"

"Because if I love someone, they'll leave me."

"Honey, that's the danger of opening yourself to another person, but in the pain of loss, there's always a lesson. Most relationships are just test-runs for the right one."

"What if I don't understand who the right one would be?"

"You're not alone. I don't think anyone does. But, honey, it's not worth this." I curled the fingers of my free hand and stroked them down his side, directly over the scars. He trembled at the caress and slammed his eyes shut.

"Don't do that." The hitch in his voice preceded a single tear.

"Oh, shit, sorry." Cora's voice nearly broke us apart, but I held tight to Chance. "Deep discussion pose. We're headed out. The cops said we can finally go." As she was about to turn away, Sierra held out her arms and made grabby hands at Chance. "Is that okay?" she asked.

Chance took the excuse to break us apart and reached for Sierra. All the harsh lines disappeared as she cuddled against him and rubbed his short beard with her chubby hands. I pushed the chair back and stood to say bye to Cora.

"You okay?" I asked as I hugged her, and she rested her cheek against my upper chest.

"Yeah, Sierra's fine. A bit too much excitement for us, but the strip never disappoints."

"That's too true. Is Grant waiting for you at home?"

"Not yet. He's leaving the airport now. He found a replacement to take his flight. I wasn't looking forward to him finding out in the air or once he landed in Paris. There's already a tally." My daughter winked at me, and I shook my head. "Is he okay?" she asked.

"He'll be fine. He got hurt at work, and now this. He's had a rough few weeks." I tried not to snort at my own understatement. Chance had had a shit year or, more accurately...life.

Cora gave me a kiss on my cheek and pulled away, then she collected Sierra from a reluctant Chance, and after a few more goodbyes, she left with my granddaughter. The defeated posture was back, and he stared off into space. I just sat down on the edge of my desk to allow him to do his thing, and then I'd see if he wanted to go home with me. No one would be able to find him there.

As I was about to break into his thoughts, Dolan filled the doorway. He barked out Chance's name, and Chance flinched.

"I respect you, Dolan, but you're not doing that. I got it handled," I warned him. We weren't much different in size, both with military combat backgrounds, and it might be a brutal fight, but I wasn't backing down.

"You got what handled? That my fucking friend is hurting himself? Or that I'm wondering if he has a death wish and needs a new career?"

"I don't have a death wish," Chance shouted. It was the first spirit he'd shown since I'd met him. He was snarky. Sometimes even bordered on flirty, but never angry. Rage was good. It meant something was still left that he felt compelled to fight for.

"Then what the fuck is wrong with you? Dammit, Chance, you get yourself shot, and now this? What about the other slip-ups you've had recently? Maybe you're not conscious—"

Chance surged from the couch. "If I wanted to die, I have plenty of razors. If I didn't want to live, I would've done it the minute I was out of your and Boss's sight. Do you know how many times I held the razor against my wrists? Plenty, and I'm still fucking here. You're not my husband anymore."

"No, I'm not, but I'm still your fucking friend. And if you

weren't quicker, how much worse would that shoulder wound be?"

"That's not what happened. What ifs don't matter when I'm still breathing."

"Tomorrow we're meeting in Vega's pit at twenty-hundred hours, don't be fucking late." Dolan turned and stormed away.

"Wanna go home with me?" I asked.

"You're not fucking me."

I shook my head. "Pretty white boys ain't my type anyway."

The eye roll made me wonder if he'd gotten a glimpse of his brain. "Good."

"My place ain't much, but no one will look for you there."

"Really?" There was a glimmer of hope in his gaze at the offer of sanctuary, some place no one would be able to find him.

"Yeah, I think you need to disappear for a bit. You can nap in my bed while I catch up on some TV I saved over the week. I'll bring you back here to get your truck before I start work tomorrow."

"I'd like that."

"Let's grab you a hygiene pack, and you can borrow something from me to sleep in."

All I got was a nod, and as always, I prepared everything for the next day while he waited quietly in my office. I didn't know why I had this compulsion to take care of him. There was something about feeling needed. My daughters were grown and independent. Rarely needed me to soothe their heartaches or need me for kissing skinned knees anymore. I didn't believe someone could fix another person. It was up to someone to deal with their trauma and find the way out themselves, but even if just for a few hours, I wanted to help carry his burden. That was something I could do for him because he needed it.

5

CHANCE

That morning, I'd leaned in the doorway of Bart's bedroom and studied him asleep on the couch. He'd looked uncomfortable, but he hadn't kicked me out of his bed or tried to *share* it with me. In my gut, I knew he wouldn't. Yet that didn't mean the thought hadn't popped into my head a few times. He'd shown me to his room, told me where to find clothes, and pointed out the bathroom. His place was small, just a one-bedroom that he said suited him fine.

He tried to feed me after my shower, but I'd shaken my head just wanting to sleep. My body was run down, and I was existing on fumes. Along with the bruised chest and the shoulder wound, everything I had hurt. I was still pissed about being accused of having a death wish. Yes, my life was sometimes unbearable, but while I had some passive suicidal ideation, I wasn't ready to end it all.

An hour passed with me standing there wearing his clothes that were too big for me, and I tried to figure out what power Bart had over me. He was the opposite of my type in the way of height and body size. He was an older man, nineteen years my senior, with deep laugh lines beside his eyes. He was commanding but careful, which was an odd combination.

"Gonna watch me sleep all morning?" Bart's voice shocked me.

"I didn't want to wake you."

"Appreciate it, but I'm not used to someone else in my space." He groaned as he sat up and threw his thick legs off the couch. He removed the head wrap he'd slept in and stretched out his back. I cringed, hearing the pops of his spine. "Too old to sleep on a couch."

"Should've kicked me out of your bed."

He shot me a glance and looked almost offended I'd think he'd do that. "Wasn't going to happen. You were sleeping good. You snore like a chainsaw, but whatever."

"I do not."

"Uh-huh, think what you like. You could've at least started coffee."

"I suck at that, too. That's why I stop and get one on my way to work."

"How have you survived this long?" he asked and placed his hands on his knees as he pushed up to walk to the kitchenette. Everything was apartment sized, including the stackable washer and dryer beside the fridge.

"Don't know, probably because, in our modern times, there's coffee shops and takeout. Did they not have those in your era?"

"Your morning attitude concerns me." He grumbled through making a pot of coffee and checking the cabinets and fridge. "I'll make you breakfast at the Outreach. I don't have anything here."

"And you worry about me? You don't even stock food, old man."

"Comes with working at the Outreach. All my meals are there."

"Who's handling breakfast today?"

"Carlos takes care of doing breakfast Sunday mornings. I take one day a week to be lazy until lunch."

"I can get a car or walk back for my truck."

"No, I said I'd take you, and that's what I'm doing. You feeling better this morning?"

I shrugged. "Weird to have a full night's sleep. My place is either too quiet, or there's running in the halls all night. There's an apartment with three college guys who love to party. I've already told them a bunch of times to keep it down, last one seems to have sorta worked. I was wearing my badge at the time."

"Cops and their badges."

"I'm a S.W.A.T. Lieutenant. I'm special." I batted my lashes at him like I'd seen some of my friends do.

"Most cops think so."

I wrinkled my nose at his tone. "You're just cranky in the morning, old bones and all that."

"And you're mouthy and probably in need of a spanking, but that isn't my thing, so look elsewhere."

I almost felt as if he'd slapped me, and I hated how much that hurt. "I-I wouldn't do that."

"Chance, come here, please." He stretched out his arm and held his hand palm side up, and I didn't know why I obeyed, but I crossed the room feeling a bit sick to the stomach. I squeaked and froze as he grabbed my waist to lift me onto the counter like my current weight wasn't over two hundred pounds.

I'd fought so hard to stay between one-seventy and one-eighty, lean and trim, a physically perfect specimen until I got support with my eating disorder. I hadn't looked it, but by clinical standards, I was anorexic.

"Honey, you can't get scared by everything I say. Have you ever known me to be mean or take out my temper on someone?" he asked, and I shook my head. He spread his hands on the counter beside my thighs, and I felt the steamy heat of the coffeemaker brewing on my lower back. "You're the only person, other than my girls, that I've let into my space...the first person to sleep in that bed other than me. I trust you to be here. For twenty years, I've been completely alone. Even with all my grumbling and insults about your atrocious kitchen skills, you still come back. I respect that. I'd never hurt you. You can flirt... you can joke...it means you feel safe. No more fear when you're with me, understand?"

"Yes, Sir."

He helped me off the counter with a nod and went over to make two large mugs of coffee. "Why did you tell me not to touch yesterday?" His question was almost absently spoken, and I didn't even know if he meant to say it out loud.

"I—" I Scrubbed my hands over my face.

"Just so you know, I know which rooms are what in the support section and what the nightly schedules are. I've seen you come out of three. If you don't want to answer me, that's fine, but if I can't touch you, I want to understand. You need to put boundaries in place."

"I became addicted to being fucked. The only times in my life I felt needed was when I allowed someone to use me. I didn't care how, one man, ten, hell, fifteen..." He shot me a glance. "The last straw for Dolan was when he caught me taking a brutal train, and I wouldn't even admit I was gay. Dolan loved me, but he stopped wanting...needing me. When he wouldn't feed my addiction enough, I went elsewhere. You know what they say once a cheater, always a cheater." I turned to lean back against the counter in front of the sink. "I thought my rape was my fault because I'd allowed hundreds of men to fuck me however they wanted. Maybe I gave off...maybe I was just meant to be a victim."

"No, you're not. You have trauma. Like we all do. You dealt with yours with sex. I dealt with mine with no sex at all. Twenty years is a long time to be abstinent."

"Twenty years, no sex...at all?"

"Your horror at my sexless life is not helping here. Sex, to me, means something. I was faithful to my wife for over twenty years. Actually, my one and only, I never once thought of straying...not even when I saw the other guys do it so easily when away from their families. Don't get me wrong, I miss it. Not the fucking but the intimacy."

"You must have loved her very much."

"I did, hell, I do. If I thought she'd have been safe with me, I would've stayed. She was my everything, friend, lover, wife... confidant when needed. We never had secrets."

"Hard to find another woman like that?"

"I don't know. For ten years, all I cared about was making myself better...told myself when I was that I'd start my life over. Didn't happen, though. What about you? Thought about starting over? You've been in group for a year."

"Sex Addict. Rape Survivor. Anorexic. Practitioner of Self-Harm. Not exactly a safe bet to start over. What would a man think when I tell him all that? Not a very pretty resume."

"Same thing, I think. You're a survivor in recovery. There's definitely some challenges, but you'd need slow, anyway. You need one of those soft caregiver types." He gave me a playful smirk, and I tried not to stare at his lips, the fullness of them. The width curved into just about the most perfect smile I'd ever seen.

"My life does have a lot of Daddies in it. Not your thing?" I asked as he handed me a mug, and I smiled my thanks.

"No, not in this life."

"But in your old one?" I asked, curious about what he meant.

"I was my wife's Dom. When I unknowingly attacked her during a flashback, I broke our trust. Afterward, she flinched whenever I touched or kissed her neck. Fear isn't always rational."

"I'm sorry."

"I am, too."

"Outside of my groups and Boss, you're the only one who knows. I keep saying I'm going to talk to Remy, but I don't know. It's like…if I'd admitted to all of it, then I'd never be able to take it back."

"After telling me, how does that make you feel, honey?"

"Scared. No one other than you knows about my childhood, not even Dolan."

"Why not?"

I took a sip of the dark, strong brew and then set the mug down on the counter. "I didn't trust him to understand. He fucked me like they did, called me a slut like I demanded…he gave me what he sensed I needed, but…" I paused because I didn't think I could give an adequate answer.

"But what? Just say it. You're on a roll."

"Have you ever seen two people making love? Just watched. The interaction. The way their eyes lock. The way they say each other's names. In my teens, it was all women my stepdad took me to. I was young. My body reacted because it didn't know any different. After that, I guess, it was that forbidden thing. It was taboo and dirty…I don't know how to explain it, Bart."

"We crave what we never had, but even in unsafe circumstances, the familiar is comfortable…there's no unknown factors."

"Yeah, that. Why would anyone want to make love to a thing like me?"

"Chance." My name held a sharp edge. "You're not a thing, do you understand?" he asked, and I automatically nodded. "You're a traumatized man who's working through all of that in your own way. If I could, I'd order you to throw away the razors, but I sense you'd find something different to replace them. Let me see," he ordered, and I lifted my shirt.

I swallowed hard as he stared at my chest and stomach. He focused on every mark, the fresh wounds and ones with the scabs falling off. His hand hovered over the softer plane of my stomach, close enough I could feel the warmth of his body but nowhere near enough to touch me. He was there in a good number of the marks. If I associated him with the pain, maybe the desire would stop, but that wasn't what happened.

"The new ones are deeper. The scars are going to be thicker. You need to use a lighter hand next time or find someone you feel safe with to do it in a controlled environment. You can't cut without them there or them doing it for you."

"That would be too much to ask. I'll be more careful." He nodded as he sipped his coffee, and we fell into silence.

I studied him just like I always did, but I didn't hide it that time. I wondered what it would be like to be hugged by a man like him. Someone not interested in bending me over or sharing me with his friends. It was so impossible, yet I wanted to know.

"Bart," I whispered his name.

"Yeah, honey, you ready to get dressed and leave?"

"Could I have a hug, please?"

He was silent for too long while he thought it over, and I was about to apologize until he set his mug down a bit too heavily. He shifted his bulk in front of me. I tensed as a massive hand wrapped around the back of my neck, and his other arm came around my waist. A gasp almost slipped free as he drew me flush against him. My flatter stomach conformed to the curve of his, and we stood there, our bodies pushed together. I was frozen for a moment as I tried to figure out where to put my hands—what to do.

"Just hug my waist, honey," he whispered as he tucked my face into the warmth of his neck.

I did as he asked and clutched at the cotton covering his lower back. My body tried to respond to the closeness, but I was too terrified of it ending. He didn't even comment when the tears started or that I held him a little too tightly or tried getting even closer.

"Shh, just breathe. We're in no hurry to go anywhere."

I didn't speak—I just stood there feeling warm and safe. Overwhelmed by being held by someone who didn't want to fuck me. Who didn't expect at least a blowjob for their kindness. I'd never recover from Bart, and I suddenly didn't feel so safe anymore, but I was too weak to break contact.

6

BART

I'd checked the clock for hours, but I gave up the later it became when there was no sign of Chance. He was due to go to what everyone affectionately called Vega's Pit. She'd always been paranoid and more than a little bit anti-establishment. But strangely, most of the Cold Case Unit was, which made their choice of profession weird. Hours later, that morning still played over in my mind.

I had friends. A lot of them, but most I didn't let close enough to think I wanted to hang out beyond the Outreach. Being alone felt safer to me. Less opportunity to form attachments. I loved my chosen family, but twenty years of self-imposed emotional and, to a certain degree, physical isolation made me miss things I shouldn't. Like I'd told Chance, I still loved my wife, but it was in the way of shared history and the deep trust we shared with me as her Dominant.

She'd loved a heavier hand than I would have offered on my own, but I loved her and gave her what she needed. When people looked at me, saw my height and build, they didn't assume Soft Dom, but that's what I was. I missed the trust and connection, fulfilling the needs of my submissive. The high I received and the Dom drop—it was just as powerful as a Sub dropping.

Except for my girls, I never let anyone into my personal space. No hugs. Not even the casual handshake. I was always in the kitchen so I could use the excuse of keeping my hands clean. That morning though, I'd pulled a stiff Chance into my arms. Tucked his face into my neck, and we'd just stood there. I'd felt the moment his fear took over, but not strong enough for him to break the embrace.

I'd had to tell him how to hug me. How much had he missed out on? What bothered me the most was he hadn't known. As if I were the first platonic hug he'd ever received.

A cool breeze from the hallway entered the warm kitchen, and I looked up. I stood frozen to find Chance in all black, a vest, weapon holstered to his thigh, and I noticed an earpiece.

"That doesn't look like you're here to work, honey."

"Nope, it was all-hands-on for a hostage situation uptown. Got called in as backup. The perks of being a sniper, I just have to take a position on a roof somewhere. Don't like the uniform?" His annoying ass did a model turn on the toes of his black tactical boots, and I shook my head.

"Not when it looks like you're about to bust everyone in my kitchen." He rolled his pretty blue eyes, and then I narrowed mine as he started batting his thick lashes. "What do you want?"

"Feed me." He pouted his plump bottom lip and gave me the most convincing sad expression I'd ever seen.

"Con artist, you think those blues are going to get you somewhere?"

"I'll starve without you. I saw a whole ass ab muscle. I'm wasting away. Bart, you don't...if it wasn't so loud, you'd hear my stomach growling."

It took everything in me not to smile at him, and I even turned away to find the rest of my team grinning as they pretended they weren't watching the brat in action. I didn't even have to say a word. They'd already started moving a plastic to-go box down the line and filling it for him. I mouthed *enablers* at them, and all they did was shrug. Quite a few of my kitchen staff had a bit of a crush on the pretty blond S.W.A.T. Lieutenant. Thankfully, none of them tried anything, but I'd warned them off a few months earlier, which I didn't know why I had. Chance was a grown man who could do anything or anyone he wanted. Wasn't my place to police his bed partners.

Carlos crossed the room and handed me the to-go container. He winked at me, and I was going to need to have a talk with them again. While the assumptions that I was gay didn't bother me, that didn't mean I wanted them to get into their heads to play matchmaker, especially not with Chance. My confusion at my feelings for the man were already a sore spot with me. I hadn't felt needed in so long he was fucking with my head.

I turned back around to find Chance grinning at me and rubbing his hands together. I set the box down, put two rolls in a small wax paper bag along with butter packets, and a thing of plastic utensils. Putting it all in a paper to-go bag, I handed it over, but when he went to take it, I held on.

"Don't make a habit of this. Pretty doesn't equal free meals."

"So you think I'm pretty?" I let go of the bag, and he chuckled. I thought that was the first time I'd heard real happiness in any of his laughter, except for when he was around the kids and they did something amusing or cute. "I'm going to soften that crunchy exterior one of these days, Bart. You can't resist forever."

"Spankings," I whispered.

"Foreplay," he whispered back. "Now that I have been gifted food, off to see Vega. Meeting's going to be late."

I took a breath, grabbed my pen and a piece of notepaper, and wrote my number down. "Here, text me to let me know what's going on. Well, use it if you need to. You know what I mean." I didn't know why I'd offered, but it had been on my mind since the night before and that morning. The scars that covered him.

The way he viewed himself as a thing. My interest wasn't sexual, but I wanted him to come to me. It was probably a mistake, but it was already out there.

He stared at the piece of paper he held, and again, I saw the emotions barely change his features, but his eyes always gave him away. "I can't do that."

"Who else are you going to trust?" I asked him, but he didn't answer, crumpling the paper in his hand.

It didn't bother me when he left without a word to me. He'd process, and he'd do with my number what he would. Accept my offer or not, it was something I could do for a friend. He was a beautiful young man who needed to heal. Boss had helped me, and I could extend the kindness to someone else.

Boss always told me I didn't have any sins to atone for. I'd made my peace with whatever God was still listening, but that didn't mean I didn't live with a degree of guilt over my past. My fear and panic, the PTSD, had urged me to make choices I thought were best for everyone involved. Once again, I'd made a choice. I'd offered my assistance, if that was a platonic hug, an ear for him to whisper his own confessions, or as a last resort, an offer to be his razor. It was his choice, but he had to make it of his own free will.

I didn't miss that each newer scabbed cut and the two fresh ones were getting deeper each time. The scar tissue thicker. I didn't know him well, but I sensed that if he didn't have someone to take over, he would lose himself in the moment. When that happened, would he have the will to step back? I was going to give him a reason to continue, no matter how much that was going to take me out of my comfort zone of the last few decades.

I knew what he needed, and it had nothing to do with a sexual release—he needed someone who cared if he woke up every morning. To worry about if he ate or slept enough. Until he called or I saw him again, I had to figure out why it mattered so fucking much.

I was surrounded by nosy people who were fucking with my head. My interest was innocent and only about being the friend Chance needed. Yes, I thought he was pretty, but anyone with eyes would think Chance was. I actually thought he looked better with the little extra weight he'd gained since I'd met him. He worked out. He told me he went to the gym almost every day but wasn't spending hours at a time working out. The first meal I'd made him, he'd only eaten half, but I knew he was still hungry. I hadn't said anything as I'd boxed it up and told him to take it home.

He had such a skewed view of himself. His self-worth and the way he physically looked, but he just didn't know any different. That was something I wanted to fix, but I knew at the end of the day, he'd have to make the decision.

"When are we going to hear you took that pretty white boy on an actual date?" I spun to find Alexa grinning at me. The young Black girl had come here withdrawn and just trying to do her community service but had turned into a brat like the rest of them and became a regular volunteer.

"I'm not interested in Chance that way, and keep that talk to a minimum. I can replace all of you."

They just laughed at me because they knew it was an empty threat. Except for the students from the local culinary school who came in on Saturdays to work the sober restaurant we ran or special events, my team was pretty solid.

To be honest, I didn't want Chance to become uncomfortable around me. To think that I wanted more than his friendship or to offer him some platonic correction when needed. I had no interest in him sexually, but why was I starting to sound like a lying broken record?

CHANCE

"**W**hat the fuck is that?" I waved toward the tower of boxes that was taller than I was and shot a glance at Vega with her babygirl seated between her feet. Lap time had been suspended until she got her stitches out.

Everyone else in the room was as horrified as I was to see the boxes. That can't be just the cases she'd worked in the last year. There was no goddamned way.

"That's six months. I'm having the others brought over from my office."

"You need to sleep more," I growled as I tested each box and found them full and heavy. "Any threats recently?" I asked as I grabbed a box and everyone followed suit.

"Not really, I mean, I'm a civilian consultant, and no one knows me beyond the computer screen. I won't say I don't get some cranky clients every once in a while. I am an expert witness on occasion to explain what I do. Forensic genealogy isn't exactly well-known."

"What exactly does your company do? I'm sure everyone else knows." I started flipping through files.

"In essence, I'm a genealogist. I have clients who come in

looking for long-lost family members, parents, and sometimes children. Most of my work centers around forensic cases, though. I'm contracted by federal and state agencies to examine DNA searching for familial links in the hopes of naming a suspect or victim. Normally, I'm just there for an assist. I do the charts, complete my reports, and send them in."

"How long have you been working with the Cold Case Unit? And what's your official job?"

"Several years. There's four precincts in this city, each one used to house a Cold Case Unit. I approached the police commissioner about an audit and reexamination of the city's epidemic of cold cases. I secured a hefty grant to go along with my proposal. After several months it was approved, and then I started entering cases into the database." As she spoke, Vega ran her fingers through Cash's hair. "The ones that actually had DNA processing done and then worked my way back to the cases that were older. During my audit, I discovered a disparity of investigation between cases where bias was clearly shown. I wasn't popular with the other units when my recommendations for reopening cases and having DNA retested and, in a lot of cases, tested for the first time."

"The mayor's office liked that they were looking good when several convictions resulted from analysis done," Remy said as he flipped through a thick file. "What they weren't happy about was the way the cases highlighted the percentage of cases that were unsolved that involved victims that were minorities and low-income. The thing is, all of the cases on the strip are in our precinct's jurisdiction unless there's a link made during investigations. When we started clearing more cold cases, the spotlight landed on us and Captain Tyson, who unofficially oversees our Cold Case Unit, was approached to make us the *only* unit in Winston Harbor. Vega, in some way or another, is linked to every cold case and a few open ones. That's a lot of possible suspects."

"So what are we looking for?" I asked.

"Well, that's the problem. We don't know. We have maybe twenty cases that deal with a sniper. None of them have the same method ours used. Only one used a controlled descent, and that case was closed. The guy is doing life without the possibility of parole at State. He was a clean confession," Robert answered as he was going through his box.

"We could have a hired gun trying to take Vega out?" I suggested and shook my head as Vega giggled.

"That's what we think, but at this point, we don't have proof. And really, our Vega is way too excited about the possibility of being a target." Stevenson grinned at a still giggling Vega.

She was insane. They were all a bit off, and the fact that I'd become one of them made me question my own mental health, which, to be honest, was sketchy at best.

"I hate to be the one to say it, but Vega needs a protection detail until we're sure of what's going on."

"Glad you mentioned that." Dolan sounded way too amused for my peace of mind. "Until further notice, you're assigned to Vega."

"Hey, I didn't—" The hard glare I earned shut me up.

"I didn't ask. We have a rookie by the name of Trey Callaghan. He has a military background and is a proficient sniper, but I haven't found a team to assign him to yet. Since you both have that qualification, you two will be working together since you know the best vantage points and what to look for. You can split the days into twelve-hour shifts. Myself or a member of the Cold Case Unit will spot y'all when needed. Since Vega is normally here, which is pretty much a self-contained panic room, or at her office, which has more security measures than the Pentagon. Stevenson and Marcel aren't on cases currently, so they'll sit on her at her office. You and Trey will be in charge of getting her from her office, home, or wherever else she needs to go."

I didn't agree or disagree, but it wasn't like he'd given me a choice in the matter. Protection detail would be better than sitting at home or stuck behind a desk or even training duties. Callaghan must be the newest rookie, but I hadn't met him yet. Which I wasn't looking forward to working with anyone that fresh despite his experience.

"Claxton will be on call at any time to assist if needed, but I'd rather not have one of my best out of the field."

I turned away to hide the roll of my eyes. In the past year, Dolan and I repaired some of the friendship we'd had before our disastrous relationship. Yet I was still trying to earn back his trust. When it came to Dolan, who knew how long that would take. At least I had Boss in my corner. As much as I disappointed him, he seemed to understand how I processed.

There were muttered curses behind me as I sat cross-legged on the floor and kept going through my box. Nothing so far stood out. Then a thought struck me. I slightly leaned back and pulled the small balled-up piece of paper from my pocket along with my phone. I glanced behind me before I entered the number and saved Bart's contact.

I shoved the piece of paper deep into my pocket and clicked on the message icon.

Chance: *What are you wearing?*

I hit send with a small smile. There hadn't been much to make me happy in my life, and I knew Bart wasn't interested. Not only was he straight, but he probably had women hitting on him all the time. I think that's why I felt safe. He had no interest in fucking me. Although, I had enjoyed the hug—maybe a bit too much—but that was my problem, not Bart's.

Bart: *Nothing.*

A groan slipped free, and I barely caught it in time. A picture of Bart without apparel tortured me for a minute. All his dark brown skin exposed.

Chance: *Send me a pic. Something to distract me from these files.*

I smirked as I hit send and set my phone aside and then threw a few more files in the *nope* pile. "Let me ask you, are you sure you haven't received—" I grabbed my phone as it went off and automatically opened the message. "Holy shi—" I cut that off, snapping my mouth closed. I'd never thought the man was cruel, but there stood Bart, shirtless, rounded belly, powerful pectoral muscles, and a smattering of hair across his chest. He was smirking, and I wanted to hate him.

Chance: *Tease!*

"Um, why is Chance drooling?" Vega asked, and I barely listened as I wished Bart had zoomed out a bit more.

"I have *never* seen him do that," Dolan answered.

"Chance," Boss yelled my name.

"Yeah, what's up?" Everyone laughing finally brought me around.

"I want his phone, and I want it now." Stevenson moved towards me, and I locked the phone before he could get close.

"It's nothing. Um, what was I saying?"

"I think you were about to ask if Vega was sure she hadn't received any threats."

I glanced at Boss to find him arching a brow at me in a silent question. Shaking my head, I put my phone away so no one could steal it and try to see Bart. That was all mine.

"Yes, um, I don't care how small. Have you been threatened recently? You naturally piss people off, but attempted murder by sniper is a big step without some warning." I tried to ignore it, I really did, but my phone buzzed.

"Check the damn message so we can get back to work," Dolan demanded.

"It's nothing. We're working." Even as I said it, I'd unlocked my phone and opened the message.

Bart: *Don't ask for it, boy, if you ain't ready for it.*

Irritated with Bart or myself, I didn't know which, I shoved my phone back into my pocket. "No threats at all?"

"Since we're ignoring the elephant in the room about who

you're hiding, no, I get the occasional client who isn't happy they're not descended from royalty like their grandmother claimed. Overall, my job is boring outside of working with y'all. Most of the time, I'm just used to establish a possible suspect. The detectives and agents do all the work. What about you?"

"Me?"

"Yeah, you were out in the open. What if you were the target?"

"I won't claim to have many friends, if any, but no one has wanted to murder me...other than Chamberlain, of course." Just mentioning Chamberlain's name made my hand go to my ribs and the scars underneath my shirt. I dropped it hoping no one noticed, but that wasn't a safe bet. The Cold Case Unit noticed everything. Other than my niece, Gabby, Boss, and Bart, I hadn't allowed anyone but medical personnel to touch me in over a year. Just the thought made me sick to my stomach.

"The only two people out in the open were you and Vega. Get in the habit of wearing your vest just to be on the safe side."

"Thanks for giving me something else to worry about, Dolan."

"Don't be a brat."

"You know I'm good at it." I snorted as Dolan flipped me off and then wrapped his arm around Boss to pull his husband closer. Boss always had that look of contentment on his face when Dolan touched him. Had I ever once felt that when Dolan had tried to be affectionate?

The simple answer was no. Yes, I'd moved halfway across the country to the east coast to get my ex-husband back, but the old me...well, I'd just hated the thought someone could turn me down. The old Chance would've snarled at Dolan being with someone older and supposedly less attractive. I'd learned a hard lesson, and one I wouldn't forget any time soon.

We continued to go over file after file. Some were federal cases that Vega had consulted on. The more I read about the types of cases she worked on, the more I wanted to know who Vega really was. She didn't look like she'd have federal clearance, and with her attitude toward any government establishment other than Cold Case, it was a wonder she'd been allowed close to the investigations.

"How did you become a consultant?" I asked without looking up.

"Well, let's just say I wasn't so quiet when I tiptoed through the federal database when I was bored one night. It may be shocking, but someone better caught me. I became a target for an investigation. Apparently, they decided they'd rather use my skills than put me in jail. Although, I think I'd do quite well in prison."

"Of course you'd think so," I muttered but looked up in time to catch Vega kissing the top of Cash's head.

"Babygirl, you ready for your dinner and bath?"

"Yes, Mami." Cash tipped her head back and smiled up at her wife.

"Go get your stuff ready. I'll be there soon."

It was odd to see a tall, leanly muscled Cash obeying her much smaller wife. Yet that was kind of normal for everyone in my new circle. Couples that shouldn't fit. Marcel and Simon were opposites. Simon drove his husband crazy with his thought process. Robert and Remy, Robert being leaner and shorter than his husband and boy. Stevenson and Doc, the age difference was apparent, but it was also the gentle way the man tended to his husband in everything, from feeding him to baths. Dolan and Boss, now that was an odd couple, but not in the way of appearance. Boss was built like a man who could take the world on and win. Yet Boss naturally deferred to Dolan in everything.

The exchange of power fascinated me, but I had such a hard time trusting people, and the rape and attempted murder by Chamberlain hadn't helped. I wondered what it was like to put your complete trust in another person. To know that they'd never hurt you. All of it intrigued and terrified me at the same time.

Just like I'd told Bart, who would want a *thing* like me? I was broken, cutting to punish myself for something that wasn't my fault. Fighting the urge to bend over for just a sliver of attention. I was only forty, but I was already too late to change. As much as I liked teasing Bart because he always gave it back tenfold, I knew there was no way, even if he were gay, that a man like him would give me a second glance.

8

BART

I was still chuckling to myself a day later after I called Chance's bluff with his *what was I wearing* text, and he hadn't sent me another since. Although that irked me a bit, I didn't know why. There was a lot I wasn't dealing with well. I'd always considered my apartment my sanctuary, but it felt empty since Chance spent the night. For the most part, I adapted to my solitary life. I had my ex-wife, daughters, granddaughters, and my friends at the Outreach, but I never believed I needed more than that.

Irritated with myself, I threw open the fridge to find it as empty as always. I'd forgotten to grab something to bring home after not eating all day. Some days, I wished I kept alcohol in the house, but drinking and me didn't mix on a good day, and I'd lost myself in a bottle after I'd started living on the streets. A knock at the door drew me away from contemplating my pitiful fridge.

I crossed the room and opened the door, freezing at the sight of Chance leaning against the wall to the right of my door. He had a black case clutched in his hands until his knuckles were white. I saw the misery and devastation on his handsome face, and his normally artfully styled hair looked as if he'd been running his fingers through it for hours.

"Something you want to give me?" I motioned to the small case.

"You told me to come to you." His voice broke as if he were trying to hold back tears.

"Come inside, boy." I stepped back to allow him inside, and once he was out of the doorway, I closed it behind him. When I held out my hand, I saw the internal battle of keeping what was in the case. I was sure it was his supplies, but he had to make the choice. Whatever he decided, nothing would be the same from that moment forward.

His hand shook as he extended his arm, and I grasped the case. I knew I could easily take it away from him, but he had to be ready. After what seemed like forever, he let go and shoved his hands into his pockets. I walked to the trashcan and dropped it inside.

He still hadn't moved when I returned to him. I stretched out my left arm and wrapped my hand around the back of his neck. He tensed as I spun him until I crowded him against the wall.

"Do you know what you're asking me to do?" He nodded. "No. People have allowed you to be quiet for too long. You use your words. Do you know?"

"Yes, Sir." His voice was barely above a whisper.

"First thing, I'm not going to fuck you. I'm not going to ask you for any payment in return. All you have to do is trust me, boy. Can you do that for me?"

"Yes, Sir."

"Now, are you ready to hear my rules that you will follow twenty-four-hours-a-day-seven-days-a-week, whether I'm with you or not?" He nodded, and I allowed that this once. "I'm very proud of you that you came to me before cutting. Your first rule is whenever you feel the need, you will call or text me to find out where I am. You will come there, and we'll work on correcting your behavior."

"Correcting how?" The high-pitched hitch in his voice as his eyes widened bordered on adorable.

"The pain gives you a release, right?" I didn't wait for him to answer. "You will lay across my lap for a spanking, but if you're going to be mine, then how I correct you is up to me. Agreeable?"

"Yes, Sir."

Warmth filled my chest at being called Sir for the first time in nearly twenty years. I'd forgotten how powerful the experience was. Being a Dominant had made me feel truly at home in my skin—in who I was. Chance calling me by my title brought back the rightness I'd lost so many years before.

"Good boy. Next rule...this I won't compromise on unless you're working and I know that...you will contact me every hour of the day from six AM when you get up to ten PM. That is your bedtime now. That only changes again when it comes to work. I will be kept informed of your mental health. Once I feel comfortable that we're correcting your behaviors, we'll lessen your check-ins. Agreeable?"

"Yes, Sir."

"You will work out no more than an hour three days a week and provide yourself with three meals a day and at least one snack in between. No more torturing yourself at the gym and forgetting to eat. You're healthy. I've already contacted Doc privately to take care of your regular doctor visits. That's an arrangement between him and me that will go no further. I wanted to be prepared if you decided to come to me." When I'd made the call to Doc, he hadn't even acted surprised by my request. Just simply told me that he could take care of Chance's exams on Saturdays at the mobile clinic. I'd asked why Doc wasn't more shocked, and he just giggled and asked to let him know when I wanted my boy to have his first appointment.

"Yes, Sir."

"Another thing I won't compromise on, Chance, is your silence. I don't need to know what goes on in group, whether you participated or not, but when it comes to me, you will tell your Dominant everything I need to know." I stepped closer, and he flattened his back to the wall. "You're not a thing to me. Being gay isn't wrong. Surviving one of the most horrific things that can happen to a person is not your fault. Your scars and trauma don't make you less than."

"Why are you doing this for me?" he asked as he kept his hands in his pockets, but I could see they were balled into fists.

I stroked my hand around to the side of his neck and placed my thumb under his chin to make him look at me. "Because not a lot has made me happy in a long time. And you, boy, make me smile. For the time being, what I listed are the basic rules for you, but I can add more at any time. Now, tell me what behaviors you need corrected, boy?"

His eyes filled with tears. "I've never made anyone happy before."

"Get used to it. Answer my question."

"I'm a survivor of rape and attempted murder. I self-harm when my body reacts. I have passive suicidal ideation. I have a sex addiction, but I haven't gone out since the assault."

"And you won't. This isn't sexual, but you belong to me, and no one else touches you. One day when we discuss it, we'll decide if you're ready to date. If I need to, I can provide you with a chastity device if you break my rule." I was almost tempted to get a cock cage for him and make him wear it when he was away from me. "Boy, tell me who owns you."

"You do, Sir." Those three words seemed to stumble on his tongue before he got them out, but soon, he'd say them easily whenever I asked.

"Remove your shirt." He didn't hesitate to pull his hands from his pockets and drag the shirt over his head.

"This is no longer acceptable." I stroked my curled fingers down his side and only lingered over the thicker scar tissue. "My boy's body will never bear another fresh mark. Do I make myself clear?"

"Yes—" He gasped as I brought my big hands to his waist, jerking the buckle free on the thick leather belt. I felt his stare like a brand as I released the button and slid the zipper down.

"I'm going to sit on the couch. You will come and lie over my lap. Sir's boy will do whatever I say, but we will practice safe, sane, and consensual at all times. Red for stop. Yellow for slow. And Green that you're okay. At any time you say Red, we stop. No questions from me. You've lost control of your body and mind, and then someone made it worse when they took what you didn't willingly give. In everything we do, your consent is paramount, but my rules aren't up for compromise."

I glanced down as I pushed his jeans over his hips to expose a surprisingly thick bush of blond curls. The waistband of his pink boy shorts held down his length and kept it hidden. When I'd met him, he was almost painfully lean in that way bodybuilders got when they existed in a deficit and were dehydrated.

"You're perfect," I whispered as I forced myself to push the seat of his jeans over the firm curves of his ass. "It's time to make your choice." He looked confused as I released him to back up and sit on my couch. I patted my thighs.

Patience was always one of the things I'd prided myself on but waiting for him to mentally debate if he were ready tore at my once positive thoughts that he needed what only I could give him. So what if I found him beautiful? I wasn't mired in toxic masculinity as I had been in the past. Affection between male friends wasn't some cardinal sin. Maybe I needed him as much as he needed me, co-dependent relationships were a recipe for disaster, but I just wanted to watch him heal. If that took months or years, I'd always be ready to act as his Dominant.

I'd missed that part of me so much, and the possibility of having it back was, in its own right, addictive. The power the submissive gifted you was one of the most precious things a Dominant received.

He'd flattened his hands against the wall and then used them to physically propel himself forward before his rational mind could rethink the decision he'd made. He paused right in front of me, our legs almost touching.

"Has anyone ever given you a corrective spanking before?"

"N-no, Sir. Dolan used to do it during"—he cleared his throat —"and a few others did it during sex."

I didn't like him talking about sex with other men, and that was completely irrational. Bending at the waist, I removed one of his boots and then the other. Socks were next and stuffed inside his boots that I set to the side. "Belly down. Adjust your pants a little lower on your thighs. Cover your groin with your hands if needed."

He looked so young standing there—nowhere near a man of forty who'd suffered horrific abuse most of his life. He was no longer connected to his body. It was a tool to be used but nothing more. Yet, he was mine to care for from that day forward until I could send him out into the world when both of us were satisfied with his progress. Even with my first submissive, married to her or not, I still made sure she had the tools to thrive when she no longer needed me. I'd do the same for him because I respected that, as bleak as everything appeared, he kept living in whatever way he could.

I held my breath as he curled his right hand in the waistband of his underwear to keep them up as he used the other to shove denim and cotton lower to expose his upper thighs. He seemed awkward as he placed one knee on the cushion, so I helped him until he was draped over my thighs. The first things I noticed were his weight and warmth. I cupped his chin with my left hand to turn him to look at me.

"Normally, I would have you count and repeat what you're being corrected for, but tonight, we'll just see what happens.

Remember, one word, and I stop. We'll work on you accepting what I, as your Dominant, think you need." I released his chin and spread my hand over his upper back, and then stroked the fingertips of my right down the indent of his spine.

He arched but caught himself. My boy was so touch-starved that he didn't know how to handle the gentle touch. Hell, had anyone ever been gentle with him? While my left was my dominant hand, I could use my right just as well. When I reached the top of his hairy crease, he froze.

"I won't touch you there, honey. I'll never ask you to take my fingers. There is nothing sexual in my care of you."

"It's just...I gave up personal grooming."

"A person, no matter what, has the right to how their body looks. Even as you're giving yourself over to my keeping, I will *never* dictate what you do with your body outside your rules. I want you to breathe deep and even. We'll start with ten and assess if you need more. Again, your Sir's discretion."

I sensed when he started his deep breaths and his body relaxed, but I knew he was prepared for the first contact. I didn't make him wait as I drew my arm back and sharply brought it forward until the sound of skin meeting skin filled the room. Repeatedly, I struck his backside, one ass cheek and then the other, counting as I increased the pressure of my left hand to keep him in place.

God, how I'd missed that. I mentally sighed as that part of me that I'd denied came back to life. His ass cheeks turned red, welted with my handprint, and the satisfaction was too intense as I paused at ten like I promised. He was still too tense, and I warned him about taking another ten.

I'd just finished saying fifteen when the first sob came. An almost painful sound as he no longer fought me.

"Your Sir doesn't want to have to correct you, but it's necessary. You'll always trust me to know what's best for my boy."

"Yes, Sir." Sir came out on a shout as my palm connected again.

After twenty, I stopped as he trembled and cried where he was sprawled on my lap. I effortlessly moved Chance's smaller frame until I cradled him in my arms. He buried his face against the side of my neck. His arms were like a steel band around my ribs as he seemed to try to get closer.

"Shh, you were so good. I'm so proud of you." I kissed the side of his head, temple, and cheek. I soothed him because he needed it. Tears were a cathartic release, and I wondered when was the last time he'd simply cried everything out. I rocked him as if we had all the time in the world, and as far as I was concerned, we did. He'd heal. He'd find his way. And that strange new part of me regretted that I'd promised to let him go.

9

CHANCE

COLD CASE
UNIT

I yawned as I walked into S.W.A.T. Headquarters, and as rested as I felt, I could've gone with another hour or two of rest. Bart had tucked me into his bed again and left me to sleep. He'd awakened me at six AM sharp to get ready for work. He'd sent me off with a long hug and a reminder of the rules he'd given me.

The previous night, I'd sat on the side of my tub with my supplies prepared, and as I started to lift my shirt, Bart had popped into my head. I'd tried to ignore the disapproval, but I couldn't. After half an hour of indecision, I'd packed everything back into my case and went to Bart without a text or call. I'd given him no heads-up in case I changed my mind and returned to my apartment to carry out my ritual.

By the time I'd arrived at his place, I could barely remember the drive there. As soon as I'd knocked, I'd leaned back against the wall and waited. When he'd opened the door, all he'd asked was if I had something I wanted to give him. The fear had almost overtaken me at the reality of what I was about to give up. It wasn't all about putting my trust and safety in his hands, but the option of no longer having my kit. The carefully cultivated collection remained with me for a year, and in some twisted way, it was the closest I had to a comfort item.

He hadn't interrogated me or ordered me to do anything. He let me decide in my own time. Yet when I had, there was an obvious change in the way he stood—in the tone of his voice as he'd given me the rules I'd live by from that moment forward.

Bart had told me I made him happy. Never once in my life had anyone said that. They praised me when I continuously ripped pieces of my soul away for their pleasure. What he'd called a corrective spanking ended with such a profound sense of peace as he'd kissed my face and rocked me on his lap. I'd lost track of time as I'd mourned everything. Was it an instant fix? No, but I did feel lighter.

"You're almost la—" I held up my hand as my reminder went off, and I pulled out my phone.

Chance: *I'm at work.*

Bart: *How do you feel?*

Chance: *Sleepy.*

Bart: *I expect you here tonight.*

Chance: *Yes, Sir.*

Bart: *Good boy. Get to work. 8 AM.*

Chance: *Yes, Sir. I set reminders.*

He sent one last reminder about whether I was with him or not that I was still his. I closed out the messaging app and locked my phone.

"Excuse me?"

"I had to send a message. Where's my partner on this protection gig?" I asked and nearly came out of my skin as Dolan grabbed my arm and dragged me to his office. I stumbled as he released me and then slammed the door.

"Chance, this isn't me as your boss. This is as a friend. What the fuck's going on with you?" I opened my mouth to give my automatic lie. "No. You don't have Deacon to run interference or

Bart. This is you and me, have the balls to fucking tell me the truth. Why?"

Once more, I parted my lips to form the words, and they wouldn't come. To tell him a lie would've saved me, but at that moment, I squared my shoulders and told the truth. "At the age of fourteen, I was left alone with my stepdad. He tried to beat the supposed gay out of me to make a real man out of me. Got me a fake ID...took me to local female sex workers to cure me. That went on for two, maybe three years. Do you know what that taught me, Dolan?" He didn't answer.

"It taught me there was something wrong with me, but when I enlisted, I learned I had control of my body, but I didn't. On the down low, I let whoever fuck me. I pretended it was because they wanted me for something other than *any hole would do*. I learned by giving it up, got me the affection I wanted. As empty as it was in my mind being desired for any reason was enough. I was in my late teens and early twenties. What the hell did I know, right? As soon as I felt I was losing their interest, I'd debase myself in any way to win them back, and when they didn't, I found the next and the next until one became two men and then groups. I became addicted to it. It fed my need until the morning after, and I hated myself again."

"There's nothing wrong in being wanted. You were my husband. I married you because I wanted you more than anything, even with the secrecy until it no longer worked for me. I loved you."

"I know...I understand it, Dolan. You couldn't hide when I felt I had no other choice. After..." I cleared my throat. "After Chamberlain, I figured he was my punishment. He saw me as the thing I was and truly showed me how disposable I was." I forced the tears back as my eyes burned, but Dolan stepped in front of me to block me from anyone who could see from outside the windows of his office.

"As your friend, I get it. Deacon and his history schooled me well. That said, as your boss, I can't worry about you out there."

"I don't have a death wish. I already told you that. I've just been stressed lately and not getting enough sleep."

"Who's the mystery man?"

"I'm not telling you that."

"Chance, I will take your phone and find out myself. You never change your damn code. Save yourself the embarrassment of getting your ass overpowered by a fifty-year-old man."

I snorted. "I'm not telling you, but it's not what you think. Everyone wanted me to find someone to talk to, and I found him. He has no interest in fucking me. I found a..." What was I supposed to say?

"You found yourself a Dom." I stared at him wide-eyed until he chuckled. "Deacon found himself a sadist after his husband was murdered. You need structure, and who's better at that than a Dominant and all their rules."

"He's not..."

"Don't lie."

"Last night, he gave a corrective spanking and laid out rules of conduct. Unless work interferes, I'm to check in every hour to let him know how I'm feeling."

"Bart is a step up from your usual."

"It's not—" He arched his brow and shut me up.

"He claimed you twice."

"He's straight. It's not sexual. He's just going to work on healthier coping mechanisms. I gave him my kit."

"Good."

"Don't tell Boss, please. I don't know if Bart wants anyone to know." I felt odd being on the other side. Was that how Dolan felt when I wouldn't acknowledge him? I understood Bart wasn't my boyfriend. He was my friend...my dominant, and that was all. He couldn't help his feelings any more than I could mine.

"Just be careful, okay, we're not married, and we burned

several bridges over the years, but we're becoming friends again. If you need me, all it would take is a call. And straighten up. No more rookie mistakes."

"For what it's worth, I promise. Speaking of rookies, where's mine?"

"Be nice, please, for all that's holy, keep that sharp tongue dulled."

"I'm hurt, Dolan." I put on my best hurt expression and laughed as Dolan rolled his eyes.

"Once upon a time, that got you wherever you wanted with me, but no longer."

"I'm sorry, Dolan, for everything. For the cheating and the lies, for how I acted after I moved here. But I didn't do shit to that one rookie. He screamed bottom, and you know that ain't my lane."

If he rolled his eyes any harder, they were going to get stuck.

"Ain't that the truth. I thought you were going to lose your shit the one time I asked."

"I was scandalized," I whispered.

"I could tell. So, back to the issue at hand. Trey Callaghan is twenty-nine. Been out of the Marines for about two years."

"But he's a rookie."

"He had to recover from an explosives attack. He was just cleared with a clean bill of health a few months ago. He applied to teams all over the country and just relocated here after he got the job. He tried the detective route but isn't really people-friendly. Be nice."

"Wow, I'm starting to get a complex here."

"Shut up and behave. I may have to casually mention your attitude within hearing distance of Bart."

"Don't do that."

"Remember that now when you want to get mouthy," he said and then turned to open the door. Jupiter's collar jangled behind me where he'd been asleep in his bed behind Dolan's desk. "Callaghan, my office now."

"And I'm the one that's supposed to be nice," I muttered as I leaned back to perch on the edge of Dolan's desk.

A tall, slender light-skinned Black man jogged from the locker rooms, and I frowned as I looked for any physical injury, an odd gait or anything, but there was nothing. Then that's when I saw it, the left side of his face had two thick scars down one side. The smaller one was cutting through his brow, and I was shocked he hadn't lost his eye. He had a bit of scruff that didn't hide a few discolored spots that had to be burn scars along his jaw and the side of his neck.

"Callaghan, this is Lieutenant Chance Bowers. You'll be working with him on this protection detail. He's familiar with all the players. Prepare yourself for some crazy."

"I'll be good, sir." His deep voice belied his slender frame.

"Play nice. I see something pretty." Dolan's smirk told me exactly who he saw, and I turned my head to find Boss headed toward the office with Gabby on his heels.

I smiled as I was left alone with Callaghan, and I cringed as a squeal rang out, echoing off the walls as Gabby noticed me and came running. I snorted hard as she completely bypassed her Pop to get to me. The scowl I earned told me I was in trouble later.

"Uncle Chance." She nearly hit me full force, and for being a tiny thing, she packed a hell of a tackle.

"Hey, sweetie." I kissed the top of her head. "Who's bossing Bart around today if you're skipping work?"

"He sent Dad on an errand, and I wanted to see Pop. I gotta get your bag."

I looked at her, feeling confused as I watched her dart away, and I followed with Callaghan beside me. The second I saw Dolan pinch Boss's chin and give him a kiss, I let out the loudest wolf whistle.

"Can I have a moment alone with my husband, Chance?"

"I'm not interrupting. You've never been shy before." I winked at Boss and the silly grin he had on his face. I saw why Dolan adored his husband so much. Boss was about the most adorable man in the world, and that was odd when talking about a bruiser in his sixties.

"Brat, this is yours." Boss held out a to-go bag. "Breakfast, lunch, and three snacks. I don't get paid the big bucks to act as an errand boy for a cranky kitchen manager. He said don't leave anything. He also said to tell you that you knew the consequences."

I felt my cheeks heat with a blush for the first time in my life as I took the bag. "I'll thank him later."

"I don't want to know," Boss muttered as Dolan grabbed his husband and daughter and dragged them away for a few minutes.

I couldn't help my laugh as Gabby whistled for Jupiter, and Dolan's faithful K-9 came running and danced around them as they disappeared. I sensed Callaghan's tension and turned to find him staring in the direction the three disappeared.

"Problem, Callaghan?" I hadn't meant the harsh tone of my voice, but it came through anyway.

"I didn't know—"

"If you need a new assignment, let me know. You're about to spend a lot of time with a gay Commander, a gay Lieutenant... well, you're going to be stuck with the Rainbow Squad until this protection detail ends. I'm sure we can find someone to replace you."

"No, no, I just, it's not a problem. I'm just surprised Commander Sharp is so open at work."

"Dolan doesn't hide his husband. If you look at his desk, you can see pictures of Boss and him on their wedding day and them with their kids."

"Boyfriend or husband send you food?" he asked.

"No, just a friend. I volunteer at the Outreach kitchen, and he thinks I don't know how to feed myself. Between you and me, he's the only reason I survive." I winked at my new temporary partner. "Ready to meet our assignment?"

"Might as well."

"Just a warning, her wife is a bit possessive, and you're about to be frisked. Just let it happen. You don't want to fight her. Cash is obsessive about Vega. We'll go over everything after we get the introductions out of the way and work out a schedule. There will be some fill-in people by way of the Cold Case Unit, but mainly it's you and me."

"I think I can handle it."

"You have civilian clothes?" I asked as I looked at his uniform.

"Yeah, should I change?"

"We're plain clothed on this one. Make sure you have your vest, service weapon, and badge. Bring your go-bag."

He nodded and turned to jog back to the locker room. Once I was left alone, I looked in the bag Bart had sent for me. Everyone knew Bart thought I couldn't feed myself. When Dolan had figured it out, I hoped no one else would. I wanted to spend more time with Bart before he realized I was too much trouble. I hoped he wouldn't, but past experience taught me a completely different lesson.

10

BART

COLD CASE
UNIT

As I unpacked the groceries I'd purchased on my way home, I listened to Chance explain in great detail how scandalized the new S.W.A.T. guy was at being frisked. I chuckled to myself as he barely got the story out through his laughter. I'd known Cash for twenty years since she was a snot-nosed punk hanging out on the strip and lying about her age so she could play in the clubs. When she'd met Vega, I'd had my doubts that was going to work.

"Then, when she checked him from the crotch down and asked if he was a Top or Bottom, I thought the kid was going to fall out right then and there. He's not going to survive this assignment. He'll be running home to wherever that is in a few weeks."

"Have some faith. You survived the introductions."

"Barely, an Amazon grabbing my ass nearly threw me into a panic." He gave me an adorable pout.

"Poor baby."

"I'm not feeling as if you're taking my trauma seriously, Sir."

"I take your trauma very seriously, boy." I closed the fridge and shifted to stand between his knees where he was seated on the counter eating an apple. "How was your day other than talking the newbie off the ledge?"

"Good. I spent most of the day wishing for a nap."

"Are you ready for your next lesson before bed?" I asked him.

"What is it?"

"You have to trust me. Do you?"

"Yes, Sir." The oddly shy heaviness of his lids made him appear almost innocent.

I grabbed the hair at the crown of his head and jerked it back until he stared at me. "We're going to work on how you view your physical self. That might be painful with how you perceive yourself, but as an end result, it'll show me what we need to correct, boy." His hair was thick and felt silky wrapped around my fingers.

"Is it okay to be scared?"

"Honey, it's always okay to be scared. Feeling that way is natural. Finish your snack and drink, and then meet me in the bedroom." I released him as my gaze started to wander down to his lips. Reminding myself repeatedly while in his presence I was a straight man who was old enough to be his father wasn't working. He was the same age as my oldest daughter.

I entered my room and went straight to the full-length mirror in the corner that I'd picked up from a thrift store earlier that day. I adjusted it until the legs were braced against the two walls and then turned on the overhead light. The next step was going to be hard for him. I was going to make him literally face himself and tell me every part of himself he hated. Being brutally confronted by his insecurities might be cruel, but I couldn't continue to allow him to view himself as a thing.

He was going to have to trust me completely for what I had planned. More importantly, I was going to have to have faith in myself for this one. Being cruel to Chance, even if it was for his own good, went against my instincts. I pushed a heavy breath past my lips and opened my closet, my gaze instantly locked on the flogger hung on the door rack.

The familiar weight of the handle fit perfectly in the palm of my hand. After he'd asked me to be his Dom, I made lists of items that I needed to purchase. The base of my skull tingled as I sensed I wasn't alone. I slowly turned.

"Boy, go stand in front of the mirror and don't move until I say otherwise."

I didn't miss that he opened his mouth to argue but obeyed and crossed the small distance. He'd already removed his shoes and socks when he'd arrived. I closed the space between us but kept us a few feet apart. He stared at me in the mirrored reflection.

"What do you see, boy?" I asked.

"You and me."

"Don't look at me. Only focus on you. What do you see?"

He shrugged his shoulders. "Myself."

"How does it make you feel?"

"Disgusted, Sir."

"Unacceptable. Remove your shirt," I ordered, and he quickly removed his t-shirt but refused to look at himself. "I didn't say look away. What do you see?"

"Ugliness," he whispered, and with a deft rotation of my wrist, I striped his back with the leather strips once and then twice. He fell forward and braced his hands on the sides of the mirror where it was mounted to the base.

I spun the hilt in my hand and came up behind him. I wrapped my left arm around him and used the end of the handle under his chin to force his head up. A man shouldn't be that beautiful. He was smooth, lightly tanned skin over a bulkier frame than when I'd met him. His little nipples were pulled into tight points by the chill in the air. I momentarily compared us and wondered why he trusted me so much that he'd bare himself.

"I see a survivor. How we cope with that survival depends on our experience. I dealt with mine by protecting my family and, in doing so, leaving them to find a normal life while I tried to drink mine away. You went with a much more visceral option, your razor. Now, your Sir is going to teach you a different way to cope." I pushed my chest flush to his back. "Remove your pants."

"I—"

"Honey, I will never fuck you." I held his gaze in the mirror as he worked his belt and then pants undone and then pushed them and his underwear off his hips. He removed his feet from the pooled fabric. "Spread your feet apart and lean forward until your hands are braced flat on the wall. Don't look away from the mirror. You're to focus only on yourself, understood?"

"Yes, Sir." His voice shook as he shifted his feet shoulder-width apart and leaned forward to do exactly what I told him to.

"You're such a good boy. You make your Sir so proud. Do you deserve to be loved?" I asked, already knowing his answer.

"No, Sir." He earned strikes of the flogger, causing red lines to form on his pale skin.

I repeated the question and received the same answer, and I increased the force of my strikes until welts started to form on his back and clenched ass. He kept lifting onto his toes. The process continued until he sobbed as he stared into his own eyes.

Coming up behind him, I draped my left arm over his shoulder, hugging his chest, tucking my hand under his arm, and jerking him fully to me. His hands painfully gripped my forearm as tears rolled down his cheeks.

"You deserve everything, baby, every good thing in the world." I spoke above his soft sobs and kissed the side of his face. "Your body is yours, and one day you're going to gift it to a worthy person who will love you so good he'll start to mend some of the wounds."

My gaze fell down his reflection, the slight curve of his softened belly to a thick above-average cock in a nest of pretty, dark blond curls. It was almost cruel how gorgeous he was. Years of self-control made it easy for me to ignore my inappropriate reaction to my submissive. But he was giving me something I'd missed so much in the last twenty years.

"An extremely lucky man will be able to call you his." And that wouldn't be me, that part I left unsaid because it wouldn't get either of us anywhere.

His head fell back on my shoulder as his sobs lessened, and he gave me his weight. I easily stretched out my arm to hang the flogger from the bracket on the mirror. With my right hand free, I spread it over his belly and slowly and lovingly stroked every scar.

"These don't make you ugly, baby." I kissed his cheek and then drew my hand down to cup his flaccid dick. He was silky and warm. It was the first time I'd had another man's dick in my hand, and I didn't hate it. I massaged him until he started to firm a bit. "How this reacts isn't a reason to punish yourself." He shivered against me, and I released him to grab his free hand and curled his fingers around his cock. "It feels good. You can bring pleasure to yourself." With my hand over his, I made him stroke himself slowly until he gasped and rubbed his bottom against me. "Look at yourself, so beautiful. How can that be wrong to feel something other than pain?"

He tried to look away, but I jerked my left hand up to grab his chin and forced him to keep looking. He was panting, and I released his hand. He jacked his cock as I used my hands to touch every part of himself that he found disgusting. The softness of his adorable belly. The scars on his stomach, ribs, and chest.

"You're such a good boy for your Sir." I watched him and felt the ache in my groin, but thankfully I didn't do more than firm slightly. Just as I noticed he was reaching the end, I grabbed his wrists and forced his arms behind his back. He whined as he humped the air. "Savor it, boy. That heat and ache, the hardness." I sucked at the side of his neck, and he whimpered. "How can that pleasure be wrong when it's consensual? That desire is yours whenever you want it."

"Sir, please."

"No. Who owns you?"

"You do, Sir." He didn't even hesitate.

"That's right, and every inch of you belongs to me...every orgasm is mine." I bit down lightly on the tendon at the side of his neck. "And I want you to learn that pleasure isn't your enemy. Need and want aren't sins. Craving them isn't wrong. I'm going to edge you for as long as I want until you realize that release isn't betrayal."

"I came when..." He paused, but he didn't have to finish.

"The same as you did with all the women your stepdad forced you to have sex with. Our bodies react. Orgasms don't equal consent. But the next time you get off, boy, it's going to be your choice and with a man who adores you. He's going to wonder how he got so lucky to find himself between your thighs. Every sound of pleasure you make for him will be a gift he appreciates. Until then, it's Sir's job to make sure you understand how perfect you are. You will never be a thing in your eyes or another person's ever again. You are a man worthy of being loved, and I won't let you go to another until you believe that."

Pain blossomed in my chest at some mystery man taking over his care. Another man acting as his Sir or Daddy. As much as I knew that wasn't my place, I was only there to get him ready to accept what he deserved. I'd never kiss those plump lips. Never know what those strong, thick thighs would feel like as they gripped my sides as he consented to allow me to fill him. No, all that was for some man waiting out there to take my boy from me.

What the fuck had I done? Years of emotional and physical distance were ruined in a matter of a week. The minute I'd told Boss I'd take care of Chance, it had already been too late. I just hadn't realized that until I no longer had the choice to step back from getting attached. The first time I'd seen the devastation in his haunted blue eyes, I'd claimed him, but I'd just successfully ignored it.

I hugged him as I smiled at him in the mirror, and he slipped his arms from behind his back to raise them to curl his hands around my forearms. The redness around his eyes faded, but the tears still stained his cheeks.

"Bart," he whispered my name.

"What, honey?"

"Don't get sick of me." There was so much pain in those five words it nearly broke my heart.

"I can guarantee that'll never happen. How about we curl up in bed, and I'll cuddle you for a bit until you fall asleep?"

"Really?"

"Yeah, I think we both need it. As intense as these sessions are for you, they're just as much for me."

I stepped back, and he turned to take my hand, and I led him to my bed. He stretched out naked, and I followed him down and then gathered him into my arms.

"Is this weird for you?"

"No. The last person I slept with was Verna, my wife. So it's a little odd to be in bed with someone again, but I think that's kinda normal."

"Why did you cut yourself off from touch?"

"Honestly, I think it was easier. As long as I didn't let anyone physically close again, I wouldn't form an attachment to them." He was warm and solid in my arms, so different from my tall, full-figured ex-wife, but, sadly, that overwhelming comfort I took in holding her was back, but it was all for Chance. "If you noticed, I don't even shake hands."

"I noticed."

I smiled as his words became slurred, and I lifted my head slightly to watch him fighting sleep—his eyelids dropped but would fly open.

"Sleep, boy. Sir will stay right here. I'll wake you at six to make you breakfast and lunch before you have to get to work."

"You'd make a good Daddy Dom."

I chuckled. "I won't say I haven't heard it screamed a time or two in my lifetime." He snarled his nose but didn't say anything else as he finally succumbed to sleep.

Selfishly I stayed there to absorb his warmth, memorizing every detail of sleeping with him. One day, he'd leave me ready to take on the world, and that's all I wanted. Him safe and happy. I just wished that would be with me. I frowned at the thought and reminded myself that it wasn't meant to be because I was a straight middle-aged man. The intimacy of being Sir for someone else was intoxicating, but I'd get over it—I had to.

11

CHANCE

"You're sitting a little stiff there, Chance." Vega's amused voice came from my right as she slid down the wall in the Pit to lean against my side. "Anyone I know?" she asked.

"No, and I'm fine. My ass is just going to sleep from sitting on this floor. How many more damn boxes do we have?" I asked to distract her from asking questions. My back and backside were tender from my flogging but nothing I couldn't handle, and to be honest, I savored the reminders of the previous night just like I had after the first spanking Bart gave me.

I'd awakened that morning to the sounds of Bart in the kitchen and the scents of him making breakfast. The scent had seemed so domestic—me curled up in bed while my man made breakfast for us. I'd felt so silly when the thought popped into my head. As much as I'd needed to get up, I'd laid there in the warm bed with the impression of his big body still in the mussed sheets and pillow. I hadn't remembered the last time I'd slept through the night other than when I was in Bart's bed.

The previous night still played on repeat in my head as I relived every second. I'd had countless hands on my dick in my day, but none had ever felt as right and safe as his. Terror had tightened my chest for a moment, thinking I'd give my feelings toward him away. My heart broke when he'd spoken of some other man who'd claim me. I didn't want anyone else.

Bart was the only man I'd looked at in over a year. I'd been dragged along to a kink-friendly club called Xanadu that my friends frequented, and none of the men there had appealed to me. None of them had earned a second glance, not even the ones who screamed brutal Top, which would've had me kneeling with a single order. I had a weird way of picking out the ones who'd fuck me to the point I couldn't walk the next day.

"Chance?" Vega called my name.

"What?"

"I said these are the last of the boxes for the year time frame y'all asked for. You okay?" She sounded concerned when she asked.

"Yeah, I just found someone to talk to, and it's sort of intense, so I'm feeling a bit..." I couldn't explain it.

"Learning new ways of coping with trauma is like hitting factory reset on a computer and then reinstalling everything without all the junk attached. It really wasn't your fault, Chance. If it hadn't been you, it would've been someone else. But when he attacked you, he fucked up. We wouldn't have stopped until we found him."

"Why?" I smiled sadly as I glanced across the room where Trey had found an out-of-the-way spot. "I was an asshole."

"We're all assholes, Chance. Have you not met us?"

I let out a loud laugh and shook my head. "That's true."

"And Chamberlain made his biggest fuck up when he came to Boss's attention. The minute he got the call that there was a victim, you were his. He would've even fought Dolan for you."

"I asked Dolan why Boss did it. He didn't owe me anything, and to be honest, he had every right to let me meltdown." My compulsion to apologize to Boss kept hitting me because I'd made the life of his boyfriend hell and then insulted his daughter, thinking Dolan was dating women. Fuck, I was an idiot over how I'd dealt with everything. Which made me feel as if I deserved what happened with Chamberlain.

"Not in Boss's makeup to ignore a victim. You're pretty much surrounded by people with sexual trauma."

I jerked my gaze to hers and saw for the first time someone who was like me. "You don't—"

She smiled sadly and shook her head. "I grew up in a very conservative fundamentalist cult. Not many people know. Doc and Remy have heard all the stories. Boss didn't get all of it. We're talking Quiverfull. Make as many babies for the Lord's army as possible. My parents sent me to conversion therapy. Corrective rapes for almost two years until they believed I'd learned the error of my ways. With my IQ, they thought I'd do well working from college to convert the gentiles and bring more ladies to the cult. Ones who were naïve and spending their first freedoms. First week away at college, I found my way to the strip."

"I'm sorry."

"Not your place to apologize. I went through the emancipation process with Boss's help, won a lawsuit against the cult and conversion camp, and started my life with enough money to take care of myself. My education was due to a full academic scholarship." She paused as she tilted her head to look up at the ceiling as if she could see her babygirl through the floor above their heads. "But I really didn't start living until I walked into my favorite club one night and saw the most beautiful babygirl playing in the band there. I was so terrified of moving forward. Would the trauma make it impossible for me to even accept what I felt she was to me? Most people think I'm crazy, Chance, and in some ways, I probably am. But I healed, I fell in love, and I adore my wife more than anything in this world. If I or Remy can find love, anyone can."

"Remy is pretty open about his past."

"That's because he isn't ashamed of it. He kinda figured

knowledge is power. If people know he's a former homeless sex worker, they can't use it against him. And also, when someone sees a person who survived and thrived, well, it helps."

"I won't even talk in group." I tossed the file I'd been holding into the finished pile.

"I never did. Boss tried, but I talked with Remy. I don't do well being stared at in group. Despite the wardrobe that looks like I bought it while tripping balls on acid, I don't like a lot of attention. It's why I chose the job I have. It's pretty much a solitary profession unless y'all are around."

"Boss tried to get me to talk to Remy, too, but I'm still...I guess I still feel like an outsider with y'all."

"You seeing a shrink, or did you go the unconventional route?"

"I guess you'd call it unconventional. He makes me feel safe. Doesn't look at me like I'm broken. He also has no interest in fucking me. That's a bit disappointing." I grinned as she laughed. "But we all have our crosses to bear." I glanced at Vega. "I don't know if I'll ever feel safe to do that again."

"You'll do it in your own time, and just so you know, not everyone believes sex equals penetration. Marcel and Simon have an extremely healthy intimacy without all the tab A into slot B bullshit. Sometimes, intimacy is the key, anyone can have sex, but people who can share a relationship filled with affection and care and respect lasts a lot longer than one based on penetrative sex."

"I'm kinda scared to try sex again. I'm addicted to it, it's the only time in my life I felt wanted, and I guess I thought I was in control...I allowed them to fuck me, so it was my choice. But it was all a lie that I told myself. Being fucked was better than being alone." I tipped my head back and then turned to stare at Vega.

"We all have our ways of coping. Some are healthy, some border on fucked up, but we do what we think is best until we learn differently. We..." My phone beeping with my reminder to text Bart cut her off.

I picked up my phone, unlocked it, and went instantly to my messages. I opened the thread for Bart and me.

Chance: *Checking in, Sir.*

I hit send and set my phone aside. I knew he was in the kitchen and didn't expect him to respond right away. Part of me had held a bit of skepticism that the check-ins would work. Instead of my phone beeping, it rang, and I jerked it up to answer.

"Hey," I said as I pressed the phone to my ear and heard the sounds of the Outreach kitchen in the background.

"Working hard, honey?" Bart asked. I loved his deep baritone that held just a hint of a rasp.

"Vega needs to sleep more and work less. We'll be going through these files for months."

He chuckled. "Good luck convincing her of that. You doing okay, though?"

"My ass is numb from sitting on this floor."

"Hello, Bart," Vega screamed too close to my ear and then eased up from the floor. "Your boy is behaving." I flipped her off. "He's making rude gestures."

"Snitch," I hissed at her as I listened to Bart laugh.

Trey had jerked his head up from the stack of files and looked almost panicked. He was going to have to loosen up soon, or he wasn't going to survive. Especially when he was in the same space as Stevenson and Doc, hell, any of the couples, really.

"I'll make a note of that for correction at a later date."

"Yes, Sir." I sighed and snarled at a giggling Vega as she returned to her workstation covered with monitors and a tower of energy drink cans.

"Do you know what your schedule is this weekend?"

My brows drew together at his question. "I'm not sure. I think Remy and Stevenson are spotting us for the weekend so we can get a little time off. Why?"

"Cora and Bettany called me earlier and asked would I watch

my granddaughters so they could have some time with their husbands. I didn't know how you felt about spending time with a toddler and a four-year-old, I was gonna warn you away, or you can take mercy on me and help me out?"

"Two wee babies scare you, Sir?"

"It's been a long time since my daughters were that age. Sierra just became comfortable enough to be away from her parents for a weekend. Leila is four going on eighteen and is *not* interested in tea parties and all the things her mother was interested in. She likes glitter polish and her hair done. My baby girls are particular about their hair."

"Well, I guess if there's food involved, I can be persuaded to help."

"What if I just order my boy to help me babysit?"

"Is that some behavioral exercise that I don't know about?" I smiled and then noticed Vega watching me with a huge grin on her face.

"No, but I adore my girls, I really do, but I missed out on a lot. My daughters loved their pretending and playing dress-up and a bit of makeup and polish here and there. But my granddaughters, this younger generation coming up? I'm lost. This is going to be the first weekend I get them to myself. I'd really appreciate the help."

"If they try to put me on the weekend, I'll beg for someone to switch with me."

"I appreciate it."

"Gabby's taught me how to do a decent manicure."

"She would. She's gotten spoiled since Dolan and Boss took her in. Okay, I have to finish up the lunches for the kids tomorrow. Remember, I expect a text in an hour."

"Yes, Sir. I already scheduled reminders so I don't get distracted."

"If you can't, just let me know so I don't worry, honey."

"I promise. Get to work. I have twenty boxes to go through,

and it's going to be a long night."

"Be careful going home. I expect a text when you leave Vega's and when you reach home, okay?"

I agreed, and we said goodbyes. As soon as I disconnected the call, I said, "Vega, help me."

"What's your Sir asking you to do?" she asked, and I glanced at Trey to find him shaking his head without looking up.

"I have to learn to do hair in three days, and what I have to buy that would work on little girls' hair."

"Watching the grandbabies, getting all serious and shit." Vega teased me as she tapped away at her keyboard.

"Don't give me shit, Vega, this is important. I can't mess this up."

"Pull up a seat, Chance. You're about to get a crash course in doing hair. Want to learn to take care of your Sir's as well?"

I didn't know why I liked the sound of that, but I nodded. "Can I?"

"Tutorials are your friend. Boss watched a bunch to learn to do Gabby's, and I've had over a decade of doing my babygirl's hair. We'll have you prepared to make a good impression. Sir could turn into Daddy. Bart definitely has potential."

I didn't comment because I didn't want to get too ahead of myself. Bart was just taking care of me and helping me to learn to cope in a healthier way. There wasn't any future there. Even if I dreamed of there being more, I didn't think I'd ever be ready to have one of those normal relationships. Just because my friends found their perfect persons, ones who were patient and loving...I still wasn't sure I was ready to accept that I could be loved.

Bart had been happily married until his PTSD became too much. He had four daughters and two granddaughters. That family shit was way too normal for me. The straight man wasn't going to go beyond playing his role of Dominant for me. I'd never be allowed into his family—be considered his. That hurt, but it was nothing less than what I expected.

12

BART

My apartment was quiet as I crossed my arms under my head and stared up at the ceiling. As much as I'd tried to convince myself Chance didn't need to be there every night, that didn't lessen the urge to have him there with me. He kept in contact, and if he followed my rules, there wasn't any need to get together for scenes constantly. Chance needed time in between to focus and heal—think about the lessons.

He had a dangerous job, and he needed to perform at the top of his game. My stomach twisted at thinking about him under threat. Vega had called to give me shit after I'd called Chance earlier that day. If someone asked me flat-out was Chance my boy—my submissive—I wouldn't lie. But I also wasn't conducting myself in a completely honest manner either.

When I'd awakened that morning, he'd been cuddled up to my chest with his thigh over my hip. We fit together as if we'd been sleeping together for years. In those moments of watching him, I'd thought about the previous night's scene. For me, it had felt like coming home. I wasn't that broken man with the bomb in my brain that could go off at any time. No, I was a man who truly desired someone for the first time in twenty years.

I closed my eyes as I pulled up the way Chance had looked, stroking his cock for me. I was a few inches longer, but we were about even in thickness. Slipping my left arm from under my head, I pushed my hand beneath the cotton of my sweats and fisted my heavy length. My back arched slightly off the bed. Fuck, I couldn't remember the last time I jerked off. At least a few years had gone by.

I removed my hand from my pants as my phone went off, reaching out to grab it from the nightstand. A frown pulled my brows together as I saw Chance's name. I connected the call.

"You okay?" I asked.

He chuckled, and I smiled. "Yes, I'm fine. Vega and Cash are in bed, Trey is taking a nap, and once he's awake, I'm headed home."

"Bored?" I held my phone in my left hand and curled my right arm under my head, relaxed to enjoy getting to hear his voice.

"Yeah, I didn't become a detective for a reason. If I have to look at one more file, I'm going to claw my eyes out."

"Can't be that bad, baby." I inwardly cursed as the endearment slipped out.

He let out the most adorable whine. "It's terrible. They delivered four boxes this evening that are all complaints filed against Vega."

I chuckled at his groan and shifted to get more comfortable. "I figured there'd be more."

"Don't curse me, Bart, please. But to be honest, the one box I've gone through, none of them screamed hire a sniper to me."

"People get pissed off by the stupidest shit, boy. Something bothering you?" The tone in his voice said he had something on his mind. As much as he thought he concealed his emotions, he sucked at it. At least for people who paid attention.

"What if I was the target? It's something Dolan said. I was out in the open, too. What if the sniper was just trying to get me more exposed by taking a shot at Vega?"

To me, it wasn't a bad theory because the shots were too close to Vega and Chance. From the security videos I'd watched, the Cold Case Unit was under cover of the tents and hidden. I'd held my breath the entire time I'd played the footage. He hadn't even hesitated to put himself between Sierra and Vega, and after he'd been hit, he hadn't slowed down once. It had sickened me that someone would put numerous people in danger, especially women and children.

"What does your gut say?"

"That's the problem. I haven't been able to trust my gut in a long time...like never."

"I don't think that's true. Your job relies on intuition as well as skill. I saw the security footage. Not once did you hesitate or slow down. So, focus and tell me what your intuition says."

"My gut tells me that if I was the target, they would've went straight for me. I wasn't covered from a direct hit at all."

"Who would have it out for you?"

"No one that I can think of. I mean, I've only lived here a little over a year and a half. I don't think I've made enemies. And the ones I thought I had, I became friends with."

"What about before you came here?"

"I'm a sniper by trade. Most of my targets never saw me. It wasn't but the last three years that I had a command position. The only person who ever attempted to murder me was Chamberlain. He took a plea deal for life without parole to save himself from death row. Taking me out would just be a vanity project."

"Only you would call your attacker hiring someone to kill you a vanity project."

He snorted. "There wouldn't be any logic in it. Dolan's the one who shot him in the groin and shattered his pelvis. He'd be a better target for revenge. Dolan put him using a cane for the rest of his life. I didn't even have to testify or do a victim impact statement. Henry did all that on behalf of Chamberlain's Winston

Harbor Victims. Convictions in the other locations were just a formality."

"But something's made you curious enough to question."

"Maybe I'm just tired, and the past week has been kinda...intense."

Had it only been a week since I claimed my boy as mine? It seemed longer. Maybe it had been. Something about him had drawn me in since he stepped foot in my kitchen all bruised and appearing as if he had the world on his shoulders. "Do you need more time between sessions?"

"No, no, Sir, I didn't mean that."

"Do you want to come over after Trey wakes up?" I inwardly cursed as soon as the question was out. Wasn't I just telling myself that he didn't have to be there every night? Hell, I'd even invited him to spend the weekend with me and my granddaughters. I hadn't planned on that, but for some reason, I'd suddenly had the urge to share my girls with him. Sierra and Cora liked him, so I knew the rest would, too. As confident as I was, I was still unsure why I wanted to spend so much time with him. At almost sixty, maybe I should have my shit together better.

"Could I?"

"Of course." Too late to change my mind. "You sleep better when someone's watching over you, and you have a lot of rest to catch up on."

"I do. You need me to stop for anything on my way there?"

"No, because a certain boy complained I didn't have anything in my fridge, so I stocked up, remember?" I closed my eyes as I took in the beautiful sound of his laughter that no longer held that edge of fakeness it had before. We still had a lot to work on, but I'd already noticed the difference. "You have a go-bag, or do you need me to dig you out some clothes to sleep in?"

"My go-bag's stocked. I figured, with my protection duties, I needed to add a few more things to it. I gotta wake Trey up in about an hour, and then I'll be over."

"Text me when you head this way, okay?"

"I can do that. Thanks, Bart…for everything."

"No need to thank me. You're not the only one getting something out of this arrangement."

"What are you getting out of it?"

You. But I couldn't say that. "I'd completely ignored a huge part of myself. Being your Sir makes me feel like me again."

He was silent for too long, and then he cleared his throat. "I'll be there soon."

"Text me, and be careful."

"Yes, Sir." He disconnected the call.

I frowned and wondered if I'd said too much, but I wanted to be honest with him or as much as I could be. Shit, I forgot to ask if he'd eaten anything. I threw the covers off my legs and got off the bed. My place was obsessively ordered because I needed control of my space. To keep myself busy instead of checking the clock to count down the minutes until he'd arrive, I fell onto my couch to see about finding something mindless to watch. When he got there, I'd ask did he need something to eat. I knew he had a complicated relationship with food—his anorexia was about control and what he put in his body, and how much he worked out was a way to have power. There was so much more to learn about Chance, and I wanted all his secrets—I needed him to trust me with all his secrets.

THE TEXT CAME thirty minutes earlier, and I knew exactly how long it took to make it from Vega's place. As soon as I heard the elevator doors creak, I got off the couch and opened my door. I leaned against the frame as I watched him make his way down the hall to my apartment at the end. He wore a white tank top and jeans that showed the powerful length of his legs.

Chance had his small duffel bag slung over his shoulder, and he was rubbing his hair until it stood up in every direction. He looked tired. The second he lifted his head, his full lips tilted into a sexy smirk when he spotted me waiting.

"Hey, honey, you look sleepy."

"How is it I'm more awake after a breach than I am sitting around Vega's house going through an insane number of files?" he asked as he stopped in front of me, and I grabbed his hips to tug him close to press a kiss to his forehead.

"You're riding an adrenaline high. Get in here. Have you had dinner?"

He slipped around me and walked straight to my bedroom, leaning inside to drop his bag just inside. "Yeah, Cash made pasta and a killer tiramisu."

I nearly groaned as he bent at the waist to remove his boots and socks. The sight of the denim conforming to his rounded muscular ass reminded me of what my handprint looked like on those curves. What was the power Chance had over me? At first, it was an almost overwhelming emotional pull. Yet that morphed into a physical one, not fully sexual, but I noticed things about him that I'd never contemplated about another man. Was it just the rush of rightness that I experienced as his Sir or something more?

"She sent you a piece," he muttered as he straightened and had a small storage container in his hand. "The pasta didn't survive. For a slender man, Trey can put away some food. I was a little later because he wanted to take a shower before I left."

"How is it having a new partner?" I asked as I turned the deadbolt and locked up, shutting off all the lights except for the lamp on one of the end tables. "He going to survive trial-by-crew?"

"Still a bit early to tell. He hasn't really been trapped in a room with all of them yet." He went to the kitchenette to open the silverware drawer, grabbed a fork, and then crossed to the couch, lowering himself to sit.

I joined him and took the dessert and utensil he offered. I cut off a piece and held it out for him. He shook his head. "No?" I took the bite myself.

"I'm not a huge fan of pasta so that's sitting heavy in my gut right now. Cash was sneaking around when I was talking to you and overheard I was coming over."

"Does that bother you?"

"No, but is that okay with you?"

"I don't have an issue with people knowing that I'm your friend or Dominant. Vega seems to have already figured it out. From Boss's grin when I handed over your food to bring you, he wasn't all that shocked either."

"Dolan did, too," he whispered.

"Baby, we're not doing anything wrong. We're friends. And being your Dominant isn't something to be ashamed of. But I know you're not used to all this."

He turned sideways and tucked his right leg under his left as he propped his head on his hand where he'd braced his elbow on the back of the couch. "I thought when I was forced out of the closet by the attack by Chamberlain that I wouldn't survive that."

"But since you were outed without your consent, how do you feel about that?"

"At first, I waited for the looks and the judgment, and then I realized Winston Harbor wasn't Houston or my hometown. My ex-husband is open about being married to a man. The Cold Case Unit, well, they're extremely out and proud." He paused as if he was trying to figure out how to explain. "I won't say that I don't look over my shoulder to see if people are staring or pointing, but I'm not traumatized by people knowing." He sighed and gave a small grin. "It was the greatest fear in my forty years... people finding out. But in the end, it was freeing to not pretend anymore. I just wish it had been my choice."

"I'm sure. Okay, I won't say I understand feeling the need to stay in the closet. Twenty years of being around the Outreach, it was never an issue with us being a safe space."

"You said you were a bit homophobic." He said it low and almost cautiously as if he'd offend me, but not much caused that at that stage in my life.

"Not my proudest moment. I wasn't yelling slurs or bashing, I just...it was just what I grew up seeing...hearing, and it made me uncomfortable."

"What changed?"

I set aside my half-eaten dessert and relaxed into the cushions. "I'd been working the Outreach for about a year, I think. I kept to myself. Came in. Did my job and left. I left one night. There was this Black kid on the basketball court. It was late...and a school night. My Dad-instincts said he needed to be home. I called out, and he turned. Someone had beaten that kid's face into pulp. He was only seeing out of one eye."

"What happened?" Chance asked.

"Some of the kids at his school. Him and his white best friend were caught kissing behind the school. In one of the alcoves where all the kids went to hide and smoke. His friend pushed him away and called him names. They stomped him. He ran away, and he was too scared to go home and see his parents. He had a brother in the same school, so he knew they were gonna find out. He was about the same age as my girls, and just like with them, I wanted to protect him." I hadn't thought about Corey in years, not since I'd received a letter at the Outreach and he'd told me about his life and husband, the job he had. How much I'd helped him.

"Did you take him home?"

"Yeah, I promised him it would be okay. Fuck, I'd hoped I wasn't lying. On the walk to his apartment, he told me that he'd told his best friend he loved him, and it got him his first kiss." I still remembered the momentary joy of Corey telling me about his first. The way the battered kid had lit up as if the greatest thing had happened to him and the way it had disappeared made me pissed on his behalf. "He'd thought it was perfect. For a split second, you should've seen the look of happiness over his first, and then it was gone. I told him there was nothing wrong with him. That he'd have dozens of first kisses in his life, and each would be special in its own way. We got to his building, and I walked up with him. His parents were frantic when they answered the door, and his mom completely broke down seeing what shape he was in."

"Were his parents okay with him being gay?"

I nodded. "Yeah, his dad was this big, hyper-masculine-looking dude just like me, but he hugged his son and just asked was he okay. The fear that kid felt over telling his parents he was gay should never happen. He made me wonder if my girls would be scared to come to me if they fell in love with a woman and feel that I would disown them."

"So it turned out okay in the end?" I nodded. "Did the ex-best friend get his ass kicked? Tell me he got his ass kicked?"

I stretched out my arm to rest over his thigh and patted the side of it as he looked angry on Corey's behalf. "I don't know that. But I do know that Corey's married and works as a counselor at an LGBT Youth Center. He told me his thirteenth first kiss was the lucky one. Corey's living a great life, and I think that's revenge enough."

"That's a really great story. Dad instincts won out there."

"It wasn't an instant fix, but being around Boss, Remy, and all the rest, I heard all the horror stories in the LGBT Youth Support group that met in the cafeteria. They were all babies and already assumed the world would hate them for who they loved. Most of them were terrified of telling their parents."

"I think my mom would have been okay."

"What was she like?"

"She was amazing. It was just her and me until I was twelve. We never had a lot of money, but she made life fun. She was the mom all my friends wanted to have. She was sick a lot that last year. They found out she had stage four breast cancer, and it had already spread by the time she went to the doctor. She was dying and still tried to be super mom, one day, she just didn't wake up."

"I'm sorry." I rubbed soothing circles on his thigh.

"I am, too. I want to believe that my life would've been completely different if she hadn't gotten sick, but that isn't what happened." He leaned forward and laid his head on my shoulder, and I didn't hesitate to brush a kiss to his forehead.

I flexed my arm until he scooted closer and cuddled to my side. At fifty-nine, I'd resigned myself to the fact that I wasn't going to have another person in my life like Verna. I'd loved her with everything that I was. Her and our daughters were all I'd ever thought I'd need. That sense of belonging I had with my girls, I had with him, and that terrified me. I'd promised him that I'd help him heal and then send him off to live his best life.

I'd never considered myself a selfish man, but as much as I wanted to help Chance, I also wanted that time for me as well. He tipped his head and pressed his face against my neck as he completely relaxed. I hadn't thought I'd give someone else that sense of peace again. Yes, it felt a bit odd that, at almost sixty, that person was a man. Yet that didn't change how I felt.

"You want to go to bed?" I asked and smiled as he hugged my arm and nodded.

"You don't have to, but would you sleep with me again?"

"Yeah, I think we could both do with a good cuddle session and sleep. Also, my back will thank you for sharing."

"Then, come on, old man." I noticed his reluctance to get up, but then he was off the couch and headed for my bedroom.

I barely suppressed a groan as he dragged his shirt off while disappearing through the doorway. By the time I got off the couch, turned off the TV and lights, put the rest of the dessert in the fridge, made sure everything was locked up, and went to join him. He was already curled up in bed. Chance had draped his clothes over the footboard.

When I lifted the covers and got in behind him, he scooted back to meet me halfway. I slipped my right arm under his head and wrapped my left around his middle. That sense of home was back as soon as he was in my arms, tucked safely against me. He was wearing nothing but pink boxer briefs. It wasn't like I hadn't had his dick in my hand the previous night and slept with him naked.

I tried to search for a sense of awkwardness in being with him like that. When someone closes themselves off completely, you get to the point where you no longer believe you need the things from your former life. Intimacy. Sex. Someone to talk to in the evenings. Share stories with a person and see how they experience it differently from the dozens of times you've told it before. I'd never told anyone about Corey or what I'd done. To me, it wasn't as if I'd done a great thing. Chance's reaction made me feel as if I'd done some great feat. To be honest, it almost seemed silly.

I had to remind myself I was there to help him heal. To be his friend. To prepare him for the right one, and as much as that hurt, I wouldn't be that person. I'd promised him he was safe with me—that I'd never fuck him. And I'd never break a promise to the beautiful man in my arms. I kissed his shoulder and relaxed as I listened to his soft snores. I'd enjoy the honor of being his safe space until he no longer needed me because I wouldn't regret the time I got to spend with him.

13

CHANCE

COLD CASE
UNIT

I averted my gaze from the wall of mirrors as I ran on the treadmill in HQ's gym. Looking at myself still made me uncomfortable, and it was odd because I'd stared at my reflection for years to make sure I was perfect. Every hair in place. No lumps and bumps, nothing soft about me. It was still hard to accept that they'd diagnosed me as anorexic. I'd always thought that was for people that were dangerously skinny—not someone who was looked at as physically perfect.

Yet after my attack, seeing myself just made me wonder what someone like Chamberlain saw to make me a victim. But hadn't hundreds of other men seen me as one or simply an easy target? Checking myself out in the mirror for more than brushing my teeth or doing my hair made me analyze that dessert I had or the cheese and bun I had for my burger. I was better, but food became a huge trigger for my body dysmorphia. Which made me question everything about my appearance to why people wanted to have anything to do with me. What did Bart see that made me worth his time and effort?

I looked at Trey on the machine next to me. Claxton and Marcel were at Vega's office, and then Remy and Robert would take over for the evening. The files had turned into a waste of time, or at least they had been so far. I was just glad to be away from them for a while. My brain still wouldn't let go of those shots being meant for me. Yet it also didn't make sense. My worst enemy was myself. I had no idea why someone would want to kill me other than the man who'd tried.

I'd noticed Trey was zoned out. His tank top and shorts showed heavily scarred light-brown skin, which made them stand out a bit more starkly. He didn't talk much, and Vega had tried like hell to get him out of his shell, but that hadn't happened. I wondered if I'd looked that awkward when I'd first been tossed into the fray that was the Outreach and Cold Case Crew.

"Do you know of any apartments for rent?" he asked out of the blue.

"You've been here months and haven't found a place yet?"

"Yeah, but I just found a room to rent, and the lady that owns the house, well, she'd kinda nosy and getting huffy about the hours I keep. I told her I was a cop when I called about the room. Since I've been here, I haven't made any friends. I'm getting kinda tired of locking myself in my room to avoid the passive-aggressive bullshit."

"I could talk to Boss."

"That's the Commander's husband?"

"Yeah, he owns some buildings on the strip. He might have some apartments available. Or I have an extra room you can rent until you figure out something else."

"No, I'm sure you..." He darted his gaze at me in the mirror.

"Don't want to live with a gay man?"

His eye roll amused me. "I have some PTSD issues, my nightmares are still bad, and I think that's one reason the landlady's looking for reasons to make me move."

"Someone raped, tortured, and attempted to murder me a year ago. My nightmares aren't much better." I nearly choked on a snort as he tripped mid-step before he caught himself. "You can deal with mine. I can deal with yours. I also keep weird hours sometimes. Once this protection detail is over, I'll be back to my team and volunteering evenings at the Outreach. We might not even see each other too often."

My phone beeped as soon as I stopped speaking, and I reached for it. I typed in my message to let Bart know where I was and what I was doing and then hit send.

"What's with that? Every hour you send a text, got a possessive boyfriend?" He actually looked concerned when he asked, and it was kind of cute.

I shook my head as I placed my phone back in the holder. "No, I have some issues that need to be corrected, and I have a friend who helps me pause and assess what I'm doing and how I'm processing in the moment."

That's the best non-answer I could come up with. Did I want to say I had a Sir who'd taken me on as his submissive to work on correcting my behaviors? That seemed a complete understatement of how I felt about Bart. I knew he was still working on getting me ready to head out into the world without him. I was dreading that day, but I respected him too much to pretend that I wasn't improving. The day that happened, my heart would break.

"Call him Sir, huh? Y'all aren't the most discreet people I've met."

"That's one way of putting it. Dolan, Sharp, is my ex-husband, my ego asked me how he could leave me, and I moved here to try to get him back. After the attack, Boss came to the hospital, and Boss took me into the fold. Getting used to the Outreach and Cold Case people isn't the easiest thing to do, especially with how close they are. It's been a year, and I'm still not exactly used to it, so don't feel so bad." I slowed my pace as I reached my tenth mile and placed my feet on the sides as I turned the treadmill off. "Want dinner?"

He was about to answer when my phone went off. Instead of a beep for a text, my phone rang. I connected the call. "Hey."

"Hey, honey, have you had your dinner yet?"

"No, Sir, I haven't. I just asked Trey if he wanted to have dinner."

"Well, go out with your friend, I was going to see if you wanted to have dinner since you had a free night, but we'll plan something for another time."

I didn't like how quickly he dismissed the invite and urged me to go out with someone else. "Would you mind if I brought a guest?"

"You know you can. I've heard a lot about him."

"Okay, if he wants to come, we'll be there soon, and if not, I'll definitely be there. I'm missing the Outreach with this protection detail."

"Whatever you want to do." He paused as I heard someone calling his name. "I gotta get back to work. Text when you're on your way."

"Of course, Sir," I said, and he disconnected the call with a growl at whoever was trying to get his attention. There was my cranky kitchen manager.

"I'll let you get to your man."

"No, come on, Bart said to bring you to have dinner with us. It's communal. So we'll probably be at a table with twenty other people. It's summer, and that means it's extra busy. We'll get showered and head out." He seemed as if he was going to change his mind. "Afterward, I can show you the apartment, and you can decide if you want to take it."

"Are you sure about dinner and the room?" I sensed he wasn't included in things much and wanted to offer me an out.

"You're good."

"Thanks. I didn't look for a permanent place yet because I didn't know if this job was going to work out. To be honest"—he sighed as we headed toward the showers—"I still don't know."

"Why?"

"I grew up in foster care, aged out, and went right into the Army. Nothing has ever really been steady, you know, and since getting the medical discharge, I'm still figuring shit out."

"Aren't we all. There's groups at the Outreach. They offer ones for PTSD, and Boss works with placement for discharged or retired vets with transition services. You can check some of that out tonight. Just keep in mind the place is loud, and kids are running around. Have you been to the strip yet?"

"Not really, except for a few call-outs and stuff, but not to just go down there."

"You're in for a treat, man. It's like a world of its own. Let's get cleaned up. I'm late having dinner, and I have to be home and ready for bed by ten." I ignored his strange look to go to one of the far shower stalls to take my shower. It hadn't even been two days since I'd seen Bart, but I was missing him.

I'd wanted to go back the previous night. Yet I'd resisted the urge to call. I had some anxiety, but it wasn't at a level I couldn't handle. My fear of wearing out my welcome had kept me at home in my own bed. Bart didn't need me to latch on and annoy him over every little thing. He took his role as my Sir seriously, and he'd do what was needed to make me secure, but he needed his own time to repair from being my caretaker. I wanted him to keep me no matter how impossible that was.

AN HOUR LATER, we parked in the back parking lot, and all the tension I'd possessed disappeared at finally returning to my safe space and Bart. Carlos was the first person I saw as I led Trey into the kitchen. He waved and nodded toward the freezer. I'd wondered why I hadn't heard from Bart when I'd texted that I was on my way. He normally made sure to send a *be careful* at least.

"Carlos, this is Trey." I introduced him to the assistant kitchen manager and a few of Bart's regular team. "Trey, if you go through that door and down the hallway, you can get to a reception desk. You can ask about some of the programs. I've got something to take care of." He nodded, and I made my way to the freezer. I knocked on the door before I opened it.

The first thing I saw was Bart with his head tipped back. His barrel chest worked hard to take deep enough breaths. His fists curled by his sides, but I didn't feel any fear. I simply let the door close, and I stayed near it until he acknowledged my presence. It took several minutes, but then his hazel eyes focused on me.

"Tell me, Sir."

"I don't know. There was nothing. I was just standing there, and it hit. It was just this overwhelming sense of loss. Give me a hug, baby," he demanded, and I didn't hesitate to walk into his open arms.

He wrapped me up tight, and I buried my face in the curve of his neck. I shivered at the chill of his skin, but I just cuddled closer. Bart kissed my neck, and I was glad we were in a freezer, or that may have been bad. He straightened until I looked up at him, and he cupped my cheeks. I shivered at the coldness of his hands.

"How was your day?"

I wanted to protest that his focus went from taking care of himself to me being okay as his top priority. As much as I needed him to be okay, I also knew that his care of me removed him from what was going on in his head. If that's what Bart needed, that's what he'd get. I wondered if he understood what I'd do for him, and that was my greatest fear. The repeat in pattern, he'd never make me degrade myself, and I knew that, but I feared I'd offer just that to stay with him.

"It was fine. I slept late. It was odd to *not* be in a rush to get up. How was yours?" I hugged his waist tighter, loving the way his rounded belly conformed to my flatter and softer one. There were still moments when the small rolls along my ribs and love handles made me calculate calories, or how many reps or miles I had to run to get rid of them. The lure of buying new supplies for my kit taunted me, but I was slowly working through those compulsions, causing them to fade. Maybe they'd never fully go away. I had to keep reminding myself I no longer needed to be perfect, not even with my healing.

"It was good. I arranged for the weekend off for time with the kids. You still good to take the weekend?"

"Yeah, I'm going to work the night shift Friday night, and I'll get relieved at about seven AM." The closer it drew to watching Bart's granddaughters meant meeting their mothers. Cora, I knew, but that was one introduction in a high-stress situation. Would they like me? Would they think I wasn't good enough for Bart? I mentally scolded myself. Bart was my friend, not my damn boyfriend.

"Good. You ready for dinner?"

"Yes, I'm hungry. I had a protein bar before my run."

"Can't have that."

"Bart, if you need a few more minutes, we can stay right here."

"No, I'm fine now, don't worry about it. The episodes I have are more manageable over the years. Twenty or thirty minutes in the freezer with some breathing, and I'm usually able to get it under control. Did Trey come with you?"

"Yeah, he's having some issues with transitioning since his discharge, so I told him where to get some information on programs and groups. He was going to check those. I told him I had something to take care of." I started to step back, and he grabbed my hips to keep me in place. "What?"

"My team has been giving me shit recently."

"For what?"

"My pretty boy."

I rolled my eyes. "Should I not come around to save you from the teasing?"

J.M. DABNEY

As he frowned at me, his thick brows drew together to make the twin grooves deeper. "Of course not, but they've been grinning and whispering among themselves. I just wanted to warn you. I know you mentioned looking over your shoulder to see if people were watching and talking about you. They don't mean anything by it."

"I know, this is my safe space...you're my safe space. Now, feed me, Daddy." I pouted up at him and batted my lashes.

He playfully growled as he spun me, tapped my backside, and then led me to the door with his hands on my shoulders. When I opened it, we walked out to be met by a wall of smirking and giggling kitchen staff.

"That's a health code violation, just in case you needed to be reminded," Carlos said in a serious tone and ruined it as he winked at me.

"If that's all the time you think is needed, I feel sorry for your wife," Bart said from behind me, and everyone laughed as they scattered.

"You know they're going to assume..." I whispered as he threw his arm across my shoulders.

"They already do, have for a year. Alexa's still asking if I've taken my pretty boy on a date yet. Apparently, Mama Sue told Boss I was in there on a date with you that night we went in for food."

I felt a little sick to my stomach. "I'm sorry."

"Honey, look at me." He pinched my chin and made me tip my gaze to his face. "What they think doesn't matter. We're not doing anything wrong. What we do behind closed doors isn't their business or even in public. If they want to assume we're dating. Let them think what they want. What they say doesn't bother me. Let's get you fed. It's getting late."

He hugged me to his side and led me toward the steam tables, and Trey appeared. His less-than-subtle shock amused me as Trey kept darting his gaze between Bart and me. Bart

110

cleared his throat, and Trey must have realized what he was doing.

Bart made all three of us plates, and then we headed out into the cafeteria. He found us a spot as I grabbed three bottles of water and three iced teas. I stopped to say hi to a few people until Bart called my name, telling me it was time to eat. Once we were settled and Bart made sure I had what I needed, he turned his attention to Trey.

The night went by slowly. Trey answered questions when asked, but for some reason, I felt like Bart intimidated him. The man was growly on a good day, but he was just a big teddy bear. There was also the thought that Trey didn't have many friends or any in Winston Harbor. If he was around much longer, he'd get adopted and pulled into the chaos that was us.

As soon as I finished dinner, I leaned my cheek against Bart's arm. He brought his left hand up to rub my hair.

"You getting tired, baby?" I nodded. "You want dessert to take home?"

"Yes, please."

"Trey, we have several desserts. Are you allergic to anything? I'll throw a few in a to-go container for you."

"No allergies, but you already gave me a free dinner."

"You can buy a dinner for our Saturday Restaurant service if you want to pay something. We have people who come in and can pick a meal from the board if they're short on funds."

"I'd like to do that."

"Talk to Carlos, and he'll get you straightened out. Come on, baby, your bedtime is soon. Let's get you ready to go."

Trey and I got up to follow Bart to the kitchen, and Bart placed desserts in two containers. I stood back as Trey talked to Carlos. With my full belly, I was ready for bed, but I wanted to be in Bart's bed. I always slept better there, but I refrained from asking. He might've said that assumptions didn't bother him. Yet that didn't mean I wanted to bring more attention to him and have people bugging the big man about what he was doing with me.

I reminded myself that my time with Bart was limited, but even before he became my Sir, I was already too attached to him. Just his presence made everything better. All I could do was remind myself that I'd be thankful for the time I had with him and wouldn't hope for more.

14

BART

M y apartment was finally quiet, but that also made me a little nervous as I finished getting ready for bed. All three had fallen asleep watching some animated movie, and Chance had been excited as the girls. I'd left them when I went to shower. I adjusted the skull cap over my hair as I debated trimming my beard, but I didn't have the motivation. My hands spread on top of the counter on either side of the sink, and I leaned in to study my face. I didn't think I was a bad-looking man. The lines hadn't gotten crazy even though the silver in my hair and beard spread more every month. As always, I was a husky guy. The belly was definitely bigger than it was when I was younger and in the military. My dad and grandfather had the same issue as they aged, but we were just naturally large men.

After meeting Trey, I'd started to compare myself to him, and that lean young man was moving in with my boy. Even with the scars, the guy was too damn good-looking and only twenty-nine. I was a few months away from sixty and a grandfather on top of that. Before I even knew what the guy looked like, when Chance had told me he was bringing Trey to dinner, I'd been irritated that I had to share.

That's what had brought on the panic and irrational rage, which sent me into the Outreach freezer. I was territorial and possessive but never jealous, and my boy had and would be spending a lot of time with Trey. Seriously, I'd never assumed I'd be one of those mid-life crisis men, but there I was. Disgusted with myself, I exited the bathroom and stopped mid-step at seeing Chance stretched out on the couch with Sierra and Leila both tangled together and sprawled across his chest.

I'd been surprised at how well he'd done with them all afternoon and into the evening. Cora's surprise was clear when she'd arrived, and Bettany had done a double-take or two at Sierra introducing Leila to Chance. He'd been a bit awkward when dealing with my daughters. I'd worried about how he'd react to my girls because we were a bit of a loud bunch—adults included when we were together. We tended to lose our minds.

My phone vibrated where I'd plugged it in on my nightstand, and I pulled my attention away from Chance and two of my girls. I picked up my phone and groaned at seeing Verna's name on the screen. I'd been waiting for it. Part of me was surprised I hadn't gotten the call after I'm sure Cora told her mother about Chance.

I connected the call. "Hey."

"Hi. How is my favorite ex-husband?"

"I'm your only ex-husband unless you have news you haven't told me."

"No, Martin is an angel."

I loved the happiness in her voice. It hadn't been there a lot after I left and asked for the divorce until she'd met Martin. He was a super nice guy and a great Sir for Verna. Provided her with the heavier hand she'd always needed that I'd tried to be for her. At first, I'd felt awkward around the new man in the family, but after seeing how well he treated Verna, I'd accepted him. Also the tall, slender, and extremely nerdy corporate accountant had surprised me when seeing him next to my full-figured pin-up style friend, and I knew he loved her before he'd even told her.

"Then what do I owe the pleasure of hearing your voice."

"That sweet talk doesn't work with me. I was married to you too long."

"That was unnecessary." I lowered onto the side of my bed.

"I haven't heard much from you the last two, three weeks. You normally at least check in."

"I've been...busy."

"Cora and Bettany tell me he's very pretty."

I groaned as she giggled. I could picture her playing with her thin gold collar, as was her habit. "I'm just acting as his Dominant, nothing more." She knew me better than anyone, and I held my breath, waiting for her to call me on my bullshit.

"How's it feel?"

"It's...like coming home. I missed it."

"Other than being with us, being Sir made you happy. You ignored that for a long time. I didn't mean to take that away from you."

"Honey, you didn't. I thought coming home and being with y'all again that everything would be fine. I'd be all fixed and back to normal, but I ignored what was right in front of me. It's been twenty years, and some things are still lingering. I do okay, though. I have a good life."

"I know that. Me and the girls understood after a while, but you need more than the Outreach."

"Now is not the time to talk about that." I glanced at the open door.

"He's still there?"

"He's currently asleep on the couch, covered in clingy girls who like him better than me. I just showered, and I was going to get him up to come to bed." I groaned as I realized what I'd said and that I'd given her perfect ammo for future use. "The pull-out couch is good for the girls, not so much a grown-up's back."

"Tried to save yourself, didn't work. It's okay to like him."

"No, it's not. I promised him I'd let him go when we decided he was ready."

"That was your mistake. You do know that you've mentioned Chance several times over the past year. You can change your mind about letting him go."

"Yeah, but I don't know. What about you? Everything good?"

"It's great. Work is crazy. I'm working on new massage oils. I may send a few for you to try on your friend. There's a sandalwood and ginger one with a jojoba oil base, and I'll send one of the anti-inflammatory ones for his bruises and a bit of numbing." Her excitement filled her voice as it became higher with each word.

"Have you gotten brattier?"

"Possibly, but you used to think that was one of my best qualities."

"I did. I apparently have a weakness for Brats."

"You're just realizing that?" I huffed. "Go get our grandbabies settled, and then go to bed. Martin will be home soon. He had a dinner meeting that I didn't want to go to. I love you, Bart. Get your shit together."

I snorted at her customary goodbye and replied with my own. "I love you, too. You and the girls are still one of the best things to ever happen to me."

We disconnected the call, and I laid my phone back down. I scrubbed my hands over my face and beard, hearing the rasp under my palms. Still having Verna in my life as my best friend shocked me after every phone call or dinner. When I'd told her I was leaving, the fight was brutal, especially since we'd never really had a disagreement during our entire relationship, not even in the beginning. I was sure that I wouldn't have wanted to survive without them as my reward for getting better. Drinking myself to death or dying on the street seemed like they would've been my only options. Yet I still didn't understand how they'd forgiven me after I'd left, even though I knew I'd done it for their happiness and safety.

As I pushed up from the bed, I smiled as I heard a whispered help from the other room. When I exited my bedroom, I found Chance trapped and a little panicked by working out the logistics of getting off the thin pull-out without waking the girls.

"Stuck, baby?"

"Quit staring and help. I've gotta piss, and Sierra's knee is digging in right over my bladder. She weighs nothing but feels like she's topping a ton right now."

"Poor baby." I crossed the room and expertly uncovered him, offering him my hand to help him up.

He stumbled, and I caught him by the waist, and then he was on the run to the one bathroom. I turned away and covered my granddaughters up. They looked so much like their mothers. My girls were in their teens when I'd made the decision to leave, but I clearly remembered them at that age. Innocent and safe, the perfect mixture of me and their mother.

I'd missed so much while trying to heal, and I didn't want to do that with my grandchildren. Missing a milestone in their lives would destroy me since I hadn't witnessed some of their mothers' big days. The ones I'd been there for, I'd hidden in the shadows. Embarrassed by my clothes or the fact I hadn't showered in days or still drunk from the night before.

"What are you thinking?" he asked and then stepped up beside me. It irritated me that he hadn't touched me or sought me out for comfort like normal with the girls around. He'd stayed on the other side of the apartment when my daughters dropped them off. Still, he wouldn't make contact even with them gone and my granddaughters asleep. It wasn't as if I hadn't noticed the involuntary aborted brushes or that lean-in wordlessly demanding a hug or cuddle.

"I remember when my girls were that age. When I'd be home

on leave, I'd noticed how much they'd grown while I was away. I was losing years and only seeing my girls mature through pictures. Their milestones over the phone. This is when I feel the guiltiest about what I did."

"You wanted them safe. Maybe you didn't do it the best way, but you worked with what you had." He took my hand and led me to the bedroom, and then pressed his hands to my chest, pushing until I plopped back onto the bed. I leaned my weight on my hands behind me on the mattress. "Your daughters love you. I could tell when I met Bettany and Cora." He straddled my thighs and rested his knees on the bed beside my hips.

I grabbed his waist and rested my forearms along his thighs. "And I loved them enough to make them safe." I tried to ignore the weight of his body on my lap. The way we fit together.

"But you completely cut yourself off, they were safe, but you were miserable." He shook his head as I started to protest. "You were. I thought any human contact was good. Some mornings, I got up for work hurting so badly I cried through getting ready. A hit or slap just my due for an empty cum shot. You did the opposite. I'm almost jealous of that." I didn't like the sad tilt to his lips that I always wanted to see smiling. "You had the love of your life. She loved and trusted you beyond everything, and even after the divorce, you remained friends and partners. Dolan was my last first kiss. Even through the cheating and lying, I still believed he was the one who'd stay. I loved him but wasn't in love with him."

"What's that mean?" I laced my fingers at the small of his back and flexed to pull him closer to make sure we were both comfortable.

"I loved that he loved me. That he chose me even though I was worthless." He covered my mouth when I would've told him to be quiet. "And then the rape happened. Chamberlain was a beautiful and flawless man, and I didn't care about the warning signs. That edge of fear in my belly. At first, I just figured it was the usual, *I don't want to be outed* bullshit. Dolan rejected me, and I needed my ego stroked. In the end, everything I was sure of, even if it was toxic behavior, imploded as I dragged myself naked from that motel room."

He seemed to zone out as if he were reliving that night, and I waited for him to process, but I gave him a gentle hug to make sure he knew I was there. I wanted him to stay as present as possible. In the early days, I'd seen that expression a lot as he performed mindless tasks I gave him in the kitchen.

"As he wrapped his hands around my throat and squeezed, I was—" He looked away for a second, and I watched his throat work as if it took everything in him to swallow. And then his attention was back, and his blue eyes were glassy with tears. "Grateful my life was ending. I wanted to die, and waking up in that hospital, I was devastated I survived. I never told anyone that. And I punished myself for it. Every moment of happiness. Every hard-on. Each mark I tried to replace with pain." He stroked the scars through his t-shirt. "My happiest memories are the deepest."

"Baby." I cupped his jaw. I didn't even know what to say because he really wanted to die. It was there in his eyes that never lied. To think I was so close to losing him before I even knew he existed.

"Don't pity me. All I'm saying is we do what we think is best with the tools experience gives us. You're protective, and you think you know best, but, Sir, that isn't always true. But we make our choices, and we live with them, or exist with them whatever the case may be."

"Tell me something else you've never told anyone." His cheeks turned pink, and I became curious. "That blush speaks for itself."

"As much as you want to believe that my answer has something to do with fucking, but no, perv. I want to know what it's like to be *in* love. Just once. Maybe find that last first kiss."

"You'll find him someday." Those four words tasted almost

bitter. As his Sir and friend, I had to do what was best for him, but that didn't mean selflessness when the time came wouldn't hurt and destroy me.

"If I do, that'll be great, but I'm not ready to accept that yet. But you have to accept that you made a good *bad* decision and stop with the guilt, Bart." He massaged my shoulders, and I lived for every freely given bit of affection or simple touch.

"I know. It's just hard. I still have the loud noise triggers, but other than that, I'm good most of the time, but it's always there. I don't want to wake up and see someone else staring at me like Verna had."

"Do you feel that way when we sleep together?"

"No, no, but I can't guarantee that it won't happen some night."

"Bart, I'm the perfect example of what happens to someone who lives in fear. Don't do that. You have your daughters and granddaughters, you have Verna, and all the people at the Outreach. Quit atoning for sins that aren't yours and thinking about the what-if."

"When did you get so smart?"

"The dumb blond stigma isn't true despite all the jokes." His bratty smirk caused me to roll my eyes.

I brought my left hand up to curl around the back of his neck and gently tugged him forward, and I pressed my mouth to his. My eyes closed at the softness, and I nipped at his lower lip, sucking softly. It took everything in me to pull back and open my eyes to look at him.

"Thanks, Chance. As much as you don't believe it, I forgot how much I needed this, and taking care of you makes me feel more me. And one day, you're going to have the most amazing last first kiss."

He nodded and then leaned his forehead on mine. We were silent after that, and I got us into bed, hoping the girls would sleep late so I could stay in bed with Chance a bit longer. I wanted to memorize every second for something I could hold onto until the next time I could see him. He'd gone through hell and deserved everything, and I was going to make sure he got it.

15

CHANCE

W hy did he have to kiss me? The forehead and cheek kisses, the few corners of the mouth ones, those I could deal with, but I hadn't had one in six years. Whenever a man tried, I'd turn my head away and avoid it at all costs. Toward the end, I'd done the same with Dolan, too.

It wasn't like I didn't consider kissing a big deal, I did, but there seemed to be something so intimate in kisses and even embraces. Sharing space with another person, trusting your physical safety with another person. I'd imagined kissing and other things with Bart for close to a year. I mean, I could've fought him or turned my head, but the minute he gently tugged me in, I couldn't resist at least one. My time with him would come to an end, and I realized I required the memories of the little things with him. So many experiences to get me through when I was no longer his boy—his friend.

Saturday night, I'd almost felt normal, Bart and I playing with the girls, having dinner, and watching TV. We went to bed like we were some typical couple. He'd awakened me Sunday morning, holding me tightly to his chest and whispering soothing words. I'd been confused until the minute I realized I was sobbing loudly. I hadn't remembered the details of the dream, but I rarely did.

I checked the dash display and saw that I was running behind on getting to Vega's. I'd picked up another all-nighter and had slept most of the day. Per my luck, I hit rush hour traffic. I sped up slightly to see if I could make up time. It had been weeks, and there had been no other attempts on Vega, and we were starting to think it was just a fluke or someone wanting to disrupt things at the Outreach.

It wouldn't be the first time the community center was a target for someone with some vendetta or bigoted belief system. I tapped the dash screen to connect a call to Trey. The rings started in my earpiece, and I waited.

"What's up?" Trey asked.

"I got caught in traffic. I'm going to be a few minutes late."

"No problem, man. I'm more exhausted from sitting around than I thought I would be. I can't wait for this detail to be over."

"Whoever the person is, they haven't made a move on Vega in a while. I'm sure Sharp is gonna reassess soon. Vega and me being out in the open may have just been a coincidence. Our shooter may have just wanted to make a statement."

"Let's hope."

I flinched at a loud bang and then the obvious sounds of a flat tire. "Dammit," I cursed as I started to slow down. "Just had a blow-out, I may be—" Another bang, and the hood flew up. I took my foot off the pedal, and then my SUV lurched as I realized I was taking fire and felt the front end lift with the force as something exploded under my hood.

I overcorrected to get the driver's side out of his scope. As the adrenaline kicked in, I felt myself go weightless, and the only thing holding me down was my seatbelt. I tried to cross my arms over my chest to keep them from getting caught in the steering wheel, but the sharp pain told me I was too late. The violence of the flips, the crushing of metal and glass showered me as I cursed. I barely heard when Trey called my name in my ear as my vehicle skidded to a stop on its roof.

All I could think was I needed to get out. There was smoke and the stench of gas. I reached for the buckle, and my wrist was almost useless. I struggled to push the button to get it to release. A grunt slipped free as I crumpled to the roof, and I held my injured wrist to my chest.

The fear threatened to take over, but I had time enough for that later. I checked my surroundings, calculated where the shots had come from, and kicked out the broken passenger-side window so that I could climb through to keep the metal between me and the guy gunning for me.

"Chance, fucking answer me." Trey's voice got my attention.

I relayed my location as I awkwardly pulled my weapon from my holster on my opposite thigh. This was not how I wanted to start my day. Especially when I knew I'd have another Dolan lecture coming my way and who knew what my Sir would do to me for endangering myself again.

"What's the situation, Bowers?" Dolan's pissed-off voice took over.

Fuck, I drew into myself as another round hit the opposite side of the SUV. Fucker was playing with me, waiting for me to run, and with the smoke and gas, he may get his chance at an open shot. People had stopped and were getting out to help, but I identified myself and told them to stay.

"Some motherfucker just took out my tire and then put two into my engine block. They're coming from the southwest. He just took another shot. I think he's waiting for me to run."

"You got cover to make a run?" Dolan asked.

"Probably won't have much choice, my gas tank is ruptured, and something's burning."

"Chance, we got eyes on you, stay low, and you can make it to the barrier. That's two layers of concrete. Unless he has a rocket launcher, you should be good." Vega's voice was strangely calm, and I needed that. "Zero is triangulating where the shots are coming from as we speak."

"If I don't make it, I'm haunting all of you." I flinched as I adjusted my stance and looked around for an escape route, but where I landed, he'd have a clear shot for about twenty feet. Fuck, this was going to hurt.

I took a few deep breaths, preparing to sprint to cover. Vest or not, whatever the sniper was using was going to go straight through me if I was too slow.

"We're en route to you. Stay alive," Dolan ordered.

I let everything go quiet, slowed my breathing, and focused on the barrier and nothing else. My body went on autopilot as I jumped up and ran, forcing my legs to pump faster, and then I dove over the barrier. I sprawled on the ground as another impact made concrete shatter and rain down on me.

"This fucker's got a cannon." I flinched as I earned a face full of debris.

"Just stay down. We have a search and rescue helicopter on its way and ready for Zero's coordinates. We're going to be coming in loud, I don't want to scare the bastard off, but I want his attention elsewhere." I heard Dolan yelling orders and a door slamming.

"I'm not going any damn place." We weren't on official channels.

"What's your damage, Chance?" Vega finally started sounding a little panicked.

"Right now, the adrenaline is kicking," I could tell by the blood rushing in my ears, and my heart felt as if it were trying to make it through my ribcage. "But except for hopefully a sprained wrist, I'm okay. Not saying I won't be in hell tomorrow. Vega, do me a favor?" I wanted someone to call Bart before he saw it on the news.

"Sure, want me to call—"

Vega's question cut off as the gas finally ignited, and my

wrecked vehicle exploded, and then sharp pain made my ears ring. The stench of burnt plastic and rubber. Flaming debris rained down on me. Then the barrier shifted as I rolled at the last minute as the mangled mass of metal missed me by a foot. I laid there exposed, and I closed my eyes as I felt the bits of metal, melted plastic, and rubber burn at my skin and clothes.

That tingling sensation traveled my spine at the pain. The same one I felt when the blade would slice into my flesh. It all came back. Everything I didn't want to think about. That fateful walk into the motel room. The sting of the needle. That sense of helplessness as I couldn't protect myself. In my head, stunned and unable to defend myself, I relived every second of what Chamberlain had done—what he'd taken, and it was as if a year hadn't passed at all.

I heard voices calling my name, Dolan, Vega, even Remy and Doc, but as I felt my lips moving, nothing was coming out—nothing but a scream that I couldn't hear.

16

BART

I was on the run and barely heard Dolan calling my name. I frantically glanced around until I spotted him outside an exam room in the ER. The minute Boss entered the kitchen, the look on his face told me something was wrong, and the first thing I thought was I was about to get news that would destroy me. He quickly assured me that Chance was fine, but he was in the ER, and they were having a hard time stabilizing him.

That's all I'd needed to hear, and I grabbed the keys to one of the Outreach's vans and made my way across the city as quickly as possible. I prayed to a God I no longer believed in that my baby was fine. That he'd worn his vest, that he cared enough to come home to me. Every second seemed to last an hour as I'd pushed the speed limit to get to him.

"Is he…" My voice broke.

"Fine. His SUV flipped a few times. He has a sprained wrist, but it may be broken. We don't know because no one can get near him. Before we got here, they said he was combative and tried to restrain and sedate him. He probably had a flashback of Chamberlain. Because he's fighting, they said policy is they need him in restraints for the safety of their staff."

"Shit." I ducked through the curtain on the other side of the open sliding door.

What I saw broke my heart. Nurses and security blocked him where he'd backed himself into a corner, using the IV pole as a weapon. He swung it wildly at anyone who came close. I eased forward, and as one of the security guys attempted to grab me, Dolan warned him Dolan himself would arrest anyone if one of them thought about touching me.

"Hey, baby." There was nothing in his eyes but fear. "Boy," I yelled sharply, and he looked at me. "You're fine. What are you when I'm here?"

"Safe, Sir." His voice broke, but he put his attention back on the people attempting to grab him.

"That's right, come here. Sir needs a hug. I was scared my boy was hurt." I kept my voice slow and steady, calm even as I melted down inside. He stared at me almost as if he didn't believe I was real, and I knew that expression too well. I'd seen it on my own face more times than I could count as I tried to convince myself I was home and no longer in a warzone.

As I neared him, I grabbed his waist with my right hand and the back of his neck with my left, and then he collapsed, sobbing as the fight went out of him. I scooped him up, and his legs wrapped around my waist, so I backed up until I could sit down on the uncomfortable bed. He buried his face against my neck, and I stroked his back, exposed by the open gown.

"It's okay. I'm right here. We have all the time in the world." I glanced at someone and mouthed for someone to get him a warmed blanket. Dolan yelled for one to be brought to Chance's exam room.

"Lay him down so we can restrain and sedate him." A grim-faced nurse ordered.

"Not happening, lady. A year ago, he was drugged, restrained, and raped." She flinched. "You coming at him with a needle while he's having a flashback isn't helping matters. He's calm now, do what you need to do. You'll just have to work around me."

Thankfully, they cleared the room, and I lifted to get farther back on the bed so that I could make Chance more comfortable on my lap. He was shaking as he hugged my neck and waist as if he thought someone would take him away from me.

"Assume the pose," I whispered and smiled as he lifted his head to press his forehead to mine. "There's my beautiful boy." I brought my hands to his cheeks, stroking my thumbs along his wet, spiky lashes. I brushed my lips to his. "Eyes on me. Where are you?"

"With you."

"That's right, and when you're with me, no one will ever hurt you again. I don't break my promises, right?"

"Yes, Sir." I grabbed the blanket from Dolan and wrapped it around my baby to make sure he was all warm, being careful of his wrist and any injuries I couldn't see.

"Good boy. You always make me so proud."

"I went back," he whispered on a sob.

"Then we'll just have to begin from square one."

"I was there, he was on top of me, and I could...couldn't fight him. It hurt—" I squeezed him as he curled into a ball on my lap as if trying to protect himself from the memories of Chamberlain.

"Chance, can you tell us what happened?" Dolan's voice was gentle, and I'd never heard that tone with anyone except Boss and their kids.

He glanced at me, and I nodded. "I was running late. I overslept." He took a breath. "I contacted Trey to let him know I was running behind. My tire went flat, and I slowed down to pull to the side when the force of an impact blew my hood up. Then a second, and then all I knew was I was flipping. I think my wrist got caught in the steering wheel. The rest I think you have on camera." He spoke in a monotone, but I could see the hell playing out behind his eyes. It was in the way he kept them locked on mine, and he clung to me with everything he had.

"Chance, look at me." Dolan's tone turned harsh, and when he tried to touch Chance, I grabbed his wrist.

"No, again, I respect you, but you won't touch him without his consent or my permission."

Dolan cursed and stormed from the room, only to be replaced with Boss.

"Honey, look at me, please," Boss whispered close to Chance but didn't try to touch him. "déjà vu, huh?"

Chance nodded but finally glanced at Boss. I just held him and was there for support as we waited for the nurse to come back. I wasn't looking forward to that, but Chance had me and Boss to advocate for him. As they spoke quietly, I shifted to get to my phone and hit my recent calls, finding the number I needed. I pressed it to my ear.

"Hi, Dad, I'm at work, but I have a few minutes." Cora's voice and the fact she was there made me relax.

"Can you come down to the ER? I know it's not your department, but Chance is here, and he needs a doctor he trusts."

"I'll be right there." She disconnected the call without asking any questions.

I fisted my hand in Chance's hair as he laid his head down and buried his face against my neck, which seemed to be his favorite spot when he wanted comfort. He completely relaxed, and the stress finally got to him.

"You doing okay, Bart?"

"I just want him to be okay. I called Cora. I knew she was on duty earlier and said she might be stuck for a double. She's coming down. I want a doctor I trust to examine him."

"He's sleeping...good." Boss smiled at me. "You want me to help you lay him down?"

"No, he's fine right where he is. This is his favorite spot when he wants a cuddle. When we're in bed, he pushes his face against my chest and has this habit of rubbing circles on the side of my belly. My baby needs to catch a break."

"Well, this guarantees he gets one."

"He mentioned that he was starting to think he was the target, but he had no idea who would want to kill him. Except Chamberlain."

"Chamberlain's in a maximum security facility, and every piece of personal mail he receives or sends is inspected. If they felt he was threatening any of his victims, they would've informed us."

"There are ways around that, and you know it." As someone who'd been part of the establishment, I still lacked trust in authority from my teens and twenties when dealing with cops.

"I know. He has to go into protective custody until we know what's going on." Boss shook his head, and I knew he'd noticed I'd tightened my hold on Chance. "You two can stay in my old apartment. Everything is still in my name. I'll call Carlos to stock the kitchen and to say he's going to be in charge for a bit."

"Boss, I can't—" Boss's patented *don't fuck with me* expression shut me up.

"What's your main priority?"

There was no hesitation when I answered. "Him."

"Exactly. And you have a strong team who can handle everything while you take a well-deserved vacation. Also, he's going to need your undivided attention right now."

I didn't disagree. We'd probably taken a lot of steps back, and Chance may be a bit fragile. There was only one certain thing I knew, I couldn't let him go. I'd fought it, but I was going to be selfless and heal him so he could have a good life. He was mine.

"Bart, he's happy with—" Whatever Boss was going to say ended as the curtain opened, and Cora came in with a thick file in her hands.

"Hi, Dad, Boss." She leaned in and turned her head to see if she could get a peek at Chance's face. "He's out. With your permission, Dad, I'd like to check his wrist?" she asked as she set his file aside.

I nodded, and she moved behind me. He flinched as she grabbed his wrist. I whispered to him and stroked his back to keep him asleep.

"Looks like a bad sprain, but I'd feel better getting an x-ray. His file also said he came in with some minor burns and cuts. Could you remove his gown and blanket so I can look?"

"Baby, I gotta lower the front of your gown so Cora can see." I kissed the side of his face as he looked at me half-asleep. "There's my adorable boy. Can you sit on the bed beside me? I won't go anywhere."

He reluctantly did as I asked.

"Hi, Chance."

"Hi, Cora."

"What I'm going to do is have you remove your gown. I won't touch you unless I tell you first. I just want to make sure your injuries are minor, and then I'm going to order an x-ray and then get you out of here. I'm sure you're ready to go home and curl up with Dad and get some rest."

I grinned as I caught Cora's wink, but when he removed the gown, I saw the change in her. I knew he wouldn't notice. As she examined him, she told him step-by-step what she was doing. I sensed she learned more than she wanted when she looked at his medical records. The time passed with me rubbing Chance's back and soothing him when needed.

"Dad, can I talk to you in private? Chance, I'll just keep him a minute. Boss is outside. I'll send him in." She spoke as she helped me get his gown back on and his blanket tightly wrapped, almost like a swaddle.

I cupped his cheek and turned him until he looked at me. "Baby, I'll just be right outside the door. No one will get near you. When we're done, we'll go home." I kissed him, and he darted a glance at Cora as if she'd be mad that I kissed him. "Just outside the door, I promise."

It took a few minutes to get up and follow Cora out, and Boss went in without a word. "What's wrong?"

"Nothing, Dad, he's fine. Everything is minor, which is surprising from what the paramedics reported at the scene."

"You saw the ER visit from a year ago."

She nodded as she hugged the file tighter to her chest. "Yes, but this isn't me acting as his doctor. With the obvious self-harm, you're his Dominant. And it's probably not my business, but I have to ask. Are you addressing that?" she asked.

"He gave me his kit. We're working on correcting his negative coping mechanisms. We may have lost some ground, but I'm taking some time off to focus on him."

"Good. I like him, Dad. He's made you happy."

"He does." I smiled, and she returned it. "Not weirded out?"

"No, you're kinda obvious. I noticed it when you introduced him...the way you interacted with him at the Outreach. You were the same way with Mom. To be honest, it's way past time you took something for yourself again. I'm going to order the x-ray so we can get you two home."

"Thanks."

"You're welcome. Go cuddle him." Cora gave me a hug, and I watched her walk away.

All my children filled me with such a sense of pride in what they'd accomplished. Cora worked her ass off to get through medical school and then a residency while pregnant and dealing with raising Sierra while her husband, Grant, was away as his job as a pilot kept him busy. Bettany, Roxie, and Tamara excelled at everything they put their minds to. I wondered what my other girls were going to think of Chance.

I leaned against the wall to take a breath before I went back into the exam room. Chance needed me to be calm and supportive, so I could break later. All we had to do was get through a few more hours, and then I could take Chance home. When I opened my eyes, I found Dolan watching me with his arms crossed over his chest.

"Got a problem, Dolan?" I asked.

"No. You may think you own Chance..." I instantly cut him off.

"I don't think I own him...I do."

"Then don't fuck with his head, man. That's all I ask."

"I can promise that. I better get back in there."

"Deacon already arranged for groceries to be stocked up at the apartment. I'm going to his apartment to pack him some clothes. Ask him if he needs anything special, and text me a list. We'll have everything ready by the time he's discharged."

"While someone sits with him, I'll go to my place and get what I need."

"Sounds like a plan. Bart, he looks really good lately. Keep him that way."

That warning was clear as he pushed through the curtain, and I followed him in. The rest of the evening went by in slow motion, and I was just ready to go home and relax with my boy. We had to talk once we were alone, but that would happen soon enough. As we waited for the discharge nurse, I got him dressed in a t-shirt and sweats that Boss always kept in his vehicle. I hugged him.

"I'll get you into bed soon, baby." I rubbed his back as he relaxed with his head on my chest and knew the adrenaline was completely gone. His injuries were minor, but it could've been so much worse. I'd process everything else later. First, I needed to make sure he was safe.

17

CHANCE

I'd slept for almost two days and everything I had hurt when I'd awakened that morning. Until I'd had my flashback and panic attacks, I'd known I was exhausted but not to what extent I lacked sleep. I'd wished to get off protection detail, and there I was, the person under protection, and it made no damn sense. Dolan was glaring at me from the corner of the couch with Boss seated between his feet. My luck Dolan decided he was going to be the head of my detail. I'd loudly suggested Claxton or Trey, anyone but him.

Even after being passed out for days, I still felt on edge after the flashback, and I didn't know how to process it. That was always Bart's job as my Sir to make sure I focused and didn't get lost, but I'd felt awkward with my ex-husband in the apartment with Bart and I.

"Baby, time for you to get ready for bed," Bart called from the guest bedroom where he'd been alone for the last hour. He was apparently setting up a surprise for me. "Say goodnight to Dolan and Boss."

"Yes, Sir. Goodnight." I barely kept myself from running across the room to escape. I moved around Bart into the bedroom and froze as I saw the bed turned down, four towels down the center. Battery-operated candles were on the nightstands and dresser.

I spun on my toes and narrowed my eyes as Bart practically slammed the door and then locked it without ever taking his focus from me. He'd been acting weird all day. I was worried he'd grown irritated that he had to be locked away with me. But I was too scared to ask and get an answer I hadn't wanted.

"I have a surprise for you. I wish Dolan wasn't here while I give it to you, but you'll just have to be quiet."

My eyes widened, and I backed up as he stripped his t-shirt over his head to toss toward his bag and then pushed his sweats over his hips. He smirked as he kicked his sweats aside and closed the distance between us. His husky body was only covered in a pair of boxer briefs, and I took in the belly and his gorgeous dark-brown skin covered with just the right amount of hair.

"You think you can do that for me, baby?"

"Do what?" I was distracted by the springy, slightly bushy hair across his chest. One of my favorite things was rubbing my cheeks over his pecs as he stroked my head at night to put me asleep.

"Be quiet," he said barely above a whisper as he pushed his hands beneath my t-shirt. He stroked over my belly to my chest. He stripped the fabric over my head. "I think you need some pampering, and Verna sent you presents."

As he tugged at the button of my jeans and lowered the zipper, I swallowed hard and looked up at him from under my lashes. I grabbed his forearms as he started to push my pants and underwear over my hips. I nibbled at my bottom lip, and I noticed him staring at my mouth.

"Can't give you a massage if you have all your clothes on."

"Massage?" I'd never had one of those. Yeah, I'd had a shoulder rub once or twice, but this would...would I be able to control myself? Would my body reacting to his care and nearness insult him? He'd told me there was no shame in getting hard. That didn't mean I wasn't still coming to grips with my renewed interest in sex and the terror of what that meant for my sex addiction.

"Uh huh, Verna makes massage oils, and other party favors for couples. Teas. Candles. Scents and stuff. She sent a few new items. She figured you'd be sore and need a bit of spoiling."

"She did?" The clear shock in my voice at Verna thinking about me and sending me things.

"Yeah. So, are you going to let me strip you so I can get you on the bed?"

"Yes, Sir."

"You're such a good boy for me." He lowered to his knees and stripped away the last of my protection.

As he lifted my feet out of my pants that were pooled around my feet, he kissed one hip bone and then the other. Thankfully my nerves kept me from getting an erection. "You know you're always safe with me, right?" I nodded because I sensed I'd always be safe with him no matter what. "One word, and we stop. I just want you to relax while I make you feel good, and then I get to cuddle you." He kneaded my tense calves. "Lay down in the middle of the bed, right on the towels." He gave my hip a soft tap, and like I always did with him, I obeyed.

I stiffly stretched out on the soft towels and stared up at the ceiling. He moved slowly around the room and then stopped beside the bed. He lifted one knee and then the other onto the mattress. I brought my arms up to rest them beside my head, my splinted wrist sore but manageable since the sprain wasn't as bad as they'd thought. He positioned me until he knelt between my spread thighs. He positioned me until my legs were draped over his, and his knees rested beside my hips.

"Now, all you have to do is lie back and let me take care of you."

I stared at him as he grabbed a large bottle of oil. I prepared for the cold oil, but when he poured some across my chest and stomach, I was surprised to find it warm. He added some to his palm, returned the bottle to the nightstand, and rubbed his hands together. He started on one leg by placing my left foot on his chest, working from my toes upward. I whimpered when he got to a particularly tight spot. A sweet scent that had this almost smoky and spicy aroma filled the room the warmer it became as he spread it over my skin.

"Bart, we have to..." My hips arched as my dick started to firm.

"If you want to stop, we can, but an erection doesn't equal consent. What did I say?"

"Bodies react, and there's nothing..." I gasped. "Shameful."

"That's right, just enjoy. And if it feels really good, then go with it. Savor it as yours. I'm just here to give you a massage to work out all those knots I'm sure you have."

I nodded as I closed my eyes, and I was shaking by the time he finished one leg and then the other. His hands were rough, with just the right amount of callouses. His touch was firm but in no way made me feel as if he were taking advantage. Like always, he just wanted me relaxed and happy. He lowered my legs back over his and started at my hips, his thumbs tracing where my thighs met my groin, then along where my cock rested but never touched.

"That feel good, baby? You need harder or softer?" he asked as he leaned forward, his belly pushing down on mine as he kneaded the sore muscles of my chest.

"Softer there." My eyes flew open as his fingers and then palms stroked over my nipples. Time seemed to stand still as he pushed his fingertips into my shoulders and down my arms, taking his time just as he did on my legs. He was so careful when he reached the brace on my wrist. Bart even massaged my good hand, stretching out my fingers as he worked out all the tension I'd carried for too long.

"Now, I'm going to work on your back, but I don't want you to move. I want you just like this, boy, and remember, we can stop at any time."

I nodded because there was no way I could speak. I was hard and aching and pushing into the cushion of his belly. Since he seemed to ignore it, I tried to put it out of my mind as well. He got close enough that his cheek brushed against mine as he pushed his arms under me, and his strong hands repeated the gentle movements. His arms beneath me had me arched into him, and my hands went to his back. The nails of my uninjured hand dug into him as he teased the top curve of my ass cheeks.

"Are we still okay, love?" he asked, and I just nodded. Rubbing my cheek against his thick beard. As he cupped my ass, his fingers dipped into my crease to skim over my hole, and my legs wrapped around him, thighs squeezing his sides. Then I froze as I realized what I was doing.

"No, baby, you're safe. You're so sexy when someone knows how to treat you right."

His body was just as warm and slick as mine, his body hair teasing my skin. He completely covered and surrounded me, but I felt no panic...no fear. I focused on how right it felt to be in his arms—beneath his big, sheltering body. Every part of me screamed that that's where I was meant to be, that he was somehow my reward for surviving. Yet there was also that dark recess of my brain that told me I was just his friend. He was just taking care of me until he sent me off to another man, but there wasn't another Sir or Daddy who I'd want more than him.

"It's your Sir and Daddy's job to treat you right. For tonight you needed a soft touch." He sucked at the side of my neck, and it stung for a second before he licked it away. "Soon, you'll have Sir's marks on you. Hand, paddle...flogger, but tonight, you're only to be shown how much I value your trust. You can have anything. All you have to do is ask."

Instead of turning away as his lips worked their way to mine,

I opened as soon I felt his breath. His fingers and thumbs sunk almost painfully into me as he rocked my hips to rub my cock against his belly.

"Is that what you want?" He didn't even wait for me to answer as he pushed his mouth to mine. The tip of his tongue met mine. He let out a rumbling groan as his hands released me and came up to grip my hair. His weight pushed me into the bed, and my heartbeat was pounding in my ears. I pulled my legs back and tried to push them between us as panic started to set in, not because I was scared but because I was about to shoot all over his belly, and I didn't want him mad at me.

Instantly his kiss gentled, and he rose to his knees to take his weight from me. "It's okay. Neither of us were ready for that yet." I felt his smile as he kissed me. "How do you feel?"

As we kept pressing our mouths together, almost as if he didn't want to stop either, but I didn't want to read anything into it. He'd edged me before, and he was still letting me go. I took stock of myself and realized my muscles were shaking from desire but also from complete relaxation.

"Can we do that again?" My question was muffled.

"Any time you want."

"Didn't think my Sir would spoil me."

"Really?" he asked as he drew his lips along my jaw and down the side of my neck, and when he reached my collarbones, he sucked hard enough to arch me off the bed. I pouted as he moved from on top of me and stretched out on his side. He rested his head in his raised hand and looked down at me. "I prefer to praise and spoil my submissive. Correction has its place but not tonight."

"Don't you find it weird to be with me like this?"

"No, you're mine, my Sub and Brat. It's my privilege to take care of all your needs, pleasure to punishment." He drew his curled fingers down the center of my chest, then my stomach, which jiggled a bit as I breathed. "It's been so long since I allowed myself this. I was always an affectionate man. Verna was never without a smile."

"She sent the massage oils, so you told her about me?"

"And she's almost giddy over it. She's been fussing at me for years about my reclusive ways."

"How did you two meet?" He looked surprised that I asked, but I turned on my side and cuddled into him like I'd done every night we shared a bed. He drew his fingertips along the indent of my spine.

"My best friend's little sister. We went on our first date the night before I had to be on a bus to bootcamp. I always found her a bit annoying. She was two years younger. I was nineteen, and she was seventeen when we got married. We had a slight slip-up with a broken condom. I'd already planned to marry her after she graduated. Her pregnant with Bettany just sped things up a bit. Most of our relationship was through letters and phone calls, dates when I was home. Bettany was born eight months later. Somehow I was lucky enough to be home for all my daughters' births." He hugged me tighter. "Verna is going to love you."

I shot him a shocked look. "I'm going to meet her?"

"Of course. Cora and Bettany have been gossiping, and I told Verna about you a few times since you started volunteering in my kitchen." I rolled my eyes, and he chuckled. "Okay, I complained to her about you."

"Now that I believe. Bart?"

"Yeah, baby?" He turned his head to get to my mouth to brush another kiss to my lips.

"I've never done this with a man before. Cuddling in bed, not worrying about a time limit of when he's going to ask me to get on all fours. I really like this...maybe too much."

He let out that rumbling bass sound that I always found soothing. "Never too much. This is something you should always demand from a partner. A giving partner will never be selfish when it comes to making you feel good, whether that's in a sexual way or not. Yes, sometimes there's a more dominant partner, like I'm your Dominant, but you have the power to stop at any time."

I smoothed my hand down his chest and over his pebbled brown nipple, and he gripped my hip. "You like when I touch you?" I tried to keep the fear out of my voice.

"I do. I told you, as much as you get out of being my submissive, I get just as much out of being your Sir. It makes us both happy, and there's nothing wrong when what two people share is consensual. I wasn't lying when I said you make me insanely happy."

I closed my eyes as I relished every second of being his, and part of me hoped that I never had to give him up. Maybe it would always be friends with a side of D/s. I wanted to ask him to keep me, but fear kept the question stuck on the tip of my tongue.

"My boy has to be sleepy, just relax and get some rest. I'm going to enjoy holding you while you sleep…I'm gonna miss this when we get to go back to our own places. I'm going to miss having you all to myself."

I didn't open my eyes as he covered us with the sheet, and he pulled me flush to him, my leg naturally slipping over his hip as he got us all settled in. This shouldn't feel as normal as it did. I wasn't automatically fixed, I had a long way to go, but with him, I knew I'd always fit. The way we just got each other was terrifyingly addictive.

18

BART

Boss stood beside me while I worked on making breakfast for everyone. I wanted it done by the time Chance woke up. My cock ached every time I remembered him under me. He hadn't realized how much he'd given away. His short nails dug into my bowed back. Strong thighs gripped my ribs as I worked the tensed muscles along the sides of his spine. Just the light brush of my fingers over his tight, little hole, and he'd held his breath. He'd wanted so much to give in, and if he hadn't become lost in his own pleasure, he would've felt my hard dick notched between his ass cheeks.

When I earned his trust enough to be able to take him, he'd be one of the most beautiful sights I'd ever seen. He hadn't felt fear, but I knew the attention overwhelmed him. It had been on the tip of my tongue to hiss *mine* and thrust against him as he rutted to release against the big curve of my stomach. There'd been times over the past few decades where I toyed with the idea of giving in just to get off but being with Chance—my boy—filled me with a sense of rightness that I'd waited for him.

"No need to look so...smug," Boss muttered at me from behind his coffee mug.

"Smug? I don't know what you're talking about." I smirked at him.

"Uh huh, that wasn't Chance in that bedroom last night sounding like you were torturing him."

"I was just giving him a massage to relax."

"Liar. You're seducing him."

"That, too. If we'd been alone in this apartment, I would've demanded he be louder. He whines like such a good boy."

"Disgusting." He playfully snarled at me, but I sensed my friend was happy for me.

I chuckled and inclined my chin as Dolan came from the bathroom wrapped in a towel and headed for his and Boss's duffel bag. The glare he gave me told me how he felt about me.

"Dolan doesn't like me being with Chance," I commented without any heat.

"He's just concerned that Chance is finding a new addiction. Dolan knows that his ex-husband has no idea what a healthy, consensual relationship is like. He just doesn't want him to get hurt."

While I respected that and loved that my boy had people who'd protect him whether he believed that or not, I wanted to make sure that Chance was able to recognize he had family. People who loved him for him and not what he could do with his body—that he wasn't just someone to fuck and move on.

"I have no intention of hurting Chance. Last night I almost told him I was keeping him, but we have some more work to do."

"If it matters, I approve."

"So do my girls, well, Cora and Bettany and Verna. My girls have been on me to start dating forever. The thing is, I told Chance when we agreed he was ready, he could find a man worthy of him. He has to choose me, Boss, completely of his free will."

The door to our room opened, and a sleepy Chance walked out shirtless, wearing a pair of my pajama bottoms cinched around his much smaller waist. He didn't even hesitate to cross the room to wrap his arms around me from behind.

"You weren't in bed." I felt his pout against my back.

"I had to make you breakfast." I turned in the circle of his arms and pinched his chin to tilt his head back. "Morning, boy."

"Morning, Daddy." He pouted, and I shook my head as I lowered to brush my lips to his. He only called me Daddy when he wanted cuddles and a soft touch. Sir was for when he needed focus. My left hand spread over his cheek and slowly moved around to grab the back of his neck. I teased the plump lower curve of his lip with my tongue until he opened for me.

As he parted those lips, I forgot we had an audience and slanted my mouth across his. My right hand fisted in the waistband of his pants, and I straightened, lifting him against my chest. A throat clearing broken by a snort brought me back, and I turned to find Boss staring at us.

"Well, the things we learn about our friends."

Chance groaned and buried his face against the side of my neck. I turned enough to kiss his jaw. I knew the old version of Chance would've jumped out of my arms at someone witnessing him kiss another man, but my baby understood where he belonged. My patience would come in handy while I waited for him to admit that he wanted more.

"Don't tease my boy. He isn't awake and at his full Brat potential yet."

Boss rolled his eyes at me and stretched out his arm as if to give me a friendly shove, but Chance grabbed his wrist before he made contact.

"Mine." Chance's voice took on an edge I'd never heard from him before.

"Sorry." Boss kept his voice soft and even, but I could see the surprise at Chance's actions.

That's when I noticed Dolan watching us, and while his expression hadn't given anything away, I could see his own shock in his eyes. Chance released Boss's wrist with a muttered sorry and then went back to cuddling my belly and drawing circles on the sides as he pushed his face back into my neck.

"Just yours, baby, I promise." I stroked the length of his bare back several times until the tension was released. "Go potty and wash your face. Breakfast is almost done."

Chance whispered okay, and I sensed his reluctance to leave me, but he wouldn't disobey me. I waited until he disappeared around the corner to the short hallway before I turned back to the stove to plate everything up for the four of us.

"What did you do to him?"

I glanced at Boss and then back at Chance's plate I was adding more fried potatoes to. "What do you mean?"

"He's possessive and...cuddly. Hell, you're all affectionate. I've only ever seen you like that with the grandkids and your daughters, your honorary nieces and nephews. You haven't even shaken hands as long as I've known you."

"I lost a huge part of myself when I left Verna and the girls. I offered Chance my presence as his Dominant. Told him he couldn't self-harm without me around or me taking care of it for him." I pushed a heavy breath through my compressed lips and wondered how long I could keep my promise. "Instead of that, I offer corrective alternatives, ones that give him the same release he gets from the pain. But I also wanted him to experience pleasure and not be ashamed of that. In doing so, I found myself again and realized how badly I wanted to keep him. So instead of preparing him for someone else, I'm teaching him to be mine. I'm just hoping I'm enough."

"You're more than enough, Bart. The old Chance wouldn't have done that. He has no concept of a person belonging to him."

"Not even Dolan?" I asked and glanced over my shoulder to find the man in question putting on his boots.

"Chance is always waiting for the person to leave."

"I'm not leaving. He'll learn to accept that."

"I hope so. He's changed so much since Chamberlain. Mostly for the good, but he still has a long way to go."

"And I have all the patience in the world. I want him to be ready, but that doesn't happen overnight."

I finished making the last plate as Chance came back, finger-combing his dark blond hair. As he glanced at me, I nodded toward the table, and he went to sit down as he waited for me to feed him. At fifty-nine, I wasn't looking for a second chance at having someone. Yet I'd started to fall for him the longer he kept showing up night after night. I couldn't believe that I hadn't recognized it for what it was.

Boss took the two plates I offered him, and then I picked up the two for myself and Chance. I went to join him at the small two-person table I'd already set with his coffee, juice, and utensils. He thanked me but didn't look up from his plate. I extended my arm toward him and curled my fingers beneath his chin to urge him to look at me.

"None of that. Remember, you make me happy and proud. As long as you're mine, you have the right to dictate boundaries. If someone else touching me makes you uncomfortable, you tell me. Now, eat your breakfast. You have to be hungry. I didn't make you a snack before bed last night."

He picked up his fork and slowly ate what I'd made him. Like always, he took small, measured bites and chewed each carefully before he swallowed. I was proud of him that he didn't move the food around to give the impression that he ate more than he had. I knew it was still hard for him. So many years of weighing and measuring food down to the gram, counting every calorie he put in his body. Even as he controlled everything, food became his enemy, and in some ways, it would probably linger for a while.

There were so many things Chance had waged war on. His weight. His sexuality and his openness about being gay. All he'd wanted to do was be in control, to have the power to do with his physical body what he wanted. Yet, in the end, he'd become a prisoner, and I wanted him to be free. I wanted to teach him that he was safe and to set healthy boundaries.

He glanced at me from under his thick lashes, and I winked at him as he caught me staring at him. The shy smile was so strange on a man who'd acted as if he'd owned the world. That's why the previous night was so important. Dominant or not, he'd learned he had control. That a single word would be all he needed to say. One night had taken his sense of self, and I was going to give him the tools to thrive. Whether that was with me or not. All I could hope for was that when I gave him the option, I'd be the one he chose.

19

CHANCE

My hands clenched and relaxed as I stood in front of the laptop while I watched the court recordings for Chamberlain's trial. I'd secretly asked Vega to get them for me, and I'd locked myself in the bathroom. Bart knew something was up because I could see he'd paid closer attention to me since Vega stopped by with the flash drive. Getting her to agree hadn't been easy. She'd fought with me and told me that it wasn't something I needed to see.

I didn't fully understand why I needed to watch the videos. During the trial before he'd taken the plea deal, the thought of sitting in the same room with him made me sick to my stomach. I could've gotten the written transcripts, and more than likely, that should've been my choice, but I wanted to see him.

The phantom taste of metal filled my mouth as I remembered him shoving the device between my back teeth to prevent me from biting. The pain in my jaw as he ratcheted it up and as it cut into the corners of my mouth. There was no video to post for my rape, but he'd relayed it in brutal clarity as he confessed to his crimes.

The slender, angelic-looking man—beautiful and flawless—

but a monster existed beneath the perfect façade. Chamberlain had shown me how unsafe I was in the world. Choice was a cruel and false sense of security. I'd never had one. All the men—the one-on-one encounters and the groups—it fed my sick need to be desired because if I was desired, then I was perfect enough. A brief respite from the all-encompassing loneliness of my existence, and that's all it had been. I'd never lived. I'd suffered through every day until I could lose myself in the emptiness of emotionless fucks.

I gagged as I looked at him and flashed back to the way he'd held my lips together as he forced his penis inside. The sexual and physical degradation of being used in whatever way he saw fit. The dildo and his own length he'd used with such force had torn me inside and out. And all I could do was lie there and wish it was over and try to block it out, but he kept talking in that smooth tone like I was any other lover.

The bite marks and bruises I'd tried to scrub off till my skin bled. My body raw for weeks until they'd faded to a sickly yellow and eventually to nothing. In my mind, they were still there sometimes. A sensory bruise that would hurt when I showered and stroked across the spot. I wanted to forget, and as sick as it might make me, I wanted to be like the others and not remember every detail. Yet I did.

I collapsed to the floor as the courtroom scenes played out. His voice droning on as per the plea deal, he stated for the record what he did to all of us. He had smiled. A satisfied tilt to his lips as he thought back on what he'd done. He felt no remorse for the lives he'd destroyed for his own ego. And I didn't want to admit it aloud, but I saw myself in him. I'd worn that blissed-out and satisfied smile after every encounter until the self-loathing light of morning came.

Before I'd taken a razor to myself, I'd used all those anonymous men and groups to do what I hadn't had the courage to do. I looked for a man depraved enough to push past my own passivity about ending my life and make that final decision for me. Chamberlain had laid bare every insecurity—every instance where my intrusive thoughts told me how easy it would've been.

"Baby, I need you to open the door." Bart's voice broke through the panic and fear, and I realized I'd curled into a fetal position. I loudly sobbed where I'd pressed my face into my knees. "Chance, baby, I'll break down the door if you need me to, but I don't know if you're near it."

Bart's voice was a torturous experience all its own. The caring and concern…that wasn't meant for me. I was a thing. A prop in the grand scheme and undeserving of happiness and life. As fucked up as it was, I should've died that night. I was no one to mourn. Not a single person would've come to an overgrown grave to lay down flowers to lament about all the good I'd done. I only made everyone miserable.

The creak of the door opening barely registered, and the edge brushed my bicep seconds before I was scooped into Bart's arms, cuddled against his husky body.

"Boss, turn it off." His words were muffled as he curved his hand around the side of my head, trying to block out the sound of Chamberlain reciting, with inhuman glee, his atrocities as if he were bragging. "Get out." Bart may as well have shouted it as hard as I flinched at the sound.

The door slammed, but it didn't prevent me from hearing the argument on the other side of it between Boss and Dolan. I couldn't make out the words, but the rage in Dolan's voice was clear.

"Baby, why did you do that? Why watch it alone?" He kept his voice calm as he kissed the top of my head. Pulling me close to his chest until I could hear the frantic pace of his heartbeat. I counted each one hoping to match the roar of mine in my ears to his, but the pain in my chest was too much as I tried to draw in a breath after every agonizing hitch of my sobs.

My brain and body wanted to latch onto him. To never allow

him to let go, but eventually, he'd have to. One day ready or not, he'd become sick of trying to fix me. He'd truly see me as the broken thing that I was, and then he'd leave. He'd find the perfect submissive that could give him what I couldn't. He'd be just like Dolan, and every other man I'd stupidly hoped wouldn't abandon me.

"Baby, calm down. You're gonna make yourself sick. Look at me, please." There was desperation in his tone as he shifted until he could grab my face to turn me to stare at him.

Through the haze of my tears, I saw his. I recognized a portion of my pain reflected back at me, and I tried to close my eyes. He shook me slightly until I focused again.

"Love, it's just you and me. Just focus right on me. Don't look away. Just keep those pretty blues on my face. I want you to breathe with me. We're going to go to the count of eight, inhale and exhale, okay, one—" He started to count to eight, telling me to inhale and then exhale for the same count until he reached one. My lungs fought the intrusion of oxygen as if my body had forgotten how to function, but he repeated several times until I started to draw in calm breaths. "Feel the expansion of your chest, and now exhale and feel it contract. Stay with me, baby, just a little longer."

Where time had seemed to come to a standstill, it began working again, and I became aware of my surroundings. The scent of Bart and the plug-in air freshener. The cool rush of the air from the ceiling vent almost stinging my hot face. I tasted the salt of my tears and the bitterness of acid, telling me how close I'd come to puking.

"That's my boy. Just keep breathing. Right now, there's nothing more important than you. I need you to calm down and focus."

A softer sob slipped free as I took stock of myself and felt the pain as my muscles unlocked and relaxed. We were both on the floor, my backside in the cradle of his crossed legs and mine wrapped around him. I'd clutched his wrist with my uninjured hand. He came into sharp focus, his broad, beard-covered jaw, his wide, full lips, and his slightly crooked nose that was barely noticeable. I stared into his hazel eyes and their bright flecks of green and yellow around the pupil. He was my safety. Nothing had terrified me as much as that realization. What happened when broken couldn't be fixed?

"Oh, baby, you don't have to be fixed. You just have to mend enough for the pain to go away." I almost looked away in shame as he answered my question that I hadn't meant to say out loud. "You shouldn't have watched that alone. Vega should've known better."

"Sh-she didn't want to give it to me. I didn't go to court. I just wanted to know why I missed the signs."

"He's a sociopath. There were no signs to notice. He was a sick man who wanted to destroy, but he can't do that anymore. You're safe right here with me."

"But for how long?" My voice broke as I asked.

"However long you need me, I am right here. No matter what you require, it's mine to give." He released my face, stretched to grab a wash rag from a basket on the stand next to the tub, and then twisted to turn on the water to wet it.

I closed my eyes as he stroked the soft, cool cloth over my hot face, gently wiping my eyes and then my stuffy nose. He washed out the rag, wrung it, and draped it over the shower faucet.

"Wanted to die…" I paused.

"I know, you told me."

"No, before. I went home with the men who told me all the disgusting things they were going to do to me, alone or with their friends. I was hoping for a razor."

"I know."

"How?"

He smiled sadly and shook his head. "No one's first thought is self-harm. There's other behaviors first. Self-destruction, putting yourself in dangerous situations, addiction, there's always something before the first cut. When the emotional release doesn't reach as high anymore...people up the stakes." He stroked his fingers through my hair and cupped the back of my head. "You tried to take control back with the eating disorder, and then after the rape, you resorted to the cutting. They were things you could hold onto...they couldn't be taken away. You had all the power, as little or as much food as you wanted. One cut or two... three, shallow or deep. They were your choice, unhealthy or not. You had to have the power over something. Chance..." I nearly broke as he used my name. He always called me boy, baby, or love, but he used my first name, and it sounded so close to the finale.

"Don't say I'm too much trouble."

"Baby, I'd never say that. You may not realize it, but you've made a lot of progress. You made friends. You started eating and exercising for health and not the numbers on a scale. You made the conscious decision to stop cutting, as difficult as that was. You have to realize once someone is hurt, there's always scars of some kind, physical and mental...emotional. Those aren't always mended perfectly, but they do heal. It's been a year, baby, you can't say it's over, and you're magically back to the old you."

"I didn't like the old me," I admitted quietly. After a year of self-reflection, I'd realized just how much I'd hated myself and to what lengths I'd gone to destroy myself. The cutting had just turned into the next level of my self-destruction. I'd harmed myself with men, exercise, and disordered eating.

"I know, but you have the opportunity to become the you that you were supposed to be before the trauma morphed you into the person you hated. Love, healing requires patience and steps and the acceptance that you're going to get frustrated. I understand why you wanted to see the court videos, but you should've never watched them without me. We should've discussed it before you contacted Vega. You broke my rules."

"Am I getting corrected?"

"Not right now. We'll add it to the tally for our next session. You've already taken too many emotional hits today." He tugged me forward until I found that spot where his scent was the strongest and most comforting. My body curved around his belly as he stroked my back in a comforting rhythm. "We'll sit here for a few minutes, but this old man's knees aren't going to like it for long. You're going to take a nap before dinner."

"Will you nap with me?"

"I'll lay down with you and cuddle you. We probably both need it. You scared me, baby, when I heard you crying, and I couldn't get to you. Don't lock the door again."

"Yes, Sir. I'm sorry."

"It's okay. Like I said, I understand, but I don't approve. We'll discuss the video later. You won't watch it again without me present."

"Yes, Sir." My words slurred, and I suddenly felt exhausted and sore. I still hadn't recovered from the last attack, and my muscles were telling me so.

Half-asleep, I felt Bart help me to my feet, my legs unsteady as he told me to lean back against the sink, and then he was up. He twined his arm around me and opened the door with his free hand. I barely registered that he led me to our room or that the mattress gave beneath me. I didn't even protest when he stripped all my clothes away and tucked me under the cool covers. As I was about to ask him to get into bed, he stretched out beside me on top of the sheet and comforter. I felt the soft brush of his lips to my forehead before everything faded as I fell into darkness.

20

BART

COLD CASE
UNIT

W e had an entire night to ourselves. Not that I didn't love my friends, but I was getting tired of being glared at by Dolan every move I made. Him and I were going to have a serious talk about Chance being mine, and he had to knock off his over-protective bullshit when it came to what I deemed appropriate correction or affection for my man and submissive. We'd had an argument after I'd broken into the bathroom when I'd heard Chance crying and then got him in bed. I'd left him after I made sure he was asleep.

He'd started in as soon as I'd closed the bedroom door behind me.

"HE DOESN'T NEED *some straight asshole fucking with his head." Dolan kept his voice low, but he might as well have yelled.*

"He's mine. I'll do with him what I want. You don't have a say in it. My boy. My rules."

"What happens when you get tired of him, or he expects more, and you just fuck off and leave us to pick up the fucking pieces?"

"I'm not leaving him. You can't coddle him, Dolan. He's gotta figure

shit out on his own. As painful as that may be for the ones who have to watch him suffer."

"Dolan, Bart can take care of Chance. Why don't the two of us leave for the evening? I think everyone needs some space." Boss stepped in front of his husband.

THANKFULLY, Dolan had agreed, and they'd left an hour earlier while Chance had still been asleep. I knew Boss had my back, at least, but they weren't pushing Chance. He needed a bit of tough love and to be made to vocalize what was going on in his head. His friends were letting him stagnate, and it was doing more harm than good. I didn't agree he watched the video of the trial alone, but I would've been there with him if he'd just asked.

That was one of his biggest issues. He didn't want to be a bother. Asking for what he needed outside of being self-destructive wasn't normal for him. He needed healthy boundaries, and again, they were tiptoeing around Chance, and it was setting a bad precedent. I heard the hinges of the door squeak, and I turned my head to glance at him coming out of the bedroom. I was disappointed he'd put his clothes on before he'd come to find me. One day he'd wear nothing but my marks and collar. He was rubbing his eyes as he crossed the room and instantly crawled on top of me. Fuck, how I loved being his comfort item because he was sure as fuck mine.

"Where is everyone?" His voice was husky from sleep and probably the sobbing he'd done earlier.

"We have the night to ourselves. Dolan and I needed some space from each other."

His head popped up to stare at me, resting his chin on my chest. "Why?"

"He wasn't your Dominant. He's your ex-husband and now your friend. We have a difference of opinion about your care."

"But I like how you take care of me," he whispered, and he

sounded so young. Compared to me, he was, but he was nearly forty-one—he had a birthday close to Thanksgiving. I'd asked so I could plan something special for him.

"There's also the danger you're in. Once this is over, we'll need to have a talk without all the other stress." I lifted my head and brushed my mouth to his. "If he'd stayed, we might have said shit that we wouldn't be able to take back. I think he's just worried, and you scared us when we couldn't get to you."

"Sorry."

"You don't have to be sorry, baby, just no more locked doors unless we discuss it. Are you ready for correction?"

He lowered his lashes in that shy way he had and then nodded.

"Use your words and tell me why you think you're being corrected?"

"I scared you, and I didn't talk to you before I got the videos."

"Good boy. Go to the bedroom and remove all your clothes. Lean over the bed and wait for me." He eased off me and did as I asked.

Once he was out of sight, I sat up and prepared myself. Part of me wanted to be lenient with him, but the other felt we were off track. With the last attack and all, I'd needed him to have time to heal. I stood and went to the bedroom; I didn't bother closing the door as we'd have the apartment to ourselves.

I paused in the doorway to find him exactly where I'd told him to be. His lightly tanned skin on display. His feet were shoulder-width apart as he braced for our next session. His cock and heavy balls hung between his spread thighs. I shook off the urge to love on him because that would come later. I continued into the room and to the corner where I'd packed the items I'd need for him.

Crouching down, I slid the zipper open, finding the restraints and short, leather paddle. When we went home, I'd have my full-sized one to use, but I'd only been able to fit my flogger, my smallest paddle, and crop in the bag along with the few restraint options. I took the items to the bed.

"Do you trust me, boy?" I asked as I stood behind him.

"Ye-yes, Sir." His voice shook, and I knew he was nervous, but he knew the rules and what to say.

I didn't say another word as I looped the leather cuff around one wrist and buckled it, taking my time to stretch the strap to secure it to the post of the metal footboard and repeated on the other side. But I was careful about his sprained wrist with the brace. I savored the sight of him stretched out, his chest flat to the mattress and his cheek on the thick comforter staring at the paddle.

"You make me so proud, boy." I stepped up behind him until I pushed my hips to his bottom, then I palmed the lush curves of his ass and pulled them apart to get a peek at his hole surrounded by sparse blond hair. "The way you trust me...I never thought I'd find that again. And I met a beautiful blond man meant to be mine." I stroked my hands upward and then curved them around the sides of his waist. "Make no mistake, Chance, you are mine." With a hard jerk, I pulled him fully against me. "Every inch of you belongs to me." My voice sounded harsh as I rubbed him against me, and he swiveled his hips flawlessly, pushing my firm cock between his ass cheeks. "Do you want that? I want you to think seriously before you answer me. You tell me yes, and I'll claim you in every way."

He whined as I released him and stepped back. I picked up the hilt and adjusted my hold until it felt just right in my palm. I turned my body to the side and spread my hand over the small of his back, my thumb nudging the top of his crease. I drew my arm back, brought it forward, and the thick leather met his bottom, and he lifted onto his toes.

"Count each one and tell me why I'm correcting you. You mess up, we start over, and I'll do that as many times as it takes for you to get it right, boy."

"Yes, Sir," he screamed as I brought it across his bottom again. Aiming for a different strip each time, the thick part of his ass, where his thigh met the lower curves of his bottom and the backs of his thighs. I paused between each to increase his anticipation. There was something about keeping my boy on edge. My heart rate increased as his voice became higher with pain, and thick welts started to form, crisscrossing his muscled, yet rounded ass.

We reached ten and stopped, then I set the paddle aside and stroked my hand over the swollen, red skin and felt the heat. I leaned over, grabbed his chin in my hand, pressed my lips to his ear, and shoved my free hand between his trembling thighs.

"I think my boy enjoyed his punishment." I stroked his hard length. He felt so good sliding through the circle of my fingers. "Do you deserve more, boy?"

"N—" he whined as I pumped his cock a few times and released him to cup his tight sac. "Sir, please."

"You want your reward now for taking your correction? Do you think you learned your lesson?"

"Please, sir, I'll beg…" I left him completely, and he fought against the straps tethering him to the bed.

"My boy doesn't beg for his Sir's affection. It's yours." I jerked the restraints free and unbuckled the cuffs to toss them aside. He didn't move, and I knew he was waiting for permission to move. "Crawl up the bed and lay down on your back."

He did as I asked and gasped as his abused bottom landed on the bed. He was breathing heavily as he laid there with his thighs spread wide. His eyes were glassy and feverish as I stripped out of my t-shirt. His gaze dropped to my belly, and then I finished taking off my jeans and underwear. I ached as my cock pulsed with the need to find release. The few times I'd jerked off since I'd become his Sir hadn't prepared me for the intensity of desire that I felt for him.

"I'm not going to fuck you, you're not ready for that yet, but I can give us what we need." I crawled up the bed until I lowered between his muscled thighs, notched my cock along his, and rolled my hips.

My mouth fell to his, braced my right forearm beside his head, and gripped his thigh with my left hand. I groaned as he arched his hips, and I shifted my knees to get the best traction. "Shit, baby, show me how bad you want it. Show Daddy what a good boy you are."

"Bart...Daddy." He parted his lips, and I thrust my tongue inside as he grabbed my hips.

We came together in an effortless dance. His cock was hot and hard against mine, pre-cum dripping and spreading between our bodies. I thrust hard against him and groaned, an almost animalistic sound as I drove his paddled bottom into the bed, and he cried out at the pleasure and pain I was gifting him.

The metal headboard slammed against the wall as he jerked his mouth from mine and arched his neck, pushing his head into the pillows, and I sucked at the muscular length of his throat. I dragged the flat of my tongue along his hammering pulse and downward to where neck met shoulder, and I bit down.

"Just wait until Daddy lets you have my fat cock." His nails dug into my back as he dragged them upward. "I'm going to make you watch as I give you every inch." I thrust hard as he grunted while I ground our dicks together. "You're mine, Chance. Tell me."

"Yours." Sweat started to slick our bodies. "Keep me, please."

"Mine," I growled, and the world outside the two of us no longer existed as I loved on him. Savored every whimper and moan, every painful dig of his short nails. My sac was drawing up tight. I surged upward, braced my arms under his knees and opened him wide, and worked our cocks together, his softer belly conforming to the curve of mine.

Through my pleasure, as intense as it was, I forced my eyes open to watch him. The way he thrashed beneath me and his body arched, tears slid from the corners of his eyes. He had squeezed them shut. The heads of our dicks sank into the soft curve of my lower belly. I'd never seen anything more beautiful than my boy—my submissive submitting and rediscovering his body. That his pleasure wasn't shameful.

He gave to me freely, and his trust humbled me. Seconds before wet heat spread between us, his blue eyes flew open, and his mouth formed into a silent scream. I completely lifted off him, took both us in my left hand, and jacked us. His fat pale cock was against my darker one, moving in the tight clasp of my fist. I cursed as I used his release to ease the way.

"Fuck, baby, I want to mark you inside and fucking out." The brutal jacking sped up as my chest heaved as I tried to catch my breath. I grunted as fire burned through my veins, and without warning, my release splattered across his pale belly and chest. I froze as I locked gazes with him.

I collapsed and caught myself at the last second as I captured his mouth with mine and played with his tongue as I massaged our lengths together until it was too painful. I rolled to my side and brought him with me. Our kisses were lazy as we calmed, and I didn't care about the mess on my hand as I stroked his bare, sweaty back and down to his welted backside, giving it a squeeze to hear him gasp and whimper in that sexy way I learned I loved to hear.

I eased the kiss but didn't break contact because I wasn't ready for the intimacy to end. "I'm loving being your Sir and Daddy. You were made for me." I hugged him to me with my right arm. "Are you okay?"

"Mmm, ask me when my brain is working again."

I chuckled as I sucked at his lower lip. "I'm not letting you go. We still need time, but you're mine. I can't let anyone else have you. Once everything calms down, I'll take you out on a date."

"Really?" His disbelief hurt me that part of him still thought that I was going to allow someone else to take my boy from me. I'd waited too fucking long to find him and myself again.

"Uh huh, pick you up and everything. Chance, I never thought

I'd have this again. It's important to me. We're going to do this right. Make it everything you deserve. And one day, when we're ready, I'm going to love you so good."

He tucked his head under my chin, and I hugged him tight as we came down from the high of his correction and our shared releases. I had to process my own reaction to loving on Chance for the first time. We fit each other so perfectly, and I hadn't expected that when he'd walked into my kitchen a year earlier. I'd never dreamed I'd have that beautiful, traumatized man in my arms, safe and content to be there. I wouldn't take him for granted. He was everything I hadn't known I needed.

I soothed him as I released him to go to the bathroom to grab a warm rag to clean him up to get my boy ready for sleep. I glanced at myself in the mirror. Nothing about me had changed. Still, the same face but so much was different. I took care of cleaning myself up and washing my hands and then went back to Chance.

When I returned, I found him on his back, shifting his hips. "I got something that'll take care of that." I lowered onto the bed and used the cloth to clean the mess on his stomach, chest, cock, and balls.

I twisted to grab the numbing gel from the nightstand and told him to get on his belly so I could take care of his bottom. He hissed at the coolness and the pain as I gently spread it over his skin. I caught him watching me from where he had his arms crossed under his head. I could see he was still wary, but I understood he needed time. We both had to process. I just hoped we had the time with the danger outside the four walls of that apartment.

We needed our life back, and it would happen, but something had to break first.

21

CHANCE

I was wrung out and bored. I'd only been locked down for a little over a week, but I was already losing my mind. When they finally found where the sniper had set up, there was nothing left behind but the distance he'd made the shot from? Not a lot of people could've hit that target. So we were dealing with a professional who knew not to leave a trace of himself. Which didn't bode well for me getting back to life per my new normal.

There was also the new dynamic between Bart and me that I hadn't quite wrapped my mind around yet. When I'd submitted to my correction, my reaction was unexpected, to say the least. I'd found freedom in every second of pain and discomfort, the rumbling of my Sir's voice. Before him, agony was simply a necessary evil, the sting of the razor or my body and muscles screaming when I overworked them to make sure I burned all the calories I ate. With Bart, the pain was cathartic in a way it hadn't come close to in the past.

Then there was what happened after my paddling. I'd nearly embarrassed myself when he'd wrapped his hand around my erection. The old me wouldn't have looked twice as the soft bulk of Bart, but everything about him drew me, not just how sexy I found the older man. He hadn't expected anything from me, and if I'd said no or even hinted at it, I knew he'd have stopped, no questions asked.

He wanted to keep me. Dates and all, and I'd never had that in the past. Even with Dolan, our dates appeared to the outside world as two friends sharing a meal. We'd never held hands or shown any affection in public, or in private for that matter, other than when sex was initiated, not that Dolan hadn't tried. All my hang-ups had ruined what could've been my first healthy relationship. As a man of forty, I felt I shouldn't feel so damn awkward about having a boyfriend or whatever I had with Bart. I was so worried about regression and ruining how Bart felt or what he saw when he looked at me. All of it seemed so fucking surreal.

Bart had to go out and take care of some things. That left me in the apartment with Remy and Robert, and Dolan. As much as I adored my ex-husband turned friend, I wasn't overly fond of him. I could see his irritation every time Bart corrected me or showed me affection. He didn't want me, and I knew that. He had an amazing husband and family—the things he'd always wanted and I wouldn't give him. Yet I didn't understand what his current issue was about my relationship. He acted as if I were too stupid to take care of myself and make healthy decisions, but our shared pasts hadn't proven I was the best at knowing what was best for me.

"I come bearing gifts." Vega breezed into the apartment, barely letting us respond to her knock.

I rushed forward to take her bag and the box in her hands, happy to have some sort of distraction even if that turned out to be files to go through. Never thought I'd think that.

"Someone must be bored out of their mind." She chuckled behind me as I carried the box to the small kitchen table. "Where's your Sir at?"

"He had some errands to run," I answered absently and flipped the lid off the box to find a messy stack of copies of handwritten notes. "What's all this?"

"All prison correspondence. Don't ask how I got them because I won't tell you."

"I wasn't going to. Why do you have them, though?"

"Well, my beautiful friend, the only true enemy you have except yourself is Chamberlain." I rolled my eyes at her and made her snort. "I figured if anyone wanted to finish the job, it was either him or one of his fans, and he has a sickening amount of fan mail. My contact shuddered at some of the *gifts* the fucker has received, and the tone of the mail, paper and electronic, has become increasingly worrying. Don't even get me started on all the platforms where they have groups where they interact. They've even started trying to doxx victims, but let's just say that doesn't work for them very well when someone pettier than them finds their information. The number of people without VPNs still amazes me in this day and age, and also doesn't use an online alias." I shook my head at her maniacal cackle. "Doesn't hurt when said petty person has a lot of over-caffeinated friends with twenty-four useable hours in a day philosophy and hasn't seen the sun in this decade or longer."

"You're saying our sniper could be in this stack?" Remy asked as he grabbed a messy handful and held them up.

"What else do we have to work with? I intercepted some chatter about thoughts on appealing the convictions, but even his defense team is dubious about that doing anything at all except getting him more attention to feed his ego. Despite all the complaints against him, he wants to claim every encounter was consensual and things just got out of hand, which would warrant a lesser sentence."

"What bullshit. We know how much he likes that ego stroked, and seeing every survivor paraded through court again would just give him masturbatory material." Robert stepped around

Remy as his husband went off to find a seat to look through the stack, and Robert took his own.

"They have him in isolation for his own protection," Vega said, and I jerked my attention to hers.

"Why?"

"Apparently, some inmates don't want to be housed with a sexual predator and serial rapist. He's not having a good time." I couldn't help being amused by her sadistic smirk. "They also have concerns he may be a danger to himself, so everything he sends or receives is inspected and cataloged. Only the materials from his lawyers are protected, but even those are scanned for any contraband down to staples and paperclips."

"What do you have other than the letters?"

"I got his parents' phone records. He makes a single call… every Sunday. His father sends sermons in email form once a week. Those are included in the stack. I was hoping for some code, but I'm not holding out much hope backwoods Preacher Daddy is much on devising coded messages. Still sent copies to a friend. The rest we need to go through. If something seems off in structure or wording, we can send them to him as well or the most fanatical ones of the bunch, but we're talking about prisoner fan mail. I don't have many hopes for high-functioning reasoning abilities. Exhibit A…" She dramatically motioned to the box.

Dolan grunted as he reached around me to grab some of his own, and I flinched as he bumped my still sore backside. He did that growling shit again and walked off. Boss was at the Outreach, so I didn't have a buffer. The door opened, and Bart entered with a tall, beautiful, extremely voluptuous woman with him.

She gasped as her gaze locked right on me. "He didn't tell me you were pretty." She glared at Bart. "Fuck, you didn't tell me he was beautiful."

Bart shook his head as the mahogany-skinned pin-up model

beside him brought her attention back to me. She even wore a skin-tight, off-the-shoulder dress with a red belt that gave her an even more hourglass shape. The stilettos she wore made her almost as tall as Bart.

"Robert and Remy said you could probably use a new friendly face, baby. Meet Verna, honey, meet Chance."

Fuck, that was his ex-wife? She perfectly matched him, and they hadn't parted on bad terms. They had a great marriage until his PTSD broke them apart. I suddenly felt very plain and awkward beside her, like I wasn't even an option.

"Bart has been bragging about you, and so have the grandkids." She gave me a friendly smile and crossed the room in her deadly high heels that made her legs look even longer. "I brought you presents. He said you were a fan of the last batch." She winked at me, and I swore my face actually heated.

What the hell was with the new blushing Chance person? I'd never acted shy in my life unless I knew it would get me something. "It's nice to meet you. Bart has told me a lot about you."

"Same. I love the way his voice changes when he talks about you. Can we talk in private?"

"Sure, um, this way." I motioned towards the bedroom Bart and I claimed and then shot Bart a panicked glance. He mouthed I'd be fine as I followed her and closed the door behind us.

"I didn't know how you'd feel opening your gift in front of people. Here." She held out a plain brown bag with twine handles and an ornate sticker on the front. "He described you. Scents you seemed to like. How you tuck your face into his neck as your comfort. I made that scent for him that you like so much for his birthday several years ago. You can put a dab of the oil on your sleeve or shoulder for when you feel anxious and inhale. It'll be slightly off since body chemistry is a factor, but it's similar enough that it should work. I do the same for the one I made my husband, Martin."

"Why are you being nice?" I asked as I hugged the bag to my chest.

"What you want to know is why I'm being nice to the first man my best friend has ever shown an interest in? Speak plainly. My feelings won't be hurt." I liked how straightforward she was and didn't placate me.

"Then why?"

"I'll admit I dreaded during our separation and eventual divorce about the person my husband may find one day. Just comes with spending decades of your life with someone. Will he choose someone exactly like me? Will he choose someone more beautiful? Thinner? These are natural insecurities that I worked through with my Sir. He validated my concerns and let me process." I noticed her playing with the gold necklace with the ornate lock. "Never thought I'd wear another man's collar, and the day Bart removed his from my neck destroyed me. But we all have to find our way to heal. When he told me he became your Sir, I knew eventually it would become more. He's talked about you in the past. No secrets or anything. He's not the type. Like I said out there." She nodded toward the closed door. "His voice changed when he mentioned you, and it was great to hear the man I used to know come back."

"He said he lost a piece of himself when he left you."

"I think that happens when two people get married and discover that their dynamic went far beyond just husband and wife. We learned to be Dominant and submissive together. But I was never the perfect submissive for him. I have a slightly more masochistic leaning than he's comfortable with, but he'd always provided me what would ground me as a good Sir does. Is this your first D/s relationship?"

I nodded. "I was an unwilling masochist. I thought I deserved it." I whispered the last sentence.

"No, you don't, but that's your lesson to learn, and it's a

process. He's going to spoil you rotten. You look like you can be a Brat."

"I may have heard that a time or two."

"He asked me to talk to you."

I shifted my feet, feeling slightly uncomfortable by her attention and the fact Bart wanted her to talk to me. "About what?"

"Despite how we parted ways, he and I are still incredibly close. And when I saw the way you looked at me...let's just say you gave away your thoughts. Comparing you and me. And he probably picked up on it, too." She tutted at me. "Cora is already aware. Bettany suspects. Tamara and Roxanne, they'll hear soon enough. We won't judge, and our daughters are aware of the dynamic their parents prefer. I guess what I wanted to do was welcome you to the family and make sure you didn't worry too much about whether you'd fit in or not. And offer you an alliance of sorts."

I grinned as she let out an almost giggle. "Alliance?"

"Bart is overprotective, and I've never met a more affectionate man. And that can sometimes be overwhelming, especially if you're not used to it. If it gets to be too much, you're always welcome to call me. Plus, I know all his embarrassing secrets, and I'm willing to share."

"And you said I'm a Brat."

"Your Sir has a weakness for them." She winked at me again. "Open your present."

I nodded and went to sit on the bed, and she lowered to sit beside me. As I pulled out bottles, she explained what they were.

"That one is great for bruises and the occasional obvious hicky. It has a sponge applicator. Just dab it on the area two to three times a day." I knew what the next bottle was. "He said you liked the sandalwood and ginger massage oil so much I made an extra-large bottle. Don't hesitate to call if you need more." I set it aside and pulled out the next one. "The oil-based cologne I make for Bart. Once again, sponge applicator, just dab a spot where you can sneak a sniff when you're anxious. Scent and pheromones play a huge part in bonding. Certain ones can make you feel safe."

There were more. Numbing gels. More sample-sized massage oils to find my favorite. There were also herbal tea packets. "This is all great. Thank you."

"You're welcome, sweetie. The teas are best for when you're alone with Bart. They're a special blend. It makes you extra sensitive and uncaring of propriety or when other people are around. Completely legal, don't worry, but definitely fun for playtime, not so much for correction."

"When he talks about you, I can tell he still loves you," I said as I set all the items beside me on the bed.

"It's more a love from companionship. The trust we shared as Sir and submissive. The romantic love faded a long time ago. He found a life at the Outreach...on the strip. He found his purpose. But in the past year, he mentioned you enough for me to take notice. I was wondering if he'd ever figure it out or accept it."

"I went to him to just be my Sir."

"And in doing so, you gave him back something he missed."

"He told me that."

She was about to speak when her phone chimed. "Time to get home. Sir expects me to be waiting for him."

"Is that stifling?"

"No. I get asked that a lot. It's freeing. Martin's entire focus is on me. He anticipates my moods. If I had a bad day. He knows when I need correction or cuddles. It's being loved and respected above all others...to always know your worth to another person. It's complete honesty and trust. A healthy power exchange relationship is the closest bond two people can ever have. He worships me as much as I do him. What could be better than that? Walk me to the door."

As we stood, she slipped her arm through mine, and then we

exited the room to find everyone staring at the door as if they'd waited for some blow-up. Except for Bart—he just watched us both with an indulgent smile.

"Once whatever this is ends, you have to bring him so we can have a family dinner. Our girls are going to love him." As she kissed my cheek, she released my arm and made her way to Bart. He kissed her cheek as he opened the door for her and told her goodbye.

He crossed the room and stopped in front of me, then he lowered his head as I tipped mine back so his lips could brush mine. "Are you okay?"

"Yeah, I'm fine."

"You don't completely trust me yet, baby, and I figured Verna could explain it better and assure you that you and I are just right. That my girls would accept you because you're mine. I'm going to put my bags in the bedroom and start on dinner while y'all get to work. Vega said she brought by an important project. If you need help to focus, just tell me, and we'll go in our room."

"Yes, Sir."

"Good boy." His mouth captured mine as he gripped the back of my neck. His strong fingers held me tight, and I opened without hesitation. He ended the kiss too soon and went to grab a backpack and a few large paper shopping bags by the handles.

I didn't take my attention from him until he disappeared into the room.

"Damn, another one has fallen," Vega whispered from too close beside me, and I turned to look down at her. "I was waiting for the tension to cause you both to explode. You're not very subtle. I knew you'd give into grabbing that living teddy bear sooner or later."

"Couldn't give a person a hint?"

"No. Zero and I found it beyond amusing."

I flipped her off as she laughed and went back to curl up on one end of the couch to pick up a thick stack of letters. I returned to the box and grabbed my own, bracing for the bullshit I was going to read. Would I become crushed under the pain like when I'd started to watch the video, or would I be able to hold it together? Only time would tell, and that was a lot of things in my life.

22

BART

Chance had excused himself to shower and go to bed early, but I doubted he was asleep. Through the evening and dinner, he seemed to collapse as he went through each letter from Chamberlain's admirers. I'd been shocked by the sheer number of letters and emails. Vega had even shown me the *Free Chamberlain* websites and the groups dedicated to freeing him while destroying the survivors. I hadn't wanted to ask how many times they'd mentioned Chance's name, but she'd leaned into my side to comfort me as if she knew what was going on in my head.

Boss was already in bed also as he had to be up early to be at the Outreach. That left me with Dolan as I tracked him with my gaze as he set the alarm system and checked the sensors on the windows. He'd even checked the ones in the adjoining apartment that had been meant for Gabby but remained empty as they'd added two rooms to Dolan's house for her and Todd. They were staying with Boss's sister, Florence, which surprised me because she wasn't the most kid-friendly person.

Dolan returned and flopped into the chair. Jupiter lifted his head from his front paws and then lowered it back to close his eyes. Dolan had taken Jupiter out for a long run to wear him out after dinner. I'd dreaded the talk we needed to have, but we hadn't had a moment alone with the Cold Case Unit, Vega, Boss, and Dolan around.

"Something on your mind?" he asked as he jotted down notes on a tablet, which he did almost every hour.

I didn't feel the need to bullshit him or sugarcoat anything. "He's mine whether you like it or not."

I didn't miss the tic in his jaw that I'd learned quickly signaled his annoyance. "Bart, I like and respect you, but Chance has a ton of trauma, and not just from the rape."

"I know. He's told me about growing up, his twenties, and your marriage and about what happened during Chamberlain's attack. He keeps nothing from me."

"Then you know he has no healthy coping mechanisms. I bumped against him earlier, and he flinched. He doesn't need..." I knew what was coming and decided to cut him off before he tried to tell me how to treat my baby.

"Whatever punishments he earns are done with loving correction. He purposely broke my rules, and he learned the consequences of his actions. And sometimes, he requires pain."

"He's had enough of that."

"You don't get it, Dolan. He cut himself because of happy memories...for feeling pleasure. He didn't think he deserved to feel anything other than pain, fear, and shame. When he came to me, I didn't intend to fall for him. But he makes me happy. Just like Boss does for you. I'd rather dole out his punishments than find he cut himself again. I don't punish him for experiencing pleasure or contentment. I praise and reward him for those. Yes, I'll admit his reward for accepting his last punishment went farther than I meant, but I'm not ashamed of that. He's your friend, and I know you worry, but he's my submissive...my partner."

Dolan cleared his throat and leaned forward to rest his forearms on his knees. "He may not be my husband anymore, but just like I told him, I married him because I loved him. I spent a decade of my life with him. As toxic and fucked up as that relationship was, I tried. Maybe I wasn't the one meant to help him, but that doesn't change the fact that I cared for him though." He glanced at the closed door. "I've watched him self-destruct, and there was nothing I could do about it. His change is so drastic that I worry he thinks it'll just go away. I'll always worry."

"He going to backtrack. He'll have good days and bad days, maybe even some horrific times, like when he was in the bathroom. But we can't coddle him. He must be able to mourn and lash out, to be selfish and set boundaries. Chance wasn't allowed to do that before, and some of those steps are going to seem over the top. And, Dolan, sometimes that's going to look like I'm being cruel, but as fucked up as that might be, it's necessary."

"I'm going to bed. I'll ease up, but that doesn't mean it's going to happen overnight." Dolan whistled, and Jupiter jumped up to follow Dolan to the bedroom.

I leaned back and rested my head on top of the back cushion as I took a deep breath. Chance was all warm in bed and waiting for me, but I needed a minute. I understood Dolan's point, and he'd known Chance longer—loved him—but Chance was mine. Fucked up time to realize that, but like I told Dolan, I wasn't going to regret anything that happened between Chance and me.

I groaned as my boy straddled my thighs and sat down on my lap. When I lifted my head, I opened my eyes to smile at Chance.

"You okay?"

"Yeah, I was about to come to bed." I curled my hands around his hips and tugged him forward until he was snug against my belly.

"You and Dolan okay?"

"We'll get there. He's just protective of you. I get it. Did you like meeting Verna?"

Part of me thought I'd taken a massive leap in bringing Verna around. I'd considered it about fifty-fifty that it would go badly, but I knew my perceived heterosexuality might turn into an obstacle. Chance's brain always went worst case scenario so easily, and I needed him to see that Verna and our girls would accept him.

"She looks like a pin-up."

I chuckled at his whine. "I have a weakness for beautiful Brats, apparently. I can tell she likes you."

"Doesn't she find this weird?" He motioned between us.

"No, baby, she doesn't think it's weird. Do you think it is? Is this something you don't want? You always have a choice. My care isn't dependent on physical intimacy or sex."

He lowered his gaze to my chest, and I raised my left hand to tip his head up. "I'm scared of it, like I'll feel the same way afterward. That I'll submit easily and then hate myself."

"If you hate yourself, that's the failure of your partner and not yours. You should be relaxed and satisfied, fulfilled emotionally, mentally, and physically. You ready for your next lesson?" I had something special planned for him. Chance had to learn that his body wasn't a weapon against him. That the pleasure he experienced wasn't a failing.

"Yes, Sir."

"Tonight isn't about Sir. Tonight, you're going to learn how being selfish is sometimes healthy."

He opened his mouth to question me, but I straightened to slant my mouth across his. I groaned at the perfect cushion of his full lips as they trembled a bit against mine. This was one of the biggest things I'd missed about physical intimacy, the making out. The learning what a partner enjoyed. Memorizing the sounds they made.

I teased the relaxed seam between his lips until he opened for me, and his shaking hands held my jaw. As I smoothed my hands up the muscles along his spine, he arched into me. A kiss and a tentative touch shouldn't cause my body to ache as badly as I did.

At first, I'd tried to blame it on touch starvation—of having no one for romantic or sexual intimacy, but I didn't know if that was completely true. I'd resisted for so long until he came along. I groaned as his muscled, rounded bottom rubbed against my hard cock. The thin cotton of our pajama bottoms wasn't a barrier.

I surged to my feet, only opened my eyes long enough to carry him back to our room, and kicked the door closed. I spun until I could push him to the surface as he tightened his legs around me.

"Boy," I growled against his lips, and I felt him tense. I wasn't ready for him to come to his senses yet. I pushed my tongue into his mouth as I trapped him against the door with my hips to free up my hands to stroke my thumbs over his tight, little nipples. Everything I had craved him, the man I was, my Sir and Daddy sides. They wanted it all. His submission. His trust. Fuck, I wanted his love. The way he trembled every time I touched him. It shot through me with an unbelievable sense of power.

He whimpered and arched his hips, and I groaned as he rubbed against my straining dick. I broke the kiss but only to drop my head to reach his neck. "You want to be Daddy's boy, baby?" I locked the door, and a sense of satisfaction hit me as he nodded.

I got us to the bed, laid him down in the center of the mussed surface, and grabbed the bottle of lube Verna had added to the first present she sent. A rumbling groan started deep in my chest as I saw him shoving his pants over his hips and kicking them away. He was all smooth, lightly tanned skin. I'd admit that he made me self-conscious. Comparing his forty-year-old, gorgeous body to my almost sixty-year-old one. The stretch marks on the front of my shoulders were noticeable on my dark skin. The roundness and jiggle of my belly. But I wanted him too much to give in to my insecurities of a middle-aged man.

I tossed the lube on the bed and then removed my own pants and underwear, braced myself to back off if he required me to. I stretched out beside him on my side and slid my right arm under his head. "Remember, you have the right to say no at any time." He nodded as I curled my left hand around his inner thigh and lifted it to drape over mine to open him for me. He added lube to my fingers when I asked, but I also saw him preparing himself for pain. "If it feels good, then just enjoy that for yourself...be selfish," I whispered against his mouth as I smoothed the slick around his tight asshole.

He gasped into our kiss as I worked the tight ring just as gently as I had the rest of his body during his massage the other night. He gave a smooth arched swivel of his hips, and I pushed the tip of my middle finger just inside. He arched violently as I gently buried my finger all the way inside. Felt him clench, and he let out a pretty whimper.

"You could get off just from me finger fucking that pretty ass of yours," I whispered against his mouth as I withdrew and thrust back inside, repeating until his thighs were shaking. I broke the kiss to glance down his body, and there was a thick pool of pre-cum spreading along his lower belly. "You ready for a second one?" I asked, but I didn't give him a chance to answer as I pulled out, but only enough to work a second finger inside.

"Daddy," he whined as I fucked in and out.

The second Daddy tripped off his tongue, my hard dick pushed into his flank. My speed went from slow and gentle to a hard slapping pace as I captured his lips to keep him quiet. The kiss barely muffled his sharp grunts as he rode my fingers. The way he rocked and rolled his hips made me imagine how he'd ride my cock, smooth and graceful.

"I can't wait for you to ride Daddy's cock just...like...that." I sensed his panic when I went from fast back to a gentle rhythm. My stomach twisted with nerves at what I had planned, but it was him, and I wanted him to feel good.

When I pulled away, he tried to grip me to keep me close, but I eased to my knees and positioned myself between his splayed legs. As I worked to loosen him, I lowered my head. He grabbed my neat twists as I licked from his balls along his thick shaft and then placed a sucking kiss to the copiously leaking head. I let out a rumbling groan at the taste of him.

One night after jerking off, I'd sucked my fingers to test if I liked the taste, but his flavor was different. With strong suction, I drew him passed my lips. It was strange, but the ache in my groin went from mild to an almost painful tightening. I could only take a few inches but used my free hand on what I couldn't get to, and I pounded his ass. The pleasure and desire were so intense as I memorized the whines and gasps, the movements as he worked himself between my mouth and fingers. Fuck, I could get off just listening to him.

I tongued his slit and was rewarded when a burst of pre-cum coated my tongue. My suckling sounds were getting louder because I wanted more, and I demanded it wordlessly because I couldn't bear to separate from him. The clenching, slick heat of his ass around my fingers made me imagine him around me. I opened my eyes to glance up at him, his face and chest red, his head pushed down into the pillow. The tendons in his neck starkly stood out as he bowed and pushed his bottom into the mattress. His uninjured hand rolled the small peak of his nipple, and I let him slip from my mouth as I kissed and licked up his belly until I could wrap my lips around it. Stroked my tongue over it and felt the tiny nub tighten further.

I sucked hard until I knew I'd leave a bruise around the flat, pebbled nipple. His eyes flew open as I removed my fingers and wiped my hand on the discarded t-shirt on my side of the bed.

"I want you to turn over, ass up, and your head on the pillow. Show me what belongs to me," I ordered as I straightened to kneel. As he obeyed, I leaned to the side to open the nightstand drawer to pull out the box of condoms I'd purchased earlier that day.

When I opened the box and pulled one out, I caught him staring at the box. "We don't have to use it, just in case." I reminded him that he could withdraw consent at any time. He'd already had his choice ripped away too many times.

I positioned myself behind him and took in the rounded curves of his muscular ass. The light bruises from his correction sessions caused me to groan. On his pale skin, they stood out starkly and the sight of them turned me on more. I scooted back enough that I could lean over, and the second my tongue stroked over his hole, he grabbed his cheeks and spread them wider.

"This pretty little hole is so sensitive." I wasn't a stranger to ass play. I'd enjoyed it back in the day, and I worked to loosen the muscle as I gripped his hips. I growled in warning when he tried to get away when I pushed the tip inside.

The sounds he made had nothing to do with fear. I smacked one ass cheek and then the other repeatedly until he was grinding against my face—fucking himself onto my tongue. He was a whimpering, sweaty mess.

"I'm gonna come," he whispered almost embarrassedly, and I reached between his thighs and took the base of his cock in the firm circle of my fingers. I tightened my stomach and sat up, and I waited until he seemed to calm a bit. Then I released his cock and blanketed his back. He searched for my mouth, and I slammed my lips onto his. I tensed as my dick notched between his firm cheeks and ground my hips against his backside. My balls rubbing his slick hole.

"I'm not ready for the night to end yet. Tell Daddy what you want."

"You."

"Where do you want me?"

"Inside me."

"Are you sure?" He nodded his answer. "Turn over. I want to see those pretty eyes while you take every fucking inch." He awkwardly rolled over beneath me. "If you want it, baby, take it." I smirked as I watched his every movement, the way his hands shook as he opened the condom.

The feel of him sliding the condom on, him pinching the tip as he stroked his hand and the latex to the base. I threw my head back on my shoulders and begged my body to not betray me.

"Think long and hard, baby, because if I take you, it'll mean something to me." I spoke as I held his gaze. "I won't fucking let you go." Even as I warned him, he added lube to the condom and lifted onto his elbow, carefully placing the head of my cock to his asshole. I nudged my hips until the broad head popped inside.

His teeth sank into his bottom lip and creases marred his brow. "Fuck, you're thick." He moaned as I sank all the way in until my balls met his ass. His pupils dilated with pleasure, and he never took his eyes off me taking him or where our bodies met. The heat and tightness had me rolling my eyes back, and again, that sense of home hit me like nothing had before.

The breadth of my hips and belly forced his legs wider to accommodate me. I held still, not just to allow him time to adjust but for me to process. For twenty years, it had been just me and my hand on the nights when I was lonely, and fantasy was all I had. This was so real. So visceral. The scent of his skin and sweat. The hair on his inner thighs teased my hips. Those sweet, needy whimpers that my boy made only for me. Fantasy had come nowhere near what I'd tried to forget while I told myself being alone was best.

"I thought I told you to take it, boy," I growled as he fell back on the bed, bent his knees to plant his feet, and I awaited the moment when he tried to kill me.

I shoved my fists into the bed beside him and braced to control myself. This young, gorgeous man wanted me, and I felt so humbled that he trusted me. My thoughts shattered with the first roll of his hips. It was hypnotic, like a belly dancer, and I gritted my teeth as he worked my cock to perfection.

"Ah, shit." I dropped my chin to my chest as he tightened his ass in a slow rhythm, releasing when he took me inside and clenching down when he retreated.

"Is that what you wanted, Daddy?" he asked, and I didn't miss his smirk.

"Just remember, boy, you act bratty, and Daddy is going to punish you." I hissed through clenched teeth as he did it again and again. My back bowed as my balls tightened, and I decided I'd let him play enough. "You asked for it," I growled as I took him with brutal snaps of my hips.

His grunts and whines, his shouts of Daddy grew as I owned him—loved him. Thick trails of pre-cum were sliding up his belly to his chest, and I shifted my hips, causing him to scream. Fire and agony worked through me as I kept aiming for that one spot, and the pounding of the headboard met his begging for more.

I fucked every sound out of my naughty brat, demanding with my body that he get louder. Fuck who could hear. I wanted everyone to know how much he craved me. How much I loved being the one to give him pleasure. He curved his fingers around the back of my neck as his eyes caught mine, and I doubled my efforts until he froze and shot over his stomach and chest. The harder I took him, the more mess he made, and the painful tightening of his ass around my cock as I forced my way through the pleasure-seized muscles threatened to destroy my control.

Scooting my knees forward, I fell forward until I braced my forearms on either side of his head. I slammed my mouth down on his, and I fucked him, giving him everything, showing him with every movement—every kiss how much I valued and needed him. I deep stroked him until he tore his mouth from mine, and I latched onto the curve of his neck where it met his shoulder. I didn't care that I'd leave marks for everyone to see. I bit and sucked, checked my work, and once I was satisfied, I pinched the bruised skin between my teeth.

"I'm gonna shoot, baby, fuck." I sped up until I was gasping for every breath. "You like your Daddy fucking you?" I growled the question. His fingertips dug almost painfully into the back of my neck, and he stared at me. Without warning, my release hit me, and I sealed my hips to his backside. I shot into the condom and ground my lower body into his, milking every second of pleasure. I fisted my hand in the long, dark blond hair on the top of his head.

"Y-yes," he stuttered as I realized the mess between his belly and mine grew as his cock jerked against the cushion of my stomach.

I nipped his earlobe with my teeth. "One day, Daddy is going to do that without a condom. Fill you so full you'll leak everywhere." He rolled his hips beneath me. "My baby likes the sound of that." I kissed along his jaw to his chin and brushed my lips to his Adam's apple. "You want to be fucking bred," I growled as I shallowly fucked him with my still-hard cock, loathing the moment I had to leave him to dispose of the condom. "I want to stay right here." I sank into him. "That tight ass keeping Daddy's cock all slick and warm. Plugging in my cum so it doesn't leak out of where it belongs."

He was hugging me so tightly that if I were a smaller man, he'd force the air from my lungs. I kissed the salt of sweat and tears from his cheek as he sobbed. When I shifted my body to get comfortable, he locked his legs around my waist as if he feared me leaving.

"I'm not going anywhere. Just breathe. When you're ready, I'll get you cleaned up, and then Daddy wants cuddles from my sweet boy. Did it feel good? Do you feel safe?" I whispered the questions and lifted my head enough to see him when he jerked his head to stare at me.

"Please keep me." His voice broke, and I knew what he meant. He didn't want the sex to be the end.

"You're not going anywhere. Me telling you that if I loved on you it would mean something wasn't a way to get you to let me fuck you. I did break a promise, though."

"What?" He looked confused.

"I told you I'd never fuck you the first night you came to me to be my boy." I kissed him. "I'm not sorry I broke it. You make me happy, Chance. Do I make you happy?"

"Y-yes, but I'm still scared."

"That's okay. I am, too." I groaned as my partially softened cock slid free, and I smiled at his pout.

"What are you scared about?"

"Same as you. Being enough. I didn't realize it, but the minute you walked into my kitchen, you were mine. You gave me pieces of myself back I'd ignored. And for that, I always want to make you safe and happy. I'm going to get us a rag to clean up. You okay until I get back?"

"Yes, I'm fine, but I made a huge mess."

I gave him one last lingering kiss and forced myself to get off him. Used my shirt to wipe up some of the mess from my stomach and chest in case Boss and Dolan came out of their room because the cum smeared across my dark skin was obvious. I pulled on my pants to head to the bathroom to clean up and dispose of the condom.

Chance was stretched out on the bed, relaxed and satisfied. I could tell by the small smile that curved his mouth, but I searched for some sign of regression. I knew we'd been intimate several times, platonic and sexual, but he still had issues to work out about not viewing sex as an act of degradation. I reluctantly left the room and froze as I noticed Dolan and Boss leaning out of their room.

"Is he still alive?" Boss asked, looking almost concerned.

I barked out a laugh. I closed the door but not before I heard Chance groan. "My baby is fine."

"Jesus Christ, I'm surprised no one called the cops," Dolan muttered and then dragged Boss back into the room and slammed the door. I shook my head as I took care of what I needed to. With a warm rag in hand, I headed to the fridge to grab some bottled water and returned to our room.

When I opened the door, I found Chance in the same spot.

His legs were still open, and my cock jerked but didn't harden as I took in his well-loved ass. After they found the threat to my baby, I'd lock him in my place for a long weekend. Just the two of us, privacy to love and correct him. I shook my head at the soft, adorable snort that told me he was asleep and went to get him comfortable.

Once he was clean, I stripped off my pants and stretched out beside him. He turned away, cuddled back to my chest and belly, and hugged my right arm to his chest. I was already addicted to this. I wonder if he truly understood how much I adored him.

23

CHANCE

D ammit, Bart needed to curb his oral fixation about visible spots, especially if Vega was going to visit regularly. My shirt collar hid most of the mark, but it still peeked above it. I covered the spot where my shoulder met my neck with my hand as I felt her stare holes into me as I flipped through one letter after another. They just kept coming. How much fan mail could one narcissistic sociopath receive in a week? Every admirer was crazier than the last. There were even notes about what items were included with the letters. Chamberlain's mail should come with biohazard stickers. There were even a few that asked for *samples,* and I nearly threw up in my mouth.

"We're not going to talk about the massive, and I mean *massive* hicky?" Vega kept poking the back of my hand with her vape pen, and I was trying to ignore her entire presence. "You can see that from *space.*" She giggled. "How badly was he trying to be quiet?"

"Oh, they weren't trying to be quiet. I'm surprised the neighbors didn't call in an attempted murder," Dolan muttered from the other side of the room. I turned to flip him off and caught him winking at me.

I glared at all of them. Outside of sex or initiating sex, I'd never talked about it, but since meeting them, they were all sex-positive, and that included not wanting sex at all. It took some getting used to. No one had any discomfort, but in my past, sex was something shameful. I'd spent so long obsessively hiding my sexuality. Bart had no qualms about his open displays of affection or telling me he was mine.

"And you thought you weren't ready?" Vega whispered and leaned in until she could place her chin on my shoulder. "All kidding aside, I'm proud of you."

I shifted my gaze in her direction. "Why are you proud?"

"I understand how hard it is to take that step. Some people are never ready. But you picked a great guy. I don't say this about many people. Bart's one of the good ones. He'll always put you first."

That's what I worried about—Bart putting too much focus on me and ignoring what he had to do for himself. I couldn't bear the thought that I'd wear out my welcome. I tried to correct my beliefs formulated by experience—that whatever a man told me, he'd always leave. "But shouldn't he take something for himself?"

"Sometimes a Dominant's purpose is the care and comfort of their submissive. I'm not saying it's that way for everyone, of course. A Dominant needs to take time to unwind and process. For me, Cash is my full focus. I feel fulfilled when she's at her happiest. Trust Bart to know when he needs a break. Even mine are still about my babygirl, cuddling and watching a movie, a night where I'm just Vega, not Mami."

"I don't want him to get sick of me." I lowered my voice so no one else could hear.

"That's something my gut says you never have to worry about, but you also have to work that out on your own. Best advice… talk to him."

I nodded and turned back to the letters and frowned as I read through one twice. "I'm no English major, but this one seems off."

"Off in what way?" Vega took the letter and scanned the piece of paper. "Do we have a pile for this admirer? Thoren Galveston?"

"Um, I think we have one." Dolan got up and went over to the corkboard where we'd been tacking the letters together in bundles by name. "Yep, dude is a bit too poetic for my taste. He's been sending letters weekly for the last four months. We traced the address, and it looks like..." He drew his finger down the notes we added as something struck us. "Forwarding service, but they won't give us anything without a warrant."

"There's workarounds for stuff like that." Vega picked up her phone and disappeared into another room, which typically meant she needed to talk to Zero.

I got up and walked over to the board. I gripped the bottom of the stack and removed the thumbtack to go through each letter. Those two had an odd friendship. Typically, when they were together, they'd be off to the side whispering to each other. Their level of paranoia sometimes concerned me.

"You doing okay with this?" Dolan asked, where he had his shoulder leaning against the wall.

"I don't know. I thought when Chamberlain pled guilty and was sentenced that it was all over except for me to get over it."

"A conviction doesn't equal instant healing, Chance. That's something you should've learned this past year."

"Yeah, yeah, I enjoyed my delusion for a while." I sighed. "You always hear about serial killers and all having fans, but..." I nodded toward the board. "This is sick. Chamberlain destroyed so many lives, and you have people sending him fan mail over his videos and saying how it was a shame his work was taken down. Like the victims weren't real people deserving of their humanity."

"There are too many fucked up people in this world. Chamberlain found his own little cult-ish following with a decade of those videos. If I could put every one of them in jail, I would. I never asked, but why did you watch the trial videos?"

I shrugged. "Mainly, I wanted to know what I missed...what made me so easy to target."

"Everyone has the potential. Training and a badge don't make you bulletproof."

"But, Dolan, I can walk into a room and pick out the one man capable of limitless brutality, but I couldn't see that in Chamberlain. Why?"

"You're torturing yourself trying to profile him. This is a bastard who flew under the radar for a decade...hell, who knows if there are victims we don't know about. Friends and co-workers never noticed, and his family...they were never in the courtroom. They never left Mississippi. Maybe they saw the signs."

"But why does someone want to take me out? No one saw my face on any of the videos, and I never testified. All I did was survive him trying to kill me." Was that meant to be my greatest sin, that I'd survived? I didn't want to look over my shoulder for the rest of my life because I'd managed to crawl from a motel room. My new start couldn't truly begin until the threats and attempts ended, and I needed a life with Bart.

"I wish I had the answer you need, but he's fucked up. Maybe it isn't even him trying to take you out but one of his followers taking that on themselves. Your attack was the beginning of the end. While his attacks were violent before, with you, he escalated. You didn't ingest the full dose of the drug. You fought back. You took his power away."

"I didn't fight hard enough." My voice broke, and I was wrapped in Dolan's arms as he pulled me against his chest.

"You were drugged. There was nothing you could do, but you survived. You just have to learn to live with that."

I hugged his waist tight and tucked my head under his chin. We'd been together for a decade, dating and married, and I couldn't remember a time where I'd just stood with him and got a hug. "You give really good hugs. I don't remember that."

Dolan's gruff laugh vibrated his chest. "My baby and kids trained me well."

"I'm really happy for you."

"I'm happy for you, too. You got your shit together when you got Bart. Kinda surprising, though."

"It was the belly. I wanted to cuddle it." Dolan snorted so hard at my answer he choked. "Seriously, though. I walked into the Outreach, and the minute I was introduced to Bart, the kitchen became my safe space. The place I went after the hell of being in group…I started to look forward to it. He became like my reward for attending."

"The old Chance wouldn't have admitted that."

"I never really liked the old Chance, and I'm still coming to terms with the Aftermath Chance."

"You'll get there. Just don't push it so hard. But if it matters, you're almost like a completely different person."

"In a good way?" I asked as I lifted my head to look at him. Dolan was one of those ruggedly handsome men that could roll out of bed and draw everyone's attention. Yes, he was arrogant and a bit of an asshole, but when I'd first met him, I'd thought that was part of his charm.

He gave me a squeeze. "A really good way."

"If I'd acted right, do you think we'd have lasted?" My gut said no because we'd started to despise each other toward the end. Some of the bridges we'd burned were still smoking, but I was grateful we'd become friends.

"I don't know. I won't say I didn't wonder about that after we'd separated. I'd asked for the divorce, sure it was the right decision for both of us. I think we all have the what-ifs, Chance. If I'd made you talk it out. If I didn't let you run away during every fight. But I don't think we would've made it. We were both too jaded by the relationship. Deacon and the kids were what I wanted…what I needed. You and I weren't on the same page, and it took me a long time to realize that. Way longer than it should've." He leaned forward and rested his chin on the top of my head. "I resented you while loving you at the same time. With everything that happened in the last year, is there any part of you that wanted a do-over?"

That was an easy answer. "No."

"You didn't have to answer so quickly." He gave me a hard squeeze, and I chuckled.

"Old Chance's ego was hurt. You didn't fall for all my tricks that worked in the past. Then I met Boss, and there's this bald bruiser of a guy that made you happy, and then a daughter. That's why I went out that night. I wanted someone to fuck me and make me feel wanted."

"Thousands of other people do the same thing every night, hooking up to share sex...again, that wasn't your fault."

"But if I hadn't..."

He shook me to shut me up.

"There's no but. Yeah, you have a sex addiction. You didn't always make safe choices when it came to sex partners but stop with the shame. You've been going to group. Whether you talk in those groups is your business, but you get something from them. Let me ask you this. Has being intimate with Bart ever made you feel bad?"

"No." I smiled. "I went to him because he wanted me to cut safely and offered to be there or do it for me so that I wouldn't lose myself. Which to be honest, I had a few close calls. But he gave me something better. I never once thought he'd want me like he does. He validates what I feel but never lets me forget there are better options. That first corrective spanking...it was freeing. There was the pain, but it was different. Not the same as what I got from the self-harm or the brutal sex."

"From what Deacon and I heard last night..."

"I didn't even think about other people in the apartment."

"That meant it was good. Take that for yourself."

"Not hating myself the morning after, well, that was my

biggest fear. That I'd have sex again and it would be like all the times before. It might sound weird coming from me, but I love the affection and cuddles. It's like having my own life-sized teddy bear. He makes me feel safe, Dolan, and I haven't felt that way since I was thirteen and my mom got sick."

"Well, enjoy it. You deserve it, no matter what you think."

A throat clearing made Dolan and I turn to find Vega staring at us.

"I will kill you both."

"Don't even try it, Vega. Deacon owns me."

"And I find Bart way too irresistible."

She narrowed her eyes and studied us as if she was looking for lies. The woman had to be crazier than she was to think me, and especially Dolan, would look at anyone else. I understood it, though. How many times had that suspicion been aimed my way?

"Fine, but your men may have different ideas." She nodded her head, and I leaned to the side to find Boss and Bart watching us.

I didn't know how we hadn't heard them come in, but we'd been focused on having our talk. Bart had to take care of an order and delivery issue and went to the Outreach with Boss that morning.

"Hey, baby." Dolan gave me one more squeeze before he released me and closed the distance between him and his husband.

My past made me question how Bart would react. I hadn't been the most monogamous or careful person. I nibbled at the lower corner of my lip. Bart turned to push his way around Dolan saying hi to Boss in a very indecent way. After Bart stretched out his arm and caught the back of my neck, he gently pulled me toward him until he could wrap me in a hug. Automatically I tucked my face against his neck to take in his scent. It was like what I assumed home would smell like, warm and comforting and always welcoming.

"Hi, baby boy, you okay?"

"Yeah. Dolan and I just had to have an overdue talk."

"Feel better afterward?"

"Yeah. We never really had the opportunity after everything calmed down. Could be we just didn't want to say anything in case we burned another bridge. More importantly, how's the Outreach surviving without you?"

"Well, which makes me feel expendable."

"Like they'd survive without you. They need the Drill Sergeant, or they'd veer off track. You have job security, the kids like your lunches better, they might organize a mini-protest." A warmth filled my chest as he chuckled and turned his head to kiss my temple.

"I'd probably pay to see that. Our kids are pretty outspoken. We have an entire army of community activists. Any progress on the letters?"

"Vega may have learned something. There's a regular fan who sends a weekly letter, but they go through a forwarding service. She was hypothetically trying to find a way to trace the address without a pesky court order."

"Hey, hey, I'll have someone procure a warrant. I'm just not patient enough to wait."

"So, what did they say?" I asked.

"Zero did a quick scan of their system, but for a sketchy forwarding service, they have some killer security measures."

"Sketchy?" Bart asked.

"Well, they normally scan the mail, and a person can sign on to read it from a browser. We noticed a few names we've come across in the past, well, more than a few. After some calls, there's some rumors on the street that they do more than forward mail. DEA and ATF have been checking out the owners. Don't ask. I won't tell you."

"We've learned it's best not to ask," Dolan said with a shake of his head.

"Any raids on the place always came up clean. Explosive and

Drug detection dogs haven't hit on anything, but there's way too much chatter about them. Zero's going to wait until everyone logs out of the system, and then he's going to scan through everything and search any records for Thoren Galveston."

"That's an alias if I ever heard one." Boss cuddled up to Dolan's side.

"Yeah, we're hoping it's his real first name and maybe where he lives, but with his skills, I don't know if he'd be that careless. This guy has had some training. The distance he made that shot from…but cross-referencing Thoren and US military records has come up empty. If he's a trained assassin, then we may have to get really unconventional on this one."

"Depending on what Zero finds, we'll come up with another course of action. Right now, Chance is safe, but we're also not getting any intel. Long-range attack. Policing his brass. No forensic evidence. The explosion of the vehicle. We didn't get any casings for comparison to the ones found during the Outreach investigation," Dolan said. I grinned as I saw Dolan slipping his hand under the back of Boss's shirt, pulling the cotton tight across the soft curve of his belly.

"Well, Zero will get back to me before he crashes in the morning. But I'll let my friend know to check out letters by this guy and see if he sees a pattern or code. I agree they're awful poetic. We're going to search Chamberlain's emails as well. Maybe we can luck out and get an IP address. Even if he's using a public hotspot, if there's a common IP, it would give us an area to focus. Zero's going to install a backdoor and set up an alert for any time Thoren signs in. I'm just wondering if he's keeping this old-school snail mail, then we might have a more difficult time depending on how many times the correspondence is forwarded."

"I just want my life back. I'm tired of being cooped up in this apartment. I miss work."

"I know you do, Chance. But even if we come up with a plan

to have you more out in the open, you're still not coming back to active duty. We have to focus on this, and you being the key figure, if he starts gunning for you in the field, we have other officers to think about."

I got what Dolan was saying, but my job was the main reason I got up in the mornings. The only thing I had that I'd ever been proud of in my life. I'd worked hard to get where I was. My personal life had suffered, but my professional one had always flourished.

"What do you want for dinner, baby?"

"Surprise me. I had my snack about two hours ago."

"You'll be hungry soon."

"I know you're probably old-school, Bart, but damn." Vega poked the bruise.

"Will you stop that," I yelled as Bart laughed.

"I had other things on my mind at the time, and quit giving my baby shit for it." He tucked the side of his curled fingers under my chin and tipped my head back. "I missed you today," he whispered right before he slanted his mouth across mine, and just like always, I forgot everything but him.

He repeatedly pressed his lips to mine, teasing me until I followed his mouth but pouting when he evaded me. "I missed you, too."

"You do your work or relax, and I'll have dinner done soon. Work or not, bedtime is still ten."

"Yes, Sir." I got one more kiss, but I sensed his reluctance to let me go.

I didn't move from where I stood. Dolan and Boss had disappeared probably to their room. Vega was curled up on one end of the couch as she scrolled through her phone and occasionally typing. Bart was working in the small kitchenette. Boss barely had a kitchen to work with, but I'd heard Boss was worse than me when it came to cooking, so I didn't feel as bad.

Bart glanced over his shoulder and winked at me, then

pointed toward the couch. I truly hadn't thought that I'd be able to go through with the penetrative sex. Not because I didn't feel safe with him. I couldn't remember wanting a man as much as I did Bart. No, my issue had been if I would have a flashback to that night. I was an extremely needy bottom. Yet, I'd worried the act would always be ruined for me. When I'd awakened, I'd taken stock of myself. Did I feel regret? Did I instantly feel the need to shower? None of that happened. I was still scared that it would happen, though. All it took was one bad day, and the flashbacks and panic would return. I dreaded the day that might happen.

I was also terrified that Bart would change his mind, that all we'd have was a short time. There wasn't any way that I could get over him seeing what we had as temporary. It was still early, less than two months since my first spanking. Yet I was already so attached. I believed him when he said if we went through with the night, it would mean something to him. Part of me was debating it all because Verna was perfect—beautiful. I was the first man Bart had been with. It was all my own insecurities and me comparing myself to the man I was before the assault.

I trusted Bart. He didn't look at me as that broken thing I'd always viewed myself as, and he told me I made him happy. As foolish as it might be, I always wanted to make him feel that way. I'd focus on my healing, and maybe those intrusive thoughts would quiet?

24

BART

COLD CASE
UNIT

The new plan of Chance going on about his life didn't sit right with me. The Thoren guy was a ghost. Zero couldn't find anyone with that name, and the IP addresses got them nowhere. All of them went to different internet cafes all over the state, and none of them had security systems on anything other than the registers and in and outside the office where the safes were. Zero was hard at work trying to get CCTV footage from the surrounding buildings, but so far, everything had turned out too grainy to determine anything.

I didn't know how they all dealt with the unknowns. The puzzles that always defied logic. I was happy to be back in my space, though. I'd gotten used to my own company—that was until Chance came along. But three weeks of being locked down in an apartment with an always rotating group of people had taken its toll on my nerves. I'd held it together for Chance, but I was looking forward to some one-on-one time with him to check to see how he was processing.

The letters and court videos, Chance had immersed himself in the case, so understandably, it would've brought up memories. The number of nightmares he'd had told me how much it still affected him. While Chance took a long bath to relax, I took care of a few chores around my apartment. I wasn't excessively neat, but everything had its place. That apartment was the first place I'd lived alone. The space I'd come to for healing, those four walls had seen me rage. They'd witnessed me hiding in corners, searching for some invisible enemy. There was a patch where I'd thrown my last bottle of booze.

All the memories there were bittersweet. Proof of my isolation. I could afford a new place but leaving the strip never crossed my mind. It worked for me. Unless I visited Verna or the kids, I never crossed the borders. I put away the cleaning supplies under the sink and then went to check on Chance. I knocked on the door he left ajar and pushed it open to find him with his head leaned back against the wall, his eyes closed.

"Hey, baby, you doing okay?" I asked as I entered and took a seat on the closed lid of the toilet.

"Yeah, enjoying the quiet. Haven't had much of that recently. How about you?"

"I'm good."

"I know you like your privacy, and being trapped with everyone couldn't have been easy."

"I adapt, and you needed me. To me, that was more important." His brows drew together with a worried expression. "Tell me."

Indecision played out over his expression, but I knew he wouldn't lie to me. "You need time for yourself, Bart. Taking care of me. Putting me first. It's going to wear you down." He didn't look at me as he spoke.

"Baby." I waited until he turned his gaze to me. "I'm fine. Verna and I had a similar talk once upon a time. When we were together, even separated by oceans or several states, I was still her Sir. That was our dynamic and our purpose. Her care and comfort were my biggest concern in our marriage, besides the kids, of course. Some people are happy with the occasional scene with a dedicated Dominant or with someone they have an agreement with in a club. Some, it's just to spice up the bedroom."

"What about you?"

"Twenty-four hours a day, seven days a week, three-hundred-sixty-five or six depending on a leap year." He snorted. "For me, that's where I'm happiest. Yes, there's times I need to work shit out on my own and have a few hours of just me. And I promise you that if I need time, just like I did with Verna, I'll always discuss it with you. A dynamic like what we have can't work without honesty and compromise."

"I just don't want you to get tired of taking care of me."

"Never happen. Ready to get out?" I asked, and he nodded. I stood and grabbed the folded towel on the sink.

He leaned forward to let the water out, then stood, letting the water run down his body. That gorgeous man let me love on him, and I had no idea what I'd done right in my life. I opened the towel and wrapped it around him as he stepped over the side. I squeezed the water from his soft hair and then gently dried him off. Just touching him—having him near made me need him. Yes, the intensity of my feelings worried me after decades of keeping everyone at arm's length, but the way I desired him had started from the moment we'd met.

"I really did miss this, Chance. Don't ever doubt this is right where I want to be. We both need time, I understand that, but I'm a man who's almost sixty. I'm not a twenty-something or even thirty-something who doesn't know what they want. I want this...I want you. We both have PTSD to varying degrees with a lot of different triggers, and we have more to learn about each other. So we can go as slow or fast as you need." I dropped to my knees and dried his legs and feet before hanging it from a hook.

I brushed a kiss just below his belly button, nuzzled the strip of dark blond hair that fanned out into a nest of coarse, springy curls, and inhaled the scent of him and me combined. I looked up at him as I circled the thick base of his dick and pulled back to open my mouth around the broad head. He let out a shuddering breath as I sucked his partially hard cock. I bobbed along the length, taking what I could and working the rest with my fist. My free hand slipped between his thighs. I pushed my fingers into his crease and played with his hole, massaging the ring of muscle.

His shaft swelled on my tongue as breathy moans slipped from him. My cock jerked inside my underwear as his pleasure became mine. Him submitting to me loving on him had been a hard-fought battle as I earned his trust. I groaned at the burst of pre-cum spilling over my tongue.

The sight of him watching me from under heavy lids, the way his lips parted to allow for his quickened breaths, showed me what my affection did to him. We hadn't fucked since that last night before I had to cater to his emotional needs with the letters and some bad dreams. A needy whine filled the small room as I released him and got to my feet. I hugged his waist and lowered my mouth to his.

Without hesitation, he opened for me. My tongue teased his, and I led him from the bathroom without breaking the kiss. There were so many things I'd taken for granted with my abstinence and periods of celibacy; kissing was one of them. As I backed into our bedroom, I released his lips.

"Damn, I forgot how much I missed this." I brought my hands to his jaw and traced his full bottom lip with my thumbs.

"Missed what?" he asked.

"The intimacy. The kissing. The touching."

"Twenty years is a long time to go without."

"I convinced myself it was for the best. There's a lot you can ignore when you're scared."

He nudged my chin with his nose until I tipped my head back so he could take his favorite spot. "What do you have to be scared about?" he asked as he slipped his hands under my tank and his fingers sunk into the curve of my stomach.

I groaned as he sucked at my neck. His confidence had grown

so much in a short time. I gripped his soft hair in my left fist as he dragged his lips down my chest, and he pushed my shirt up until it bunched under my arms.

"You're not answering me," he whispered right before he pinched my nipple between his teeth.

"Shit, baby." I released him to remove my shirt and toss it aside. "Of hurting someone else I care about."

I dropped my gaze to him as he knelt at my feet, pulling down my sweats and wrapping his hand around the base of my dick. In slow motion, I watched his lips part and move in. Then I noticed the moment the fear came. I'd barely felt the brush of his breath, the softness of his lips before he gagged.

"Baby, you don't have to do that." With my hand cupping his chin, I gently urged him to stand, and when he did, I backed up until I could sit on the end of the bed. I pulled him down to straddle my thighs. "Hey, Chance, look at me, please," I whispered as he opened his eyes, and they were glassy with tears. "I'm like any man. I enjoy a good blowjob, but only if the person giving it is, too." I stroked the slight scars that were barely noticeable on the corners of his mouth from the device Chamberlain had used to keep Chance from biting.

"I trust you." His voice broke.

"Trust isn't always enough. It's an act you associate with pain and degradation."

"It used to be one of my favorite things. One of the few sex acts that I liked. I'm tired of him taking things from me."

"Love, maybe you'll want to try again in a week, a year, hell, never, but whether you suck my dick at any point in the future doesn't change how I feel about you."

"I-I'm sorry," he stuttered out and dropped his attention to my chest.

I didn't like when he tried to shut me out. I cupped his jaw and forced his head up. "You have nothing, and I mean nothing, to be sorry about." I gave him my best reassuring smile. I used my thumbs to tug at his bottom lip and leaned forward to brush my mouth to his. "There's other things you can do with this mouth that I love."

"What?"

"Being snarky." I nipped at his bottom lip as I felt him smile. "Calling me Sir." I stroked the corner of his smile with my thumb as I kept my lips against his. "Smile and laugh. I really love those." His eyes shot open, and he stared at me. "Is that shocking?" He nodded. "Baby, I waited a long time to see you smile and hear you laugh for real."

"Didn't take you for a sweet romantic man."

"We all have layers. Only two people have gotten this from me. You snuck in under the radar, though."

"You did tell me you thought I was pretty," he whispered shyly and batted his lashes like the brat he was. "It was the supermodel stroll in my uniform, wasn't it?"

"I also mentioned something about spankings."

"Foreplay," he said against my lips and then smiled.

"Why do I put up with you again?" I asked.

He tipped his head back as if thinking about it. "I do that thing with my hips you really, really like." He demonstrated with a smirk, and I groaned as he rubbed his dick against mine.

"That is definitely a perk." I forced my voice to sound bored.

"I think Daddy is being mean." He pouted.

"I'd never be mean to my boy. Daddy is for caring. Sir is for correction." I locked my arms around him as I stood, turned, and tossed him on the bed. He bounced a few times before settling his head on the pillows.

I stripped off my sweats and then crawled onto the bed until I could rest between his thighs. Bracing my right arm beside his head, my left hand stroked down his side until I could hook it under his knee and pull it high on my side. I stroked his damp hair from his forehead. "I adore you, Chance, I really do. I know all your demons. I accept them as much as I do every other part of you. Now, give me a kiss. I need a few of those before we go to bed."

He tipped his chin up until his mouth met mine. Kissing him got better every time. There was a shyness to his tentative kisses, the ones he gave me when he was testing if I'd allow him. He was so unsure, but soon Chance would realize there wasn't much I wouldn't do for him or give him if he'd ask. I wanted to be cautious. Give him space to make his own decisions, to make the first move. If he'd accept his newfound confidence, my boy would be unstoppable, and I couldn't wait to see that.

25

CHANCE

I glared at Claxton over the top of the book I'd tried to read for the last hour. He was being a bigger dick than normal. Since him and the girlfriend broke up, he'd had a stick up his ass. Having to watch me wasn't helping his disposition any. I wasn't saying that he wasn't a good guy, Claxton was laid-back normally, but something was off the past few months. He wasn't hanging out as much as he used to and turned down most of the invites to Xanadu when he was fine going before. We weren't close enough for me to interrogate him about his new attitude, especially when we hadn't started off friendly in anyway.

"Problem, Claxton?" I asked without removing the book from in front of my face. Remy, Doc, and Vega were determined to expand my reading choices into more interesting realms. People would be surprised to know that I had more than a few functioning brain cells and preferred my non-fiction, maybe a little speculative fiction thrown in. My friends determined I needed some spice in my life. Bart gave me plenty.

"Can I tie you outside and see if anyone takes a shot at you?" he asked.

I batted my lashes at him and gave him my most innocent

smile. "Kinky. Didn't think you were the bondage sort, but sorry, my Sir wouldn't appreciate it." I winked at him, and he let out a menacing rumble. "Aw, sounds like a puppy doing their first growl."

"I can shoot you and get away with it. I'd blame it on the mystery sniper."

"Should I mention you as a suspect?" I asked.

"I'd chance it."

"I think you need to get laid," I commented and closed my book to toss it on my desk next to where I had my feet propped on the corner.

He scratched the side of his neck where my faded bruise lingered. "I think you're getting enough for both of us."

"Jealousy." I smirked.

"I liked you better when you were an arrogant asshole instead of some Sir's boy."

I pouted as I worked hard to get one tear to fall, and he picked up his phone. "What are you doing?"

"Going to send a picture of you being a brat to your Sir."

"I'll tell him you made me cry. He's overprotective. Who'll win? His perfect boy or you, the grumpy bastard?"

He huffed and threw his phone down. "I need new friends."

I frowned as I caught his oddly hued eyes, somewhere between green and honey, shifting to the side, and I followed to see who had caught his attention. Trey was coming from the gym and shower area. "Got a thing for pretty ones, too, huh?" I whispered so Trey wouldn't hear.

"No, I just don't know what to do with our newest rookie, and Dolan, in his great wisdom, has decided I'm the Rookie Wrangler."

"Liar." I barely breathed the word and earned another glare.

"Just because all my friends are gay doesn't mean I am."

"I think you protest too much. You might like it."

"Again, I liked you better before."

I chuckled. "I didn't, but we all have preferences." I glanced at Trey one more time until he disappeared into the locker room and then turned back to Claxton. "He's a great officer. He's just having issues adjusting to a new place with all new people to mesh with. We're a tight team and friends, so he's a bit on the outside. Once he feels he has a place on a team, he'll settle right in."

"I've cycled him through, and he hasn't meshed with anyone."

"Give him to me," I said, and Claxton stared at me like I was insane. "What? I like him. We know we can work together well, and he's my roommate, so assign him to me."

"I don't know. You'll teach him bad habits."

I flipped him off. "Listen, you need a partner for him, you want to think about it, fine, but in the end, you're going to assign him to me anyway. You like him too much to work with him."

"You think you know everything."

"Not everything. Okay, be possessive. He's assigned to my protection detail. When that's over, you can make a definite decision, which will be my team."

"I'll think about—" The sound of the alarms blaring broke off whatever Claxton was going to say.

"Suit up," Dolan bellowed as he appeared from the elevator. He ran toward me, carrying a vest and jerked me out of my chair.

"What's going on?" I asked as he roughly secured me in the body armor and shoved another plate in for two layers of protection.

"Bomb threat. Everyone remove your name patches now, masks in place." He was yelling louder to be heard over the blaring alarm. "Someone is gunning for one of us. That means he'll go for any of us, stay low, stay tight, and take cover once you step outside those doors."

"Dolan," I snapped, and he looked at me. "Just let me go out. Plain sight."

"No, you're not sacrificing yourself on my watch."

I felt like a fucking kid as Claxton pulled the mask over my head and positioned it until it covered my cheeks and then slammed my helmet on. And then a strange earpiece appeared and was placed in my ear.

"Chance, my man, guess what? I'm your friendly partner today." Vega's voice sounded in my ear. "Dolan is currently equipping you with a small camera. First person shooter action here, man." Her maniacal voice almost made me forget that I could die that day. "You're a sniper. Walk it for me. Tell me best positions. What would you do? I'm trying to get satellite access to scan the area."

As soon as I was dressed like I was a kid, I ran to the armory for my weapon. Taking deep breaths, pacing them out like Bart had me do when I panicked. With thoughts of him, my mind cleared. My Sir/Daddy would be disappointed if I fucked up. A sense of peace came over me as I joined the entire S.W.A.T. unit waiting in a phalanx to open the large garage access door. An armored van behind us for us to retreat to if we started taking fire.

We worked as a singular unit as we would if we'd initiated a breach. Everyone went low, scanning the exterior before walking into the mid-afternoon sun. The sudden glare blinded me for a second, but I felt three taps to my lower back that let me know Dolan was at my Six. It used to be the signal we used in public when I couldn't...wouldn't acknowledge him. A sense of regret came over me for what I'd done to Dolan, but I pushed it away. I'd make amends later.

"Chance, we're on a private frequency, just you and me, your Sir if you want him to be, but I need you focused on the mission and not your Sir, but if you two dirty talk, I could be persuaded. My own personal show."

"Ha. Ha. Ha. You got jokes."

"Tell me what you see, man."

"Nothing. Our unknown sniper probably hoped for more

chaos and not us coming out as a unit." We broke formation into several separate units, and I went left with at least Dolan behind me. I raised my rifle, placed my eye to the scope, and my world shrunk down to nothing but the crosshairs. "He'll want a position high enough to get a clear shot. He probably reconned the area in the last few weeks. If he's as good as he thinks he is, he'll want cover, but a position that also allows for a swift exit."

"Would he want an open position like at the Outreach and highway, or would he want more cover?" I heard the clicking of keyboard keys sounding in the background and a low bass voice that had to be Zero muttering. "Zero wants to know what direction would be best for an unobstructed line of fire."

I panned from right to left, then left to right, searching for anything—a flash as sun struck a scope, but there was nothing. "We're covered on the east and west by cement walls that lead into the vehicle access." I moved farther until I was no longer covered, and I was out in the open.

I shook off the hand on my shoulder. I knew it was Dolan trying to pull me back, but I needed a better view. My heart pounded in my ears. I controlled my breathing even as my mask moved with my inhalations and exhalations. I felt Jupiter's powerful body against the side of my leg as I moved farther out. Just as I broke the first row of cars, the resounding noise and force of an explosion threatened to knock me off my feet. One vehicle, then another, lifted with the force as I dropped to my belly.

"He's trying to herd us to the northwest." The scent of burning rubber and the acrid scent of hot metal filled my nose.

Jupiter and I worked as a unit as I commando crawled, and suddenly the shade of a vehicle covering me blocked me from sight. I heel-kicked the undercarriage, and it pulled to a stop. I started at the top of one building and worked my way down. Chaos ensued, but I ignored it all.

My only job was to find the sniper's nest. Each window

showed a glare until I noticed a dull pane. I needed a better look, so I kicked the undercarriage, and the van started moving. I heard a shout above me as another shot rang out, and the unit shuddered with the force of the impact.

Just a bit closer. I mentally pushed myself so I didn't pause. *Just show me your face.* The movement was almost invisible, a figure cloaked in black, but he overcompensated, probably worried about the time he was remaining in one position, but there it was, a barely there flash. I scanned the building and saw the name.

"Harpon Building. Thirtieth floor," I said as asphalt fragmented six feet in front of me.

"We have units on the way," Vega said as she typed more. "Floors twenty-three to thirty-one are down for renovations. Chance," Vega whispered my name.

"Yeah?" I asked absently.

"Leave him a mark to remember us by."

She was right. I was tired of running from a fucking ghost. I'd had enough of that in my forty years. He had to leave something behind, and I was going to make sure it happened. I placed my index finger over the trigger, inhaled, squeezed, and exhaled. My weapon recoiled, and the window above the removed panel shattered. It was nothing more than a shadow in my scope, but I saw the slightest movement. I aimed. I just needed a drop of blood—that's it. If he wasn't in the system, we'd have something to compare to when they found a suspect.

Sirens and smoke, yells of shots fired, and the address of the Harpon Building, but I ignored it all. Nothing and no one existed outside me. I crawled from under the vehicle. Vague shouts of my name and *get down,* barely registered. It all happened in slow motion. Existence slowed down. My heart was beating a steady rhythm in my chest. I licked my lips—nothing was real outside my scope. I'd trained for over half my life for my job. My rifle and crosshairs had always been my comfort zone. The place I'd felt I could do no wrong.

I flinched as one shot after another pounded the pavement as I ran for the nearest car, then I braced my arms and weapon. If I knew nothing in this world, this was mine. I counted down, picturing the repetitive slide as he slid the bolt back, reloaded one projectile, fired, and then repeated. Everything was silence and peace, it was a strange warmth, and I gently squeezed the trigger and aimed into the shadows. Once, twice, and then a third time until no more shots were returned.

"Chance, shooter is down. S.W.A.T. unit arrived. Paramedics are on their way." Vega's voice was a surreal, dream-like drone as it filtered in.

I relaxed and straightened, pulled my mask down, and glanced at the carnage around me. Six vehicles lay in fiery ruin. One of the S.W.A.T. vans was dented from the force of bullet impacts, and Trey was jumping down from the driver's seat.

"Any injuries on our side?" I asked Vega.

"No. It seems he was more focused on getting you out in the open than doing damage to anyone else. Bomb squad is en route to check the rest of the vehicles and building for more explosive devices. But more than likely, he just wanted to clear the building. It looks like a fucking warzone."

"Vega, call Bart and let him know I'm okay before he sees it on the fucking news."

"Zero is already doing damage control. You're getting a spanking for this one. Look up. You're already caught."

I glanced upward to find news helicopters hovering above and groaned. Just what I fucking needed…Bart to see it on some breaking news broadcast. I was in so much trouble. That was if Dolan didn't kill me before Bart got near me with his paddle.

"Any ID on our suspect?"

"No, looks like he'll live…unfortunately, but maybe he'll talk. They searched him. Apparently, he didn't have any ID on him, and he's not talking."

"Chance," Dolan bellowed behind me.

"Maybe a spanking isn't the worst of your worries. Zero and I can make you disappear." She sounded too amused as I heard the connection end, and I turned to find Dolan and Claxton coming for me.

I should be used to being in trouble by now.

26

BART

If there was one thing I'd avoided like the plague was ending up in a police station, but there I was, seated on a small couch in the Cold Case Unit as everyone stared at me like I was about to go off. The minute Carlos had yelled at me to turn on the small TV in my office, I'd been doing the weekly order for the community pantry. I'd almost ignored him until he'd appeared in the doorway with a concerned look on his face.

I'd turned on the TV to find breaking news with an aerial view of the outside of the S.W.A.T. headquarters. It looked like a warzone. Cars were burning, some resting on their roofs, dozens of S.W.A.T. officers taking defensive positions, but as much as that terrified me, the sight of my boy standing in the middle of it all was my breaking point. His body was almost too still as he braced his rifle and body against the side of a small car.

He wore a mask and helmet, but I'd have known Chance anywhere. I could feel the intensity of his focus as he aimed. It was almost as if nothing existed for him. Not the danger. Not the wreckage of vehicles. It was just him and his rifle and a mission to complete. My heart was getting too much of a workout, and as

I was about to call someone—I didn't know who to contact—my desk phone rang.

Zero informed me that my baby was fine and that the sniper was taken down, but that didn't change the fact that I knew he put himself between the shooter and the rest of his fellow officers. Experience and what I knew about Chance, told me he had barely any caution when it came to his own personal safety. No matter how much I tried to instill in him my need for him to be safe, he was all instinct on the job.

"Where the hell is he?" I rumbled to break the silence. S.W.A.T. headquarters was pretty much a crime scene. The entire building was in lockdown until everything was cleared inside and out.

"He's finishing reports, and Dolan's going to bring him here."

"What do we know? What can you tell me?"

"Someone got a digital scan of his fingerprints while they prepped him for surgery. Gavin Savage. Twenty-year military veteran. Sniper. Intel is sketchy, but when you have hackers for friends, not everything is impossible to find out," Robert answered me.

"He got a dishonorable discharge a decade ago. Apparently, him and Chamberlain have similar hobbies. Several women in his unit and under his command lodged complaints of assault and inappropriate behavior. After some digging, he was a fan of Chamberlain's work."

"So, it's over?" I asked Remy.

"We're unsure. He's not talking, so we have no idea if this was a solo mission or if he got some orders from Chamberlain." Remy sipped his coffee.

"But why try to take out Chance?" I just didn't get the need to take out someone who didn't testify against you.

"We don't know. That's the issue. Because what if Chance just took out one threat, and there's another one waiting to take Savage's place?"

"Chamberlain is petitioning for his sentence to be overturned due to ineffective counsel. Maybe he's trying to get rid of witnesses," Marcel said from where he was seated at his desk. "Simon's digging into what's going on, but he has to be careful. Gladys and him have been doing some research on the case, looking for whatever loopholes Chamberlain's trying to slither through."

"He confessed. Took a plea deal. What did that have to do with his lawyers' fuckup?"

"We don't know his end game. While most of Chamberlain's survivors don't remember all the details, they remember enough to identify him. Chance remembers everything and would be a powerful witness. All it takes is one sleazy defense attorney to find one piece of evidence for reasonable doubt." Stevenson rubbed his hand over his hair and cuddled Doc on his lap. "All of us agree that it's highly unlikely, but the justice system isn't always balanced."

"Have any of the other survivors gotten threats?" I asked.

"We've worked through the list of known victims over the last few weeks. No one reported anything strange. But—" Remy paused, and I saw him grimace, and then Robert was rubbing his back.

"What? Just say it. I can't get any more stressed than I already am."

"Chamberlain never made a mistake. He had the process down perfectly. Any forensics were degraded by countermeasures or complicated by the locations, hundreds... thousands of samples to process per case. Something was different about Chance. While Chamberlain was violent and brutal in his execution, he was always aware of what he left behind. At first, we assumed it was his connection to Boss and Dolan."

"But you don't think that's it anymore?"

"Don't take this the wrong way, but as excellent as Chance is at his job, he was a well-cultivated target. But, and this is where we're lost, Chamberlain focuses on perfection. Symmetry. Innocence. While Chance is perfect and aligns with our theories on why Chamberlain chose the victims he did, there's nothing innocent about Chance, and almost two decades older than his usual targets. When we looked closer, Chance was stalked for at least several weeks. Any and all activity on his phone and computer were monitored. There's some shit we kept from Chance." Remy glanced around the room.

"What did you keep from him?"

"We thought it best for his healing," Marcel tried to explain, but the tone was pissing me off.

"That's not answering my question."

Remy sighed and seemed to deflate further. "Vega found an encrypted file on Chamberlain's computer. There were thousands of images. Chance coming out of clubs, some when he was in the clubs, there's images of him during sex acts at a local rough trade club. It's a file that can be used to discredit Chance."

"There's images of him…" My voice broke.

"He was grateful that there was no video of the attack. Him finding out there's photos of him as the recipient of several trains…Chance, well, he thought he was always on the down-low. No one knowing he was gay, and then there's Chamberlain, who could've exposed him. Also, an attorney could say that a consensual-nonconsensual encounter took place. Say that Chance had a rape fantasy and then called foul afterward."

I felt sick to my stomach. Disgusted by the bastard Chamberlain was and how far he was willing to go to destroy anyone he encountered. Chance had cultivated anonymity in order to feed his masochism and sex addiction. This would send him into a spiral. I didn't know if I had the power to bring him back from that.

"If he had this file, then why not use it at trial?"

"That's the unknown. It would be easy enough to bring that into question. For Chance's attack, he was charged with first-degree sexual assault, attempted murder, and assault with a deadly weapon. Experts testified that Chamberlain's injection would've killed Chance. The dosage was enough to start paralyzing his respiratory system within minutes."

I called Doc's name as I looked away from Remy. "What's your opinion?"

"Chamberlain is too controlled. I went over any medical files that were forwarded to me. He was exceptionally careful with how much sedative he used. He had it almost down to a perfect dose by weight. He wouldn't have made that mistake. He purposely tried to kill Chance."

"What was his damage?" I asked and fought the urge to take the question back.

"Chance was brought to the ER, after assessing his injuries, a rape kit was administered. During said examination, his rectum was found to require stitches inside and out. He was penetrated by the assailant's penis and by a foreign object, in this case, a dildo without prep or lubrication. And by the size of the dildo, I would've expected more damage." Doc swallowed hard and cleared his throat. "During further examination, he was found to be covered in bite marks that broke the skin in some places. He was beaten and tortured. The corners and inside of his mouth, along with his tongue, had cuts and tears from the metal device used to keep Chance from biting or screaming for help. He suffered chemical burns from being doused in bleach. After all that, Chamberlain manually strangled Chance until he lost consciousness. A few minutes longer, we would've found a corpse in that motel room."

I dropped my head to my chest and began to breathe deep and even as I felt the panic build. I fought the urge to vomit on the floor. Soft, small hands gripped my forearms.

"Hey, Bart, listen to me. Your boy survived something that should've killed him. He's a fighter and survivor no matter how much he doesn't believe so." Doc squeezed. "You have a badass boyfriend. He's safe. He's happy. He's healthy, and he adores you...trusts you with not only his body but his heart. Treasure that."

"I-I do, but how much more can he take?"

"He'll take as much as he needs to and beyond that. That's where your care comes into play. That's what a good Sir does."

"Bart, we do have an issue?" Remy spoke.

"What issue? The shooter was found and hopefully says Chamberlain hired him."

"Claxton went to the scene. Yes, Savage is a helluva sniper. One of the best, according to his military records, but he's also impulsive. He planted explosives on vehicles outside a S.W.A.T. headquarters. Called in a bomb threat. And decided to take out Chance in the ensuing chaos. He didn't assume Chance was better."

"Better?"

Marcel stood and shoved his hands in his pockets, and Remy made a go-head motion. "Chance is one of the top-rated snipers in the country. He was highly decorated when he left the military. His records are sealed, and when anyone asked, we got the *we're not at liberty to discuss* spiel. Through a single scope and experience, he spotted Savage's position, and if you watched the news, he went deadly calm."

"Marcel, what are you saying?"

"I'm saying that with a few questions for the right people, sealed records don't mean shit when it comes to people who can't keep their mouths shut. We're worried there's a team...one to handle any contingencies about taking out a target like Chance. Savage didn't appear to have an exit plan. The other two attempts, there was no trace of the sniper or snipers. Remy profiled Savage. He's impulsive. He's a psychopath with no moral compass. He's indiscriminate when it comes to targets. Zero's access to his military and psych evals shows that he was a ticking timebomb."

"And you think Chamberlain has hired an entire merc team to take Chance out?" This was getting more insane by the minute. As Chance had said, there was no logic to a hit on him, and I'd started to agree.

"We don't know, and what we don't know is opening up way more questions than we have answers to. We're trying to find a list of known associates. People who've worked with Savage in the past. Vega has pushed her contact to work quicker on the letters and emails to see if there's a pattern that matches Savage's, but we can only go so fast with our very limited information. But we've also discovered that in the past six months, Chamberlain has been having a steady stream of lawyers visiting him, not the ones who are listed as his official counsel. We're running background checks on all his visitors, but again, we need time."

"Remy, he might not have more time if your assumptions are right."

"Bart, we know that, but as frustrating as it is for you, it's more so for us. Chance is our friend…a member of our family, and that means we're personally involved. We're getting pushback from the higher-ups because they believe we're too close to the case and can't be objective. A lot of our work has been off the books." Robert called my name until I looked at him. "We're not much for rules, man. We know where to bend them just enough so they don't break, but we're getting stonewalled when it comes to official channels. Vega and Zero are taking a lot of risks, and we're waiting for all our luck to run out."

"Then what the hell are we supposed to do?" I demanded as I thought about Chance continuing to be in danger. More time to look over his shoulder with no relief in sight. He was strong. He was healing, but there was only so much even the strongest person could take before they broke.

"We're waiting for Savage to get out of surgery, and then we'll go talk to him. Depending on how hard he pushes back at us, we'll come up with a better plan. Just give us more time." Marcel gave me a sad smile.

I didn't know if I had more patience in me. I wanted mine and Chance's life together to start. I wanted him safe. As much as it killed me to rely on Remy and everyone else to do their thing, I was tired of my boy being the target of who knew how many people.

Everyone's phone went off, and I knew it was a group text they all belonged to. "Chance and Dolan are on their way here," Remy said as he was the first to check his messages. "Bart, just keep doing what you're doing, and we'll work on everything from our end."

I nodded, and Doc gave my arms one more squeeze before he straightened and returned to Stevenson's lap. I collapsed back and scrubbed my hands over my face. I'd waited too long for Chance to lose him. I couldn't deal with that thought. Two decades of isolation and loneliness disappeared when a gorgeous yet battered blond walked into my kitchen. As selfish as it might make me, I couldn't fucking give that up.

27

CHANCE

COLD CASE
UNIT

Bart greeted me with a hug and a kiss and checked me over, but he maintained a strange silence as we headed back to his apartment. Once inside, he ordered me to take a shower, and I'd instantly gotten sick to my stomach. I'd been waiting for the moment that he became tired of my bullshit. Maybe what everyone viewed as my recklessness had finally pushed him over the edge. To be honest, most of the time, my job was routine. There was planning and execution, and there was training and recertifications.

The past year things had just been more chaotic. I wasn't ready for Bart to tell me to get lost, but I also didn't want to pull out a *Chance Special* and beg and offer to do whatever he wanted. I wanted my Sir, my Daddy, fuck, I just wanted Bart to keep me despite how much trouble I was. I could find another job, but I loved the one I had. But I loved Bart more. The revelation nearly made my legs collapse beneath me.

Everything I thought I loved always left, my mother's illness took her from me, but she still left. In my neediness, I tried to convince myself I loved Dolan, and that hadn't worked out either. I'd even had a few here and there that I thought could overlook the toxic person I used to be. The lengths I would go sexually to keep them prolonged their interest until they walked away, too.

When I figured I couldn't hide in the bathroom any longer, I exited with a towel around my hips and scrubbed my hand over my damp hair. I frowned to find all the lights off except for the bedroom one. There was always a nightlight or at least a dimmed lamp on as Bart didn't always like shadows when he was stressed. If anything, that day would've made him feel on edge.

I cautiously peeked around the doorframe into his room. My brain was no longer calling it our bedroom, and I was falling back into the trap of distancing myself before the final hit came where he told me I needed to go. Bart stood at the foot of the bed with his back to me. He'd changed into pajama bottoms.

His dark skin shown under the overhead light. I was going to miss the feel of him. The softness of his belly and the springy tease of his body hair. He was everything I hadn't thought I'd wanted or deserved. Bart gave so freely, and I hadn't been able to hold onto it as long as I'd craved. I flinched as he bent his arms and wrapped his hands around the back of his neck, massaging the muscles.

"What was the rule about your silence, boy?" he asked without turning around.

"That you wouldn't compromise on me being quiet, Sir." I stayed frozen in the doorway until he turned and dropped his arms to his sides.

"Chance—" I shook my head because I didn't want to hear it.

"I'll get dressed and leave. I'm sorry I was so much trouble. Thank you for—" I was already headed to where I'd dropped my bag, and Bart's rough hand grabbed my upper arm. He spun me around, and I involuntarily raised my hands to deflect blows.

"Fuck, baby, don't do that." I was shocked when his voice broke, and his devastation was clear in his expression at my move to protect myself from him.

I opened my mouth to apologize, and if I'd expected rough,

almost violent, something punishing, he gave me the opposite. His mouth gently came down on mine. His tongue teased the seam of my lips until I opened for him. I was too scared to touch him. I fisted my hands behind my back.

He eased the kiss but didn't pull away. "Touch me, Chance, please."

My fingers slowly uncurled, and I shook with fear and confusion as I hugged his waist. The only thing keeping my body from responding was my brain misfiring and telling me this was Bart saying goodbye. He was too good to be cruel when he sent me away.

"You're giving this old man's heart a workout lately," he whispered between kisses as he pulled the knot from my towel, and it fell around my feet. "Sir and Daddy need a break."

"Okay, I'll sleep on the couch if you..." He grabbed my hips and jerked me to him.

"I didn't say I didn't need you. I just said your Sir and Daddy need a break. There's something I need to tell you, and it's just between Bart and Chance."

"Are you breaking up with me?" I asked and frowned as I felt his smile against my mouth.

"I didn't wait twenty years for you just to give you up. But Sir is reserving the right to punish you tomorrow." He nipped and sucked at my bottom lip. "I was thinking."

"Yeah?" I asked as I lifted onto my toes. I brushed my mouth against his and shivered as his hands spread across my lower back and then moved lower to cup my ass cheeks.

"We're due for a real date. What about Friday night? There's a club—" He let out a heavy sigh when I tensed. "Not that kinda club. I've been a pacifist for twenty years, but the thought of anyone else touching or assuming they can have you makes me extremely enraged. No, a friend has a blues club, nice and quiet, we can have dinner before and then I can dance with you. I've been thinking about that."

"You're not leaving me?" My voice shook as I spoke.

"I'm not like the others, baby. You were honest about your past. You may think you're not worth the effort, but I'm going to teach you to demand everything you deserve, especially from me."

I nodded my head and lowered my chin, then I glanced up at him from under my lashes. "What do you have planned?"

"What do I have planned for tonight?" he asked as he brought his left hand to my cheek and traced the curve of my lower lip with his thumb.

"Yes."

"I thought we could find a movie to watch," he whispered as he teased my lips with his. "Maybe have a good old-fashioned make-out session before we go to bed."

Fear and insecurity fled, and my cock firmed and ached. For too long, I'd experienced shame for my need. That sex was nothing more than degradation, something that disgusted me the next day because of the things I allowed men to do to me.

"Baby, what's going on in that head of yours?" He used his thumb under my chin to tilt my head back so he could see my face.

"I never thought I'd be with a man like this and not be sickened by myself." He tightened his hold on me as I stepped back, there was something I'd been keeping from him, and I wanted to confess. "Remember when I said my happiest memories were the deepest?" I asked as I took his hand in mine and stroked his fingertips over the thickest scars.

"What made you happy?"

"You," I whispered, and he jerked his head up from where he was staring at my scars.

"Baby." The endearment was nothing more than a sigh as he brought his hands to my belly and almost lovingly traced the self-inflicted imperfections. "There are so many. Tell me."

I pointed to one over my heart. "This one was the first time I imagined you kissing me." And I moved to the next one. "The first time I dreamed of us in bed." I went through the list and listed all the silly things I'd punished myself for when it came to him.

The minute he dropped to his knees in front of me, his lips touching each tangible memory. "Why, love?" The break in his voice threatened to bring back my insecurity.

"I didn't think I deserved you. I was terrified you'd see it and would treat me differently." I gasped as he sucked at my skin, licking away the sting. "Bart," I whined as he nuzzled my thick bush and brushed kisses along my length until he drew the head of my cock between his lips. "Fuck." I gripped his hair in my hands and ordered myself to keep my hips still.

I locked my knees as my thighs shook at the wet heat and the gentle suction as he bobbed along my length. The soft drag of his calloused fingers and palm up my belly, my chest, and then he wrapped it loosely around the front of my throat. A shuddered moan escaped me as he teasingly dragged his teeth on my sensitive dick.

I dropped my chin to my chest as he traced my lips with his fingertips, and I opened, prepared to gag, but I sucked his middle and index fingers in. He pushed down on the back of my tongue, and my cock jerked. Before Bart, I'd never truly enjoyed what was done to me. I endured it. Focused on the other men's pleasure, and while I got off, I was never truly satisfied.

"Fuck, Daddy," I cursed as he slipped his fingers from my mouth and released my dick, and before he was fully on his feet, I dropped my mouth to his. His deep, dark chuckle was nothing more than a rumble as I shoved his pants down his hips.

"I love when you call me that, almost as much as when you say Sir." He grabbed my face in his big hands and started backing up, and then he spun us until he could lower me to sit on the bed.

Without him having to ask, I scooted backward until I spread out in the middle of our bed. He was so gorgeous and good, and he was all mine. I wrapped my hand around the base of my cock and stroked as I took in the warm, dark tone of his skin, the curve of his belly and lower to his heavy cock and balls. My body restlessly moved on the bed as I focused on my man while he stripped away his pants.

"I'm going to love you so good, baby," he growled as he opened the nightstand on his side of the bed and grabbed the condoms and lube. He threw the items down beside me and then crawled onto the mattress, stretching out between my widespread legs.

"I like when you love on me, Bart," I whispered as I lifted my head to reach his lips. "You're perfect." I sucked at his bottom lip.

I lost myself in all the kisses. They became my most favorite thing, and then the touches. My heart beat an almost terrifying rhythm. I twisted and writhed beneath his bulk, and our bodies turned slick with sweat. I hooked my calves around the back of his thick thighs and rutted my dick against his. Every move felt natural as we loved on each other with lips and hands, and my short nails digging into his back. As always, he groaned at the bite of pain.

He shoved his left hand beneath me to grab my ass cheek, and I arched as he thrust against me. His right hand fisted in my hair as he held his mouth suspended above mine.

"Look at me, baby," he ordered, and I forced my eyes open.

His eyelids were heavy, and his eyes were glassy. His perfect lips were swollen from our kisses. I kept my gaze locked with his as he rolled his hips and his balls rubbed against mine. I wanted him forever. I craved the safety and happiness he instilled in me so easily.

"I'm gonna get you ready." I could only answer with a nod. Against my will, I reached for him in a panic as he pushed up and off me. "Chance, I'm not going anywhere. I just have to stretch you. You should never feel pain when I love on you."

My chest worked with every labored breath. He went through the motions of rolling on a condom and then adding slick to his fingers. I held my breath at the first cool press of his fingertips. My arms shot upward, and I fisted the pillow under my head.

Pressure and a slight burn as just the tips popped inside, he twisted them, rubbing the lube just inside my asshole. For a year, I'd believed I'd never feel that again. That I'd never feel safe enough to let a man inside me, even just to prep me.

"You should see how good you look wrapped around my fingers."

I squeaked as he added more lube and pushed deeper, only to retreat and repeat the motions until I swiveled my hips to ride them. Fucking myself and uncaring that Bart would see my neediness. He valued it and me, praising me when I demanded pleasure from him. He made me enjoy my body again—a celebration and not the lead-up to the morning after self-loathing.

I was vocal, moaning and whining, calling his name, and through it all, I stared at him. He made me his full focus. Bart didn't calculate how long until he could get off. My ecstasy was his.

"I could get off just watching my sexy man take Daddy's fingers like a good boy." I whimpered as he almost pulled all the way out and then shouted as he slammed them back inside, the force pushing my ass farther off the bed. He leaned over me and brushed his small smile to my mouth. "When you're thinking clearer, I wanna have a serious talk about no more condoms." My cock jerked, and my knees squeezed his sides. "I think my baby likes the sound of that."

There was no way I could respond. Even with PrEP, I'd never gone without a condom, not even with my ex-husband. The only time was...I forced the thoughts away. He no longer belonged in my head. I pouted as the fullness of his fingers disappeared but was quickly replaced with the head of his thick cock. My thighs shook, and as he sunk all the way to the base, I let out a sigh.

"I'm so humbled you allow me inside you...it's like fucking coming home."

He started an easy, deep rhythm. The tenderness—and I knew it was only in my head, but love in the way he took me—made tears burn my eyes. We came together perfectly, as if we'd been doing that our entire lives and not just months.

"I'm never letting you go." He groaned between each word, punctuating them with a slow thrust of his hips.

I wanted to believe him. I needed what we had to last. Even when he fucked me, I knew he valued me and that I wasn't just a body to use. He pushed up on his hands and hovered over me as he loved on my hole. I gripped the backs of his biceps as he increased his pace, rocking me and the bed with his thrusts until nothing else existed but the overwhelming pleasure.

The wetness of precum spread across my lower belly, and each slam of his hips caused my cock to jerk and leak more. I drew my legs upward, pushed my heels into his ass, and I held my breath when he stroked over my prostate. The pressure built in my face. My chest ached as I looked down between our bodies to see the curve of his belly and, below that, his latex-covered cock appearing and disappearing.

I pushed my left hand between us and placed my index and middle finger on either side of my hole, feeling how much he split me open. Squeezing my fingers together caused him to groan, and his pace stuttered. I panicked as if I did something wrong until he jerked from me, manhandled me onto my hands and knees.

Just as I was about to beg him to fuck me, he pushed back inside, spread his hands across my upper back, forced my head down, and then he used me in the best possible ways. Sweaty skin slapping together, then a groan-inducing grind. I submitted to him, just as I always had, but I did it with the certainty that he'd savor my submission and not use it against me.

I embarrassingly whined and grunted, begged and pleaded,

and then I felt the tightening of my balls. A shiver worked along my spine, and I prepared for the intense pleasure.

"Daddy, fuck me harder." He was always careful, but I wanted harder, rougher, nastier. I wanted the things I'd craved in my former life but wanted to wake in the morning savoring the reminders instead of scrubbing them away.

He blanketed my back and pressed his lips to my ear. "Be careful what you ask for, boy."

"I don't think I stuttered, Sir." I suddenly felt insecure when my challenge was met with a terrifying rumble, and his weight disappeared from my back. I opened my mouth to apologize, but nothing came out, not a sorry, not even a breath.

"You want Sir, you better not regret it tomorrow." His tone was dangerous, and I barely braced myself before he was fucking me. During sex, I got Bart or Daddy, but Sir was for scenes…for correction. "You want to be fucked? I'll make sure my boy doesn't sit right."

My back bowed upward, and I dragged the pillow under my chest, gripping it almost like a comfort item as he destroyed me. The sting of his smacks to my hips. He pounded into me, and I feared how much I loved it. Without warning, I shoved my face into the twisted covers and screamed as I shot onto the pillow.

"Goddamn, boy, that's…tight…hole…is…like…a… fucking…vice."

All I could do was brace as my release didn't seem as if it wanted to stop. The more brutally he rammed into my prostate, the harder my cock jerked with every spurt. The intensity of it made me fight him, clawing at the sheets to get higher on the bed. I sobbed, and tears wetted my cheeks, and then his lips brushed my temple.

"Easy, baby, it's okay." He shallowly fucked into me as he soothed me. "Ah shit, love." He buried his face against my neck as he shook and his hips jerked, and he whispered my name. I tensed as he rolled us to our sides, and he tightly hugged me to his heaving chest. "You're mine, Chance, only mine." He turned my head until he pressed his mouth to mine, and I opened so easily.

Time passed in gentle petting and tender kisses; loving words whispered as he brought me down. I whimpered as he slipped free, and I loathed the emptiness. I gripped his thick thigh, felt the coarse hairs, and rubbed my ass against him.

"Baby, give your old man a minute. I'm not as young as I used to be. My recovery time is embarrassing."

I snorted into our small kiss and loved the feel of his smile. I made Bart happy, and I always wanted to be the one to make him feel that way. That I'd always be just his.

28

BART

I'd laid in bed that morning watching Chance sleep and berated myself for not opening my damn mouth. It was three words. Yet they'd change everything. Was he ready to hear them? But I was also questioning myself. Why at that moment? Why Chance? I didn't have the answers.

I'd spent thirty-nine years as a straight man and twenty as a celibate or abstinent loner who wouldn't even shake hands. My boy had changed everything for me. He went from being unable to meet my gaze to coming out of his shell to show a bratty nature I found irresistible, and then I'd seen the scars. Everything in me wanted to take his pain away, but I hadn't realized how much that compulsion would change me.

The minute he told me that I was the cause of his deepest scars, something in me broke. My stomach tightened and a lump formed in my throat. He'd wanted me for a year, and I hadn't noticed. I'd always prided myself on figuring shit out. With Verna, I'd anticipated all her moods and needs, but with Chance, I hadn't noticed anything. If I'd opened my eyes and paid attention, would we have found our way sooner? Although, my intuition told me that my baby wasn't ready until recently. If the shooting hadn't happened, would we have ever moved passed tentative friends? One thing I hated more than anything was questioning myself and the sudden uncertainty of who I was.

I threw aside the inventory checklist, removed my reading glasses, and then scrubbed my hands over my face.

"Bad time?" Remy's voice made me open my eyes to find him leaning against the doorframe. The big, husky man was so different from the first time I'd met him. He'd been scarily underweight and always covered in bruises or holding himself stiffly to ease some hidden injury. He'd survived hell, and like with all the kids, I was as proud of him as if he were one of my own.

"No, what's up?" I asked, and a knot formed in my belly as he stepped inside. He closed the door behind him, and as I reached for my phone, his chuckle stopped me.

"Your boy is fine as far as I know. I just wanted a private word with you about him."

I narrowed my gaze with suspicion, and he rolled his eyes at me. "You here to question my motives?"

"No. I wanted to see how you're doing with him."

"Why?" Remy lowered into the single chair in front of my desk, and he appeared to be trying to find the right words. "I've known most of you since y'all were punk kids coming in for your condoms before a busy night on your corners. Just say it."

"I always loved your bluntness. You'd never bullshit us."

"Y'all were way older than your years, so I didn't see a reason."

"Chance is…" He sighed. "I see a lot of myself in him. Working closely with him and him becoming part of our family, well, I know how I worried about Robert dealing with me at first. You've been reclusive for all the years I've known you. I wanted to offer my wisdom of being a damaged, former self-hating person in perpetual recovery."

"Robert loves you. He always went above and beyond because he knew you were worth it. Chance is worth it. I'm not trying to pay for sins by being his Sir, and I—" He raised his hand to cut me off.

"I didn't ask if you were looking to pay for sins. All I'm saying is that being with someone like Chance isn't the easiest thing. A year isn't enough time. I'm still dealing with my trauma almost thirty years later. Love doesn't fix the damage. It just makes the scars a little less ugly."

I cleared my throat and leaned back in my desk chair, listening to it creak, and took my turn gathering my thoughts. "He makes me happy, Remy."

He smiled. "Anyone who sees you around him knows that. But even Dominants need to take a breather or get advice. I thought we'd broken you of that toxic masculinity."

I didn't bother saying anything about his last comment. "I've been here twenty years. I've always been able to separate here from my apartment. Boss brought me this boy who was beat all the hell. I could see he was dying inside. The Outreach sets you up with knowledge most people don't want to have. One night... he was late getting to the kitchen about a month after he started volunteering, so I walked out front and saw which group he came out of, eating disorder, and then as the weeks went by, I saw him exiting the sexual assault survivor group, sex addiction...before I even heard his story, I knew some of it."

"Did he tell you about the rape?"

I nodded. "He tells me everything. I never anticipated falling for him. All I wanted was him to self-harm as safely as possible. I offered to be his razor, but when the time came, I wanted to be his Sir instead. What Chamberlain did to him...I'm so fucking pissed, and my baby just accepted it as some punishment... someone seeing him as a victim and getting what he deserved. His trauma caused him to make unsafe choices." I felt my eyes burn.

The previous night came back to me and the way he'd reacted, automatically assumed that I was breaking it off with him. I knew I shouldn't have taken it personally. My baby didn't know any better, but that didn't mean it didn't hurt any less. Other than cheating or breaking my trust, I didn't see where he could do anything else that would drive me away. I knew his so-called *body count* bothered him, as if I'd look down on him for that. I didn't care about shit like that.

"He thought I was breaking up with him last night. I grabbed his arm as he tried to change and pack his bag. He covered his head to protect himself from me. *From me*, Remy." It had brought back memories of Verna flinching away from me after I'd attacked her in my sleep. That sick feeling in the pit of my stomach that another person I loved believed I'd hurt them.

"Fear isn't rational, Bart. Our brains make us react. Even when we want to die, our primitive survival instinct kicks in. That's what made him crawl naked from that motel room."

"He told me the happiest memories are the deepest scars on him." I didn't go into detail. While I probably needed advice, I wasn't ready to pour my soul out to Remy.

"It's a twisted behavioral exercise in a way. If we associate the good with pain, we can desensitize ourselves to the pleasure and the good in life. Since he didn't think he deserved to be happy, he tried to change what he compared it to. It's like you with the drinking after you left Verna."

"What drinking?"

He snorted at me. "Bart, we were in the same addiction group."

"I forgot about that. Verna and the girls were my everything, and I feel the same way about Chance. That kinda scares me, Remy."

"Why? Because he's the first man you've ever been attracted to?"

Did I want to lie? No. "Partly. But my brain is asking why Chance."

"Sometimes the gender of the person doesn't really matter.

There's just something about them that calls to you. I was in love with Robert for two years. He was my everything, but I knew he'd never see me the way I did him. He doesn't know why me, but he never questions his feelings for me."

"I don't question my feelings for Chance. But I just..." I scrubbed my hands over my beard. "He's healing, and I don't want to put pressure on him because I suddenly caught feelings, and I promised I'd let him go when he was ready." I'd told him repeatedly that I was going to keep him, but I was unsure if he believed me or not. When he asked me to keep him, that was enough for me.

"Like you're letting that pretty man go anywhere. I heard a story he grabbed Boss's arm when he went to touch you and claimed very clearly that you were his. Where would be the pressure in telling him? Because there's one thing you're forgetting." Remy paused, and the longer he was silent, the more irritated I became. He knew exactly what he'd done.

"Dr. Kaufmann, please share your great wisdom."

"Asshole." He sneered at me, and he looked almost cute. No wonder his Daddy loved him so much. "Chance is waiting for you to leave."

"What?"

"Think about it. He instantly assumed you found him to be too much trouble, right?" He didn't wait for me to answer. "He apologized, didn't he? He tried to give you a way out. But he also wanted to leave before you sent him away, Bart. Chance has a skewed perception of himself. For the first forty years of his life, he used his body as a tool. That's all it was. It was simply a vessel he employed to get him the attention and sex he needed to feel wanted. Desire became a trap. He wanted out, but he wanted the instant gratification that desire afforded him. I know him too well. My body made sure I was fed. Had a nice warm place to sleep. Bodies are viewed as commodities and are judged on how attractive those are."

"I made him stand in front of a mirror." He was going to get the PG version. "I asked him how he felt seeing himself. His answer was disgusted. That he wasn't worthy of love. Yes, as his Dominant, I have to be careful in the way I correct him. That he knows I don't want to hurt him, but that he earned his punishment by breaking our agreed-upon rules of conduct."

"I think he knows that, and your friends definitely do. You never take your eyes off him, not since you met him. If he's around, you lock onto him to make sure he's okay. Boss and I were just wondering when you'd notice."

"My crew wasn't just giving me shit."

"No, everyone who's known you knew your severe touch aversion, but you loved being in Chance's space when he was working with you. You touched him, maybe it was just a brush while moving through the kitchen, but none of us but you and Chance were clueless."

I closed my eyes and thought back on the previous year. Chance in my space became one of my favorite parts of the night. There were times I'd spread my hand across his lower back, barely a touch. Yet no one else had ever made me ignore my rule. I'd had so many opportunities to make the move to start dating again, but it had never felt right.

"He feels right."

"Explain."

I kept my eyes closed as I pictured my boy and the bratty behavior that had begun to come out not long after he started volunteering with me. There had been a few odd compulsions to brush his hair back. I'd started viewing him how I had Verna the first time. Slightly annoyed, but her playful Brat won me over, and it had happened twice. I'd never anticipated a second chance. A clearing throat pulled me from my thoughts, and I opened my eyes to find Remy smirking at me.

"Have you ever met someone who just feels right? You just want to get lost in their presence. It's a sense of happiness. You don't know where it came from, but it's there, and it makes all the pain…frustration…all the hardships you went through worth it to get you to that point."

"Then what are you so afraid of?"

"That's the question, right? And my answer is I don't fucking know."

"I don't think it's required. Fear is healthy, but don't let it ruin shit between you and Chance. You've been good for each other."

"Do you know where my boy is?" I asked.

"Nope, I think Claxton is on Chance duty today, or maybe Trey."

I snarled my nose without thinking about it, and Remy arched his brow. Trey was handsome and lean. Even with the scars, it just gave him a bit of an edge and kept him from being downright pretty. That didn't mean I hadn't studied Chance and Trey side by side and seen them as a way better fit than me and my boy.

"What's going on?" Remy asked.

"That young, handsome man is spending too much time with my boy, and they're living together."

"Don't even go there, man."

"He's gorgeous and younger. My kids are older than Trey is. Hell, Chance is the same age as my oldest."

"Are we having a mid-life crisis?"

"No, yes, fuck, maybe," I growled at Remy as he laughed at me. "It's not funny. I never had these issues before."

"Well, for what it's worth, Chance worships at your feet, and I don't believe he even thinks about your age. That's probably all in your head."

"I know." I pushed out a heavy breath. "I really do. But I've only done this one other time in my life. So don't blame me that my boy has me all fucked up. Also, you know what happened between Verna and me." I shut up because I didn't know how to explain that edge of fear that one unconscious action could destroy what I'd built so far with Chance.

"Bart, you have PTSD. That's not something that goes away. It's something you manage. When you had the incident with Verna, it hadn't even been two years since you retired. I'm not going to say that it won't happen, but I do believe Chance is well-equipped to deal with it."

"I don't want him to deal with it, Remy. I want him safe when he's in bed with me."

"Maybe start going to group again or sitting in on one of the partner groups."

"I'll think about it. My evenings are reserved for Chance. Which means I have to get this paperwork done. I was going to make him something special for dinner."

"Then I'll leave you to it. Roo has a therapy appointment, and I need to pick her up soon to get there." He pushed up from the chair, and I stayed seated.

"She doing okay?"

"Yeah, she's fine, but she has a lot of trauma to work through. And Robert and I think it's good for her to have someone to talk to that's not us, and Roo loves her art therapy. She's wanting to take classes, and she's developed an interest in sculpture. She's only eight, but she's pretty sure about what she wants to do when she's a grown-up."

"But you don't want your baby to grow up too fast."

He sighed, and that was the sound of a man who wasn't adjusting well to his baby growing up. I knew it well—I'd experienced it four times over. "It doesn't seem like it's been that long since she became ours."

"You and Robert were the perfect parents for her." He shyly whispered thanks, he'd never been the best person to accept compliments, and as I watched him walk out of my office, the years faded away.

I remembered a skinny and broken Remy, looking for anything to make him happy. As the years passed, the changes were slow, but the minute he'd met Robert, anyone could see how far he'd come. It was so odd how I'd adopted so many young people. How proud I was of them with every milestone. I'd made a good life for myself, and I wanted to make it better. I just had to show Chance what he meant to me.

Fucking up wasn't an option, but I had to figure out why I was so terrified of Chance's rejection. We were a pair. Yet he was perfect for me, and I was determined to confess and tell him exactly what I wanted our future to be.

29

CHANCE

COLD CASE
UNIT

The hospital loomed in front of me as I leaned back against the grille of my new SUV and stared at the building. I'd ditched my escorts, Trey and Claxton, but they needed some alone time anyway. I hadn't told Bart where I was going. I'd already resigned myself to my Sir's punishment, but I wanted to look at the fucker who tried to kill me. A little over a year had passed since my rape, and I was tired of living in fear.

Bart told me he wanted to keep me. Even said he'd take me on dates, but as always, in the back of my mind, I was waiting for the moment I became too much. I wanted to believe him, I did, but all the others had left before. I closed my eyes, tipped my face up to the sun, and took a few deep breaths.

"Not the best place for meditation." Cora's voice coming from my right made me open my eyes to find her smiling at me. "If this wasn't my place of employment, I wouldn't even come here." She neared and turned to lean back beside me.

"The guy who tried to kill me is inside, well, one of them."

"And you seem like such a nice guy, but you definitely live with a target on you. What do you expect to happen if you go inside? Answers?"

"I really don't know."

"Your Sir isn't going to be happy, but since Dad isn't here, it means you didn't tell him your plans."

"You calling your dad my Sir is a bit weird."

She laughed and shook her head. "Not to kids with parents who are open and honest. Our sex talks included the usual stuff but also in-depth conversations on consent and what can be better to explain consent than the safe, sane, and consensual power exchange. Also, Mom and Dad were always Sir and submissive, we didn't have a name for it, but we knew they were different after we spent time with the parents of our friends."

"I know you already saw my scars." She nodded but didn't speak. She was a lot like Bart. "I needed healthier coping mechanisms, and Bart...well, he offered to help as a friend."

"You two don't seem *friendly*. Dad's extremely possessive of you."

I glanced at her to see if she had a problem with Bart and me. His girls, including Verna, were important to Bart. He'd do anything for them, but if they didn't like me, would Bart move on? Just another thing for me to worry about—his kids didn't like me, and he broke up with me. She was just smiling, her hair hidden under a bright head scarf with perfectly smoothed and curled edges.

"Possessive?" I asked.

"Very. I knew he was interested when he introduced you at the Outreach at the beginning of summer. When he was near you, his mannerisms were the same as they were with Mom when I was little. It was the first time I saw my old dad in the way he smiled and carried himself. But do you know what sealed it for me?"

"No."

"When I walked into his office, he had his forehead pressed to yours. He hasn't initiated contact or shown affection to anyone other than family in decades. And when I realized he'd mentioned you countless times in the past year, I knew it was only a matter of time before he went all Sir and claimed you."

"I was drawn to him from the minute I met him, but I never dreamed he'd find me worth liking, even as a friend. I spent a lot of time embracing my self-destruction to the detriment of my overall health. As I got older, it just got worse. But after the rape, torture, and attempted murder, I spiraled worse. Boss thought I needed a distraction after it happened and took me to the kitchen. He introduced me to Bart. He was calm and so self-assured. He was my first crush, which is weird for a forty-year-old man, but I hid it because I liked the way being around him made me feel. Even in a busy kitchen, I enjoyed his nearness."

"Dad has that effect on people. We, mostly me, were mad at him for a long time for leaving. I'm the baby and spoiled. He was the rock, there was nothing he couldn't make right, but I learned a hard lesson that dads aren't superheroes."

"How did you get over that?" I knew he'd spoken to me about the years after he'd left because he wanted to protect Verna and the girls, but I knew he still had guilt for not being able to *man-up* and be okay.

"I saw him at the Outreach. I was in my early teens, and Mom took us there to see him. He wasn't ready for us to sleep over yet. The nightmares...night terrors were still bad. At the Outreach, we saw slivers of our old dad. I was still too young, but I knew something had changed, and we had a long talk. And I realized that he'd left so he could get better and be the Dad we needed. Tweens and teenagers are not the best at critical thinking."

"Some adults aren't either."

"So, is this a healthy curiosity or lack of critical thinking?"

"Maybe a mixture of both. I'm tired of feeling like a victim."

"You're not a victim." The certainty in her tone reminded me so much of Bart.

"Then what am I?"

"A survivor. When Dad called the night you came to the ER, I saw your file. The list of your injuries. Yes, you have some destructive coping mechanisms, but Dad assured me he was working on that when I asked since you were his."

"Why aren't you bothered by your straight dad seeing me?" I asked, but I was unsure if I wanted an answer.

"If he's with you, he's not altogether straight, but power exchange, even if it starts off as platonic, it breeds intimacy. You have to develop an unquestioning trust to submit your well-being to another person. That turned into something more. And you might not think so, but you're really good for Dad. It's like seeing the man I grew up with again. You became his everything...his purpose. Fight for it." I was unsure what to say. "Also, I want to make jokes at Dad's expense about his younger boyfriend and midlife crisis."

"Brat."

"My husband loves it. So, are we going to meet the guy who tried to kill you?"

"We?"

"Us Brats have to stick together. And as much as Dad won't agree with it, as long as you resign yourself to the fact that you're getting punished, I'll support you. Besides, Martin needs a fellow co-parent. He's overrun with girls."

I chuckled at her bratty expression and only tensed slightly went she wrapped her arm around mine and then leaned into my side.

"I also owe you. Sierra. I could've lost my baby, and I know a lot of people would've stepped in, but you did. You put yourself between her and danger, and I kinda love you for that one."

My chest expanded with a gasp at her saying she loved me. Less than a handful of people had loved me in my life. I felt a lump form in my throat, and she straightened and dragged me beside her.

"Besides, if he's in ICU, then you're going to need an escort. I'll distract everyone while you do your thing. Do you know what floor and room number?"

I nodded, and we made our way inside and up in the elevator. When we stepped out of the car, I uncovered my badge on my hip, and she swiped her ID to get into the locked unit. She released my arm and stepped in front of me to block me from the nurses' station.

There was a uniformed officer outside a room at the end, and I squared my shoulders. He stood up when he saw me, his body language telling me he was on high alert until he noticed my badge.

"I'm here to ask the suspect some questions."

"He's not supposed to have any visitors, but I'll give you ten minutes. The doctors are still keeping everyone out."

I nodded and told him thanks as he opened the door, and I stepped through. All hospitals smelled the same, sickness and antiseptic, bland meals. I paused as I noticed the foot of the bed and took deep, even breaths as I tried to pull the mask into place that I'd used for most of my life.

After I took the last few steps, I could see there was a thin man on the bed. Nothing special about him. His greasy hair was plastered to his head, and there was a faint scent of body odor as if no one had washed him since he'd come in. I leaned my shoulder against the wall and crossed my arms over my chest.

"You don't look like I expected, but probably that big gun of yours made you feel more like a man." I smirked as he jerked his head up and groaned. "Hurts, huh? Should've aimed better, though. Maybe I need more time at the range."

He was just a man, not the monster I'd assumed he'd be. Part of me thought when I saw him that fear would take over, but he looked like hundreds of other men I'd encountered.

"I might've not got ya, but I ain't the only one."

Something to look forward to, more targets on my back, just great. "Mysterious. Not as much fun when you're not behind a screen talking about your lord and savior, Chamberlain, and your target can hit you back. You're going to have a great life in prison, attack on a S.W.A.T. Unit, attempted murder of not just me but dozens of others. Maybe you can be a roomie for your bestie. I don't know if you're his type, but he's been locked up for a year. His standards could've gone down."

I softly chuckled as he snarled his nose. "I ain't no…"

"No, no, no, it's the twenty-first century, enlightenment, my friend. I'm sure as a *fan,* you watched his gay ones, too. Ashamed it got you off?" He cut me off when he jerked at the cuffs that kept him restrained. "Not a good feeling, huh? Being tied up and trapped. Anyone could do whatever they wanted to you. Don't like being on the other side? I read your file and all the complaints against you, a little boy playing at being a big man. Now you know how all those women felt being helpless."

"They wanted it, liars, every last one of them. Quick to get on their knees, even quicker to file a complaint when they got caught since they liked sucking me off so much. They got what they deserved."

The door opened behind me, and Cora walked in. She mouthed for me to get lost.

"Mr. Savage, how are you doing today?" She passed me reading his chart. "Seems your wounds are healing nicely, sir." She glanced at me. "Could you leave us alone for a few minutes while I check my patient?"

"Sure, doctor, not a problem. I was just leaving. I'll be seeing you around, Savage."

I backed up and out the door. I caught sight of a few detectives I recognized coming toward the room and took an alternative route to an opposite exit. The anxiety I'd expected at seeing him hadn't hit me. He was just a man—a pathetic one who had a false sense of importance when he was nothing more than a bully. My demon was Chamberlain. That was a ghost that wouldn't go away. No matter how many years passed, I'd never be free.

Once I made it to my vehicle, I got in and checked my phone.

Bart: *Boy, check in. You're late.*

Shit, I quickly typed out a message that I was on my way to the Outreach and that I'd be there soon. I wasn't looking forward to confessing what I did that late afternoon, but I knew the rules, and I'd broken them. I could just hope that he wouldn't be too mad at me.

30

BART

As soon as Chance entered my kitchen, I knew something was up. Before he opened his mouth, I sent him to my office with an order to close the door and stand in the corner until I came for him. I didn't know what he'd done, but in my gut, I knew I wasn't going to like it. I finished preparing for dinner service as I ignored all the looks from my crew as they kept darting their gazes from my office door and then back to me.

They wanted to ask, but they wouldn't. It wasn't as if Daddy or Sir hadn't slipped from Chance's mouth more than once when he visited or volunteered with me. I hadn't kept my relationship with Chance a secret, and I'd taken the jokes because I knew my crew couldn't resist.

"Carlos, you're in charge. I have something I have to take care of," I said as I removed my gloves and then washed my hands.

"I'm on it, boss man." He went into organizing mode as he began ordering everyone to take the trays out to the steam tables in the cafeteria.

I tried to prepare myself for what my boy had to tell me. I paused at my office door for a few minutes and then opened it, stepping inside. Chance wasn't in sight, but I found him in the corner that was blocked by the door. No one would've seen him unless they entered. He was standing there with his nose in the corner and his hands behind his back.

Corner time wasn't Chance's favorite thing because it made him think too much. He couldn't distract himself with other things. That's why I did it. He had to decide how he wanted to approach me and tell me he deserved his correction.

I closed the door, making him flinch, and my heart broke. He still feared me, I knew he was instinctual, and it would take time, but outside punishment, I'd never touched him with the intent to hurt him. Even when I caused him pain, he understood I didn't like it, but it was for his own good.

"Chance, turn around but stay there," I ordered as I sat on the edge of my desk.

"Sorry, Sir."

"What are you sorry about? This is more than being late with your check-in."

"I went to the hospital."

I surged to my feet, and he cowered. "Baby, have I ever touched you in anger?"

"No, Sir." I barely heard him answer me.

"Why did you go to the hospital?" I knew why he went. He wanted a look at the man who tried to kill him, but again I'd have gone with him, but he wanted to do it on his own. He was my boy...my baby, but he was a grown man, and I understood, but I couldn't allow him to break our rules, ones he'd agreed to.

"I just wanted to see him...to understand why."

He fidgeted and wrung his hands together. I knew what he wanted. He wanted to touch me, but I didn't allow him close because if I could pull him to me, our talk would be over.

"Did you get what you needed? Was it worth defying me over?"

He jerked his gaze upward but kept his chin lowered, and I

could see him peeking at me from under his lashes. His plump bottom lip quivered as he fought tears.

"I don't like when you're mad at me."

"Baby, I'm not mad at you. I'm disappointed in you keeping secrets from me. This was the one I wouldn't compromise on. What should your punishment be?"

"Sir, but I already stood in the corner for an hour."

"That was for you to think about your actions and how you'd tell me what you did. Your real punishment happens when we get home."

"But, Sir…" He pouted out his lip more and batted his lashes at me.

"Brat, get your ass over here." I opened my arms, and he was instantly in them, wrapping his around my waist and tucking his face into my neck. My baby's favorite spot. I hugged him to me and gave him a squeeze as I lowered my head to kiss his shoulder. I grinned as he cuddled into me more and brought his hands around to the sides of my belly. "How did you even get in? I heard it was a locked ward until he was moved out."

"Cora snuck me in."

I groaned as he giggled. Just what I needed, Verna, my daughters, and my baby all ganging up against me. Brats formed a really tight unit, and they were scary in packs.

"Of course she did. I don't know how my son-in-law puts up with her. Cora is like Brat concentrated."

He leaned back, and I looked at his beautiful face. I brought my hands up to cup his jaw. I still wondered what the handsome, younger man saw in me, but I wasn't going to question it too much. Letting him go wasn't an option for me. I lowered my head until I could brush my lips to his. We shared a few soft kisses, and I hated I had a few more hours until I could be alone with him.

"Can I trust you to go home and behave until I get there?"

"Daddy, don't say that."

I arched a brow, and he rolled his eyes. "You have to stop looking so cute when I'm supposed to be irritated with you."

"But, Daddy, do you know how many times I imagined you and me and this office?"

"Do tell, baby."

He hummed and slid his hands under my shirt. "Well, there was that time I messed up that casserole you wanted me to make, and you were mad at me, and I thought about you ordering me to your office to *talk* to me. You spanked me and made me suck you off." He nudged my chin with his nose until I tilted my head back. "You're the perfect size to choke me just right, Daddy."

My cock firmed, and I willed myself to keep control. Lube and condoms weren't far away, but I wasn't going to fuck him in my office with all my crew knowing he was in there with me. Not that they weren't already speculating.

"Baby." I gripped his hair in my left hand as he sucked at the side of my neck.

"You know ya wanna, Daddy." I tensed as he rubbed my hard-on through the fabric of my jeans and gave me a nice, firm squeeze.

I winched his head back and slammed my mouth down on his, my tongue pushing passed his soft lips. I grabbed his hips and lifted him as I spun us to place him on my desk. Wedging myself between his muscled thighs. My brain kept yelling *mine* and to tell him I loved him, but the words wouldn't come. I wanted the perfect moment. Not when we were being intimate or when everything was high stress, but I wanted him to know he was it for me. No one else would do.

A chuckle slipped free as he started to work on my belt. "No, baby, no office sex, especially when everyone knows we're in here." He whined. "With that said, none right now, but I reserve the right to bend you over my desk in the near future."

He paused for a few minutes holding eye contact and smirked. "It's the near future. Can we do it now?"

"Brat," I growled.

"I like when you call me that. Do I still make you happy, Bart?"

"Very happy, baby." I brushed his hair back from his forehead. "You and my girls are the best things to ever happen to me."

"Really? I rank with the girls and Verna?"

I frowned and saw the insecurity in his pretty eyes. "Of course." I stroked his scruffy jaw with my thumb and couldn't believe how much just being allowed to touch him was enough.

"I like belonging to you," he whispered and tried to lower his head to hide from me.

"Only mine, remember that. I don't share. Every inch of you is just for me. Do you understand me?"

"Yes, Bart. Are you sure we aren't going to have office sex?"

"Very sure. If you take your punishment later, I'll reward you."

"Fine, I'll be good...for now."

We jumped as several people started banging on the door, and then it flew open. I rolled my eyes to find my entire crew squeezing into the doorway with Boss and Dolan behind them. Chance turned to lean back against my chest, and I grabbed my right wrist in my left hand to hold him until I had to let him go. I hadn't missed physical contact with someone. Well, maybe I just hadn't noticed until Chance. Any other touch had always made my skin crawl.

"Dammit, we thought we'd find something interesting." Alexa waggled her brows.

Chance chuckled, and I grumbled at her. "The door would've been locked. My eyes only. Why the hell aren't you working?"

"Because we're nosy. Dolan and I were informed Chance was visiting." Boss winked at me.

"He came by to say hi, and he's going to go home and wait for me after I feed him."

"You're so cute with the boyfriend." Carlos pretended to wipe away a tear. "It's like you're all grown up now."

"Ha, ha, ha, y'all are so hilarious. Now get back to work."

They all waved, but Boss and Dolan only stepped out of the way before entering. I checked to see if there was something I had to worry about, but all they did was smile as they looked at us. I loved that he didn't rush to get away from me. Chance was still dealing with coming to grips with being outed against his will, but he was doing better. He'd changed so much since I'd met him and a lot since our arrangement turned into a relationship.

I turned my head to press my lips to his ear. "I'm so proud of you, baby." He hugged my arms to his stomach as he nodded to acknowledge what I said.

"We were actually wondering if you wanted to have dinner tomorrow night. Vega invited all the kids to her place to give everyone a child-free night."

"We'd love to, but I already planned us a date. It's past time for our first official one. Carlos is going to take over dinner service, and I'll handle the breakfast chaos."

"Then another time. Chance, are you coming to group tonight?" Boss asked.

"Yeah, and, Boss, I wanted to talk to you about something really quick."

I reluctantly released Chance as he and Boss left, but not before I got a quick kiss. That left Dolan and me alone. We'd gotten over a bit of the issues between us, but I still hadn't relaxed.

"Do you know what my boy is probably conspiring about?" I asked.

Dolan chuckled and shook his head. "When it comes to Chance, I wouldn't put anything by him. How's he doing?"

"He's great." I kept the fact he went to the hospital to myself. "We're still working on a few things, but he seems more relaxed."

"Relaxed? Man, you turned my ex-husband into a cuddler, and I never thought that would happen."

"Does that bother you?"

As he shook his head, he let out a gruff laugh. "No, we were never going to work, but it kinda became a habit rather than a relationship. The Chance you have is not the Chance of a year ago, but it's a good change. Okay, I promised the kids a night of movies and junk food with Pop while their dad sits in on his groups."

"Have fun. And, Dolan, thanks."

"You're welcome. Just keep taking good care of him."

Finally, I was alone, and I crossed my arms over my chest. I was hoping tonight was the right time. I'd planned the perfect date for him, bought him something to wear, and I was going to show him how important he was to me. It hurt that he still wasn't confident with me. It was in the way he'd been shocked I'd considered him one of the best things that had happened to me.

I left my office to finish work while he did his group. Then we'd have dinner before I'd take him home, and the rest of the night would be just us. I loved having my baby all to myself, and that intensity scared me a bit. Twenty years of apathy when it came to romance and relationships made the quick shift odd, but I refused to fuck things up with Chance. I'd waited way too long to find and claim him.

31

CHANCE

COLD CASE
UNIT

"**I** *want to give Bart a blowjob.*"
Those words had slipped free as soon as I had Boss alone. And Boss being Boss, he hadn't missed a step. To some, not being able to give oral wasn't a huge deal, but I'd always enjoyed it. Bart said it wasn't a dealbreaker, and I believed him. Yet I wanted to do that for myself. We'd had sex, and I trusted him enough for that, but I flashed back to that night any time I thought about it.

"*Is this for you or for Bart? Because knowing him, he's not going to make you do something you don't like or causes you distress.*"

"*For me. He said it doesn't matter to him, but for me, it's another thing Chamberlain took. It was one of the few things I enjoyed about sex. But the one time I tried, as soon as Bart touched my lips, I gagged. I've sucked his fingers, and it wasn't a problem.*"

"*Chance, honey, trauma responses aren't always logical. I had a gun shoved into my mouth and down my throat, never had an issue with oral, but I didn't want to bend over for anyone. Remy couldn't bottom or give his back to anyone. Sucking your partner off is an issue for you.*"

"*I know, but we've had sex.*"

"*I'm well aware. You're not a quiet one.*" Boss snorted as I rolled my eyes at him.

"I trusted Bart enough for that, then why can't I do the other thing?"

"Our fears don't care about what we want to do. Okay." He dragged me into his office and closed the door.

I fell into the chair he motioned to and waited for a lecture. Boss loved his lectures. He only ever did them out of love. I knew that, yet I wanted to know how to get over my fear.

"I'm going to give you some advice. Next time you and Bart are intimate, don't think about sucking him off. When you're kissing and touching him, maybe play in the general area. Ease into sucking him. A considerate lover won't push. There's more to blowing someone. Just forget about the dick."

"Um, my Daddy has one you can't forget." I laughed as he groaned and threw his head back.

"Bart is one of my oldest friends, and I don't need to know about his dick."

"Shame, he's extremely brag-worthy."

"Chance," he yelled my name, and I gave him my most innocent expression. "Back to what we were talking about."

"Me sucking Bart's dick."

"I question my life choices."

"Fine, fine, I'll be good."

"Play with his nuts...his ass, work your way up to licking his cock, back off when it gets too uncomfortable for you, and go back to teasing him. Have you ever topped before?" My shock gave me away. "Okay, okay, don't freak out."

"Dolan asked me once, and I couldn't."

"Honey, what's your aversion to topping?"

I shrugged my shoulders. "I don't know, I just never saw myself in that position. When I was younger, my stepdad tried to cure me by forcing me to have sex with women..." I looked away.

"Honey, look at me." He touched my cheek until I turned my attention back to him. "Sex has always been made into an unenjoyable experience. I'm sorry for that. You don't have to top, if it's something you don't like, but it's your body. And you have this fucked up relationship with it. If it comes down to wanting to give Bart oral, then you'll find a way, and if it's an act that's always tainted for you, there's no shame in that. He'll adore you no matter what."

I could only hope that was true. After our talk, I went to my group, and I even talked about my new relationship, but I didn't name names. From some of the smiles on the faces of the regulars to the Outreach told me they knew who I was talking about. Then after dinner, we'd gone home. When I'd asked about my punishment, he told me my corner time was enough, and he'd cuddled me the rest of the night.

Although, my conversation kept circling in my mind all day and up until I'd arrived at Bart's place for him to get me ready for our date. I'd asked all day what we were doing, and he'd just tell me to be patient. That's how I ended up standing in front of the full-length mirror naked as I waited for him as ordered.

My gaze was locked on my reflection. I didn't view myself as a thing as often. I was more than the slight softness of my belly, the little love handles. I stroked my scars, paying close attention to the thicker ones. Almost everything I'd punished myself for envisioning doing with Bart were replaced with actual memories. I might not love the scars, but I wasn't as disgusted by them.

"Hey, baby, you ready to get dressed?" Bart asked, and I smiled as I caught sight of his husky, naked body in the mirror.

"Yes, Sir." When I went to turn around and go to him, he shook his head and told me to stay.

He pulled two garment bags from the closet, draped them over the bed, and I frowned as he removed something from the top drawer of his dresser. I didn't relax until I felt the warmth of him against my back—his belly conforming to the curve of my lower back.

"You're so beautiful." A shy smile curved the corners of my mouth as he stroked his curled fingers down my cheek, the side of my neck, and spread over the center of my chest. "How did I get so lucky?" he asked as he brushed a kiss to my cheek but never broke the eye contact we held in the mirror.

I didn't care how innocent the touch was, Bart always made my pulse pick up. "You really think you're lucky, Sir?"

"I would never tell you a lie. A real man knows how his baby needs to be treated..." I arched as he stroked his hand lower over my stomach. "How their baby needs to be touched and loved. Do you trust me, boy?"

"Always," I whispered without hesitation, and I gasped as he cupped my cock and balls in his hand.

He chuckled as I pouted when he released my dick and circled around to stand in front of me, then he lowered to his knees. That's when I saw what he had in his hand. A cock cage.

"Sir," I whined, but he shook his head.

"You'll wear this for me the rest of the night until we get home."

I was about to protest again, but it was cut off by a deep groan as he wrapped his lips around the head of my cock, sucking me to the back of his throat. I curled my hand around the back of his head, the wet heat disappeared, and I hissed as cool metal enclosed my dick.

"You're so pretty when I keep you on the edge. No Sir could have a better submissive than I do."

I shivered as it was locked into place, and he rolled my balls in his big hand and licked between the metal bars to my dick.

"But, Sir, I was good all day." The weight of the cage felt odd. No one had ever used a chastity device on me before. Another first I experienced with Bart, and every time it got better. Each kiss, touch, hug, and moments of intimacy—they broke down the walls I kept in place to protect myself. Not having to brace myself for unwanted pain was the hardest lesson I'd had to learn.

"And you're going to be a good boy for me the rest of the evening." He kissed my belly. "Now, I have to get you dressed."

It was like cruel foreplay. He dressed me in silky pink briefs, adjusting me with agonizing slowness. Next was a gorgeous charcoal suit with a pink dress shirt. High-polished dress shoes. No tie. He stroked his fingers across the front of my throat. There was something sexy about being completely dressed while my Sir tended to me naked. I trembled as he wrapped his hand around my throat.

"One day you're going to wear my collar, everyone is going to know you're taken….that your Sir values you above all others." He pinched my earlobe between his teeth.

My knees nearly gave out at him telling me I'd wear his collar. "Can we stay home, Sir?" I asked, but I'd beg if he wanted me to. I rubbed my ass against him as the cage painfully pinched my cock.

"No, boy, you're getting your first date," he rumbled as I reached back to grab his thighs. "I want to show my baby off."

I whimpered as he abandoned me and stepped back. I looked at myself. My cheeks were flushed as I tried to catch my breath, and I spun away to watch him get dressed. Such a shame to cover how handsome my Sir was. I was torn between wanting to experience a date where I was out and with a man who was proud I was his and begging him to just stay in so I could have him to myself.

"Damn," I whispered under my breath as I saw him wearing a perfectly tailored black suit with a crisp white dress shirt, and he was putting on his watch.

He glanced at me and winked. "Do I pass inspection, baby?"

"I don't know if I want other people looking at you."

"You're good for my old ego. Let's go. We have reservations for dinner. And it's past your dinner time."

The night that followed was perfect and romantic, something I'd sworn I'd never needed, but with Bart, it was just right. To him, I wasn't just a body to use. Not just something to bend over and fuck with no care. I felt special and loved. He held my hand and pulled out my chair at dinner. Bart touched me with so much reverence that it was almost too much after an entire life of being unwanted except for sex.

In the past, I would've scanned the room. Searched for anyone who was looking and speculating, but no, the only important person was seated across from me. I didn't feel like a jaded and broken forty-year-old man. With him, I was special and worth the effort. My value wasn't judged by the cut of my abs, the numbers on a scale or measuring tape, or what I was prepared to do to degrade myself for a moment of empty affection.

He ordered for me, and when the food arrived, made sure I was set with everything I needed before he even glanced at his own plate. I wanted everything with him. Unlike in the past, I wanted everyone to know I was taken. I wanted to say I love you and know the sentiment was returned. Yet I was still scared, the newness of the devotion I felt for him was overwhelming, but I never wanted to give it or him up. I just needed to find a little more courage to do what he was teaching me—demand what I wanted, and I needed Bart with everything I was.

32

BART

COLD CASE
UNIT

Fuck, I was hard as a fucking rock after dancing with Chance all night. He followed so perfectly. I'd taken him to a Queer-friendly club to end our night. None of my friends there even batted an eye as I introduced him as mine. I knew all the assumptions about my sexuality because of where I worked and my group of close friends, but I'd expected more shock over me breaking twenty years of being single. The long-standing joke about my reclusive ways circled the strip and Outreach for years.

The music had played as I'd held him in the middle of the dance floor, stealing kisses as he watched me shyly while I teased him all night. I knew every time he hardened inside his cage because he'd gasp and try to rub against me to get greater stimulation, but I had plans for him when we got home to our bed. When I'd suckled at the side of his neck, he just nodded when I asked was ready to go home.

I'd led him from the dance floor to help him on with his jacket and then ordered a car. On the ride home, he hugged my arm as I rested my forearm across his thighs. I'd wanted everything perfect for Chance to enjoy his first date. When he'd asked earlier if we could just stay home, I'd almost agreed because he looked sexy all the time, but in the suit I bought him, I'd wanted to instantly strip him.

He didn't protest the cock cage as much as I'd thought he would, but he trusted me to take care of him. When we arrived at my building, I got out and offered my hand. There was something about his shyness that made me feel powerful. Even after everything that happened to him, he let himself be vulnerable with me.

My phone beeped in my pocket, and I groaned, hoping it wasn't anything that'd fuck up my baby's night. I held his hand until we reached my door, and I let him go to unlock it and turned the knob, pushing it open for him to go first.

I pulled out my phone, swiped the screen, and tapped on the message. I chuckled as I saw a picture of me and Chance in the club.

Vega: *Aw, look how cute you two are!*

"What's so funny?"

I handed over my phone, and he looked at the screen. "Vega has spies everywhere, but you look exceptionally handsome in a suit, Sir."

"Not as much as my boy does. Plug that in for me. Answer her if you want." I shook my head at his shock at me telling him he could reply to a text. I didn't understand the urge of younger men to lock down their phones so their partners couldn't go through them. Different generation, I guess. "I'm going to lock up and grab a few waters. I'll meet you in the bedroom. Strip down and wait for me at the end of the bed."

"Yes, Sir." He plugged in my phone and his. Since he wasn't back to full active duty, he didn't have to be attached to it.

I opened the fridge and looked over my shoulder to see him disappear into our room. He may think the night was over, but we weren't even close. I'd arranged for Carlos to handle getting the kitchen ready so we could sleep in. I grabbed two bottles, closed the door, and crossed the room to my door.

Pausing in the doorway, I couldn't take my eyes away from Chance. The suit jacket was draped over the end of the bed, and he was working the buttons on his shirt loose to expose lightly tanned skin. I could watch him all day, every day, and it wouldn't be enough. I'd always joked with my friends over the years, pairing up and becoming obsessed with their partners. I'd had the same obsession with Verna, but this was different. I was older and wiser and knew to appreciate my limits.

It hadn't escaped my notice that my nightmares were few and farther between. I'd wake up from them but not instantly on alert. Before him, I hadn't realized the full extent of how much I'd healed. I'd never be the old me, but I was okay with that. I just needed my man safe when he slept in our bed.

I stepped into the room as Chance started to remove his pants, exposing the pink silk of his briefs that were cupping his rounded, muscled backside. He glanced at me, and I set the water on the dresser. Shrugging off my jacket and tossing it aside, I unbuttoned my cuffs and slowly rolled up my sleeves, one arm then the other. My baby had frozen, and I smirked. I swore my baby catered to my ego. I'd never considered myself a handsome man or someone who a person like Chance would find attractive. Typical thoughts brought on by getting older and no longer possessing the toner body of my twenties and early thirties.

"Finish undressing, baby." I made myself stay in place. "After that, I want you to bend over and place your hands on the bed."

I praised him as he did what I asked. He shifted his feet farther apart, and his caged cock hung heavy. I stepped up behind him to grip his hips and pull him back against me. My thick dick notched between his ass cheeks.

"You were such a good boy tonight. Your Sir was extremely proud of you." I stroked my hands up his back, and he arched into my touch. I drew my hands back as I dropped to my knees behind him.

I spanked the firm curves of his ass and then pulled his cheeks open. I leaned in to lick over his hole. The light hair tickled my tongue. I ate his ass as I savored every moan and whimper he made and how much he trembled. I went lower to suck his balls, and he fell face-first into the mattress. I removed the key for the lock and continued playing with him as I removed the cage, which fell to the floor.

I ordered him to stand and turn around. When he didn't immediately obey, I spanked him several times until he was facing me. His face was flushed, and he had tears on his cheeks. I brought my attention to his cock. He was hard and copiously dripping pre-cum, so I licked at the drops, and he let out a deep, tortured groan as he tensed to the point of shaking.

Practice had made perfect. I opened my mouth around his head and sucked until he nudged the back of my throat. I loved the weight of him on my tongue, the hot silky length. But nothing was better than when he allowed me to sink into him, trusting me that I'd never hurt him.

I was so lost in giving him all the pleasure he could take that I barely registered when he was digging his nails into my shoulders. And I slowly released him and leaned in to kiss his lower belly, and then got to my feet.

"Too much, love?" I asked as I lowered my mouth to his, and he nodded. "I want to tell you something, but I don't want you to get scared, okay?"

"Bart, don't..." I saw his eyes filling with tears.

"Chance, don't do that." I wiped them away with my thumbs. "I love you."

"Wh-what?" He stared at me as if he'd never seen me before.

"I love you, Chance Bowers, just you, not what you can do for me, *just you*." I kissed him and felt his lips quiver under mine. "I wanted you to have your first date. I have no intention of hiding you. Everything about you is perfect, even the pieces you find ugly."

"Y-you lo-love me?" He barely got the question out.

"Yes, is that okay? You don't have to say it, not until you're ready, but I wanted to make sure you knew I'm keeping you. You're it for me. I know you're still unsure..." He fell to his knees in front of me and frantically worked at my belt and the fly of my pants and started to pull them down until my cock slipped free of my underwear. "Baby, you don't..." I gritted my back teeth until my jaw ached as he swallowed me to the base.

I brutally gripped his hair as I lowered my chin to my chest. His kiss-swollen lips were stretched by the girth of my dick. I almost told him to stop as he gagged, but he just relaxed, and buried his face in my thick pubes. The pressure as he swallowed repeatedly made my thighs shake.

In my head, I was begging for control. I wasn't ending our night by coming down his throat. Holding the sides of his head, I forced him to slow down.

"Sir is in charge here, boy. Do you need me to put your cage back on and have you stand in the corner?" I controlled him, moving him along my length at a slower pace until I pulled him off me. I dropped to my knees, pulling him to straddle my thighs. "There's another thing my baby can do with that mouth I love."

"Did you get your results?" he quietly asked as he kept brushing kisses to my mouth and then lower to my neck.

"I did. Why?" He'd already shown me his paperwork from his last test six months ago, and I hadn't been with anyone since Verna. I was positive I was negative, but I wanted to show him in case it made him more comfortable, especially after years of living on the streets. I'd seen his stress as he tested month after month. He was on PrEP, but it didn't protect against other STIs.

"Because I heard two people in love usually do away with protection."

"Fuck." My cock jerked as I took his hips in a bruising hold.

He didn't say it, but it was close enough. I had no problem waiting until he was ready.

"Bart, I love you, but I'm scared."

"What are you scared of?" I asked as I worked to get us onto the bed.

"Everyone who loves me leaves."

I stood as he sat on the end of the bed, and I leaned over to place my fists on the mattress on either side of his thighs. "I will never willingly leave you. I promise you that. We'll fight, we'll be mad at each other, and we'll do thousands of things every other couple does, but nothing you do will ever make me leave. I trust you just as much as you do me."

"You're overdressed, Daddy," he whispered and then leaned forward to stroke his tongue along my bottom lip.

"Is that right? My pants bunched around the middle of my thighs ain't working for you, baby?"

"Oh, Daddy, it's definitely working for me."

I chuckled as I toed off my shoes, removed my socks, and shoved my pants and underwear all the way off. I stepped out of the fabric. "What do you even see in me?" I asked as I crowded him until he scooted up until his head was on the pillows. "You're beautiful and young. You could have your choice of men." I kissed him as I settled between his thighs and braced my weight on my forearms beside his head.

He gave me a small smile as he rubbed the sides of my belly. "The old Chance had all the options, a lot of ones I didn't want to have. Men fucked me because I was willing to degrade myself for them. You care." He brought his hands up to my face and cupped my jaw. "You don't make me feel dirty. I've never woke up after you've loved on me and scrubbed my skin raw until I bled. You've always made me feel safe since the second I met you."

"I love everything about you, Chance, even the so-called ugly parts. I always want to be your safe space. Now, let me love on you."

"Thank you for loving me."

"Baby, don't make it sound like a hard job. I waited so long for you and never even knew it."

When he tried to look away, I captured his lips and silently sealed my promise that he would always be mine.

33

CHANCE

I'd awakened with Bart's head resting on my stomach, he'd told me he loved me, and I hadn't questioned if he meant it or not. I stroked my hand over the top of his head, the silk of his skull cap smooth under my touch. The night he'd planned for me was perfect, and I was excited to wake up, but that had quickly disappeared when I'd gotten the call from Dolan to report to his office. I'd been okay until he'd told me to bring Bart with me.

Bart already knew about my trip to the hospital, but Dolan was clueless, or I'd thought he was. When we'd entered headquarters, my stomach seemed to drop as everyone was there, including Zero, and he avoided being associated with cops at all.

"Baby, whatever this is, we'll be okay." He held my hand tighter and leaned to the side to brush a kiss to my temple.

I wanted to believe him, but this was a group meeting and there was a board with three men projected onto it. They could've been my brothers.

"Sorry to get y'all out of bed so early." Dolan looked almost guilty.

"It didn't sound like we had much choice," I said as I took a seat, and Bart lowered to the one beside me, but again he didn't release my hand. I tried to appear calm and relaxed when I was anything but. To be honest, I didn't know if I could handle any more hits because they kept coming.

"We learned some new information after Savage was interrogated. First, I should kick your ass for sneaking into the hospital, but right now, we have bigger issues." Dolan glared at me.

"What did Chamberlain do now?" I asked.

"Vega." Dolan stepped aside, and Vega took his place in front of the board.

"As we suspected, Savage wasn't the first shooter at the Outreach or the highway. That shooter is still unknown, but Savage said since that one failed at his objective, he didn't receive the rest of the payment. Savage was brought in when our unknown shooter skipped town. Our unknown was a professional that was hired. The partial payment depleted the funds for the hit ordered on you."

"So why was Savage brought in?" Bart asked as he gave my hand a squeeze.

"Because Savage was cheap, and as a fan of Chamberlain's, he wanted to step in when it was spread that the first attempts failed," Remy said from where he was seated on Robert's lap. "Savage didn't care about the target or what you did to Chamberlain, Savage confessed, well, more like bragged about two other homicides. The detectives hurt his ego, told him what a half-assed job he did, and with absolutely no impulse control, he flipped out and confessed, but he gave us some very useful information."

"What intel did he pass on?"

"Let's get a few things out of the way. When we started out on the investigation and Chamberlain became our suspect, there were two lost years from his life, ages eighteen to twenty. At twenty, he resurfaced and attended college. We always wondered what he did in those two years. When he was arrested, the issue just dropped." Vega turned to the side. "We looked for similar unsolved homicides during the time frame that he was off-grid. I found three missing person cases turned murders. They were three openly gay men in towns surrounding Chamberlain's hometown. One disappeared during Chamberlain's senior year of high school."

"So he murdered before?" I asked and frowned.

"Yes, but small southern towns with almost zero openly gay residents...they were barely investigated. In the reports—" Marcel slid three files towards me, and I released Bart's hand to pick them up. "Friends and family said they had risky social lives. They were meeting anonymous men on dating platforms. Pretty much, they wrote it off as they met up with the wrong men and things went bad. The usual morality police claiming they'd done it to themselves."

"What's linking them to Chamberlain?" I asked as I flipped through one file after another. They were thin as hell, with almost no forensic evidence listed.

"As you know, murderers normally target people in a geographical area that they're comfortable in. Chamberlain's father ministered in all three towns. He'd go along with his father on those trips. We found someone willing to talk to us. Throughout high school, people thought Chamberlain was just a weirdo. Socially awkward, unremarkable. There was a string of peeping tom cases and suspected stalking. Everyone thought Chamberlain was responsible. No outright evidence, only assumptions. There were also attacks. Someone would grab people off the street and fondle them." Remy sounded frustrated, but most of us were. When Chamberlain pled guilty, we thought we were done with ever hearing his name again outside support groups. At least I had.

"Was he questioned for those?" Bart rested his arm across the back of my chair, and I leaned into his side.

"He was brought in, but in the end, it was the same old

bullshit. He was the minister's kid, so they wrote him off pretty quickly, but the rumors just grew. We had Remy expand Chamberlain's profile."

I glanced at Dolan and then to Remy.

"I made some calls, looked at his school records, and talked with people who knew him. As we already knew, his paraphilia began early in life. He had no control over his life. His mother coddled him, and his father held him to a high standard. He needed be above reproach. Something Chamberlain failed to do on a consistent basis."

"He was a mama's boy and loathed by his father. Doesn't turn every person into a serial rapist and killer." Would I ever be rid of Chamberlain? It seemed the farther I got away from him, the closer he always seemed to get, and I was fucking tired of it.

"No, it doesn't, but it's part of the process to move someone in that direction." Remy leaned forward and rested his forearms on the table. "We have a narcissistic sociopath. Someone incapable of relating to people on any healthy or humane level. To him, he develops an attraction to a person, but that person isn't perfect enough, and in his head, he has to make them compliant, and to him, making them completely helpless gets him off. But we're getting ahead." Remy cleared his throat. "Senior year of high school, Chamberlain returned from summer break a completely different person physically. He'd lost weight...put on lean muscle. His skin was clear. His hair and clothes were flawless. His personality disorder became masked."

"Chamberlain reinvented himself but remained the same." Great, apparently, pretty masked everything in this world when it came to serial killers and rapists.

"Yep." Marcel opened a file, and a photo glided across the table.

I noticed the eyes and leaned back. Bart caught the picture before it could touch me. Turning my head away, I started to breathe deep and even, focusing on each one as I counted.

"Baby." Bart's lips brushed my ear. "You're safe."

It took everything in me to turn my head and look at the image. The eyes were the same, but other than that, the Chamberlain I'd met looked nothing like the picture. He was slightly overweight, his skin marred by painful-looking acne, and braces peeked through the grimace that I assumed was supposed to be a smile. He looked so unassuming, just like the outcast in any high school.

"That was him before. And three months later, he was almost unrecognizable as the same person. His behavior, not so much. We found a list of teachers and called around until one was willing to talk with us. Chamberlain had always made her uncomfortable, even more so after the transformation."

"What did she tell you, Remy?" If he showed signs, why the fuck hadn't anyone said anything? That would've saved over a hundred people their safety and, in some cases, their lives.

"Chance, I need you to breathe for me." I started to protest Remy telling me to breathe until Bart laced his fingers through mine and brought my hand to his mouth. He brushed a gentle kiss to my knuckles. "Okay, the teacher who refused to go on record said that he became aggressive with some of the female students and even a few of the teachers. It was as if he expected absolute submission because he'd reinvented himself. I'm assuming she was one of the ones being harassed, but she wouldn't confirm. She said all the girls were blonde and petite, almost like porcelain dolls. Too pretty to be real. There were reports of inappropriate contact. All that was pretty much swept under the rug because of his father. All they did was give them different class schedules."

"He just kept getting away with shit. No wonder he thought he was untouchable." Bart was flipping through the files one-handed. I noticed he'd turned Chamberlain's picture over so I wouldn't have to look at him.

"Exactly, but we found out where Chamberlain was for two

years. He was institutionalized off and on." Vega spoke up. "Each stay corresponds with a disappearance. It was a version of locking the weird, creepy uncle in a backroom and not letting him out...making the kids who visit not approach him for any reason."

"Is there any way to definitively tie Chamberlain to the three unsolved?" I asked but was sure I already knew the answer.

"Vega had them pull the forensic evidence. She offered to pay for all the testing out of pocket if needed. Depending on how degraded the samples are, we'll see. From the reports, the bodies were found in a medium state of decomposition and in the elements. To be honest, even with the advancement of DNA testing, we're unsure if we can. But this proves our theory that he'd started his assaults and murders earlier. What we don't understand is why he reverted to drugging instead of killing. Maybe assumed that sexual assaults would draw less attention? It's a crime that's met with too much skepticism." Remy had worked Sex Crimes before transferring to Homicide, and he wasn't shy about voicing his opinions on how sexual assault cases are mishandled when it comes to advocating for the victims.

"He did pick naïve victims who would more than likely feel shame and not be as willing to come forward." Robert spoke as he looped his arms around his husband's waist. "Cops and the Queer community haven't exactly seen eye to eye in the past or even now."

"One thing you haven't answered is where's the money coming from?" Bart held me closer.

"Chamberlain could've hidden the money away and given access to his lawyers, but that would open an entirely new can of worms. I don't feel as if his lawyers would've exposed themselves for a client none of them were happy to have," Robert answered. "Anyone who saw the trial videos or read the transcripts knew that he showed his ass in court."

"All we're getting is more questions and less answers. I want my life back. I'm tired of looking over my shoulder. I want to be back at work." I sighed. "I can't let it all go or try to move on if I keep worrying about the next shooter he sends my way or one of his obsessed followers decides to do it on their own. What about me is so fucking special he can't let it go?"

"He's delusional, Chance, all he cares about is feeding his own ego. Currently, he's in closed management. Outside of access to his lawyers, he has no contact with anyone other than through all those letters. We've tried to break it down. Overall, you're as far from his victimology as someone can get."

"Chance," Zero called my name and took my attention away from Marcel. "Can I speak with you privately? If your Sir wants to come with, that's fine."

I nodded, but I tightened my hold on Bart's hand, and we got up to follow Zero into Dolan's office. He had his laptop set up on the desk as Bart closed the door behind us. I glanced out the windows and saw everyone watching us closely.

"They're going to be pissed I did this, but information is power. As you know, I was able to find out he was tracking you for several weeks before he even made contact with you. Vega and I found images on his computer, a lot of them." He turned his back to me and typed for a few seconds before he stepped away and then motioned to his laptop.

I moved away from Bart to see the screen, and I nearly gagged as I started to swipe through photo after photo of me. Some were of me going about my day. Nothing particularly newsworthy, but it was just the fact he'd been that close to me so many times. There were ones of me arriving and leaving the gym, but some of the pictures showed me naked in the locker room. My body far different from my current one.

The photos that brought tears to my eyes were ones of me being fucked. Men lined up one after the other. A man bending me over and another shoving his dick in my mouth as groups of men waited, jerking off as they watched me. Tears burned my eyes, and acid burned as I dry-heaved, and my legs started to give out until strong arms grabbed me around my waist.

"Baby, stop," Bart whispered in my ear, but I couldn't stop tapping the next, one after another.

The tears were falling so quickly that I could barely see the screen. I'd spent decades of my life hiding, and there was proof of everything I'd done in the hopes of finding someone who would put up with me—who would stay. I didn't care if they stayed for the wrong reasons. I'd just wanted to be wanted. To be normal, but it was all there clearly on display. I zoomed in on my face in one of the pictures, and the absolute devastation and horror were clear in my expression. No one could've missed it, but man after man, group after group, had ignored the pain.

I'd destroyed myself, suffered through my anorexia, ignored my sex addiction, and tried not to think of all the times in my life I'd had sex when I hadn't wanted, starting from the age of fifteen.

"Chance, I'm sorry." Zero's voice broke.

"Baby." Bart cupped my opposite cheek in his left hand and turned me away from the screen. He held me tight enough that it was hard to breathe as I sobbed. "Hey, you're going to make yourself sick."

"You saw—" I broke further as every dream I'd started to believe was real seemed to collapse around me.

"Chance, I love you." He pressed kisses to my cheek, the corner of my eye. "Nothing will ever change that. Not those images. Not the eating disorder. Not the sex addiction. None of that changes that you're mine."

I stiffened as the world shifted, and I found myself sitting on Bart's lap. The scent of his cologne. His beard oil. The roughness of his hands and the softness of his lips. The fact he told me he loved me. They were all the background of screams and sobs, mourning all that I hadn't realized I'd lost. The falsehood that my life and what I did with any of that was my choice. The memories of my past, the flashbacks of my rape, sometimes felt so surreal, as if they'd happened to someone else, but the proof was on the screen.

How much I'd lied to myself was clearer than I wanted it to be. I really was that thing, and no matter what anyone told me, how much they tried to reassure me, I was still nothing.

34

BART

COLD CASE
Unit

Once Zero had opened Dolan's office door, I'd carried Chance straight to his truck and drove us home without a word to anyone. He hadn't said a word to me, and I was worried about what was going on in his head. They'd told me the pictures existed, and I was shocked by them, I wouldn't lie. Chance's reaction to them broke me, though. When we made it home, I'd tucked him into our bed and made sure he was warm. I could hear the shouting and arguing on the other side of the door.

I stepped out into the main room to find Dolan and Zero eye to eye, Boss and Vega trying to play referee.

"What the fuck were you thinking?" Dolan shouted.

"He had a right to fucking know. You were coddling him. He's a grown-ass fucking man!" Zero gave as good as he got. "Rape doesn't mean you're too broken to think or make decisions for yourself."

"Shut the fuck up before you wake him." My tone was calm, but I may as well have yelled. I couldn't say I wasn't enraged. The pain my baby was in still filled my head. In every photo he flipped through, I could see the self-hatred and disgust he had for himself. A few showed he'd gotten off, his release covering his belly, but as I told him, erections and orgasms didn't equal consent. "There were definitely better ways to introduce the proof Chamberlain was stalking him, but he did need to know."

"Is he okay?" Vega asked.

"He's passed out. We'll assess how okay he is when he wakes up."

I feared we would be back to step one, but like I told him, nothing I saw or he told me made me feel differently toward him. He was still my baby, my Chance, and if we had to repeat the process to get him back, then that's what I'd do. No one survived his life without trauma and everything that went along with that. I was disgusted by the lack of care all those men subjected him to when it was clear to anyone who looked that they were hurting him in every way.

"What the hell was the point of the slideshow?" I asked Zero.

"Chance brought Chamberlain back to the beginning. His first attempts at hunting, three suspected first kills. He stalked Chance for a reason, and that reason is he wanted the high of the first time. Every high pales in comparison to that initial hit."

Vega stepped up close to Zero and shook her head. "Chamberlain is like an addict. That first rush of feel-good chemicals...the dopamine and adrenaline. He rode that trip until the crash came. He got depressed. Maybe suicidal, which led to him being institutionalized. But he quickly found a way to get it again. It just wasn't the same. And like with any addict, the dose has to get higher each time, or it's not satisfying. With Chance, Chamberlain went back to his roots. He thought he could recapture the thrill."

"He got off on being that close to Chance. Chamberlain could've taken him at any time. But Chance is physically fit and a S.W.A.T. Officer. He needed to take him when he was weakened enough that he couldn't fight back." Boss mouthed sorry to me, and I shook my head. "That evidence is just Chamberlain's way of having something to hold back...when he was ready, he could've exposed Chance to public ridicule. When Chance decided not to be in court or do a victim impact statement, it robbed him of his plan to humiliate one of his victims one more time. It wouldn't have been as effective if Chamberlain couldn't witness it."

"You're saying that he's punishing Chance by using his fans and intel from the stalking to keep torturing Chance? What the hell are we going to do to fix that? That's all I want to fucking hear."

"Savage failed. There's no more money trail that we can follow. Chamberlain's broke as far as we can find, and his parents are nearing bankruptcy. They mortgaged their home and almost emptied their savings *helping* with lawyer fees and private detectives." Vega approached me and leaned into my side, and I rested my arm across her shoulders. "We don't have any proof that they assisted in hiring hitmen. I doubt they'd even know how."

"We've been running tracking software. Getting our hands on every piece of mail. Peeks into the groups and forums. Any mention of Chance or anything alluding to Chance in some way is almost non-existent. I saw the more hardcore fans are still looking at ways to get him out, but through random financial searches, his *fans* aren't the well-off sort. A lot of them are distancing themselves as names were being outed as viewers of the videos. If they want to take out one of us, I have no problem destroying them by any means necessary. People don't fuck with our family." Zero's voice still held an edge, and as much calm as he portrayed, from the clenching and relaxing of his fists, his anger was very much still there.

I wondered if Chance truly knew how much his friends loved and wanted to protect him. He'd never had those things growing up or through adulthood until Boss had taken Chance under his wing.

"We're going to leave and let you take care of Chance. We just wanted to make sure you two got home safely." Vega patted my belly. "Tell your baby we love him."

"Will do." I leaned way down to kiss the top of Vega's straight, black hair.

Hugs were exchanged, and a few more words, but the more they talked, the faster I herded them toward the door. Once everyone was gone, I locked the door and turned on the nightlights and the dimmest lamp. To keep myself busy for a few minutes, I prepared a snack for Chance to have when he woke up and was ready to eat. I'd just grabbed some water bottles to take to the bedroom so I could nap with my baby when a knock sounded at the door.

I cursed under my breath as I set the bottles aside and crossed the room, I lowered my head to see through the peephole, and my brows drew together to see Trey on the other side. Unlocking the door, I turned the handle and pulled it open.

"Hey, what's up?" I asked.

Trey looked almost uncomfortable being there. "I heard about what happened earlier. I figured he was bedding down with you. So I grabbed him a few things he might need." He held up a bag.

I stepped back and motioned him inside. "Thanks, I'm sure he'll appreciate that. He's sleeping, and he'll probably be that way for a while, but you're welcome to stay."

"No, no." He handed me the small duffel bag. "I don't want to impose. I just wanted to check and see if he was okay."

"Not okay, but I'm sure he'll get there. Want something to drink?" I asked, and he shook his head and looked everywhere but at me. "Are you okay?" I dropped the bag beside the closed door of the bedroom.

"I'm not sleeping that great." He cleared his throat. "I-I've been going to a few of the groups, but nothing's an instant fix, right?"

"No, it's not. I've been out of the military for over twenty years and some days are still bad, but not as bad. Manageable, I guess, would be a good word. We all heal on our own time frame. Some of us learn that a little too late."

"Oh, there was also some mail for Chance that I threw in his bag. There was one from a lawyer's office. I thought it might be important. I better get going."

"Trey…" I waited until he looked at me. "Groups are great. The resources at the Outreach are excellent, but if you need to just talk to someone, you can call me." I found a pad and pen, wrote my name and number down, and ripped off the bottom of the sheet. Straightening, I turned and held it out. "This is a no-pressure offer. I know what it's like, and sometimes you just need someone to rage to that understands."

"I-I appreciate that. I got out a few years ago, then it was healing from the explosion, the graphs and physical therapy, but I was never really comfortable with talking to a shrink or anything."

"Remy isn't licensed, but he's a good one to talk to…his approach is much more relaxed."

"I'll keep that in mind. S.W.A.T. seemed the perfect fit for me. I just don't integrate into groups easily, and I don't think, other than Chance, that I've really made any friends. With the PTSD and…"

"And what? No judgment here."

"I never came out. It just never seemed like a big deal because I've never really wanted anyone. Being here, around the Commander and Chance and everyone else, I don't know."

"You're trying to find your place. It's not an easy thing to do."

"No, especially not when you're covered in scars, and that's all men seem to notice."

"The right one will see them but won't give a shit." I reached out and patted his cheek.

"Thanks. Chance really loves you a lot. I can see why. I'll leave you to take care of him. If I didn't pack something special that he needed, just tell him to text or call me."

I thanked him and showed him to the door. When I'd called Carlos to let him know Chance and I had a meeting, he said just to take the entire day off. I was glad he'd volunteered to cover for me. I'd spent the last twenty years working seven days a week, but Chance was my priority, and some missed time from the Outreach wasn't stressing me out. My baby needed me.

With everything locked up and lights on so there wasn't any shadows for either Chance or myself, I picked up the water and went to the bedroom. I eased the door open to find that he hadn't moved since I'd tucked him in. I stripped down but put on sweatpants and went to stretch out beside him. He instantly turned to tuck his face into my neck, and I stroked his soft blond hair and then down his cotton-covered back. I thought about stripping him but decided not to mess with him so he could rest.

I had my own thinking to do, prepared to fight my baby when he tried to leave me. He wasn't going anywhere. I didn't tell him I loved him to just turn around and abandon him for a past that didn't matter to me except for the damage it caused him. I smiled as I cuddled him close and planned a family dinner so I could introduce him to the entire family, my other two daughters, their partners, and Martin. My family was his, and they were going to love him.

35

CHANCE

COLD CASE
UNIT

The pounding in my head awakened me, but the comforting scent of Bart and the gentle stroke of his fingers along my bottom lip and jaw made me cautiously open my eyes. I feared I was still dreaming, and he wasn't there.

"Hey, baby, I was waiting for you to wake up." He brushed his lips to each cheek, one corner of my mouth, then the other, and then a soft kiss before he lifted his head but didn't go anywhere. "I was wondering if you'd sleep through dinner."

All I could do was shake my head. I didn't want to say anything to break the spell. I needed his weight and warmth against my side, the loving touch that told me nothing had changed. Yet, I knew it all had. Was I existing on borrowed time with him? Would he slowly distance himself from me before letting me go completely?

"No, love, I know what's going on in that pretty head of yours. My love isn't conditional."

"But you saw, Bart, it was right there." My voice cracked, and Bart just smiled down at me.

"What I saw was a man who wasn't enjoying a second of what was done to him. Even if you were fully into it, I still wouldn't think less of you. Number of past sexual partners has nothing to do with your current relationship. Body count limits are bullshit insecure people throw up. What I saw was fear and pain." He used his thumb to swipe at my wet lashes. " If you don't believe me, that's fine, we'll start back at step one, but that won't erase the fact that I love you. I've said those words romantically to only one other person, and it's not something I take lightly. When I said them, it meant I'm in for the long haul." He kissed me again. "I won't say it didn't bother me, but not for the reasons you think. I'm pissed about every person who made you view yourself as something you weren't."

"You still love me?"

"Maybe more than yesterday. While you were sleeping, I was planning a family dinner. You haven't met all my girls and their partners yet. Roxie is dating someone, but she's not ready to bring them around yet. She just says they, so we know no details."

"Why aren't you mad at me?"

"Because you did nothing for me to be mad about. You have an addiction. Sex is just as much of a habit as drinking or drugs. Why would I judge you when I'm a sober alcoholic? There are days when I think one drink won't hurt but know that one drink wouldn't be enough. I threw my last bottle of liquor against the wall so hard I embedded it in the drywall. I left it there for nearly a month." He laughed, but it held no mirth. "I sat in my recliner every night staring at it until I fell asleep, and it was the first thing I saw every morning."

"I can't believe you—" I tried to turn away, but he grabbed my chin.

"No, baby, you look at me when you talk to me. You're not hiding. You have nothing to be ashamed of or to be sorry for. I'm dreading when you go home."

"What?" I asked as I cuddled into him.

"I love you being the last person I see every night and the first I see in the morning. Fuck, being your Sir and Daddy, your man, makes me happy. The way you allow yourself to be vulnerable with me makes me feel powerful, like the old me before the tangled wiring. And I don't know what you see in an old man like me."

"The first time I saw you, I knew I was safe and you being hot was just a bonus." I smiled as he chuckled, and I allowed myself to relax, to just be present with him. All my fucked up thoughts were best left for another time.

"I always want you to feel safe with me, Chance. And I want you to meet my girls and Martin. I want to show you off."

I shyly dropped my gaze to his bare chest and then realized that I was still fully clothed. "You didn't get me ready for bed, Daddy."

"You needed your rest, and I didn't know how you'd react to awakening to someone taking your clothes off. Flashbacks and panic attacks are tricky."

"You said dinner earlier. You missed work."

"Carlos told me to take care of you. You're my priority. I've worked seven days a week for twenty years, except for the occasional emergency day off. I'm due a few days here and there. Especially when I get to spoil my beautiful baby."

I wrapped my arms around his neck and used my weight to push him to his back. I draped myself over him as he stroked from my hips to my shoulder blades and back down again. He was the first man in my life who I'd wanted to just be with. Some nights making out before going to sleep. Cuddling on the couch. Sharing dinner. Everything I assumed a normal relationship was like, but something I never thought I'd ever deserved.

"Why don't I give you a nice long bath, and then I'll make us some dinner? There's a few movies and shows you've mentioned you want to watch. We can have a nice quiet night to relax. Your day was way too stressful for my liking."

I squeaked as he sat up, and my legs went around him. I held on tightly as he got off the bed. Not once did I open my eyes or worry about him dropping me. When he carried me into the bathroom, he softly told me to let loose. He turned on the water, plugged it, and then turned back to me to start stripping away my clothes. My eyelids fluttered open, and the love and devotion in his eyes—his expression left me speechless.

He whispered for me to lift my arms when my t-shirt bunched in my armpits and around my chest. I obeyed like I always did. He gave my lips a quick, playful kiss before he lifted my shirt over my head and gave me another one when I tossed it in the hamper.

"My boy is adorable. Part of me wishes I'd recognized my feelings sooner so we didn't waste a year, but I know it happened when it was supposed to. You had some healing to do, and I had to figure out why I was so drawn to you."

"Did you figure it out?" I asked, and then gasped as he undid my belt and pants, pushing them off my hips until they fell to pool around my feet.

"You triggered my Sir. Twenty years of ignoring something that was a huge part of myself, I'd forgotten what it felt like. Why do you think I offered you a non-sexual power exchange arrangement. Sir wanted to take care of you."

"You wanted me even then?"

"The first night...the one where you arrived with your kit. I promised I'd get you ready for a man who deserved you, and as soon as I said it, I felt a loss that it wouldn't be me."

"Did it make you uncomfortable because I'm a man?" I asked, and he shook his head and then looped his arms around me.

"I won't say I didn't wonder why it was so easy to picture you as mine. As a person, I wanted you as my submissive but also as my partner. Apparently, I didn't hide it well because everyone knew before me. I just want you, love, and I'm going to make sure that you always want to be mine."

All I could think about was him seeing those pictures and finally learning I wasn't worth his time and effort, his love, but he still did. He wanted me. He wanted me to meet his other two daughters. Bart had no shame in telling everyone, and that made me awe-struck that a man like him wanted me forever. I realized out of all the men I thought I could get to stay, none of them had a care for me. After the bridges I'd burned with Dolan, I was shocked we'd become friends.

I remained silent as he turned off the water and helped me into the tub. He held my hands as I lowered. He grabbed a rag and the soap that smelled like him. Before he started washing me, though, he took care of my hair. His hands felt amazing on me, his fingers massaging my scalp.

"Trey stopped by while you were asleep."

"He did? Is he okay?" I asked.

"He seemed fine. He did say he was still having some issues adjusting. I offered to be there if he wanted to talk…I gave him my number. I hope that's okay." He turned the water back on and used a cup to rinse away the shampoo.

"It's fine, Bart. He's a nice guy, but I don't think he's ever had a place to belong."

"Not for long. Vega will adopt him any day if she hasn't already. Do you like him?"

My brows drew together at his question, but he wouldn't look at me. "The scars kinda kill the pretty vibe, yet that doesn't mean he isn't beautiful." I lifted my right hand out of the water and stroked Bart's bearded cheek. "But he has nothing on you." I caught his smile, and I leaned in to brush my lips to his. "Does it bother you I'm nineteen years younger than you?" I asked as he finished washing me, but he let his fingers linger over my scars.

"A bit, but mainly because a man who looks like you could have anyone you want. I'm an oversized kitchen manager. My romance skills are totally rusty."

"But the other skills are majorly on point."

He rumbled at me. "I'm just a piece of meat. I see how it is." He dropped a kiss on the tip of my nose and then leaned his forearms on the side of the tub to sit back and watch me. "It's a good thing you're adorable."

"Bart," I whispered his name.

"Yeah, baby."

"I do love you even if I don't understand why you love me back."

"One day, you're going to understand. But remember, I have all the patience in the world, and I can wait." He leaned in again to give me a kiss. "I love you, too. You want to soak some more or watch me cook dinner?"

"Watch you cook, shirtless. You deprived me of the view at the Outreach."

"I think they'd frown on the manager being some thirst trap for you."

"Then they're mean."

"Come on, boy, Daddy has to feed you. You didn't get lunch or your snacks."

I allowed him to help me out of the tub, and he dried me off and dressed me in a pair of his sleep pants. When I told him I didn't understand, it was the truth, but for once, I wanted to be selfish and hold onto him. Because if he taught me anything, selfishness could sometimes be a good thing.

36

BART

"Daddy, what's this?"

I looked away from the TV as Chance was coming back from the bathroom and noticed his bag there. We'd had dinner, cleaned up, and had already watched three episodes of some show he'd wanted to see, and we were about to move on to a movie. Other than background noise or some show or game, I rarely turned my TV on, maybe once a week.

"Trey said he packed a few things for you that you might need. There was also some mail, a letter from a law firm, and he thought it might be important. That bag was awful heavy, though."

"The books that were on my nightstand. Shh, don't tell anyone," he whispered as he approached me with the bag tucked under his arm. "Non-fiction. Vega and Doc, even Remy, are trying to make my reading, in their words, more fun." He sat down beside me and threw his legs over mine as he unzipped the bag. "I do have these fun book covers with half-naked men on them." He whipped out one of the books, and I snorted at the stretchy cover over one of the books that showed two men in a tastefully represented compromising position.

"Only you, baby." I took it and opened it, a Fred Hampton biography. "Nice reading material."

"Don't let the blond hair fool ya." He winked as he started going through the stack of mail and threw all but one of the envelopes on the coffee table. "Or the pretty face." He pouted at me as he tore the end off and pulled out a letter.

Instantly concern hit me when all the color drained from his face, and he started to shake. I took it from him, and a rumble vibrated my chest as I read the letter. Chamberlain.

Hello Beautiful. I see my friends didn't get to properly deliver my message. It's disappointing how people can't follow through on the simplest of instructions. Did you miss me, Chance? You cried so pretty for me. If you could've just died like I planned, it would've been the perfect scene. My messages may not have reached as they should've. Yet I assure you that at least one will. I can make it all stop, though. All you have to do is one little thing. I put you on my visitor list. If you ignore my polite invite, maybe I'll just have to send a messenger to someone who's easier to track down.

I stopped reading, wrapped my arm around Chance, and picked up my phone. Vega had added me to the insane group text she had and sent one to get everyone there that Chamberlain had sent Chance a letter. Notifications popped up, Dolan and Boss were on their way, Vega, too, and Robert and Remy. I didn't bother answering and tossed my phone back on the table, along with the letter. Shoving the bag off my baby's lap, I tugged him to me and seated him on my thighs.

"Hey, breathe for me. Everyone who can is on their way."

"Why...I just want it all to stop."

"I know, Chance, I want that, too." My phone rang, and I just hit speaker. "Hastings."

"Hey, Bart, it's me," Simon spoke. "Chance got a letter from Chamberlain? How was it sent?"

"Through a law firm." I read the firm's name, and Simon told Marcel to get him his laptop.

"Those aren't the guys who were in charge of his defense. Chance being one of us, I followed everything closely. I'll make some calls to find out more about them. But anyone with half a brain cell knows you don't allow an attacker to contact his victims, especially if the offender wants out. Witness intimidation…tampering with witnesses."

"Why would he send it?" I asked as Chance cuddled tighter to my side, rubbing my belly for comfort.

"It's getting pretty clear Chamberlain wants to make an attempt at a new trial. Not going well for him, though. Too much evidence against him. We've discussed it, and we can't figure out where the obsession came from. We know he gets off on seeing the aftermath of the damage he caused, but this definitely goes deeper than that."

"If they sent me that letter, then Chamberlain knows where I live. Trey moved in. What if—" Chance's voice broke.

"Trey will be fine. Someone will take him in until we can figure shit out. Don't worry about that." Simon tried to sound reassuring, but we were dealing with a lot of unknowns.

"Chance will stay with me for a while. I don't want him anywhere else anyway." I kissed my baby's forehead.

"Sounds like a plan. Someone will get me the letter and envelope, and I'll do my thing. I'll leave the rest of it for the cops of the family." He said goodbye and told us if we needed, he'd send Marcel.

I just let the call end and pinched Chance's chin to make him look at me. "I'm proud of you."

"Why?" he asked softly.

"You didn't have a full-blown panic attack at seeing the letter."

"But I couldn't finish reading it."

"You didn't have to, but you didn't shut down, and that's why I'm proud of you. Let me hold you while we wait for everyone to get here." He relaxed onto my chest, and I patted his hip.

"Do you think Tamara and Roxanne will like me?" he asked.

"Yes. Are you worried they won't?" If he didn't want to talk about the letter until everyone arrived, then we'd discuss everything but.

"Yeah. Not only is their dad bringing home someone new, but said person is a man and their age."

"Well, Roxie came out as pan about ten years ago. I think we'll be fine. Also, Martin is a decade younger than Verna. My girls will love you just like they did when Verna brought home Martin because their parents are happy."

There was banging on the door, and I eased him off my lap to go and answer. "Y'all made good time."

"Sirens and flashing lights." Vega practically giggled as she skipped around me, and I turned my head to watch her until she was curled up on the couch with Chance. He allowed her to snuggle with him. She was in complete Mami mode.

"I can't believe her scooter kept up. I'd give her a ticket if I wasn't impressed." Dolan walked around me, holding tightly to Boss's hand.

Remy and Robert were attached as always. Remy leaned in for a cheek kiss, and I shook my head. Chance didn't like when other people touched me, and I knew a lingering sense of insecurity brought on the discomfort.

"It's okay," Chance said, and Remy kissed my cheek loudly, making my baby laugh.

I closed the door, and by the time I turned around, everyone was passing around the letter.

"We can't do this," Boss said. "Putting Chance in the same room as Chamberlain will give that fucker wank material."

"But I can't let him keep coming, sending one person after another until someone gets caught in the crossfire."

I took the seat on the other side of Chance, but he needed a bit of extra comfort, so I let Vega love over him as I held him to my side with my arm across his chest.

"What would be the point of sitting in the room with him?" Dolan asked.

"Do we even know what's going through his head? I want it to stop, Dolan. I'm tired of being on a desk. Looking over my shoulder all the damn time."

"He wants five visits, Chance. Can you tell me that you can stay in the same room with him for five visits, an hour or more a piece?" Remy asked as he lowered onto the coffee table and rested his forearms on his knees.

"What's your opinion, Remy? You did the profile?" Chance asked.

"Like it's always been, he wants to see how broken you are. He needs to see your fear of him. He's been on a suicide watch. I think he's descended into a major withdrawal phase. Chamberlain is also not getting the respect and accolades that he did when he was posting his videos. He's no longer the hunter. My opinion, I think you need answers, but my concern is that you're not far enough into your healing to be able to handle it."

"I'll be there. He'll handle it fine. My boy will just need some special treatment post-meetings."

My heart said to keep him as far away from Chamberlain as possible, but my head told me he needed to confront his attacker, at least for a few hours. I knew the why haunted Chance. What made him the so-called victim. I wanted him to hear my support. Whether he visited or not was a decision he had to make.

As his Sir, it was my job to ground him. To be present and anticipate what he needed. Caring for him was where I was most confident.

"Boss," Chance whispered his name.

"Honey, I'll support whatever you need, I have to be at the Outreach, but all I am is a phone or video call away. We'll do some remote groups. I only ask that you're alone when you attend. Everyone knows you and won't mind in the least."

"Zero is so ready to nuke Chamberlain from the face of the

earth. He fucks with you too much...Zero will search out every avenue of support or money trail until the fucker won't be able to buy a pack of gum from the commissary." Vega threw herself forward and wrapped herself around Chance and me.

I felt Chance tense, but then he quickly relaxed and hugged Vega tighter. Until recently, Chance hadn't seen himself as a true part of the family. He hadn't belonged to one that loved and cared for him since his mother passed away. I'm sure it was overwhelming for him, and he'd have my girls and partners soon, too. I wanted to give him everything.

"If you want, Remy and I will go along. Roo can go to stay with Amber and Savvy. That way, you have some backup while you're there."

"I can be ready to be in the air at a moment's notice. You just have to call," Dolan offered.

I sat back as comfort for Chance as they made plans, but I also worried about how he'd handle everything once he was in the room with Chamberlain. There was so much at stake, and I needed it all to work out in Chance's favor. I wanted him to be able to go back to his life before Chamberlain decided my baby needed to be taken out.

37

CHANCE

COLD CASE
UNIT

Vega had rented us a nice hotel suite for Bart and me, Remy and Robert, and Simon came along to act as my legal counsel. I dropped the bag that had mine and Bart's stuff beside the door and walked over to the large window. We'd taken a late flight, and Sir wanted to get me food before it was time for me to go to bed. I wasn't hungry, but I had to have something, or I was going to make myself sick.

At eleven the next day, I would be escorted into a meeting room at the prison and would be left alone with Chamberlain. Guards and everyone would be watching from the observation room, so I'd be essentially trapped with him. I'd thought I was ready, well, not ready, but my confidence lagged mid-flight.

"Hey, baby."

I turned at the sound of the door opening, and Bart entered with a take-out bag and a box under his arm.

"What's in the box?" I asked as I approached him and took the bag.

"I don't know. Vega had it sent to the hotel for us. The front desk person said it just arrived."

"I'm a little scared." I grinned as he nodded to agree with me.

"She addressed it to Sir Bart Hastings. I'm sure the lady didn't assume I was royalty."

I snorted as he came over to the bed. I sat down to see what he'd gotten me for dinner. I approved of the sandwich and salad. That was probably all my stomach could handle. "Well, open it and see what mischief Vega is up to...and to think she's the Mami and Domme. She'd succeed at world domination if she was a Brat."

"Not going to disagree." He used one of his keys to break the tape on the box. He let out a booming belly laugh as he started pulling items out, and I was thankful I hadn't started eating yet.

A small leather paddle, restraints, and flogger. A mini keep Chance in-line kit. He handed me the letter. I ripped the envelope and pulled out the single sheet of paper. Everything we'd need, according to her, was included. I should've experienced more shock at the care package, but what could I say? It was Vega.

"Figured a kit couldn't be brought on the plane with you or even if you thought of it, but Mami did. Corner time won't be intense enough." I paused reading as Bart shook his head. *"Check your bag on the way home. Also, there's a present for you two."*

Bart pulled out a smaller box. He handed it to me as I set the letter aside. It was two bracelets, and the package said that if the person wearing one touched the sensor, the other one would light up. I'd seen them advertised for long-distance couples. A sticky note on the side of the shiny box said they were already set up and paired. So I wouldn't feel alone in that room.

I'd never even thought about that. Bart wouldn't be right there, and I knew he'd watch over me, but this was something tangible. I lowered my chin to my chest, and the rough pads of his fingers slipped under my chin and made me raise my head.

"Talk to me?" he asked as he removed his touch and then cleaned up, placing all the stuff back in the box.

"I was an asshole to everyone. Why do they care...they invited me into their family."

"Because most of them know what you went through to some degree."

Even though I didn't understand that, I nodded. Vega had shared her story with me, but I kept that to myself. I'd spent most of my life pushing everyone away—not belonging to anyone in any true sense. When my mother was alive, I understood family —the two of us just fit. Family units had lost their meaning since.

"Remy starved himself for years to maintain an unhealthy weight because he made more money on the street that way because it made him androgynous. Doc covered his insecurities with sarcasm and flirting, fucking men who made him ashamed of his needs and boundaries. Boss cut himself off completely after his husband and Sir was murdered, and then went to a Sadist because that's what he thought he needed to cope. We've all got trauma and our own ways of dealing with it."

"Boss told me that he would've even fought Dolan to take care of me. I mean, I get it. I've been around long enough to know how everyone works and the community the strip and Outreach provides. It's just hard to really understand for me. When my mom died, the only person who cared for me was gone."

"But you told me you thought Dolan would stay."

"All a delusion, but Dolan leaving was my fault. He'd put up with the secrecy and cheating until I was just too much. All he'd wanted was me to be out, and to me, that was the worst thing in the world. In hindsight, I get it. I really do. It's hard being forty and realizing that everything you were sure of was wrong. I'd always thought I was smarter than that...swore I was self-aware enough to know what was best for me."

"Baby, we all have those moments where we wake up and figure out we need a change. Sometimes that's in your twenties, and other times you're fifty-nine and find out that you wasted twenty years."

"Wasted? But you do great things at the Outreach."

"I do, and I'm proud of all the shit I've accomplished because of the Outreach. I went from sleeping in an underground homeless camp to being Kitchen Manager. But if you asked me at thirty-eight where I saw myself, this wasn't what I pictured."

"Do you regret it?" I cautiously asked because I didn't want to learn I was one of the things he regretted.

"No." He stretched out his arm and stroked my cheek, and I leaned into his touch. "When I retired, I thought I was superhuman and ignored a lot of the red flags that I needed help. Because I thought I'd just need to man up and everything would be back to normal." He dropped his hand to my inner thigh where I had my legs crossed. "I mourned losing Verna, my kids. While what I did worked out in the end, I still had to repair the damage I'd caused."

"Do you think you'd still be with Verna if you'd done things differently?"

"Honestly, yes, because she was the love of my life for twenty years, but I also see her with Martin, and he's absolutely perfect for her in every way. He was...is an amazing stepdad and grandpa to the kids. Yet you also have to think, we didn't spend a ton of time together when I was deployed or whatever. We were two completely different people. Being together every day, maybe we'd have naturally grown apart. The thing is, when I look back, I can't imagine it working any other way. The Outreach gave me purpose and a place to start healing, groups of people who understood me, and eventually, it gave me you. What could be better than that, huh?"

I covered my face with my hands to hide my smile and the fact my cheeks felt hot. Bart was everything I'd wanted but denied I needed, and he chose me, which made it even more surreal.

"You're adorable when you get all shy." I giggled as he leaned in to kiss the side of my neck and tickled me with his beard. "Eat your dinner, love. I don't want you hungry. I should've remembered to bring you snacks."

"Don't do that," I whispered.

"Do what?"

"Think that you did something wrong because you didn't provide me with a snack. I don't think I would've been able to eat anyway."

"How are you feeling about the meeting tomorrow?" he asked as he pointed to my food.

"Not as confident as when I said I'd do it. It hit me mid-flight that I'm going to sit in a room across from my rapist." I took a tentative bit of my sandwich—it was plain but just right.

"I don't want you to do it."

"Then why did you say you'd support me?"

"Because me not wanting you to do it is not the same as me backing you on something you feel you need to do. You want to know the why, Chance. The what-ifs are lingering, and I think you need answers. As your Sir, I'm there to support you... emotionally, mentally, and physically. But as a Sir, I also have to take into account what's best for you. This is going to be scary, and you may regress, but it's my job to help you cope with that in a healthy way. To offer you an outlet, even if that outlet is helping you feel pain. I don't like hurting you, but sometimes pain is the only answer."

"Don't I stress you out?" I asked, and then I took another bite of my sandwich and opened the container with my small salad, adding my dressing. My relationship with food still wasn't the greatest, but I was able to ignore the estimation of calories over the small cup of dressing. The number of miles I needed to run to get rid of the carbs from the sandwich.

"No, you haven't caused me one moment of stress. Outside factors have, but not you personally. What did I tell you?" he asked as he stood, grabbed Vega's gifts, and walked over to where

I'd left our bag. He crouched down and started going through the bag, pulling out our toiletries.

"That I made you happy."

"And one thing I will never do is lie to you. Secrets have a way of ruining shit, no matter the relationship. We're still working on stuff. We've known each other over a year, but as a couple, we're new."

The suite had a private bathroom, and Bart disappeared into the room for a few minutes before coming out, removing his t-shirt. All that dark brown skin on display. The belly that had turned into my favorite thing to cuddle.

"Have I told you recently that I have the sexiest Daddy and Sir out there?" I finished off my dinner, packed up my trash into the bag, and downed the bottle of water he'd gotten me.

"You may have mentioned it a time or two. Can I ask you something?"

"Of course," I said as I slipped off the bed to throw everything away and stripped down to my underwear.

"Why didn't you ever have a Dominant before?"

"I never really thought about it. Dolan had an extremely dominant personality, but we—" I glanced at him, and he rolled his eyes.

"Baby, I've told you about Verna. You've met her. Dolan is your ex-husband, and I'm not that insecure."

I pulled the covers down and crawled onto the bed to get comfortable while Bart got ready to lay down with me. "We never did all the Daddy and Sir stuff. I know he's Boss's Daddy now, but I just wanted to be fucked...degraded. He gave me what I needed, but when he told me what he needed, well, I freaked out. And what he wanted wasn't like excessive. He just wanted me to be out, but there was that one time he asked me to top, and I was all nah-uh. Would you ever want me to do that?"

"Not if you're not comfortable with it, but I wouldn't say no if it's something you want to do. I'm well aware I can say no if it's not for me." He did a belly flop onto the mattress, crossed his arms on my stomach, and then rested his chin on his forearms to look at me. "Consent goes both ways. You'll hear Red from me if we need to stop. Submissives aren't the only ones who can safeword when needed."

I played with the twists of his hair and then stroked the backs of my fingers across his cheek, tracing the curves of his lips. "Bart, do you really think I'm doing the right thing? Maybe I'm not ready."

"I have all the faith that you are. Yes, it's gonna be hard. This is the man who raped, tortured, and tried to murder you. Anyone would be terrified to meet them afterward. It's the reason a lot of survivors don't testify because they don't think they can sit in the courtroom having to see the person...have their attacker stare at them."

"I'd had sex hundreds of times when I didn't really want to. I've been brutally fucked, smacked, spit on, and covered in cum from groups of men. Knowing it was going to happen didn't change how disgusted with myself I felt afterward. Chamberlain was just one in a long line."

"But, love, you walked into clubs with the express purpose of being degraded, and maybe part of your brain thought Chamberlain would be like all the others. He wasn't, though. You connected with someone like thousands of people do, yet he tried to murder you."

"I get that, but—" I sighed heavily as he stretched his arms out beside me and tilted his head down to kiss my belly. "It also made me realize how close to dying I'd come over the years. Walking into a room and instantly knowing which one would hurt me became an unwanted talent. I saw Chamberlain, and I got none of those vibes from him."

"I watched the trial videos."

"What?"

"One day, when you were at headquarters, I watched."

"Why didn't you tell me?"

"I wanted to be prepared if you ever asked me to sit down with you and watch again. The way you reacted in the bathroom, I guess I needed to be ready to just be there for you. He showed no emotion but satisfaction when he stood in court and told the entire room what he'd done. I've been around almost sixty years, and I don't think until I saw him that I'd ever seen true evil. The things he said he'd done to you..." He swallowed hard and cleared his throat. "I can't imagine doing anything other than loving on you. You survived, and you're recovering. That's why I think you're ready, and even if you break, in this room just like at home, I'll do what's required to make sure you're okay because you and my girls, I'd do anything for y'all."

He pushed his left arm under me, and I squeaked as he rolled onto his back, blowing a raspberry on my soft belly. I squirmed down until I curled up against his side, with my head on his shoulder as he held me tight. He crossed his arm over his chest and gently caressed my cheek until I tipped my head back to look at him.

"I need you to always be this happy, Chance. When you're really smiling and laughing, and just confident, I know I'm doing something right. And I'll remind you as many times as you need me to."

At a loss for words, because I could see the truth of what he said, and knowing his only concern was me being happy and healthy, nothing else mattered. I stretched until I could push my lips to his. We shared a few kisses, and then I cuddled back into him, pushing my face against his neck. I couldn't imagine being anywhere else, and I was slowly coming to realize that I'd gotten something right, and I wasn't going to let go. Twenty-six years was long enough to suffer.

38

CHANCE

COLD CASE
UNIT

That morning I'd barely been awake when I made a run for the bathroom. Bart being the caring Daddy he was, held my head up, washed my face, and placed a cold rag on the back of my neck. I was cold and clammy, and all he'd done was kiss the top of my head and take care of me. He'd bathed and dressed me and placed a few swipes of his cologne on my inner wrists so I'd have his scent to calm me.

Bart had tried to hide it, and although I could tell he was almost as nervous as I was, he went into Sir mode. He'd held my hand all the way to the prison, only letting me go as we made it through the security checkpoints and met up with Chamberlain's attorneys. My entourage of Remy, Robert, and Simon were behind Bart and me. Sir never let go of my hand no matter how many looks we were getting, especially him.

I'd have to plan something special for him to thank him even though I knew he wouldn't want that. How to spoil my Sir was a problem for a later date. We were led into an observation room, and through the two-way glass, I could see two chairs and a table bolted to the floor with a metal loop welded to the table for Chamberlain to be restrained.

The warden was a grim-faced man who looked like he hated everyone, but his voice was kind. "I know a private meeting was requested, but I wouldn't agree to it without an officer in the room. He's simply there for Lieutenant Bowers's protection and won't interact unless the inmate becomes threatening. The inmate will only have an hour per visit. If he becomes belligerent or destructive in any way, I will cancel the rest of the week. Are you okay with this, Lieutenant Bowers?"

"Yes, sir." I was proud of myself that my voice didn't break, but that probably had more to do with Bart rubbing comforting circles on my lower back.

"The inmate is being searched and will be here shortly. I only agreed to this because you requested it." The warden looked at me. "I've spoken with your legal counsel, and while I don't understand after reading the files, I respect your right to confront him. Don't make me regret it. Officer Carmichael has final say if the meeting will continue for the hour agreed upon. I hope you find what you're looking for."

I nodded, and the warden left, and we were left in the small dim room. Bart wrapped his arm around my waist and spun me into a corner to block me from the room. I looked up at him, and he lowered his head. His mouth brushed mine, and we ignored someone clearing their throat.

"I won't be in there with you, baby, but just remember I'm right on the other side of the glass. You survived Chamberlain. You lived when he tried everything to make sure you didn't. He's just another inmate. What are you when I'm with you?"

"Safe, Sir," I whispered.

"That's right. This is just five hours of your life. After those are up, we can go home, but he'll rot in that cell of his."

"Yes, Sir, but what if—" His fingertips stroked my wrist where the bracelet was, and the scent of him lingered.

"You do what you need to do to find your answers. Beyond that, I'll take care of you."

The sound of chains was almost tinny sounding through the speakers. They'd be able to see and hear what was going on. Bart and my friends knew, but there were strangers, Chamberlain's attorneys. There were people who would hear everything he'd done to me, and I wasn't sure I was strong enough not to break in front of them all.

"He's just a man, Chance, an evil one, but just flesh and blood, no more, no less."

I nodded, and his fingertips pushed under my chin and tipped my head all the way back until he could capture my lips. As I always did, I submitted, but with Bart, that submission was valued. The tip of his tongue teased mine, and we broke apart as I heard Remy's laughter. I found I'd wrapped myself around Bart.

"Keep it G-rated. I think you're making the homophobes uncomfortable."

I leaned a bit to the side to see the room, and the officer and Chamberlain's legal team did seem to squirm a bit. Bart's lips brushed my ear. "We'll finish that when we get back to our room."

I smirked as he nipped at my lobe and then stepped away from me. I'd lived through one of the most violent things a person could go through. I wasn't the Chance that Chamberlain met and tried to kill. I'd found family and love, a man who wanted only me. Yes, I was scared, but I wouldn't let it show until Bart's presence made it safe to do so.

"Bowers, I'm going to take you into the room. The inmate has requested not to be secured to the table since he's not going to be left alone with you. He makes one move that either myself or my officer deems aggressive, we'll chain him to the table. Or you can ask for it at any time. My officer has been instructed that he will take your lead on this, but we get final say."

He allowed me to get a few words and hugs of support, and then Carmichael led me from the room. As soon as we were in the hall, he glanced at me.

"Just so we're clear, my husband would be pissed about me being called a homophobe."

I snorted as he rolled his eyes which looked odd on a man who looked like he could bend steel bars with his bare hands.

"If it makes you feel any better, his life sucks in here. This is the hour he gets for rec, so as soon as this is over, he goes back to his cell. Good luck." As he unlocked the door and pushed it open, I stepped inside.

Almost instantly, I felt my knees turn weak, but I controlled myself quickly. He looked thinner. His thick hair was dull where it framed his face. The beige of his clothes made his pale skin look sallow, and the fluorescent lights didn't help.

"Chance, you've gotten fat." Chamberlain snarled his nose.

"Good thing your opinion doesn't matter because my boyfriend loves it." I glanced at my wrist in time to see the brightening on my wrist, three slow fade ins and outs. I glanced at the glass. I couldn't see him there, but I knew he'd be right on the other side to watch me closely.

"Boyfriend." He tsked. "You could've done so much better. Old and fat, a kitchen worker, really?"

Rage burned in my chest at his insulting Bart. He could verbally abuse me all he wanted, but my Sir was not up for ridicule. "Chamberlain, you can say whatever the hell you want about me, but leave my man out of it. You can go back to your cell without these little meetings you wanted so badly."

"But don't you want to know why? Why you were so special?"

"No." I lied easily.

"I don't think that's true. Please, have a seat." He motioned to the chair across from him, and I shook my head.

"You sent that letter to get me here, but I'm fine standing." I made my way to the opposite corner, crossed my arms, and leaned my shoulder against the cold cement block wall. That fear and nausea still burned in my gut, but I inhaled as the scent of

Bart wafted up to me. His voice was in my head, telling me I was safe.

"That's just rude, Chance. I had such higher hopes for you, but what I learned about you, you really have no self-respect. Did you see my souvenirs? Did your boyfriend?" His slow, arrogant smirk nearly made me gag.

"I saw. What did you expect to do with all those images?"

"You should've seen the videos. You were made to be on camera. The raid ruined my plans to upload. Oh, how many times I got off watching you. Would you like details?"

"Dolan should've aimed a bit more to the center," I commented, and his hand almost flexed as if he were looking for his cane. I knew the shot had shattered his pelvis and dislocated his hip with the impact. "They didn't let you keep your new accessory?"

"My messages I sent you should've been clearer."

"Why don't we call them what they were? You tried to kill me again, four times total. You shot one of my best friends and endangered a child for what, revenge? You fucked up when you took Dolan's man. You made that mistake. No one would've mourned you if you'd bled out. I definitely wouldn't have. I know a lot of people who would've celebrated."

"You enjoyed it, Chance. You resisted, but that was just your way of teasing me. If you'd just submitted, I wouldn't have gotten so mad at you."

"So when you shoved your dick and a massive dildo up my ass to the point I tore and bled, was all my fault because I made you mad? You forcing the metal device in my mouth and ratcheting it up until the corners of my mouth split was just my due?" I clenched my fists as he closed his eyes as if he was pulling up the memory and getting off on it. "Now, I see the purpose of you wanting this visit. You just want to get off on the damage you caused. The profiler said that was the case, but all I could think was what about me got that twisted brain of yours fixated on me?"

"All you had to do was be good and die, but no, I should've been more careful to check before I left. I should've known it was too good to be true. You wanted to die. I was just going to give you what you wanted. How can a man be blamed for that? A mercy killing. That shouldn't even be a crime."

"If my death wouldn't have been a crime, what about the others? Innocent kids. All they wanted was a connection, and you took advantage of that, all for some views and praise. You made us part of a group none of us ever dreamed of belonging to, and to make matters worse, you posted what you did to them. Are you mad at me because I didn't just lie there and take it? You're not so virile when your victims are conscious. Maybe you can't get it up at all when they're awake?. The ones who died during your attacks? Did you even care, or was it as long as the body wasn't cold, you were good to go?"

I forced a smirk as he surged to his feet, and the officer in the corner rushed forward, slamming him back onto the chair. He jerked out of the officer's grip, and the officer glanced at me, silently asking if I was okay. I nodded, and he went back to the corner.

"I hit a nerve." I chuckled coldly. "You know you could've saved yourself dying in prison if you'd just gotten yourself a sex doll. I heard they're realistic and made to order."

"You're insulting me."

"Very astute. Although, after seeing your high school yearbook photos, I'm not surprised you'd have issues with a conscious person." He clenched his hands on the tabletop, and his pale skin turned red. I knew if the guard wasn't in the corner, he'd come for me.

Chamberlain was just a bully who wanted to torture representations of all the people who'd turned him down. He'd changed himself, morphed into someone who no one would look at and say monster, but that's exactly what he was. Yet he was also self-absorbed and arrogant enough that he wanted to show his work to the world. Not only did he make the videos for his own jerk-off fantasies, but it was also, at its core, a way to shame his victims even if they'd never discovered the site.

"They were all quite willing." His voice was horrifyingly calm. "They were just ashamed they enjoyed it so much."

"Delusional. In the grand scheme, they were innocent... babies, sheltered. You destroyed that innocence for your own pleasure. You're just obsessed because a grown man got the best of you. Put you in prison. But do you know the true moment you fucked up?"

"No, please, enlighten me, Chance."

"You underestimated a man you'd never met or what lengths he'd go to protect his kids." I moved across the room and stood at the side of the table. "You were outsmarted by an old, gay man you'd snarl your nose at. He's rough and abrasive but beautiful in every way. You'd anticipated no one would care, but he was there in the aftermath, showed grace and love, that they were worthy even when they swore they weren't. Some of those people you thought you destroyed, with his support, went on to find love and have families. They thrived despite you. I thrived despite you." And as soon as the words were out, not all of the weight, but a lot of it, disappeared, allowing me to breathe easier. Yes, I'd been broken, but I survived. I'd started to recover from decades of trauma.

"Does your boyfriend know what you are?" He leaned in, but I didn't give an inch. "How many men you let spit on you and knock you around? How they lined up for a go at any hole they wanted?"

My wrist flashed, and I smiled as I caught sight of it from the corner of my eye. "Is that all you have? Really? Slut-shaming me? I'd expected more from you, but that was my mistake. Better make this meeting count because as soon as I leave, I won't be back."

He jumped from his chair. "I'll fucking kill them all. No matter what I have to fucking do, they will all die, and I will make sure you're there to see every death." Foam gathered at the corners of his thin mouth, the guard wrapped his arm around Chamberlain's throat, and the door flew open, Carmichael rushing in as Chamberlain fought to get to me.

They dragged him away as he kicked and screamed. Bart was rushing through the door with everyone else behind him. He grabbed me and pulled me against him. The minute I was in his arms, my legs collapsed, and he was the only thing keeping me upright.

"Chance, are you okay?" Remy asked, and I opened my eyes to find him standing beside Bart on one side and Simon on the other. Simon stroked my hair back from my forehead.

"Yeah, yeah, I think it...I was fine, and then I just wasn't." I'd made a habit of that, though.

"Understandable," Remy whispered.

"Should I inform his lawyers you won't be back?" Simon asked.

"No, but if he has access to carry out his threats, Remy, I need to know what to ask. How do I trip him up?"

"Baby, why would you come back?" Bart nuzzled the top of my head and then brushed a kiss to my forehead.

"Because I have to protect my family. I have to make sure you and the girls are safe...that my family is good. If I can do anything to discover if he's hiding something, who he might still send after us...I need to do something."

"Okay." He cupped my face and made me look at him. "We'll come back. You were so good, baby, strong."

"I didn't feel very strong."

"That's the fear hitting you, but my baby held it together, and

I'm proud of you for that, but you also know that I'm there when you need to break."

I nodded and closed the distance between our mouths for a quick kiss. "Remy, you think you can help me?"

"I can. I'll come up with some questions this afternoon, and we'll go over them at dinner. But right now, I'll leave your Sir to take care of you. You two need some time, so let's get back to the hotel. I heard Vega sent you a present." Remy winked at me.

Shortly, we were headed out of the prison and getting in our rental. On the way back to the hotel, Bart cuddled me to his side. Even though he was praising and tenderly touching me, I was dreading when the adrenaline disappeared, and I fell apart.

39

BART

W hen Chance and I came back to our room, he'd passed out for a few hours, and I'd curled around him from behind to hold him until he finished his nap. Pride had filled me when he'd held himself together. I knew he'd faltered a few times but hadn't shown it. Chamberlain hadn't been at all what I expected after seeing the videos. I was sure prison had taken its toll on him.

The man who'd stood up in court and detailed his crimes exuded arrogance in a designer suit and a hundred-dollar haircut. Just as Chance had said, appearance-wise, he'd been an exceptionally handsome man, almost bordered on the looks of a model. I could see how Chance would go to a motel with him. Overall, he looked like a normal, successful man, but we all knew looks could be deceiving.

What I hadn't expected was standing on the other side of the glass, watching my baby face his rapist and being unable to do anything about that. I couldn't barge into the room. I couldn't take the bastard's head off. Not being able to make it all better for Chance filled me with a sense of powerlessness I hadn't felt in years. Intellectually, I knew erasing his pain was impossible.

Although, that didn't mean everything else inside of me wanted to reverse time. The fucked up thought I'd had that if it hadn't happened, he'd never have been mine. What kind of man did that make me?

I sensed him starting to wake up, and I turned onto my side to rub his back and massage his neck. Just the way he liked when he spent the night, and he'd snuggle in for a few more minutes until I made him get ready for work. I felt his lips pout against my chest, and he made that little disgruntled sound I found adorable. For a man who had to be awake at a moment's notice, he was not easy to get moving on a regular day.

"Hey, love, did you sleep good?" I asked as I kissed the top of his soft hair. He had a few bad dreams, so I'd held him through each one and whispered to soothe him, and they passed. I'd expected more, but we still had, at most, a week there. He'd been emotionally worn down after the meeting, and when he reset, it could still hit him.

"Yes, did you sleep at all?" He tipped his head back as he asked, and I dropped a kiss on his lips.

"No, I wasn't tired, but I didn't want to leave you in case you had a nightmare."

"Did I?" He spread his right hand on my chest and twirled his fingers through the hair there.

"Just a few restless spots, but you didn't wake up. Are you doing okay?"

"I don't know. He looked different until he opened his mouth. I still don't understand why me. Why does that bother me so much?"

"I think anyone who's attacked in a senseless crime would wonder why. What they could've done differently. I think it's a normal part of the healing process."

"But am I doing the right thing, Sir?" he asked as he pushed me to my back and lifted to straddle my hips.

I grinned as he started rubbing circles on the sides of my

belly. "I'm your Sir and your Daddy, but you're a grown man. Do you feel like you need this to move forward?"

He tipped his head back, and I gripped his thighs, feeling the hairs tickle my palms and fingers.

"I don't know."

"Acceptable answer."

"How is not knowing a good answer?"

"Because, baby, we're not all-knowing. You also have to decide what's going to happen if you don't get the answers you need."

"I know, Daddy." He pouted at me. "But I've come a long way. I feel I've made progress with my groups and you, you being the biggest factor. Sad thing is, though, looking back, I barely remember the time before Mom died. All the bad overshadowed the good and robbed me of the memories. They say trauma affects memory."

"Tell me something you remember about your mom."

His full lips pulled into a beautiful smile.

"Mom used to dress up as Santa. Beard, belly…the entire suit. She did it every Christmas. There was never a lot of presents, but we'd watch all those holiday movies, and she'd splurge and make us a traditional meal. One year, she rented a snow machine. I think I was seven, and I'd written Santa for one of those white Christmases I saw on TV and in the Christmas cards. It was set up behind our trailer, and in the window behind the tree, I could see snow falling."

His face brightened with the memories, and with the happiness, the tenseness of his muscles disappeared. One year I'd have to take him somewhere snowy, Winter-Wonderland-type of setting. Another positive memory to block out the bad ones.

"What else?"

"She'd take me camping."

I chuckled. "I can't see you as a camper, love."

"You'd be right." A heavy sigh slipped out. "I haven't gone since I was a kid. She couldn't take a lot of vacation time without messing with our money. She'd put change in a jar all year and take an extra day off with her usual two days in a row. Our tent was more duct tape than anything. I think she'd picked it up from a thrift store."

I laid there as so many emotions went across his face, from bittersweet to happy. Most people would say Chance didn't physically show how he felt, but it was there for anyone who cared to pay attention. My baby was an open book for the most part until he felt he needed to shut down to protect himself.

"We'd get those dollar packs of hot dogs, you know the ones. They're even questionable for hot dogs. We'd cook over the fire on sticks. Get stuff to make s'mores. We tried fishing, but neither of us was really good at it, and I don't think Mom wanted to clean the fish." A joyful sound slipped free. "We ate more sandwiches and cheap hot dogs than anything. Oh, and those popcorn packs that you normally cooked on the stove, and I thought there was nothing better than the way the foil puffed up. We'd swim and just be for three days. I still remember she smelled of those body sprays, jasmine blossom and vanilla sugar cookie." He looked down and away.

"What? Say it."

"People always joke about those scents, but Mom liked to feel pretty. She'd buy herself dresses but feel guilty over a two-dollar dress. All of it was from secondhand stores, but she'd pull out her sewing machine. She didn't have much, so it was discount store makeup and body sprays." He paused again. "I sometimes go to the store, and I'd take the top off those, spray just the tiniest bit, and sniff them. The scent always comforted me. For a short time, I could remember her." He cleared his throat. "I think she'd be disappointed in the man I became."

I lifted my arm and stretched it out until I could reach his cheek. "I don't think that's true, but we also can't be sure what your life would've been like if she'd gotten better. Just like I'm not positive that I'd still have my old life."

"But a different path, and I wouldn't have met you. I didn't think walking into the Outreach would change everything. After the assault, I was curled up in the hospital bed. It's where I officially met Marcel. He told me he had a victims' advocate coming to see me. When Boss pushed the curtain aside, my heart sank."

"Boss is an advocate first. It's the reason the Outreach has kept going for so long."

"How did you meet Boss? I don't think I ever asked for the story."

I knew he didn't want to talk about himself, so I let him change the subject. If he wanted to hear me talk, then my baby would get what he needed.

"That was a long time ago."

"I'm sure you remember, Daddy. Tell me." He pinched my belly and pouted at me. He definitely had the power of the pout, and he knew it was one of my weaknesses.

"Okay, my retirement money kept going into our joint account for Verna and the girls. She'd always stayed at home and had a home business, alterations, those kinds of things. It's how she started with her oils and stuff. So I was doing odd jobs to make money, but it's hard to stay clean on the streets, and the change for washing clothes could be used for something cheap to eat. Some of the others told me about the Outreach. I could get a meal, shower, wash clothes. I didn't believe them when they said it was all free. Nothing was free. Strings were always attached."

"Shocked you?" he asked.

"There were a lot of vets, way too many on the streets. Mental health issues, trauma, but I was new. It was the first time in my life I was homeless. I'd never experienced being cold or hungry unless it was on some mission. The worst part of it all, I couldn't see my girls. They always made everything better. They were safe and happy, and I felt I couldn't do anything wrong in their eyes."

"Verna would've understood if you just needed—"

I shook my head. "I know that, but also, my brain was scrambled back then. The girls screaming and running around. They'd drop something. Verna would fuss at them. It was all so overwhelming. I went for a lot of walks." I felt guilty for my irritation at all the noise and chaos. "I felt so weak."

"PTSD doesn't care about everyday things."

"True. One night, I'm lonely, and I can't stand my own self. I packed up my bag and left my narrow stall-type room that was partitioned off with wooden pallets. There I was, standing outside the Outreach door, and I was about to turn around when this short man, built like a damn tank came out of nowhere. He asked me what I needed. I told him I needed to shower and wash clothes, but I didn't want a handout."

"Boss put you to work, huh?"

"He did, but only after I showered and started my clothes. I picked some clothes and stuff from the community closet. That first night, I washed dishes and prepped the ingredients needed for the next day. I got a hot meal and all my clothes and sleeping bag clean. After that, I went back to my tiny stall. At first, it was just a few days a week, then full-time. I still stayed on the streets even after he gave me the job. The former kitchen manager had an issue with drugs and sometimes just didn't show up, and Boss would send someone to get me."

"Why did you stay on the streets even with the job?"

"I was sending everything to Verna except for some pocket money. After attending groups and spending time with Boss, I wanted to have a place to bring my kids, even if it was just for a few hours. My kids were scared of me, I was sometimes dirty, and I smelled like cheap liquor. Verna said I needed to make changes, or she couldn't bring the girls to see me. So, I saved up enough for the apartment and tried to be normal, but alcohol was my only companion for almost five years."

"Normal is overrated, or at least that's what the family tells me."

I snorted at his bratty eye roll. "Definitely."

"Bart?" He spoke my name softly and leaned forward, braced his hands on the pillow on either side of my head.

"Yes, baby?"

"I'm humbled that you love me back."

I grabbed his face in my hands as he tried to look away from me again. "No, that should be the other way. Everything you've been through. How your trust and faith in yourself was dimmed, I was lucky enough to earn that." I lifted my head to brush my mouth to his, nipping at his bottom lip. "We still have work to do, both of us. After we're done with Chamberlain, it's just going to be you and me. A boring, normal couple."

"I can't wait." He dropped a quick kiss on my lips. "I love you. I've only ever said that to one other man, but I didn't know what it meant until now."

"I love you, too. What about we go out? It's almost time for your dinner."

"But, Daddy, you'd have to get dressed. That would be a shame."

"There you go stroking my ego again."

He hummed a bit. "If we stay in, I could do more than stroke your ego."

"We can get room service." I grabbed him around the waist and flipped him to his back, his laughter filling the room. Free of stress and real, unlike the man I'd met that first night. There was nothing in the world better than the sound of my baby and my girls' happiness. That would always be my purpose.

40

CHANCE

COLD CASE
UNIT

J ust like the day before, Carmichael escorted me to the
meeting room. Chamberlain was already in there waiting
for me. I paused beside the door and leaned my head back
on the wall. I just needed a minute. I'd played a good game at
being okay with Bart. He always had final say on something that
would affect my mental health. He was a great distraction, but as
soon as I had to leave him behind, it felt as if the floor just went
out from under my feet.

"Why are you doing this?" Carmichael asked, and I opened my
eyes to find his staring at me.

"I'm getting asked that a lot."

"Are you answering truthfully or just bullshitting your way
through?"

"Mostly bullshitting." I smiled at his gruff chuckle. "Bart wants
what's best for me, and I'm just drawing straws, hoping I don't get
the shortest one. I'm in law enforcement, a S.W.A.T. officer. It's
the only thing I ever really took pride in. I need to know why
Chamberlain saw me as a victim."

"I get that. I was a cop before this. Sex Crimes. I did that for
five years. My mother is a survivor of domestic abuse and

partner sexual assaults. I'd never understood the why either, but I thought working the cases would give me some insight."

"Did it?" I asked.

"No. Offenders see it as a power move...the ultimate degradation...their right to take because, men, right? I took too many reports, collected too many kits, and then after...the treatment a rape victim receives...they drop it. Quit cooperating because they know they won't get justice. I spent a year after quitting molding a bar stool to my ass."

"Did you learn anything at all?"

"That humanity is lacking and that innocent until proven guilty applies to the offender but almost never to the victim. Why did they have that extra glass of wine on a first date? Why did they take that shortcut instead of staying on the path? An offender claiming their victim didn't say no. They weren't mindreaders. It's always the same."

"Pessimistic."

"My husband would say the same thing and has on many occasions."

"What's he think of your job?"

He smirked and shook his head. "The warden likes it fine when he can watch me on the security cameras my entire shift."

"The warden?"

He let out a loud laugh and shook his head. "Your gay ESP didn't pick it up?" I shook my head. "It's not common knowledge, husband of the warden walking among prisoners...not always safe. But this is a private area, and you asked."

"Why did he agree to let me see Chamberlain?"

"Because I told him to. Everyone has the right to confront the person who hurt them. My mother always wanted to know the why. Why did my father beat her...why did he force her to have sex? He died in a barfight before she healed enough to want answers. The unknown still haunts her. She's never trusted another man again. There's always that suspicion. She was fooled once, she refused to have it happen again. That man of yours loves and respects you, supports you, but it's still something a survivor has to face on their own."

"Thanks."

"For what?" he asked.

"For understanding."

"This is one thing I wish I didn't understand, but I respect your need to know. You ready?"

"As ready as I'll ever be."

"We can end this at any time. Just tell my officer you're done. I'll leave you to take a breath. Besides, make the fucker sweat." He winked at me and went the short distance to enter the observation room.

Remy had prepped me for hours the previous night to ask the right questions. We'd agreed Chamberlain was going to die in prison, retrial or not. Not every case was brought against him, and they were still working on the evidence to charge him with hiring hitmen to take me out.

Vega and Zero had assured me that he no longer had any resources he could tap into. Any fundraising to assist him in getting out had steadily dwindled and dried up. My friends and their accomplices had flooded the forums and groups with the truth about who Chamberlain was, which seemed to help. His cult-ish followers weren't inclined to have their personal habits exposed for friends and family to see. A lot of accounts were deactivated, but files of information remained in the event someone thought they'd try anything else. Yet that hadn't lessened my need to know for me.

For over a year, I'd lived my life in limbo, and I was tired of putting everything off. There were doubts that the sniper in charge of the first two hits would ever be found. With no money to offer, he'd moved on to more profitable jobs. I spun away from the wall, placed my hand on the knob, and took deep breaths as I turned it.

One more visit, that's all he'd get from me. After I walked out of that room at the end of the hour, I was determined to move on with my life, answers or not. I was tired of living in the past—in my trauma, and my obsession with the *why* kept me from going forward. Schooling my features, I stepped inside and closed the door behind me. The electronic lock beeped as it engaged. I glanced at the officer, and he gave me a small nod.

"You're late." Chamberlain sounded put out like I'd messed up his busy schedule. I didn't give a fuck.

That didn't mean that lingering sickness didn't build in my stomach at seeing him. He looked different than the previous day. His hair was neatly combed, maybe even trimmed. He'd shaved the peach fuzz from his face. That didn't help the almost sickly pallor of his pale skin.

"No, I'm not. You're just lucky I'm here. I had better things to do today."

It took everything in me to pull out the chair across from him. I made sure that no part of him could touch me in any way. I laced my fingers and caught the flash of the bracelet, but I didn't turn around to glance at the glass behind me.

He rested his forearms on the table and leaned forward. The arrogant smirk sickened me. "You can tell me you miss me? We both know you do."

"Make this visit count because, after today, you won't get another second of my time."

"But don't you want to know why you were so special, Chance? Why I followed you for weeks?"

"Not gonna lie and say I wouldn't like to know what your sick brain thought was so special, but that's your choice to tell me. I'm not going to beg you for answers because that's what you want."

"Does your boyfriend know how hard you came for me?"

My fingers clenched around each other. I kept reminding myself that release didn't equal consent, yet the more I looked at him, the harder my heart pounded in my chest. "My boyfriend knows everything you did to me. I don't lie to him."

He let out a heavy sigh and leaned back in his chair. His body language opened the distance between us, and he started to cross his arms over his chest but caught himself. There was one thing I'd learned, appearances were everything to Chamberlain, not just the way he looked but also the people he associated with. Crossed arms implied defensiveness.

"You know you could do so much better. Lose that, what, forty pounds you've gained. You've let yourself go, and it's such a shame. Not to mention the fat, old boyfriend. Is he desperate? I mean damaged goods."

My jaw clenched involuntarily, and I grimaced, which let him smell blood in the water. "You apparently found something to be obsessed with. Were you desperate?"

"You've seen my work. I could take anyone I wanted. Do you know they cried even while unconscious? The occasional scream and whimper. How many would love to know how they moaned? How many times they got off when I was inside them?"

Saliva built up in my mouth, and my body got too hot, sweat popping up on my back. I wrung my fingers until the joints hurt, the slight pain focusing me. That tingling sensation traversed my limbs as my brain started thinking about the sting of my razor. A sensory memory of the blood almost tickling as it traveled down my skin. The crimson spreading along the waistband of my pajama pants.

"But none of the others were as special as you, Chance. And do you know why?"

"No, gift me with your wisdom." I was shocked when my words came out strong and unbroken.

"You wanted to be degraded, craved it. You might have looked like you were fighting me, but, oh, no, Chance, you were riding my cock, begging for it. A video of you would've been my masterpiece, my perfect opus, and it's my only regret that you couldn't see how beautiful you were as you pretended not to want it." He let out an obscene moan. "You know what gets me off the hardest when I lie on my bunk at night? Oh, I'm sure you'll deny wanting to know, but it was how you clamped down on my cock as I wrapped my hands around your throat. The second you were almost at the edge of death, you made a mess of both of us. Do you still remember what my cum feels like inside you? Do you think of what I did to you while you let your boyfriend fuck you? It's me you want...I gave you exactly what you wanted, does he?"

Years of rage and helplessness burned bright in my chest, and the world came down to him, nothing but a pinpoint, and the next thing I knew, I was being grabbed from behind. Chamberlain chuckled as he wiped the blood from the corner of his mouth and the back of my hand stung.

A strange voice whispered in my ear to calm down, and I angrily nodded and pulled out of the officer's hold.

"Now, now, Chance, did I hit a nerve?" His voice was low, almost intimate, just like he'd spoken to me and every other victim he'd attempted to destroy. "I always assumed I wanted absolute control, but the way you pretended to fight me, it was better than every limp, unconscious body I used however I saw fit. I never understood how hot fighting for dominance could be, and when I get out of here, I'm coming for a repeat."

The glass shook behind me as I heard something connect with it. I jumped to my feet and turned my back on Chamberlain. I spread my hands on the glass and stared at my own reflection but knew my Sir was right on the other side.

"Ah, the boyfriend doesn't like hearing he's going to be second best. I bet he loved seeing the photos of you. When he figures out what a disgusting little slut you are, he'll move on. Isn't that what all the men in your life have done? Move on once they get to use that nasty hole of yours? Does he imagine how many men have fucked you?"

I listened, but my only focus was on the glass and my Sir on the other side. My bracelet lit up three times. I knew what those three flashes meant without him ever saying a word. *I love you*. After I calmed myself a bit, I turned and leaned back against the glass. I needed to be as close to Bart as I could get at that moment.

"You'll never get out of here. Your parents are on the verge of bankruptcy. Your followers don't like having their secrets exposed. Savage, well, he's a whole different issue for you. I hear he's going to talk to save his own ass. Like you, he's a big man when his victims don't fight back. Also, there's three new cases that can be linked to you...three homicides. Capital murder. You're going to die in this fucking prison or strapped to a table with a needle stuck in your arm. And what did it get you? A bit of twisted fame. Like with anything, you're going to be forgotten because you're nothing but that pimple-faced, overweight teenager."

The officer who'd returned to his corner moved forward as Chamberlain jumped up from his chair and slammed his hands onto the table.

"If it makes you feel any better, you destroyed me. Is that what this meeting was about? Needing to see the one victim who could remember everything you did to them so you could see the aftermath? Gloat? Tell me everything you did and try to convince me I enjoyed it. I survived despite you, Chamberlain. I found family. A man who loves me." He snarled but fell back into the chair. "He loves me despite me thinking I was nothing more than a thing worthy of all the disgusting things I allowed men to do to me."

With nausea filling my throat—burning right before the vomiting began—but I ignored it. I approached the table, spread my hands over the surface, and leaned in.

"You're right. I'm damaged goods. I'm a thing unworthy of anything good in my life. That may never change. The man I love may leave me one day when he sees I'm too much trouble. But you're still going to be sitting in a cell wishing for the glory days of when you elicited fear and pain. Do what you want, trying to kill me for the rest of my life, but get a good look because I'm not coming back. You no longer matter, I survived you, and that's all that fucking matters."

I quickly straightened and calmly as possible walked to the door. I thanked the officer as he opened it. Seconds after the door closed, blocking Chamberlain from seeing, I gagged and heaved. My body bent in half as the minimal amount I'd had for breakfast splashed on the cement wall and the floor at my feet. My stomach violently clenched as blood rushed in my ears, and the world around me ceased to exist except for the pain and horror of my life—every piece of me that was broken and stolen. Peace and self-respect were torn away in chunks until nothing more than a shell remained. And no matter what changed, I would always be that thing that disgusted me.

41

BART

COLD CASE
UNIT

Hours earlier, I'd physically carried Chance away from Chamberlain and the prison. He'd shut down, refused to speak to me or anyone, and he didn't protest when I stripped him, bathed, and then brushed his teeth. I'd picked him up and put him to bed. Yet all he did was stare at the ceiling, and nothing I did brought him around.

Simon, Remy, and Robert tried to calm me down as I posted up next to the bed. I'd lost it as I'd observed Chance and Chamberlain, him threatening to finish what he'd started with Chance. The C.O. had grabbed me from behind as I'd punched the glass and told me Chance had to do what he had to do. The minute I saw Chance's face through the glass, I knew we'd regressed. All his progress disappeared.

The more Chamberlain spoke, the more enraged I became, and I was helpless to do anything. I'd supported my baby's need to know, but I hadn't fully understood what Chamberlain had done until I listened to him talk with such disturbing glee. It was one thing to see the videos, read the reports, but it was another to see Chance in the same room as his attacker.

I needed Chance mad—I needed him to fight. My next move

had to be carefully executed. Either we went home together, or I was about to ruin everything.

"Are you sure about this?" Robert asked as Remy and Simon walked out of the door, bags in hand, to move to another room.

"No, but he forgot everything he learned in that room, and I can't have that."

"One of us will text you with our new room number. We won't be far if you need an assist. Do you have everything you need?"

"Yeah, thanks for watching him while I went out."

"We're family. We take care of our own. Good luck."

I nodded because I was sure I was going to need more than luck on my side. After I was left alone, I moved furniture to make space in the center of the room and laid out everything on the coffee table. Stripping down to nothing but my jeans and removing my shoes and socks, I made sure there was water, a few sodas, and some snacks for later.

Preferring a lighter hand in dealing with my sub, I refused to cut him. Even though I'd promised earlier that would be something I'd do, I couldn't bring myself to etch another bad memory into his skin. I craved to love on him. Show him with my actions that I valued his trust and submission above everything else, but I was about to veer into unfamiliar territory with Chance.

After I'd centered myself and committed to what needed to be done, I returned to our room. I paused in the doorway to watch him cuddled under the sheet and comforter, a pillow hugged to his chest. His attempt to cover his soft sobs failed. Squaring my shoulders and straightening my spine, I crossed the room and fisted the fabric in my hand, and jerked.

"Get out of bed, boy." The harshness of my tone caused him to flinch, but he obeyed.

His body language screamed defeated, his shoulders slumped forward, and his head was down with his eyes averted. I stepped up beside him, grabbed his soft hair, and jerked his head back. He gasped in pain. Tears and confusion filled his gaze, but his expression remained blank.

"You keep your eyes on me. Do you understand me?" He nodded, and I jerked his hair harder. "Use your words. Do I need to remind you of your rules?"

"N-no, Sir."

"Go into the living room and assume the position," I ordered as I abruptly released his hair, and he stumbled forward.

His body was bare, and my hands fisted to keep from reaching for him, tenderly caressing him until he melted into me but first, I needed my Chance back. I entered the main room in time to see him lower to his knees and splay his hands on his muscled thighs. I picked up the crop as I started to circle him. I tapped his upper back.

"Back and shoulders straight...head up." When he didn't comply quickly enough, I increased the force of the tap until he surged upward at the sting. "What are you, boy?" I asked as I stopped in front of him.

My baby wouldn't move his gaze above my knees. I tapped him under the chin until he was forced to tip his head back. I lowered to crouch until we were eye to eye. I flipped the crop upside down and used the hilt to keep his attention on me.

"I believe your Sir asked you a question, boy."

"Bart—" His voice broke. "Do-don't make me—"

I grabbed his jaw and squeezed until my fingers dug into his skin, and tears flowed down his cheeks.

"Answer me." I made my voice as cold as possible even as it broke me.

"I'm disgusting, Sir." He jerked out of my hold and curled forward until he pressed his forehead to the carpet.

I tossed the crop aside and crawled around behind him. I moved in close enough until I could completely blanket him. He fought me as I hugged him. He screamed and cursed, clawed at the carpet to get away from me, but I wouldn't allow that to happen. Too many people in his life refused to fight for him. I wasn't going to be another one.

I placed my hand on his opposite cheek and roughly turned his head until I could place kisses on his temple, cheek, and the corner of his mouth.

"Baby, I'm not letting you go. I'm going to fight for you even if that means I have to go head-to-head with you. I love you."

Painful-sounding sobs wrecked his body as he arched until the back of his head pressed against my shoulder. I let him mourn no matter how hard it was for me to not be able to instantly fix what was wrong for him. My left hand fisted in his hair so that he couldn't hide from me again. All I could do was try to hold him together as he fell apart. As he raged at Chamberlain and countless unknown men in his past, his stepfather, and even his mother dying and leaving him.

Minutes or hours passed as I held him and cried myself, waiting patiently for my baby to come back to me. He turned his head as if searching for my mouth, and I kissed him and tasted the salt of tears. I broke the kiss and rested my forehead on his temple.

He murmured something I couldn't make out. "What, baby?" I asked as I hugged his sweaty yet chilled body closer to give him warmth and comfort.

"How can you stay?" The question was barely above a whisper.

"Because, Chance Bowers, you are worth every second of my love and care, no matter how worthless you think you are. You're not. You're mine. Special. One of the best things about my life."

"But everything he—" He went quiet.

"He's a sick, demented man not worth our time anymore. You're stronger than he'll ever be. You survived being in a room with him for two days. You faced your fears, and we're done with him. We'll go home. You'll go back to your job, and when you come home, you're all mine."

"Bart, but I broke."

"It was going to happen sooner or later, love. You had to mourn."

"But you heard everything."

I straightened, bringing him back against my chest, and then manhandled him until he was kneeling between my legs. I ignored the twinge in my old knees as I lifted my hands to hold his beautiful face.

"And I saw the trial videos. I read the reports. I saw the images Zero shared. None, and I mean none, of those changes how much I love and adore you. I borderline worship you. And I will say this again, I will fight for you. Unless you truly want me to go away, I'm here to stay, and I'm keeping you." I peppered soft kisses all over his face, his skin splotchy and tear-streaked, and he was sniffing hard. "You're a mess, love, but you're my mess."

"I don't understand." He started crying again.

"Maybe not right now, but we have all the time in the world. We'll start from the beginning again. You'll go to your groups. You'll go to counseling. We'll go together as a couple, so I better know how to care for you. I'll go to a group for partners. Whatever you need, I'll do, but I need you to fight, Chance. I need you to get angry. I need you to scream and rage, whatever you have to do to get it out."

"Do you really still love me?"

The disbelief in his voice saddened me. The cruelty of one man had taken my baby's comfort in knowing that I loved him unconditionally. I loved him a hundred percent because you can't love someone without appreciating the ugly parts as much as the pretty ones.

"More than anything. And we're going to have a good life out of pure spite. You'll be bratty and push the rules. You'll probably gang up on me with our girls and Verna. Somedays, you might not even want to get out of bed, and I'll cuddle you until you're ready. I'll tell you I love you every hour of every day until you believe me."

My eyes closed as he threw himself at me and tucked his face into my neck. He inhaled the scent of me, and all I did was stroke his back. I savored another day of touching him—of knowing that even though he was scared, he still wanted to be mine. Yes, our lives wouldn't be easy, we'd both have our hellacious days, but we'd have each other.

I'd give my baby everything he needed to grow and heal, to find the man he wanted to be. I groaned as I shifted to sit on my ass, brought him onto my lap, and rocked him. I kissed his shoulder as the tension disappeared, and he melted into me. Being his comfort item was my purpose—my life had led me to the Outreach and to him, and while I'd always live with some regrets, I wouldn't be sorry that I'd made it through. In the end, I had Chance and a good life. I had a family that couldn't wait for him to be one of us. I would give my baby everything he needed, no matter what those things were.

42

CHANCE

B art's chuckle made me jerk my gaze to him to find him watching me closely as I'd given myself a mental pep talk. We'd just pulled up outside Verna and Martin's house, actually the home where Bart had lived with his ex-wife and raised their children. I'd talked a good game up until we'd parked, but I wasn't so sure I could get through dinner. A few weeks had passed since we'd returned from seeing Chamberlain, and I was handling that two days of mental hell better than I was about doing family dinner with Verna and the girls, along with their partners.

"We can cancel and try some other time." Bart came closer to lean against the vehicle right next to me.

"I was fine, and then I…wasn't fine."

"Baby, I get it, I really do. I think if I was meeting your mom, I'd feel the same way."

"I think she would've loved you."

"I'd hope so, and I'm sorry I'll never get to see the woman who raised my baby." He slipped his arm between my chest and the side of the vehicle and then tugged me to him. "I know this is new. Dolan never had contact with his parents, so this is the first meet the boyfriend's family event, but you're going to do great. Verna and the girls are excited. Sierra has been asking was Grampy bringing you all day. Cora and Bettany have been texting to make sure because my granddaughters can't wait to see you again."

"Really?" I asked.

"Yes, really. I know you're nervous, but I really want everyone to meet you...make it all official. And I think they also want to make robbing-the-cradle jokes at my expense."

I snorted so hard I hurt myself at the exasperation in his tone. "It's your fault for being a brat whisperer."

"My girls do take after their mother, and she's always said I have a huge weakness for Brats. Look at my newest one." He winked as he leaned in and dropped a playful kiss on my lips. "My last one."

He moved lower to kiss my collar that he'd given me the night before. I'd melted down when he'd told me to stand in front of the mirror. I wasn't a fan of the mirror sessions, but nowhere near as much as I hated corner time. He lifted the chain over my head and then secured it around my throat. The weight of it was strangely comforting, and the look of pure happiness as he'd given it to me was a moment I'd never forget.

"Are you ready?"

"As I'll ever be."

He laced his fingers through mine, and we walked along the sidewalk until we reached the walkway that led to the front porch. It was one of those houses you'd see in shows about happy families. Hanging baskets lined the eaves. Rocking chairs and a porch swing, and the windows glowed with a warm, yellow light. We'd barely stepped onto the first step when the door flew open.

I released Bart's hand just in time to catch Sierra, and Leila wasn't far behind. I barely got them both picked up before five tall, strong women filed out, Cora and Bettany smiling, Roxie and Tamara looked like Verna, and then Verna stepped into the middle. It was a phalanx of beautiful women, who, when you looked closer, were the perfect mix of their parents.

"Sorry, they've been staring out the window since you two pulled up." Verna spoke first and closed the distance as I settled Sierra and Leila on my hips and carefully held them. Verna leaned in and kissed my cheek and then went to Bart.

Just like Boss and Dolan, I tried to pick out any jealousy, but it wasn't there. I could see the love between them, but it was that of former lovers and best friends. I spoke to his granddaughters as I waited for Bart and Verna to be done greeting each other.

"Cora, Bettany, you remember Chance. Cora, I'm sure you do." Cora giggled as her father glared at her.

"I have no idea what you mean." Cora looked so innocent.

"Uh huh, Chance, meet Roxie and Tamara." He motioned to them to indicate who was who.

"I'd shake hands, but—" I bounced my precious cargo on each arm.

"It's great to finally put a face to the stories. Mom's been bragging about you since she met you." Tamara gave me a friendly grin.

"Hi, Chance. No wonder Dad's been keeping you to himself." Roxie winked at me, and I chuckled as Bart groaned when she gave me a once, then twice over.

"Quit flirting with my man." Bart playfully growled at her and then placed his hand on the small of my back.

We followed them inside, Leila wiggled to get down, and I leaned over to place both on their feet, but Sierra held on tight, so I kept her. The girls introduced me to their husbands, Tamara's boyfriend and a tall, slightly shy woman Roxie called her person. I asked about pronouns, and the stranger smiled and said she/her.

Everyone wandered off to what I assumed was the living room, but I froze as a beautiful, slender man came up beside Verna and pressed a kiss to her forehead. He was graying at the temples, and he had bright blue eyes behind wire-framed glasses.

"You're Chance? It's a pleasure to meet you." He glanced at Bart, and when I noticed Bart nod, Martin extended his hand for a shake. "My girl has told me so much about you." He released my hand, and his attention was instantly on Verna. "Are you okay, love?"

"Yes, Sir." The brash woman seemed almost shy.

"Verna was nervous about you coming to visit finally. She's been a bit manic today, making sure everything was just right," Martin explained with an indulgent expression, one I'd seen on Bart's face plenty of times.

"I'm sure everything is great. I nearly had a panic attack when I got out of the car." When I said it, Verna caught my gaze with hers. "This is my first meet the family ever."

"It's natural to be nervous, Chance, but Bart has said nothing but great things about his boy."

I instantly leaned into Bart's side, and Sierra rested her head on my shoulder. "Is she ready for bed?"

"Too early for that, but she was so excited she didn't have her nap. She'll be overly tired later, but Cora and Grant are sticking to her regular bedtime. We already have a room set up for the girls to sleep when it's time. Can I get you anything to drink?" Verna asked.

I glanced at Bart. "We'll both have iced tea," he answered for us. "Chance is back to full duty tomorrow." He didn't mind if I had a beer or whatever with everyone, but during work, he'd made a rule no alcohol unless I was off-shift the next day.

"Congratulations. Are you excited?" Verna asked as she dragged me away from Bart and toward the back of the house. Bart and Martin were laughing behind us.

"Nervous, I've been off active duty, and I missed it, but I've liked having more time to spend with Bart." She let go of my wrist as I stopped beside the island, and she went to the fridge to grab a glass pitcher and then to a cabinet for glasses.

"I brought you in here to have a minute before we go into the living room. Martin is so self-assured, but he was nervous when he'd met Bart and the girls, too. I thought you might need a minute."

"Thanks for that. I'd met everyone but Tamara and Roxie and the partners. I don't know why I was so nervous."

"You're meeting the children of your Sir and partner. I'm sure that's nerve-wracking. Meeting Martin's parents, that was intense. I was a Black woman a decade older than him with four children. He hadn't dated a Black woman before, so there I am, arriving at a massive estate to meet his conservative parents. Turns out they're not so conservative, but the lead-up was definitely scary."

"How did you meet him?" I asked as ice clinked into the glasses.

"My best friend since childhood worked in his office. We were going to have lunch. She'd told me about her new boss, said he was plain and standoffish. When I met him, I thought he was handsome and stern. I love stern." I chuckled as she winked at me. "She called me one day and nearly screamed into the phone he was asking about me and that he'd demanded my number. We went out on a date a week later."

"Was it weird to date again after being with Bart for so long? You don't have to answer."

" I hadn't really thought about dating again after Bart left. I mean, I had four kids, and my body showed it. I'd always been tall and curvy, but the girls definitely made the hourglass bigger. Bart was my one and only, and the thought of exposing myself to someone else scared me a bit, but I thought, what could one date hurt, right?"

"Apparently, it worked out."

"It did. Not that it was easy. I'd been with Bart since I was sixteen, and there was the matter of being a submissive. Dating again at almost forty hadn't been in my plans. Our first dinner, he plainly told me that he was a Dominant and that it was a huge part of him, and as much as he wanted to see where things would go, that had to be a lifestyle I shared. Seemed like fate. I was left a little off-balance when Bart left. Martin didn't go straight into being my Sir. There's a certain amount of trust and conversations that need to happen." She shrugged her shoulders. "I think insecurity is normal. How are you doing with it all?"

"Good, Bart is perfect."

"What? You frowned a bit."

"Nothing bad. I'm just coming to terms with the old Chance and the new me. The old me wouldn't have looked at Bart twice, and that makes me sad. I would've missed out."

"People change. It's the way the world works. I have these since you've got her."

We moved through the house and into a large living room. Cora was at Grant's feet, his hand under her hair, massaging the back of her neck. Roxie was seated on the floor with her head resting on her girlfriend's knee. Martin and Bart were in two chairs on either side of the fireplace with a pillow beside his feet. Tamara and Bettany made themselves at home on the floor, each leaning back against their partners' chests. Verna placed the two glasses on a small round table next to Bart's chair. Bart patted his thigh, and I settled on his lap. He kissed the back of Sierra's head where I was sure she was having the nap she wasn't supposed to have.

"What is it you do, Chance?" Grant asked.

"I'm a Lieutenant with the Winston Harbor S.W.A.T. Unit. I'm a sniper by trade, though. Winston Harbor is my first command position." I caught Verna lowering to her knees to the cushion, and Martin leaned to the side to kiss the top of her head. They looked happy, everyone did, and it was so odd to me to be around truly emotionally healthy people. It wasn't until I'd met Boss and all the rest that I'd remembered what family was.

"How old are you?" Roxie asked. I instantly saw the mischief, and Bart groaned.

"I'll be forty-one mid-November."

"Dad, we didn't take you for the mid-life crisis type to date younger, way prettier men." Tamara started batting her lashes, and then I noticed all the girls were doing it, including Leila.

"It's forty-one, not twenty-one, a respectable age," Bart rumbled, but I heard the amusement in his voice, and I relaxed as he patted my hip.

"Are you sure? He doesn't look anywhere near forty-one. Do you have ID?" Bettany acted like she was going to come search for my wallet, but her laughing husband held her back.

"And I told him y'all would behave? No respect for your elders."

"And you're elder, elder..." Cora squeaked as I caught Verna poking her.

"Hey, I'm only two years younger than your dad. Ease up on the elder."

"Don't embarrass your mother, Cora." Martin sounded stern, but he sure didn't look like it. The smile on his face and the way his eyes lit up said he was amused.

"Sorry, Da." She wasn't sorry in the least.

Brat understood Brat, apparently. I smiled as Sierra let out the softest, cutest snore, and I glanced at Cora. "Should I wake her up?"

"No, she's been good all day. We'll wake her up when it's time for dinner. She's always been a good sleeper, but she was excited to see her Papa Chance again."

I gasped, and my eyes burned as I held Sierra closer to me. I turned to hide my face in Bart's neck so I wouldn't embarrass myself by crying.

"Hey, baby, what's wrong?" He carefully pinched my chin and

worked to get a look at my face without waking up the little girl in my arms. I shook my head. "No, we don't keep secrets. What's wrong?" he whispered.

"She called me Papa Chance." I kept my voice low so people wouldn't hear, but the entire room had gone silent.

"Of course she did, you're mine, and that means my daughters and granddaughters are yours." I lifted enough for him to softly kiss me a few times. "My family is yours."

"I didn't...think about that until..." I put my face back down.

"I love you, Chance. This was your welcome to the family dinner. I thought you understood that."

I sort of had, but to be acknowledged like that hit me. After decades of being unwanted to suddenly being surrounded by family overwhelmed me and threw me off balance. I tightened my arms around Sierra when I felt like she was slipping, but I relented when I noticed it was Cora taking her. She leaned down and kissed my cheek—one after another—Verna, Roxie, Tamara, and Bettany all repeated the caress, but they didn't move away. They stood in front of the chair in a half circle.

"Chance, sit up, please."

I was nervous by the almost insecure tone of Bart's voice. He was always confident about being able to take care of me. I caught Verna holding out a small black bag. Bart took it, and Verna and the girls were almost bouncing.

"Baby, don't look like that, I know we haven't been together long, but I love you so much. I wanted to share this moment with Verna and our girls." He pulled the strings on the bag to loosen them. "Put out your hand, palm up."

I obeyed like I always did with him, and cool metal fell into my palm, and I completely stopped breathing. It was two thick black bands. I tried to bring my attention back to Bart, but I couldn't.

"Chance Bowers, you wear my collar, and I want you to wear my ring. I want you around for the rest of my life...to make a home for us." His touch was gentle as he placed his fingertips on my opposite cheek and urged me to look at him. "Baby, breathe."

I gasped as I noticed my chest had started to hurt. There was that loving expression I'd never dreamed of seeing on another person when they looked at me. No one had ever made me just feel like I was right—that I belonged. I wasn't judged on my past. He'd never made me feel as if I were broken beyond repair.

"When you're ready, I want you to marry me, but until then, I want everyone to know you're mine and taken, that I was lucky enough to earn your trust."

"Bart…" I glanced at him and then at Verna and the girls, Sierra and Leila, too.

"We want to keep you." Verna smiled at me.

"So, what do you say, Chance? Want to keep making me happy for the rest of our lives?" His breath teased my ear.

I was still in shock. Being adopted by Boss and all the rest of the Cold Case and Outreach people was one thing, but Bart wanted to marry me? Verna and the girls wanted to keep me, too? Rough fingertips turned my head, and I met Bart's gaze.

"You really want to keep me?" I asked.

"More than anything. It won't be easy, we both have things we're still working on, but I want to be your safe space…the person you come home to…to make everything better."

"Yes."

I waited for him to say something, but he just slammed his mouth onto mine. I barely heard the whistles as I hugged Bart's neck, squeezing the bands in my hand until they cut into my palm. Someone finally wanted me, no matter how much trouble I thought I was.

EPILOGUE

CHANCE

COLD CASE
UNIT

F uck, my husband was trying to kill me. I panted for breath as I sprawled over Bart's chest and belly. My thighs shook where I straddled his hips with his big dick still buried deep. Always my favorite way to start my day, and he knew it.

"Still alive, baby?" He sounded amused, and I snarled at him.

"I think you try to break me before I go to work every day."

"Maybe I just want all those young guys who think they can take what's mine to see my husband well-loved and fucked."

At his words, I straightened and realized my mistake as soon as I took him all the way to the base. My eyes rolled at the intense pleasure. After a year of marriage, he still had the power to destroy me in the best ways possible. We hadn't had a huge ceremony, just our families and Boss had gotten ordained to marry us. He was the one who'd gotten us together, and I'd figured he was the best person for the job. The party we had turned into an entire block party. Almost everyone on the strip had shown up.

"Why would I want anyone else when I have an extremely sexy husband at home?"

"You take your ring off at work."

I rolled my eyes. "Only when I'm in the field is your ring in my locker." If anyone else accused me of taking my wedding band off, I would've melted down, but my Sir doing it just annoyed me. I think he provoked me just so I'd break the rules, and he'd get to take a paddle or flogger to me.

Almost three years had passed since I'd met him, and I still wondered how I'd gotten lucky enough to get him. I wouldn't say that the frequent scenes and corrective punishments hadn't helped, but I'd never be fixed. Almost thirty years of conditioning didn't change overnight or ever. Bart still loved me anyway. He had his nightmares, and occasionally, I'd have to lure him out of the walk-in freezer at the Outreach. But really, we were slowly healing together, and at the end of the day, we understood each other's quirks.

"I love this." I stroked over his belly. "I love you. I wouldn't have submitted to you being my Sir so easily if I hadn't."

"You still happy with that?" he asked.

"Yes, Sir, especially when Daddy comes out to play." He groaned as I rolled my hips forward and back, and he pushed his head into the pillow. My husband was always in control, but I savored the moments I got the upper hand. "I live for when you try to fuck the Brat out of me, Daddy."

I groaned as our alarm went off to signal we needed to get up soon to get ready for work. We'd developed a habit of waking up an hour or two earlier than needed to have a lazy morning together.

"I love the Brat side too much to fuck it out of you, but I will admit the challenge is pleasurable."

"You still happy with me?" I asked, and he instantly brought his left hand to my cheek.

"Always. At sixty, I sure as hell didn't see myself here, but I won't regret that. You always make me happy, Chance."

"Even on the bad days?" I leaned into his touch.

"Especially those. You trust me to see your pain and tears...to be the one who gets to take care of you. You do the same for me. We have a few more challenges than most couples, but that just makes it worth it. But just think, this weekend, you get a break from my over-affectionate attention."

"But I need Sir and Daddy cuddles. The belly is the only reason I gave you the time of day."

"Piece of meat, just what every husband wants to hear."

"You know you love it." I pouted at him. It was always Bart's weak spot. "Is Cora sure she wants to give us the baby for the weekend?"

Cora and Grant had welcomed another daughter, and they were all determined to make sure the girls always outnumbered the boys. I'd been there since she'd had a home birth, and I was the first to hold the tiny, screaming baby. Our grandchildren loved to spend time with Grandpa Bart and Papa Chance. At odd times that still tripped me out. Sometimes it felt like the old Chance hadn't existed.

"You do fine with our other grandchildren. You don't like our newest granddaughter?"

I rolled my eyes at him, and he smacked my hip for my bratty behavior. "You know I love her, but she's so tiny."

"Our granddaughters have abandoned me for you. Flora won't be any different." I hid my shy smile, but he caught my chin before I could look away completely. "Your stepdaughters love you, too, Chance. Even Verna is looking at you too fondly. So glad she's a submissive and you're gay."

I snorted and whimpered as his cock slipped free, and as always, I felt empty the second he left me. "Never thought I'd be a stepdad, much less a granddad."

"It looks good on you, baby. All I ever want is you happy and safe."

"I've always been safe with you. You still okay with me going out with Trey, Vega, and Doc tonight?"

"Of course, but you know the rules."

"I know, Sir." I grinned. "Why would I want anyone other than you touching me?"

"I trust you, not so much everyone else."

"There's a reason I wear your ring and collar, Sir, and I wear them with pride." I brought my hand to the chain around my throat with a metal lock with a B and C engraved on it. My uniform shirt easily hid it, unlike my wedding ring, so I always had a piece of him with me.

He stroked his hands over my chest, and the dark bruises caused by his mouth and teeth, the pale lines of my scars except for the deeper ones, were nothing more than faded reminders of the past I didn't want to return to. I wouldn't say it was easy but loving him was.

"I hope you'll always wear them with pride."

"You never have to worry about that. I'm leaking everywhere. I gotta get in the shower. Join me?"

"Love, you know what happens when we shower together?"

"I do. Why do you think I asked?" I threw my leg over and jumped off the bed to head for the bathroom. "Daddy, your boy is very needy, and I have a really long day ahead."

I pouted and backed the rest of the way into the bathroom and turned on the light. I squinted and looked at myself in the mirror. Damn, I was a mess—stubble and sweaty hair stuck up in every direction, but I couldn't be happier. I smirked as I ran my fingertips over the bruises and impressions of my Sir's teeth in my skin. The me before Bart would've went into a panic at the marks, but Bart's claim looked perfect where it was.

"You okay, baby?" Bart asked as he came up behind me and wrapped his arms around my waist. He gave a slight tug, and I leaned back against his belly and chest.

"Perfect."

"Yes, you are," he rumbled the words against the side of my neck, and I tilted my head to give him better access.

"And people thought I was arrogant before. You just make it

worse." I joked as he growled against my skin, and I giggled as his beard tickled me.

"We found our redemption together, and we made it okay for each other to not be so perfect. I love you."

"I love you, too, Bart, and you gave me everything I never thought I wanted."

I'd waited almost forty years to figure out my shit, and all it took was meeting a group of people who accepted me and then the man who would bring me peace and safety. Nothing was better than being loved by Bart and being able to call him my husband, my Sir, and my Daddy. I hadn't done much right in life, but for once, I couldn't wait for the future and everything it would bring.

ABOUT THE AUTHOR

Two time USA Today Bestselling author J.M. Dabney is a multi-genre published writer of Body and Fat Positive Romance & Fiction. They live with a constant diverse cast of diverse characters in their head. They live for one purpose alone, and that's to make sure everyone gets the happily ever after they deserve. There is nothing more they want from telling their stories than to show that no matter the package the characters come in or the damage their pasts have done, that love is love. That normal is never normal and sometimes the so-called broken can still be beautiful.

The author is Non-Binary and uses the pronouns They/Them.

ALSO BY J.M. DABNEY

Cold Cases Unit

Cold Cases and Second Chances

Cold Cases and Dark Secrets

Cold Cases and Bitter Enemies

Cold Cases and Bruised Hearts

Cold Cases and Sweet Redemption

Cold Cases Coming Soon

Cold Cases and Deadly Lies

Cold Cases and Zero Witnesses

Masters of the Zodiac

(Multi-Author Series)

Pisces

Sappho's Kiss Series

When All Else Fails

More Than What They See

Dysfunction it its Finest Series

Club Revenge

Soul Collector Prophecy

Twirled World Ink Series

Berzerker

Trouble

Scary

Lucky

Brawlers Series

Crave

Psycho

Bull

Hunter

Executioners Series

Ghost

Joker

King

Sin & Saint

Trenton Security

Livingston

Little

Gage

Pure

Masiello Brothers

The Taming of Violet

3 Moments Trilogy

A Matter of Time

The Men of Canter Handyman

Black Leather & Knuckle Tattoos

Chance at the Impossible

Bloody Knuckles Bar & Grill

Clipping the Gargoyle's Wings

Standalone

By Way of Pain (Criminal Delights - Assassins)

Christmas, Bloody Christmas (By Way of Pain Xmas Story)

Waited So Long

An Odd, Little Girl

Claiming Whisper

Adoring Beast

A Yuri Sorenson Mystery

Not Another Statistic

Permanent Freebies

Has the Honeymoon Ended? (Brawlers Short Valentine's Story)

Once Upon a Bear Claw

The Scars She Bears (Executioners Short)